Praise for MY LEGENDARY GIRLFRIEND

'Comic. . .fizzy. Here comes the male Bridget Jones'
Mirror

'Can't help but win you over'
Company

'Wonderfully contagious, humorous and astute'
The Bookseller

'Gayle handles the tale impressively and in the almost-Biblically desolate Will, he has created a character who would cheer Holden Caulfield up'
GQ

About the author

Previously an Agony Uncle, Mike Gayle is a freelance journalist who has contributed to a variety of magazines including *FHM*, *Sunday Times Style*, *Just Seventeen* and *Bliss*. MY LEGENDARY GIRLFRIEND is his first novel.

MY LEGENDARY GIRLFRIEND

MIKE GAYLE

FLAME

Hodder & Stoughton

Grateful acknowledgment is made for permission to reprint
excerpts from the following copyrighted works:

It's A Wonderful Life® is a registered trademark of Republic
Entertainment Inc.®, a subsidary of Spelling Entertainment
Group Inc.®

Quotation from WILD PALMS by William Faulkner reproduced
by permission of Curtis Brown, London, on behalf of
Random House, Inc.

The lines from *Ferris Bueller's Day Off*, a Paramount Pictures
Release, are reproduced by permission of Paramount Pictures

The line from *Gregory's Girl* is reproduced by permission of
Bill Forsyth, c/o Peters Fraser Dunlop

The line from *Bugs Bunny* is reproduced by permission of
Warner Bros.

Copyright © 1998 by Mike Gayle

First published in Great Britain in 1998
by Hodder and Stoughton
A division of Hodder Headline PLC

Flame paperback edition 1999

The right of Mike Gayle to be identified as the Author of
the Work has been asserted by him in accordance with the
Copyright, Designs and Patents Act 1988.

1

A CIP catalogue record for this book is available
from the British Library

ISBN 0 340 75043 X

Typeset by Palimpsest Book Production Limited,
Polmont, Stirlingshire
Printed and bound in Great Britain by
Clays Ltd, St Ives plc

Hodder and Stoughton
A division of Hodder Headline PLC
338 Euston Road
London NW1 3BH

For Claire

For Clara

Acknowledgements

I would like to thank: for their help, Philippa Pride and all at Hodder, Jane Bradish Ellames and Emlyn Rees and all at Curtis Brown; for their encouragement, Joe and Evelyn Gayle, Andy Gayle, Phil Gayle, Jackie Behan, The Richards clan, Cath McDonnell, Charlotte and John, Liane Hentscher, Emma and Darren, Lisa Howe, John O'Reilly, Pip, Ben, Rodney Beckford, Nikki Bayley and the Four Winds regulars; and for their inspiration, Mr T, Dave Gedge, Kevin Smith, Mark Salzman, Xena, Richard Roundtree, Clive James, Oxfam and anyone who ever asked Mike.

Please sir, I want some more
– Charles Dickens, *Oliver Twist*

Sometimes you get what you want,
Sometimes you get what you need,
Sometimes you get what you get
– My Mother, *Pearls of Wisdom*

FR1DAY

'Mr Kelly, which football team do you support?'

As I strolled along the edge of the pitch clutching a football underneath each arm, I considered fourteen-year-old Martin Acker and his question carefully. He had been the last of my pupils to leave the pitch and I knew for a fact that he'd lingered with the specific intention of asking me his question, because amongst other things, not only was he genuinely inquisitive as to where my footballing allegiances lay, he also had no friends and had selected me as his companion on that long and lonely walk back to the changing rooms. He was quite literally covered head to foot in Wood Green Comprehensive School football pitch mud, which was a remarkable achievement for someone who hadn't touched the ball all evening. Of his footballing prowess, there was little doubt in my mind that he was the worst player I'd ever witnessed. He knew it, and he knew that I knew it, and yet I didn't have the heart to drop him from the team, because what he lacked in skill, he more than made up for in enthusiasm. This was of great encouragement to me, proving that for some, the futility of an occupation was not in itself a reason to give up.

While Martin was hopeless at playing soccer but excelled in its trivia, I, on the other hand, could neither play, teach nor fake an interest in this most tedious of distractions. Owing

3

to PE staff shortages and the need to impress my superiors, the mob of fourteen-year-olds that made up the year eight B-team was entirely my responsibility. The headmaster, Mr Tucker, had been much impressed when I volunteered for the task, but the truth was less than altruistic: it was either football or the school drama club. The thought of spending two dinner-times per week, aiding and abetting the kids to butcher *My Fair Lady*, this term's production, made football the less depressing option, but only marginally so. I was an English teacher – created to read books, drink cups of sugary tea and popularise sarcasm as a higher form of wit. I was not designed to run about in shorts on freezing cold autumnal evenings.

I peered down at Martin, just as he was looking up to see if I'd forgotten his question.

'Manchester United,' I lied.

'Oh, sir, everyone supports Man U.'

'They do?'

'Yes, sir.'

'Who do you support?'

'Wimbledon, sir.'

'Why?'

'I don't know, sir.'

And that was that. We continued our walk in silence, even failing to disturb the large number of urban seagulls gathered, wading and pecking in the mud, by the corner post. I had the feeling Martin wanted to engage me in more football talk but couldn't think of anything else to ask.

Martin's fellow team-mates were bellowing and screaming so loudly that I was alert to their mayhem before I even reached the changing room doors. Inside, chaos reigned – Kevin Rossiter was hanging upside down by his legs from a hot water pipe that spanned the room; Colin Christie was snapping his towel on James Lee's bare buttocks; and Julie Whitcomb, oblivious to the events going on around her, was tucked in a corner of the changing room engrossed in *Wuthering Heights*, one of the set texts I was teaching my year-eight class this term.

'Are you planning to get changed?' I asked sardonically.

Julie withdrew her amply freckled nose from the novel, squinting as she raised her head to meet my gaze. The look of bewilderment on her face revealed that she had failed to understand the question.

'These are changing rooms, Julie,' I stated firmly, shaking my head in disbelief. '*Boys*' changing rooms, to be exact. As you are neither a boy nor getting changed may I suggest that you leave?'

'I would, Mr Kelly, but I can't,' she explained. 'You see, I'm waiting for my boyfriend.'

I was intrigued. 'Who's your boyfriend?'

'Clive O'Rourke, sir.'

I nodded my head. I hadn't the faintest clue who Clive O'Rourke was.

'Is he a year eight, Julie?'

'No, sir, he's in year eleven.'

'Julie,' I said, trying to break the bad news to her gently, 'year elevens don't have football practice today.'

'Don't they, sir? But Clive said to meet him here after football practice and not to move until he came to get me.'

She dropped her book into her rucksack and slowly picked up her jacket, as though her thought processes were draining her of power, like a computer trying to run too many programs at once.

'How long have you been going out with Clive?' I asked, casually.

She examined the worn soles of her scuffed Nike trainers

intently before answering. 'Since dinner-time, sir,' she confessed quietly. 'I asked him out while he was in the dinner
queue buying pizza, beans and chips in the canteen.'

Hearing this tale of devotion which included remembering
details of a beloved's lunch was genuinely moving. My eyes
flitted down to my watch. It was quarter past six. School had
finished nearly three hours ago.

'I'm afraid you've been the victim of a practical joke,' I said,
spelling it out, in case the penny hadn't dropped. 'Somehow I
don't think Clive's going to turn up.'

She turned her head towards me briefly before examining
her trainers once again. It was clear she was more heart-
broken than embarrassed, her eyes squinting, desperately
trying to hold back the tears and her lips pressed tightly
together, attempting to lock in the sobs trying to escape.
Eventually, she allowed herself the luxury of a carefully con-
trolled sigh, rose and picked up her bag.

'Are you going to be all right?' I asked, even though it was
obvious that she wasn't.

With tears already forming in her eyes she said, 'Yes, sir,
I'll be all right.'

I watched her all the way to the changing room doors by
which time her grief was audible. Some teachers might have
thought no more of her but not I. Her image remained in
my head for some time because in the few brief moments
we'd shared, I had realised that Julie Whitcomb was closer
in kind to myself than anyone I'd ever met. She was one of us
– one who interpreted every failure, whether small or large, as
the out-working of Fate's personal vendetta. Clive O'Rourke's
name would never be forgotten, it would be permanently
etched on her brain just as my ex-girlfriend's was on mine.
And at some point in her future, mostly likely after completing
her journey through the education system right up to degree

level, she'd realise that a life pining after the Clive O'Rourkes of this world had made her bitter and twisted enough to join the teaching profession.

The sound of a small boy emitting a noise roughly approximating, *Whhhhhhhoooooooorrrrrraaaaaaahhhh!!!* signalled that Kevin Rossiter had changed adrenaline sports and was now racing around the far changing room, naked but for his underpants on his head. I couldn't begin to fathom his motivation for such a stunt, let alone find the required energy to tell him off this close to the weekend and so, sighing heavily, I slipped unnoticed into the PE department's tiny office, closing the door behind me.

Rooting around in my bag I discovered my fags, slightly crushed under the weight of my year eights' exercise books – I had one left. I mentally totted up those that had fallen: five on the way to work, two in the staff room before registration, three during morning break, ten during lunch break. It was difficult to work out which was the more depressing thought: the fact that I – who had only in the last three years made the jump from social smoker to anti-social smoker – had managed to get through enough cigarettes to give an elephant lung cancer or that I hadn't noticed until now.

As the nicotine took effect, I relaxed and decided that I was going to stay in my small but perfectly formed refuge, until the last of the Little People had disappeared. After half an hour, the shouting and screaming died down to a gentle hubbub and then blissful silence. Pulling the door ajar, and using my body to block the smoke in, I peered through the crack to make sure the coast was clear. It wasn't. Martin Acker was still there. He was dressed from the top down but was having difficulty putting on his trousers, mainly because he already had his shoes on.

'Acker!'

Bewildered, Martin scanned the entire room nervously before locating the source of the bellow.

'Haven't you got a home to go to?' I asked.

'Yes, sir,' he said dejectedly.

'Then go home, boy!'

Within seconds he'd kicked off his footwear, pulled on his trousers, pushed his shoes back on, grabbed his things and shuffled out of the changing rooms, shouting, 'Have a good weekend, sir,' as he went through the doors.

The newsagent's *en route* to the tube was manned by a lone fat Asian woman who was busily attempting to serve three customers at once, while keeping an eye on two Wood Green Comprehensive boys, lingering with intent by a copy of *Razzle*, which someone far taller than them had thoughtfully left on the middle shelf. When my turn came to be served, without taking her eyes off the boys, she located my Marlboro Lights and placed them on the counter. It was at this point in the transaction that I got stuck; Twix wrappers, torn pieces of silver paper from a pack of Polos and fluff were the nearest items I had to coins of the realm. The shopkeeper, tutting loudly, put my fags back on the shelf and started serving the man behind me a quarter of bon-bons before I even had a chance to apologise. As I brushed past the boys, their faces gleefully absorbing the now open pages of *Razzle*, I berated myself for not having used my lunch hour more wisely with a visit to the cash machine on the High Street. Smoking myself senseless in the staff room had seemed so important then, but now, penniless and fagless, I wished with my whole heart that I believed in moderation more fervently.

Stepping out into the cold, damp, Wood Green evening, gloomily illuminated by a faulty lamppost flickering like a disco light, three women, approaching from my right, caught my attention, due to the dramatic way they froze – one of them even letting out a tiny yelp of surprise – when they saw me. It took a few seconds but I soon realised why these women were so taken aback: they weren't *women* – they were *girls*. Girls to whom I taught English Literature.

'Sonya Pritchard, Emma Anderson, Pulavi Khan: come here now!' I commanded.

In spite of everything their bodies were telling them, which was probably something along the lines of, 'Run for your lives!' or 'Ignore him, he's the teacher that always smells of Polos,' they did as they'd been told, although very much at their own pace. By the time they'd sulkily shuffled into my presence they'd prepared their most disconsolate faces as a sort of visual protest for the hard of hearing.

Pulavi opened the case for the defence. 'We weren't doing nothin', sir.'

'No, sir, we weren't doing nothin',' added Sonya, backing up her friend.

Emma remained silent, hoping that I wouldn't notice the furtive manner in which she held her hands behind her back.

'Turn around, please, Emma,' I asked sternly.

She refused.

'Sir, you can't do anything to us, sir,' moaned Sonya miserably. 'We're not under your jurisdiction outside of school.'

I noted Sonya's use of the word 'jurisdiction'. Normally I would've been impressed by any of my pupils using a word containing more than two syllables, but 'jurisdiction' was the type of word only ever employed by characters on shows like *Baywatch Nights* – which was more than likely where she'd got it from. 'Judicature', however, was the sort of word shunned by TV private eyes, tabloid newspapers and teenagers alike, and definitely would've earned her my deepest admiration.

'Okay,' I said, feigning acute boredom, 'if that's how you want it. But I wouldn't want to be you on Monday, though.'

It occurred to me that perhaps I was being a bit of a bastard, after all; they were right, this wasn't school time and this wasn't any of my business. The only answer I could think of to defend myself was that being fagless had turned me into a grumpy old sod who enjoyed annoying teenagers.

'That's not fair, sir,' moaned Pulavi rather aptly.

'Welcome to the real world,' I chided, rocking back on my heels smugly. 'Life isn't fair – never has been and never will be.' I turned my attention to Emma. 'Now, are you going to show me what you're hiding or not?'

Reluctantly she held out her hands in front of me, revealing three cigarettes sandwiched between her fingers, their amber tips glowing wantonly.

I tutted loudly, employing a carbon copy 'tut' of the kind my mother had used on me for some twenty-five years. All week I'd found myself doing impressions of people in authority: my mother, teachers from *Grange Hill*, Margaret Thatcher – in a vain attempt to stop them from running riot.

'You know that you shouldn't be smoking, don't you?' I scolded.

'Yes, Mr Kelly,' they replied in sullen unison.

'You know these things will kill you, don't you?'

'Yes, Mr Kelly.'

'Well, put them out right now, please.'

Emma dropped the cigarettes – Benson and Hedges, if I wasn't mistaken – on the pavement, and extinguished them with a twisting motion of her heel.

'I'm going to let you off this time,' I said, eyeing Emma's shoes sadly. 'Just don't let me see you at it again.'

'Yes, Mr Kelly,' they replied.

I picked up my bag and began to walk off, momentarily feeling like a Rooster-Cogburn-John Wayne single-handedly sorting out the baddest gang of desperadoes this side of Turnpike Lane, but after two steps I stopped, turned around and surrendered.

'Er, girls . . .' I called out. 'I don't suppose you've got a spare ciggy, have you?'

My good work went up in smoke. I'd balanced my job's requirement for discipline against that of my desire for a nicotine rush, and the Cigarette had won. As smokers, my pupils understood my dilemma; that is, once they stopped laughing. Pulavi delved into her moc-croc handbag and offered me one of her Benson and Hedges.

'You smoke Benson and Hedges?' I asked needlessly, taking one from her outstretched hand.

'Yeah, since I was twelve,' she replied, her face half hidden by her handbag, as she searched for a lighter. 'What do you smoke, sir?'

'Sir probably smokes Woodbines,' joked Sonya.

'Marlboro Lights, actually,' I replied tersely.

Pulavi discovered her lighter and lit my cigarette.

'I had a Marlboro Light once,' chipped in Emma. 'It was like sucking on air. You wanna smoke proper fags, sir. Only poofs smoke Marlboro Lights.'

Once again they all dissolved into fits of laughter. I thanked them and attempted to leave their company but they insisted they were going in my direction. Linking arms, they trailed by my side. I felt like a dog owner taking three poodles for a walk.

'We're going up the West End, sir,' said Emma bustling with energy.

'Yeah, we're off on the pull,' added Pulavi, smiling the kind of filthy grin that would have put Sid James to shame.

'Yeah, we're going to the Hippodrome, sir,' said Sonya. 'D'you fancy coming with us?'

Their question made me think about going out, not with them of course – that would've been unthinkable – but going out in general. I didn't know a single soul in London, and had nothing planned for the weekend, so it was still some wonder to me why, when a few of the younger teachers in the staff room had asked me if I was free for a drink after work, I'd told them I was busy.

'You've got no chance of getting in there,' I said, shaking my head knowingly, partly for their benefit but mostly because I was still reflecting on the sorry excuse of a weekend I had in store for myself.

'You're joking, aren't you?' squealed Sonya. 'We go there every week.'

'Don't you think we look eighteen, sir?' asked Emma.

For the first time during the conversation I recalled what had alarmed me so much in the first moments of our encounter. I knew them to be fourteen-year-olds, but the girls trailing after me were far more worldly than their biological years indicated. Emma had squeezed her frankly over-developed chest into a bra top, barely large enough to cover her modesty, matched with a short silver skirt. Sonya wore a lime green velvet cropped top, combined with an incredibly short blue satin skirt that, whenever she moved her upper body, raised itself an inch higher, instantly revealing more thigh than was strictly necessary. Pulavi had opted for a pair of leopard-print hot pants and a sheer orange blouse, through which her black Wonderbra was clearly visible to the world at large. I was truly mortified.

I thanked them again for the cigarette and rapidly conjured up a girlfriend I was in a rush to get home to. This was exactly the kind of moment which Fate liked to introduce into my life, to let me know there was still plenty of room for things to get worse before they got better. The girls began giggling and in a matter of seconds reduced my self-confidence to zero.

As I entered Wood Green tube station I checked my back pocket for my travel card. It wasn't there. Neither was it in any of my other pockets. Trying not to panic I rapidly developed Plan B:

1. *Try not to dwell on how much it will cost to replace travel card.*
2. *Buy one-way ticket to Archway.*
3. *Do not even consider worrying until 7.00 a.m. Monday morning.*

It was some moments before it occurred to me that Plan B was flawed by the fact that I had only sweet wrappers and pocket fluff to my name.

It began to rain as I put my card into the cash machine and punched in my Pin number: 1411 (the date and month of my ex-girlfriend's birthday). I checked my balance – £770 overdrawn. The machine asked me how much money I wanted. I requested five pounds and crossed my fingers. It made a number of rapid clicking noises and for a moment I was convinced it was going to call the police, make a citizens' arrest *and* eat my card. Instead it gave me the money and asked me in quite a friendly manner – as if I was a valued customer – whether I required any other services.

On the way back to the tube, I passed Burger King on Wood Green High Street. Emma, Sonya and Pulavi were inside, waving at me animatedly from their window seats. I put my head down and did my best to give the impression that I hadn't seen them.

At the station I bought a single to Archway and placed the ticket in the top pocket of my jacket for safe-keeping. As I did so, my fingers brushed against something: I'd found my travel card.

I reached the southbound platform of the Piccadilly Line just in time to see the back of a tube train flying out of the station. I looked up at the station clock to see how long it would be until the next one. *Ten more sodding minutes.* When it finally arrived, I sat down in the end carriage, put my travel card and ticket on the seat next to me where I could keep an eye on them and promptly fell asleep.

The train lurched into a station with a jolt, awakening me from an incredibly gymnastic dream about my ex-girlfriend. While mentally cursing the train driver for cutting short my reverie I looked up in time to realise I was at King's Cross – my stop. I grabbed my bag and managed to squeeze through the gap in the closing doors.

The second part of my journey on the Northern Line, as always, was uncomfortable. All the carriages were so littered with burger wrappers, newspapers and crisp packets that it was like riding home in a rubbish tip on wheels. The only pleasant event that occurred was the appearance of a group of exquisite looking Spanish girls getting on at Euston. They chattered intensely in their mother tongue – probably about why the Northern Line was so dirty – all the way to Camden, where they alighted. This seemed to be the law as far as the north branch of the Northern Line was concerned – beautiful people got off at Camden; interesting people got off at Kentish Town; students and musicians got off at Tufnell Park; leaving only the dull, ugly or desperate to get off at Archway or thank their lucky stars they could afford to live in High Barnet.

Halfway up the escalators at Archway, I searched around

in my top pocket for my ticket and travel card. They weren't there. My hugely expensive one-year travel card was now stopping at all stations to Uxbridge on the Piccadilly Line. I shut my eyes in defeat. When I opened them seconds later, I was at the top and thankfully no one was checking tickets at the barrier. I let out a sigh of relief and thought to myself: *Sometimes, life can be unusually kind.*

Opening the front door to the house, a depressing atmosphere of familiarity overwhelmed me. For five days this had been home. Five days, but it felt like a decade. I pressed the timer switch for the hallway light and checked the mail on top of the pay-phone. As I put the key in the door to my flat the lights went out.

7.20 P.M.

'Ahhh! You've been burgled!'

These were the words my ex-girlfriend, Aggi, used to turn and say to me every time she saw the state of my bedroom. It was our favourite running gag which, in spite of its asthmatic tendencies, used to have us in stitches every time.

Aggi and I split up exactly three years ago, not that I'd been counting the days or anything. I was aware of precisely how long it had been because she dumped me on my twenty-third birthday. And despite everything I'd done to forget the day I was born and the occasion of her dumping me, the date remained locked in a brain cell that refused to die.

I was woken that fateful day by the sound of silence; Simon and Garfunkel got that spot on: silence had a sound. Back then at my parents' house, if anyone was in and not comatose, silence never got a look in. Every action of the occupants was pursued without regard for the sleeping: washing machines at six in the morning, clinking cutlery, breakfast television, 'Have you seen my shoes, Mum?', shouting, and occasionally laughter. Living in the aural equivalent of Angola, I quickly learned to filter out the white noise of lower-middle-class family life.

Later, when my parents had gone to their respective places of work (he: Nottingham City Council; she: Meadow Hall

17

Retirement Lodge) and my kid brother, Tom, to school, the house was allowed to drift back into a restful peace. My brain, no longer filtering out anything more threatening than the occasional starling chirping in the garden, woke me up – silence was my alarm clock.

On top of my duvet lay a solitary brown manila envelope. Whenever post arrived addressed to me my dad would leave it there before going to work. I think he hoped the excitement of seeing it there would somehow galvanise me into action. It never did. Nothing could. At the time, I didn't receive many letters because I was a hopeless correspondent. It wasn't so much that I never wrote letters, I did frequently, I just never posted them. At any one time there were dozens of sheets of notepaper littered around my room with barely legible 'Dear so and so' scrawled across them. With nothing happening in my life I had very little to say beyond 'How are you?' and to have documented even the smallest slice of my mundane lifestyle ('Today I got up, and had Frosties for breakfast . . .') would have left me too depressed for words.

I was well aware of the contents of the envelope on my bed before I even opened it, as the day in question was Significant Wednesday, the bi-weekly religious festival that heralded my salvation – my Giro. My parents were, to say the least, not the happiest of bunnies when I, their first born, returned to the family nest to languish on the dole. Four years earlier they'd driven me – along with a suitcase, hi-fi, box of tapes and a *Betty Blue* poster – off to Manchester University, expecting me to gain a first-rate education, an ounce or two of common sense and a direction in life. 'We don't mind what you do, son, as long as you do it to the best of your ability,' they'd said, not bothering to hide the extreme disappointment in their collective voices when I announced that I intended to study English and Film Studies. 'Whatever for?' asked the two-bodied, one-headed guardians of my soul. Neither were they impressed with my explanation which basically boiled down to the fact that I liked reading books and I liked watching films.

Three years later, I concluded my journey on the educational conveyor belt and quickly gained a realistic perspective of my position in the world at large: I was over-educated in two subjects that were of little use outside of university without further training. Having only just scraped a 2:2, and bored with the education process as a whole, I bundled 'further training' into the box marked 'out of the question'. Instead, I applied myself to reading a few more books, watching a lot more films and signing on. I maintained this pattern for a year or so, until the bank got tough with me during a short-tenancy in a shared house in Hulme. In a two-pronged attack worthy of Rommel, my bank manager withdrew my overdraft facility and made me sign an agreement to pay £20 a week into my account to bring the overdraft down to 'something a little more reasonable'. And so, like a homing pigeon, I returned to the parental home in Nottingham and holed up in my bedroom, contemplating the Future. Both parents pulled any number of favours to help me get on the career trail, while my Gran telephoned with regular monotony informing me of jobs she'd seen in the local paper. Needless to say all their hard work was wasted on me. I wasn't interested in a career, I had a roof over my head and, I reasoned, as long as I had the love of a good woman being poor didn't much bother me.

I say 'much', because occasionally my impoverished state did in fact work me up into a frenzy of bitterness. Fortunately, I learned to express my powerlessness by scoring as many points against Them – as in 'Us and . . .' – as I could. These minor acts of guerrilla warfare included the following:

- Obtaining a NUS card under false pretences.

- Using the aforesaid card to gain cheap admission to the cinema.

- Altering out-of-date bus passes.

- Damaging fruit in Tesco's.

- Driving a car without road tax or insurance.

- Drinking complete strangers' pints in night-clubs.

I did anything which, generally speaking, kept my mind alive and made me feel like I was chalking up another point on my side of the great scoreboard of life. But it was Aggi who kept me sane. Without her I would have dropped off The Edge.

Aggi really was quite brilliant, the most wonderful person I'd ever had the pleasure of meeting in my life. When we first started going out together I used to walk her home and while we were kissing and hugging good-bye on her door step, my favourite thing to do was to concentrate my whole mind on capturing the Moment – her smell, the taste of her mouth, the sensation of her body pressed against mine – I wanted to photograph it and keep it forever. But it never worked. Within minutes of walking through the damp streets of West Bridgford, with drizzle in my hair and an ache in my loins, she was gone. I could never recreate the Experience.

We met in a charity shop during the summer break. Aggi was eighteen then and had just finished her A levels, while I'd just completed the first year of my degree. She worked at an Oxfam shop in West Bridgford which I'd been frequenting on a twice weekly basis, because of its high turnover of quality junk. I'd been waiting patiently for the doors to open since

9.25 a.m., but as the shop didn't officially open for another five minutes, I'd whiled away the time pressing my nose against the glass door pulling faces purely for my own amusement. Aggi had noticed one in particular – my impression of a gargoyle in mental distress – and had opened the doors two minutes early, laughing as she did so. We were alone apart from an old lady at the back of the shop listening to *Desert Island Discs* as she sorted clothes. That day Aggi wore a short-sleeved green dress with small yellow flowers on it and a pair of sky blue canvas baseball boots. The overall effect was, to be truthful, a little twee but somehow she made it look marvellous. I positioned myself in front of a few old Barry Manilow albums and pretended to look through them, because the rack that housed them was the ideal location for me to steal as many glances at this incredibly beautiful girl as I liked.

I was sure that she would feel my eyes watching her every move, because after a while I gave up all pretence of being interested in any of Barry's greatest hits and just gazed at her longingly instead. I smiled as I approached the till with my sole purchase, an Elvis mirror, the type found only at fun fairs, where something skilful with an air gun, dart or hoop has to be done to win one. Thanks to Aggi, I'd cut out the middle man. Elvis was mine.

'The King of Rock 'n' Roll.'

Those were the first words she ever said to me. I went back every day that week and over the following months and subsequent conversations we got to know each other well.

Me: Hi, what's your name?

Her: Agnes Elizabeth Peters. But it's Aggi to you.

Me: Why do you work here?

Her: My mum works here sometimes. I'm bored of staying at home so I help out sometimes, it's my contribution to helping humanity evolve. (Laughs) Plus it looks good on CVs.

Me: What do you do?

Her: I'm about to go to the Salford University to do Social Science.

Me: Why?

Her: (Looks slightly embarrassed) Because I care about people rather than money. I think it's wrong that people in this day and age should be homeless. Call me old-fashioned but I'm a socialist.

Me: Do you believe in platonic friendship?

Her: No. 'Platonic friendship is the moment between when you meet and your first kiss'. Don't applaud, I didn't say it first.

Me: Do you think Elvis really is dead?

Her: (Laughs) Yes. But his memory lives on in the hearts of the young, the brave and the free.

Me: What's your favourite film?

Her: This might sound a bit pretentious but I think film as a medium is nowhere near as expressive as the novel. Having said that I must admit a distinct liking for Audrey Hepburn in *Breakfast at Tiffany's*.

Me: What's the weirdest thing you've ever thought?
Her: If there are an infinite number of parallel universes, containing all the alternate decisions I could've made, how would my life have turned out if I'd accepted Asim Ali's proposal of marriage when we were six?

Me: When was the last time you cried?
Her: Probably when I was six, after turning down Asim Ali. I don't know – I don't really do emotional histrionics that often.

Me: Do you love me?
Her: I love you so much that when I think about how I feel about you my brain can't begin to comprehend it. It's exactly like infinity. I don't understand it, but those are the limitations of my love.

Between the first question and the last was a period of about five months. We got together between 'Do you believe in platonic friendship?' and 'Is Elvis really dead?' which was the opening topic of conversation on our first proper date, in the brightly lit, overcrowded, not-in-the-least-bit-romantic lounge of the Royal Oak. Deep down, I always liked to believe that I knew things wouldn't work out between us. Nothing could have been that perfect unless it had its première on terrestrial television. The thing that swung it for me, the one thing that made me so sure, was our first kiss. It wiped away my fears and insecurities in an instant.

At the end of our first date I'd been unsure about where we stood with the boy-girl relationship thing. Yes, we'd held hands occasionally and flirted a great deal, but we hadn't kissed, at least not properly. At the end of the night I'd kissed her lightly on her left cheek, as I would my Gran, and made my way home after I'd made her promise to see me again. I'd spent the entire week prior to our next date in a tortured state of limbo. What had happened, exactly? We'd gone out together, yes, but had it only been a date for me? Perhaps for her it had been nothing more than a night out with a nice guy? Had I spent the last seven days dreaming of her unceasingly, while she could barely remember my name? I wanted an answer. I needed an answer. I even called her once to ask her, but my courage had faded and I'd put the phone down. I couldn't think of how to say what I wanted to know, which was basically: Am I your boyfriend?

'Am I your boyfriend?' is the kind of question a nine-year-old asks another nine-year-old. It had no place in a sophisticated relationship. I knew the rules – I was meant to be cool and relaxed, laid back and casual. At first maybe we'd 'see' each other (which meant that she'd still 'see' other people), then maybe we'd date (which would mean that she wouldn't see other people even though she might want to) and then finally we'd be boyfriend and girlfriend (by which time she wouldn't want to see other people because she'd be happy with me).

When the day of our second date finally arrived, we met outside a record shop, Selectadisc, as arranged. The plan, such as it was, revolved around spending the afternoon in the square outside the town hall feeding the pigeons (her idea). Only it didn't happen like that. The first thing she did on seeing me was to wrap her arms around me tightly and kiss me so fervently that I literally went weak at the knees. I'd never felt passion like it before. And this was the best bit: *she* looked straight into my eyes and asked *me* if she was my girlfriend. I said, 'Yes, you are my Legendary Girlfriend.'

The end of everything we had, everything we were and everything I'd hoped we'd be, also arrived with a kiss, one which I found myself reliving two or three times a day years later. It was my birthday and I'd only been back in Nottingham for a couple of weeks, while Aggi had been there all summer since graduating and was waitressing in a restaurant in town. We'd arranged to meet outside Shoe Express in Broad Marsh Shopping Centre. Aggi had got there before me, which should've set alarm bells ringing as she was frequently punctual but never early. She was empty-handed but the significance of this didn't occur to me until much later.

We had a glorious afternoon celebrating my twenty-third – maybe a little too glorious – wandering in and out of stores pretending to be a recently married couple furnishing our love nest. The conversation and humour made me feel alive, really alive. It didn't matter that I didn't have a job, future or money – I felt at peace with the world. I was happy.

Driving home I sat next to Aggi in her mum's Fiat Uno as we made our way through the city centre. Ten minutes before we should've been at her mum's house she pulled into Rilstone Road, a cul-de-sac near Crestfield Park, and stopped the car. Undoing her seat-belt, she turned her body towards mine and kissed me. There was no mistaking it – it was a 'good-bye' kiss.

It was a 'this isn't working' kiss.

It was a 'this is hurting me more than it's hurting you' kiss.

All I could think was: 'This is The Last Kiss.'

She said that for a long time she'd felt that I wanted more from her than she had to give.

She said I needed someone who could guarantee to be around forever.

She said that, while she did love me, she didn't think that was enough any more.

She said that she was twenty-one and I was twenty-three and that we should both be living our lives to the full but instead we'd got stuck in a rut.

She said that for a long time she'd had the feeling that we weren't going anywhere.

I said nothing.

At 5.15 p.m. I'd been a perfectly happy young man with everything to look forward to. By 5.27 p.m. my life was over. It took twelve minutes to dismantle three years of love.

I got out of the car, slamming the door behind me, walked to the nearest cashpoint, took out £50 and headed for the Royal Oak. There, despite my embarrassingly low threshold for alcohol, I drank three double Jack Daniels, a Malibu and Coke (out of curiosity) and a double gin and tonic (because it was the first drink I had ever bought Aggi).

On a whim, I got a taxi back into town and continued drinking, despite throwing up twice. Around midnight I ended up in a club called Toots, with a group of people whom I vaguely knew. Much of what then happened is hazy, although I do recall stealing at least three strangers' pints. Some weeks later, while bruising peaches in Tesco's, I was pounced upon by a fat, angry Irish girl who filled in the rest of the details. She claimed to have been at the club that night and said that I'd danced with her, shirt unbuttoned to the waist, to Abba's 'Dancing Queen'. According to her version of events, half an hour later she discovered me in a stall in the Ladies', lying curled at the side of a toilet bowl, crying desperately. My good Samaritan, worried that an earlier refusal to kiss me had had this effect, put me in the back of a taxi, but not before I'd thrown up over her shirt and told her that I loved her.

7.45 P.M.

It's a soul-destroyingly depressing fact that when you live in a place on your own, nothing moves. When I'd left the flat on Friday morning it had resembled Dresden after a flying visit from the RAF. Suitcases lay open, their contents spilled out across the floor. Cardboard boxes full of junk occupied valuable floor space. Soiled underwear lay abandoned in the oddest of places – the window sill, on top of the wardrobe, underneath the phone – while dirty crockery bred rapidly all around. And now, some twelve hours later, things were still pretty much the same. Maybe the air was a little staler or the dust on the TV a bit deeper, but on the whole nothing had changed. Back home in Nottingham, however, if I left my room – sometimes for as little as an hour – something always changed. Usually it was because my mother had kidnapped the dirty clothes off the floor, or sometimes because of my kid brother's general snooping; once, even my Gran got in on the act – playing detective. Inspired by a report on Young People and Drugs on *This Morning with Richard and Judy*, Gran had decided my sleeping in late and general lack of motivation was a result of drug abuse. In search of hard evidence she set about my room, but the nearest she got to crack was a yellow and blue tin that said Myoxil, and even then she still insisted on taking it to Boots to check it really *was* athlete's foot powder.

Dumping my bag on the sofa, I contemplated cleaning the flat. It was the sort of idea – along with ironing, visits to the launderette and letters to friends whom I hadn't seen since university – which I was inclined to conjure up when I had nothing better to do. The idea, however, was taken no further because I spotted a novel in one of the boxes which I'd given up on months ago, and decided that now was as good a time as any to finish what I'd started. I was about to pull out the sofa-bed – in order to delude myself that I was going to recline and read, rather than recline and sleep – when I decided that I might be hungry. There was nothing that my mother, or for that matter a dietician, would've construed as 'proper food' in the kitchen, but I lit up a cigarette from the emergency pack stashed in my suitcase to stave off immediate hunger pangs, and checked out the fridge for the sheer hell of it.

The yellowing refrigerator in the corner of the kitchen gurgling vociferously, as if suffering from a heavy bout of indigestion was, at a guess, probably a decade older than myself, as was virtually everything in the flat. The cooker, wardrobes, sofa-bed, carpet – the rigours of age had consumed them all to such an extent that it had rendered them useless unless you had the know-how. For instance, to get a ring on the cooker to work, the control knob had to be turned on and off twice; to open the wardrobe door, pressure had to be applied to the top right-hand corner. Had I noticed all that was wrong when I first saw the flat, I wouldn't have taken it, but at the time getting a roof over my head had seemed more important than checking wardrobe doors, and my landlord, Mr F. Jamal (at least that was the name I wrote on the rent cheques) had known this. His skills in interior design were so shoddy that he must have graduated with honours from the Rachman school of landlords. Every surface in the flat had been painted in cheap cheerless white emulsion some time in the last fifty years, which the passing of time and countless smokers had managed to downgrade to a pale orangey-brown. The only furniture in the room was a sofa-bed in fawn velvety material pitted haphazardly with cigarette burns; a tile-surfaced coffee table against the far wall which had the TV perched on it; and two small white Formica wardrobes along the wall opposite the window. To try and cheer the place up – an impossibly futile task – I had stuck my favourite photo of Aggi on the wall near the sofa-bed and an Audrey Hepburn poster on the wall in the bathroom.

I'd spent two solid weeks searching for accommodation. They were the second most depressing weeks of my life, requiring me to get the 07.15 National Express coach from Nottingham to London four times, in order to traipse around the slum districts of the capital. In this time I learned the two laws of looking for accommodation in London:

1. **Never trust a landlord while he's still breathing.**
2. **The only good landlords are four dead landlords.**

The only place I saw, could afford and which didn't have drug dealers in the vicinity was Flat 3, 64 Cumbria Avenue

– aka – N6. A luxurious self-contained studio flat with own kitchenette, bathroom/shower

– aka – a glorified studio flat, minus the glory, on the second floor of a decrepit Edwardian house in crappy Archway.

To be truthful, Mr F. Jamal hadn't advertised my abode in *Loot* or any other free ad newspaper. He hadn't needed to. He had a kind of word of mouth thing going amongst people in the know in the lower end of the accommodation food chain, so much so that his many properties were consistently snapped up within seconds of becoming available. I, however, became aware of his legendary status not by being in the know – but through Tammy, my friend Simon's girlfriend. She'd told him about Mr F. Jamal after I'd been moaning to Simon about the difficulty I was having. I'd looked at nine places, all complete and utter toilets 'five minutes' from the tube, the worst of which was a place in Kentish Town. The landlord arrived half an hour late for our appointment, by which time five other people had turned up to view the place he'd promised me first refusal on. It wasn't anything to shout about, just a double room with a shared toilet and kitchen. He told the assembled crowd that the man living there had changed his mind and wanted to stay, but he was going to put an extra bed in the room and did anyone want it. At this point I'd walked off in disgust but three of my fellow house-hunters were desperate enough to stay behind. Tammy gave Simon Mr F. Jamal's phone number. One call later and I was signing the lease. I had thought about thanking her for her effort, but as Tammy and I couldn't stand each other I hadn't bothered. I'd assumed her assistance was some kind of perverse tactic to get one over on me.

I opened the fridge door and peered in. The light didn't come on. I suspected it probably hadn't done so since the Apollo Moon landings. Peering amongst the abandoned items within: marmalade, margarine, tomato ketchup, a five-day-old can of beans and an onion – I spied a jar of olives and smiled heartily to myself.

Lying on the sofa in the main room, I lanced an olive while attempting to write my name on the cushion with my index finger – all the down strokes followed the flow of the material so half of it was missing. Time flowed by. I ate another olive and stared at the ceiling. More time flowed by. I ate another olive and tried to read my book. Yet more time flowed by. I ate another olive and let the brine drip off the end of the fork onto my chin and dribble down to my neck. At this point I decided it was time for action. I considered all the things that needed doing and chose the least painful: a begging letter to the bank. On a page of notepaper using a green Berol marker pen I'd stolen from school, I wrote:

Dear student banking advisor,

Having recently qualified from a teacher training course I'm now ready, at the age of twenty-five (nearly twenty-six) to take my place as a fully functioning member of society. I have a job but am living in London, and it is so ridiculously expensive to live here that I'm not sure why I bother. To this end please would you extend my already extended overdraft a bit more, because otherwise I may faint from starvation in front of a class of fourteen-year-olds.

Yours forever,

William Kelly

I chuckled aloud. I was just about to add 'PS and don't think that I've forgotten that you stitched me up when I needed you most', when I noticed the red light of the answering machine blinking away.

Next to the Walkman, I considered the answering machine to be one of man's truly great achievements. It allowed you to keep abreast of the latest developments in your social life *and* screen calls. Brilliant. My love for this particular piece of technology was inspired by a message Aggi left on my Aunt Susan's when I was house-sitting for her in Primrose Hill during the summer vacation of my second year. At the time, Aunt Susan lived in London, where she was beauty editor on *Woman's Realm* or some other similar magazine that had knitting patterns.

Aunt Susan, it must be said, was more unlike my mother than I thought possible for people who had shared the same womb. Twelve years younger than my mother – almost a generation apart – she had more in common with me. She hated work, was one of the first in her road to have cable television, and adored the third series of *Blackadder*. She used to tell me that she'd never get married because then she'd have to grow up. The summer after I came to house-sit, however, she got hitched, had my cousin Georgia, gave up journalism and moved back to Nottingham. On the occasion in question, she'd gone on holiday with Uncle-Bill-to-be, and said I could do whatever I wanted with the house as long as the police weren't involved. Fortunately for her all I did was watch videos, eat crisp sandwiches and walk her dog, Seabohm – hardly activities worthy of the scrutiny of the local constabulary. I'd been out walking the dog on this particular day, when I returned to the house to discover there was a message for me from Aggi:

You're not in! This is not how it was supposed to be. All I wanted to say was that I dreamt about you last night. We were in a field and the soundtrack to 'Singin' in The Rain' was playing in the background. We lay on our backs just staring at the moon. I want you to know I won't stop loving you. I promise you, I won't.

I listened to it over and over again. I wanted to keep it forever but it was sandwiched between a call from a PR called Madeline inviting Aunt Susan to the launch of a new range of Boots nail varnishes, and one from my mother checking to see if I was eating properly. When my aunt heard Aggi's message she said, and I remember this quite clearly: 'That sounds like Ms Right to me.' When I got back to Nottingham, I asked Aggi about the message but she refused to discuss it. That was just her way.

I played the messages back:

Venus calling Mars. Come in, Mars! Why are men so bloody competitive? Discuss. Hi, Will, Alice here. If you have an answer to this eternal conundrum, or indeed just fancy a chat with your best friend in the whole wide world – call me now!

Er, hi. This is Kate Freemans here. (Voice falters) I used to live in your flat. (Starts crying) I was just wondering if there was any mail for me. (Attempts to stop crying, instead snuffles loudly) The temp agency I was working for posted my cheque to the wrong address. I'll try and ring later. (Begins crying again) Thanks.

Listen, I've got something really important to tell you. Call me as soon as you can. It's urgent. Really urgent . . . oh, it's Simon by the way.

Will, it's Martina. I don't know why I'm leaving this message, I think your machine is broken, this is the third one I've left this week. Assuming that you've got it fixed, hello for the first time since Saturday night! Er, ring me, please. We need to talk. Bye.

Hello. This is Kate Freemans again. I'm just ringing to say sorry about my message. Just ignore it, okay? I'm really sorry.

My first thoughts were about the girl who used to live in my flat. It felt weird hearing a stranger's message on *my* answering machine, let alone one in which she was crying. As she hadn't left a number there was little I could do bar sit and wonder why my answering machine had reduced her to tears. Next up, I thought about Martina, even though I didn't want to. There was no way on earth I was going to return her call because she, as far as I was concerned, was a first rate nutter of the *Fatal Attraction* variety and I had no intention of playing Michael Douglas to her Glenn Close in her sordid little fantasy. I checked my watch. It was too late to catch Simon now, as I knew for a fact that his band would be on stage at the Royal Oak. Anyway, the message was so typically Simon – overblown and melodramatic – that it completely failed to pique even an iota of interest. And so by process of elimination, Alice's was the only message left worth returning, qualifying on the grounds that it was the only one that made me feel better.

I'd first met Alice on my sixteenth birthday. I'd been standing in the Royal Oak, discussing the finer points of the British soap opera compared to its weaker, less attractive Australian cousin, with two attractive fourteen-year-old girls who had taken it upon themselves to follow Simon's first band, Reverb. The girls had got it into their heads that Simon was good-looking and interesting, and I was busily trying to persuade them that I was a far better option, when I felt myself slipping away from the conversation. While my body gibbered away on terra firma, the important bit that made all the decisions focused its attention on a girl who looked like the French foreign exchange student of my dreams – dark-red hennaed hair, a beguiling smile and beautifully tanned skin – standing alone at the end of the bar observing Reverb's exceptionally abysmal cover of The Buzzcocks' Ever Fallen In Love. My brain alerted my body to its new discovery and both made their excuses to their captive teenage audience.

Chatting up girls had never been one of my strong points. Some people had that certain something needed not to look like a pillock while doing it. Simon, for instance, had it in abundance. I, however, didn't. On most occasions I would've resigned myself to this fact, content to gaze longingly at her rather than take up my desires and run, but this time was different. In a matter of half an hour I was convinced that this girl was the person I'd been looking for all my life – there was no way I was going to give up without trying.

At the end of the gig I approached her, using Reverb's performance to open up the conversation. She told me she thought they were terrible but the singer was quite cute – I was devastated. Right on cue, Simon, guitar in hand, strode across the room and introduced himself. 'Who's your friend?' he asked me 'casually'. I told him I didn't know and she smiled, offered her hand to him and introduced herself: 'My name's Alice. Alice Chabrol.' And that was that. I wasn't so much edged out as completely ignored. Admittedly I did receive compensation by way of a birthday kiss, 2.2 seconds of red-lipped perfection pressed against my cheek with the delicate touch of an angel's wing.

Simon and Alice went out for a total of two weeks before she came to her senses and realised that he could never be as interested in anyone as he was in himself. 'I hadn't thought it was possible,' she'd told me over coffee the day after she'd dumped him. 'Everything he says is *me me me*.' Alice and I, however, became best friends. Over the following years I fell in love with her several times but never felt compelled to tell her, there was no reason to – she never seemed the slightest bit interested in being anything more than friends. If I'd seen the faintest glimmer of hope I would've gone for it, but faced with Alice's lack of interest and the memory of her choosing Simon over me I gave up, thus cultivating the following theory:

Kelly's First Law of Relationships:

No woman who finds Simon attractive will ever be interested in me.

As if to prove this as fact, when Alice went to university at Oxford she fell for Bruce (a surrogate Simon if ever I saw one), a Maths postgraduate who bore more than a passing resemblance to Steve McQueen in *The Great Escape*. With the exception of his total expertise in every field known to impress man, his most annoying trait was his ability to make me feel like a eunuch without even trying. He wasn't so much a man as a hyper-man, masculinity dripping from his every pore. He worked out three times a week. He knew what an exhaust manifold was. He owned an autographed photograph of Bruce Lee. Honestly, even Sean Connery would've felt like a bit of a girl around Bruce.

Fortunately my blossoming inferiority complex began to fade once I came to see Bruce as my best friend's boyfriend instead of six feet four inches of tosspot, and Alice as my best friend rather than the woman I most wanted to see naked. I adapted so well to my new role that my earlier mini-infatuations – which at the time had seemed more important than life itself – now felt like boyish crushes from a bygone age. I still didn't like Bruce, but it was no longer personal. When you have a friend of Alice's calibre, you come to realise there's no way anyone in ownership of a penis will ever be worthy of her.

After Alice got a job as marketing manager for British Telecom, she and Bruce moved to Bristol and led the kind of life that involved expensive restaurants, shopping trips to Bond Street and weekend breaks in Prague. I considered being jealous of her quite a few times but I couldn't. Though she earned more in an hour than I used to get in my entire fortnight's Giro, she was still the same person inside: kind, patient and understanding. As a rule, I disapproved of successful people, especially those of my generation, but I couldn't resent her. Success not only suited her, it appeared to be made for her.

*   *   *

'Hello?' said Alice.

'It's me,' I replied.

'Will! How are you?' she said, genuinely excited. 'How's the job?'

'Oh it's crap. Kind of just what I expected only worse.' I felt a yawn rise up from deep inside me. I attempted to stifle it by gritting my teeth. 'Much worse.'

'Is that possible? I thought your motto was "Think of the worst thing possible and multiply it by ten".'

'Obviously I didn't think things could be worse than even *I* could possibly imagine them,' I replied, reflecting on how, since Aggi, it had become my personal philosophy to look on the dark, half-empty, who's-nicked-my-silver-lining side of Life.

'It's horrible,' I said, noticing that the photo of Aggi had fallen down. 'A total nightmare. I can't coast or take it easy for a second, otherwise they'll skin me alive. I can't show any weakness. The kids, they can smell weakness from a mile off. Once they catch a whiff it sends them wild. They're like a pack of hyenas pouncing on a wounded antelope. Sarah, another newly-qualified teacher, broke down in tears in front of a class on Thursday.' I fiddled with the Blu-tac on Aggi's photo and put it back up. 'I give her another week before she's looking at other career options.'

Alice laughed.

'It's not funny, you know.'

'No, of course it's not funny.'

It wasn't the least bit amusing because I'd had some bitter experiences of my own during the past week. On Monday three year-eleven boys had walked out of my class; Wednesday I'd returned to the staff room to discover that one of the little gits had spat a huge 'greenie' on the back of my jacket;

and Thursday I'd left my bottom year-eleven set's English books back at the flat.

'It can be like that,' said Alice adopting a tone of voice reminiscent of a reassuring rub on the small of the back.

I wasn't comforted. I wasn't happy. I was fed up. And Alice would never understand this. She had a 'career', whereas I had a 'job' and that was the difference between us. 'Careers' are about personal challenges, whereas 'jobs' are about survival. Granted, Alice's chosen occupation might have been stressful at times, but her targets were realistic and she had the grand resources of a multi-national at her disposal. As a teacher, I had to deal with ludicrously ambitious targets, zero resources, school inspections and sociopaths who thought spitting on a teacher's back was right up there with Monty Python's parrot sketch.

'How do you do it?' I wondered aloud.

'How do I do what?'

'You know,' I said, searching for the right word. 'That . . . work stuff. How do you cope with it all?'

'Experience, Will, experience,' said Alice warmly. 'I don't want to seem patronising but come on, Will, you put a lot of this pressure on yourself by expecting results too fast. I've been working four years now, but this is the first job you've ever had.'

Alice, to be frank, was being more than a bit of a cheeky cow, as she was well aware that I'd spent an entire summer working in the Royal Oak. I knew what hard work was: I'd shifted barrels of beer, brought up huge crates of mixers from the cellar and worked twelve-hour shifts, all of which I reminded her.

'It wasn't the whole summer,' said Alice, sniggering. 'It was four weeks, and you got sacked for continually being late, if I remember correctly.'

She was right, not just about my employment history but about my attitude to work. I wanted everything to be perfect straight away, because the thought of it taking time and patience to learn how to control these animals made me feel sick.

During the course of this part of the conversation I'd become aware that something about Aggi's picture didn't look right. It was only as Alice told me some gossip about a mutual acquaintance who had been caught shoplifting, that I realised the photo was sloping a little to the right. I took it down to readjust it but creased it in the process. This was my favourite picture of her – taken before she'd had her bob; her long ringlets of auburn hair, which at times overwhelmed the delicate features of her face, were tied back leaving her beautiful green eyes, kissable lips and delicate nose on full display. She was leaning against a wall outside the university library, reading *The Beauty Myth*. She looked perfect.

My feet began to itch. I took off my sock and gave my toes a rub.

'Do you think you'll stick it out?' asked Alice. 'I mean, you sound pretty stressed out.'

I told her I didn't know and explained the crux of my problem – teaching in the training year was nothing like teaching was now. This was For Real. The kids were depending on me to help them pass their exams. The ramifications of my being a crap teacher were terrifyingly immense.

'Imagine thirty kids fail their English GCSE because of me – thirty kids who will get a rubbish job or no job at all sucked into the poverty trap. Five years later, half of them will have kids and be living off social security. Multiply that by a couple more years of me teaching, and before you know it I'll be responsible for increasing unemployment in the UK more than any government, Conservative or Labour, since the war.'

'You're overreacting,' said Alice. 'You've got to face facts, Will. You're a grown-up. Grown-ups have responsibilities.'

'You know what I mean,' I said, while pulling off my other sock and rubbing between the toes on my now naked foot. 'These kids won't know anything unless I teach it to them. What if I'm a crap teacher?'

I sensed Alice was having problems seeing my perspective. Too tired to continue making my point, I changed discussion topics. Over the next half hour – in which time I'd put my socks back on but taken my trousers off and draped the duvet around me – Alice told me how she was working out of the Peterborough office for a month and living in a Novotel in the city centre because of a project she was overseeing. The only time I'd ever been to a hotel was when Aggi and I had saved fourteen coupons from the *Daily Telegraph*, which had got us a half price night at the Nottingham Holiday Inn. We stole the shampoos, shower caps and even the miniature kettle before vacating the room the next day. It had been brilliant. I was about to remark how cool it must be to live in a hotel at someone else's expense when it occurred to me that Alice probably saw things a bit differently.

'What about Bruce?' I asked, remembering the times I'd really missed Aggi, like when she went on holiday to Austria for two weeks with her mum, or when she had her wisdom teeth out and had to stay in hospital on my twenty-first birthday. Both times I'd missed her so much I literally thought I'd die. 'Isn't he missing you?'

'Yes, he is,' she said sadly. 'At least I think he is. That's what my message on your machine was about. I think he feels threatened by the fact that things are going so well at work for me at the moment. He's been throwing himself into his work as if he's got something to prove to me – I don't know – that he's the main bread winner. As if I cared! He's been working late most nights, even some weekends. Once this project is over I'm going to ask for a transfer to a less frantic department. Maybe then he won't feel the need to compete and we can just be happy.'

I got the impression that Alice was unsettled for the rest of our conversation – I wished I hadn't reminded her of Bruce's absence. Hiding her sadness under the guise of a merry gossip she told me about the gym she'd joined and how her friend at work, Tina, was having an affair with her supervisor, and how she and Bruce were planning to go to New York over Christmas.

Before she finished the call she brought up the subject of my birthday.

'I know you hate birthdays, Will.'

'And Walkers prawn cocktail crisps . . .'

'But I . . .'

'And totalitarian governments . . .'

'. . . really wanted to . . .'

'And sticky-outty belly buttons . . .'

'. . . do something . . .'

'And Alfred Hitchcock films.'

'. . . special . . .'

I ran out of things to hate.

'I hope you don't mind,' said Alice.

I tutted softly and told her I didn't. She refused to elaborate on what 'something special' would entail, said good-bye, and promised to call me on my birthday. As I replaced the phone I whispered a small prayer of thanks to whoever was responsible for introducing this angel into my life.

10.01 P.M.

Peak time Friday night. Office workers, labourers, cleaners, architects and all, wash themselves free of the fetid stench of Work. This was the moment they were finally allowed to forget they were office workers, labourers, cleaners, architects or whatever, and remember, perhaps for the first time in five days, that first and foremost, they were people.

All week I'd been a Teacher. But what I wanted now was to be a Human Being.

I should've been out there with the office workers, labourers, cleaners and architects.

I should've been getting my round in.
I should've been making jokes about my boss.
I should've been onto my sixth bottle of Molson Dry.
I should've been dancing somewhere.
I should've been out on the pull.

But I wasn't . . .

While everyone in the Western hemisphere was *out* having a great time, I was *in* having a crap time. This of course explained why none of the second-division friends in my sodding address book – people whom I only ever contacted

45

when really, really desperate – were in. Of the six calls made I got one no answer, two requests to enter into dialogue with answering machines and for the rest, I got the unobtainable tone. I refused to leave any messages on the grounds that there was no way I was letting anyone – least of all friends I rarely spoke to – know I was in on a Friday night and desperate for their company, while they were out starting their weekends with a bang.

I looked at my watch and wondered optimistically if it was telling the wrong time. I called the speaking clock:

At the third stroke it will be Ten-o-six-and-fifty-seconds.

Not altogether dissimilar to the time on my watch.

At moments like this, when loneliness seemed like my only friend, the only place safe to hide from the world at large was under the sheets. It was time to get out the sofa-bed.

The sofa-bed was pretty diabolical as a sofa and not that much better as a bed; the fact that these two nouns were joined together by a single hyphen failed to make the object they described any more comfortable than Dralon-covered paving stones. I threw its two cushions to the floor to reveal the depressing sight of the bed's underside. It always required more strength than I thought I had to pull the bed frame out. I took a deep breath and pulled. It slowly creaked into action, unfolding stubbornly.

Leaving my socks and shirt on, and pulling the duvet off the floor, I lay on the bed and tried desperately to forget the cold and the reason I'd retired there in the first place. The need to hear another human voice became paramount in my mind.

I turned on the radio on my hi-fi, hoping that *The Barbara White Show* would be on. I'd been listening to her show on Central FM all week. Barbara White was the 'larger-than-life' host of a phone-in show where assorted nutters, losers, weirdos and plain helpless cases called in with their problems. Barbara – a woman about as qualified to advise as I was to teach – listened, made the appropriate sympathetic noises and then came up with answers so facile she honestly had to be heard to be believed. The fact that she was American was probably the only reason she got away with giving such screamingly obvious advice.

Barbara was talking to Peter, a student from Newcastle-under-Lyme, who had just finished his A levels and had got into his local university to study Engineering. He wasn't happy, though. His girlfriend of seven months was going to university in Aberdeen and he was worried that the huge distance would drive a wedge between them.

It occurred to me as I listened to his pitiful story that Peter was being naive in the extreme. He'd been in a relationship for less time than it takes to make a baby and here he was wanting to make commitments. If I'd been his age I would have been over the moon at the prospect of hitting university as a single man – able to do what I want, when I want, with thousands of like-minded individuals who also think they've just invented sex, alcohol and staying up past 2.00 a.m.; people who'd want to party, party, party 'til they were sick and then party some more. Peter was guaranteed to have three years more exciting than my next ten.

I was so entrenched in my bitter attack against Barbara's caller I managed to miss most of her solution. All I heard her ask was, 'Do you love this girl?' and he replied he didn't know – he thought he did but probably wouldn't be sure until it was too late. As Barbara announced she was going to a commercial break, the phone rang.

I knew it wouldn't be Simon – his gig didn't finish until eleven; it was too late for either of my parents; I'd just spoken to Alice and as far as I knew no one else had my number. The odds were, of course, that it was Martina, because my life was like that: too much of what I didn't want and a permanent drought of the things my heart desired most. I hoped with all my strength that it wasn't Martina, because as well as not feeling up to listening to her complain about how terrible her life was, I especially didn't want to dump her, at least not right now.

Ring!

Please don't let it be Martina.

Ring!

Please don't let it be Martina.

Ring!

Please.

Ring!

Please.

Ring!

Please. Please. Please.

Ring!

Please. Please. Please. Please!

I answered the phone.

'Hello?' I held my breath and waited for the first sounds of Martina's placid yet disturbing voice.

'Hello,' said the female voice on the other end of the phone, which clearly wasn't Martina's. There was a school-girlish enthusiasm about it that would've been refreshing had it not been me she was talking to. *Whoever this person is*, I thought, *this call is going to disappoint her*.

'Can I help you?' I asked politely.

'You can indeed,' she replied. 'I'm sorry to call so late but I thought if you're anything like me it's better to have a call late at night rather than early in the morning. My mum tries to ring me at seven in the morning sometimes just to tell me I've got a letter from the bank. Mind you, I'm never in at that time these days because I'm on my way to work, but if someone rang me on say, my day off, then boy, would they be in big trouble.'

She was rambling. The more she rambled the more adorable she sounded.

'I was wondering,' she continued, 'whether you could help me. I used to live in your flat up until a week ago . . .' She paused as if reaching the punch-line. I suddenly recognised her voice. She was Crying Girl from my answering machine. 'I was wondering . . . has there been any post for me? I'm expecting a cheque to arrive. I was doing a bit of casual office work for a temp agency and they've sent my cheque to my old address, even though I'd told them a million times that I was moving to Brighton.'

'Mmmm,' I said, thinking it sounded sympathetic.

There was a long pause.

I was about to offer another 'Mmmm' to fill the gap in the conversation when she spoke again. 'Well . . . is there any post?'

Instead of answering her question I deconstructed her voice. It was quite pleasant, really. The sort of voice that made me feel at ease; it was a bit well spoken at the edges but far from aloof. No, this girl sounded like she was definitely worth investigating, especially as there was the small point of her tearful message. I wanted to ask about it but couldn't quite work out how to do it.

'Sorry?' I said.

'Is there any post?' she repeated. 'I'm sorry for phoning so late but the cheque's quite important. I need it to pay this month's rent.'

I finally woke up. 'Oh, sorry. No, there's no mail for you. There's a big pile of stuff downstairs that no one's touched all week. People who used to live here ages ago, I think. But I've been through it and I didn't see any addressed to this flat.'

'Really?' she said disappointedly.

'Really. Tell me, what's your name?' I asked, quickly adding: 'So I can check again, if you like,' so that it didn't sound like a chat-up line.

'Katie,' she said. 'Or Kate rather.' She laughed. 'No, that's Kate Freemans, not Kate Rather!'

'As in the catalogue,' I quipped and then desperately wished I hadn't.

She laughed.

'Right,' I said. 'I'll just be a second while I nip downstairs and check them again.'

'Oh, thanks,' she said gratefully. 'It's nice of you to go to all this trouble.'

I put the phone on the bed and raced down the stairs in my boxer shorts, socks and shirt ensemble. Picking up the discarded post, I shot back upstairs, slamming the door behind me.

'There's loads for Mr G. Peckham,' I said, breathlessly shuffling through the letters. 'He's got a lot of stuff from the AA.' This was small talk of the tiniest variety, but I didn't have any other choice if I wanted to keep talking to her. 'There are two letters for a K. D. Sharpe, all with New Zealand stamps, and the rest is boring junk mail stuff. Sorry, nothing for a Kate Freemans.'

'Well, thanks for looking,' she said stoically.

'Maybe it'll turn up tomorrow,' I replied in a cheery tone which was very un-me. 'The post's pretty crap around here. It's my birthday on Sunday and I haven't received a single card yet. If they don't arrive tomorrow I won't have any on the day.'

'I'm sure you will,' she said, her disappointment at being cashless seemingly evaporated. 'How old will you be?'

'Do you really want to know?' I knew it was a stupid question the moment it slipped off my tongue and into the conversation. She wasn't going to say no, but it wouldn't be a truthful yes, either. She wasn't honestly going to give a toss about how old I was.

'Yes,' she said, so clearly, so confidently, so joyfully, that I was totally convinced she'd told the truth. 'But don't tell me. I'll guess. Are you thirty-one?'

'No.'

'Older or younger?'

'Younger.'

'Twenty-nine?'

'Lower.'

'Twenty-six?'

'Got it in one! Well, three actually. But well done anyhow. How did you guess? Do I sound twenty-six?'

This, of course, was stupid question number two. Where all this inanity was coming from I couldn't begin to guess, perhaps, I mused, I'd become a portal between Earth and Planet Stupid.

'I don't know,' she said. 'How does a twenty-six-year-old sound?'

'Although technically speaking,' I explained, 'I'm not actually twenty-six until Sunday, they do happen to sound a lot like me. The male variety, of which I consider myself to be a prime specimen, tend to whinge a lot about receding hair

51

lines, loss of physique, life, work, love-life (or lack of love in their life) while constantly harking back to some golden age, usually their university days. It's quite a monotonous sound but comforting all the same.'

Kate laughed. With my hand on my heart, and a finger hovering over the self-destruct button marked, 'Cheesy Similes', I swear that her laughter perfectly captured summertime – the sun on my neck, birds singing in trees and cloudless skies – all at once.

'And what about you?' I asked. 'How old are you?'

She didn't speak.

'Okay,' I said. 'You're twenty-one or twenty-two?'

'Nope.'

'Higher or lower?'

'What do you think?'

'Lower.'

'You're right.'

'Twenty?'

'Er, nope.'

'Nineteen?'

'Yup,' she said. 'But I'll be twenty in November.'

There was a long pause.

The long pause grew longer.

The long pause grew so long that unless one of us said something soon, the only thing left to say would be good-bye. I panicked and said the first thing that came into my head.

'Ahhhhh.'

There was another long pause.

'What does "Ahhhhh" mean?' enquired Kate, mimicking my 'Ahhhhh' note perfectly.

I hadn't a clue what to say next and was running out of plausible ideas at an alarming rate. 'Nothing really. Well not much anyhow. It's just that . . . I used to know a Katie at junior school. She was the fastest runner in the whole of our year until she was ten. It was amazing. I've never seen a girl go so fast. I've often wondered whether she ever made it to the Olympics or anything like that. You're not that Kate, are you?'

''Fraid not, Mr Spaceman,' said Kate.

'Spaceman?' I repeated.

'I don't know your name.'

'No, you don't, do you?' I thought of making one up purely for my own amusement, but somehow the honesty and the purity of her voice shamed me into not being so pathetic. 'Names are irrelevant. They're just labels. I mean, how can you tell what a child should be called before they've even had a chance to do anything?'

I was well aware of how pompous it sounded, because I'd thought exactly the same thing when I heard Simon say it to a girl at a party. The reason I was employing its use now was that I desperately wanted to ape the fantastic results he'd got using it.

'Don't you like your name?' asked Kate.

'It's all right,' I said nonchalantly. 'But it's not the name I would have chosen.'

She laughed, which wasn't exactly the reaction I'd been looking for. I asked her what she found amusing and she said something about boys being all the same and then asked me what name I would've chosen, which proved unfortunate as I couldn't remember which name Simon had used.

'I . . . I don't know,' I said nervously. I jammed the phone up against my ear with my shoulder, leaving my hands free to frantically tear the letter I'd written to the bank into little pieces.

'I think I'd call you James,' she said playfully.

I was intrigued. James? I listed all of the cool Jameses I

could think of: James Bond (shaken but not stirred cool), James Brown ('soul power' cool) and James Hunt (daredevil motor racing cool) – in spite of my list and the fact that the odds were a million to one against, I couldn't help feeling she had a different James in mind. James Baker, to be exact, a small lad in the year below me in junior school who perpetually had scabs around the edge of his lips.

'Why James?' I asked defensively.

'I don't know,' she said whimsically. 'You just sound like a James. But if names are irrelevant why did you ask me what mine was?'

'Because I wanted to know how wrong your parents were.'

'And how wrong were they?' asked Kate guardedly.

'Only quite wrong,' I answered. 'Not far off the mark, I suppose. Three out of ten for effort.'

The rude streak that dwelled within me had risen to the surface. I'd like to pretend that my obnoxiousness was part of my seduction technique but it wasn't. It was sheer blatant crapness. My mouth always ran away with itself, intoxicated by the power it wielded. It happened any time I came face to face with genuine niceness, as if scientifically testing the limitations of my chosen subject's pleasant nature – to see how far was too far.

'Are you trying to be offensive?' she asked, more stunned than hurt.

'No, I'm sorry,' I said, apologising profusely. 'Forgive me, I'm stupid. It's just . . . it's just that I'm just having a bit of a rough time at the moment.'

'What's the matter?' asked Kate, genuinely concerned.

I tried to stop myself but couldn't.

'It's my girlfriend,' I said. 'She dumped me.'

'Oh, I'm sorry to hear that. I know how you feel. It's terrible when things like that happen. I feel terrible. Your girlfriend's just dumped you and here I am wittering on about cheques.'

'Oh, don't worry,' I said cheerfully, momentarily forgetting my grief. 'It's not like she's just done it.'

'So when did it happen?'

'Three years ago.'

The whole story came out. During the appropriate breaks in my narrative, Kate made supportive 'uh-huh' noises which made me feel even worse. Here I was wasting the time of an interesting, velvet-voiced and quite possibly good-looking girl, telling her about my ex, when any man with any sense would've been trying their best to chat her up.

When I'd finished my story, roughly an hour later, without pausing she told me that I ought to be strong. She herself was recovering from a recent break-up of a relationship.

'That's why I was crying on your answering machine – thank you for not mentioning it, by the way – phoning the flat reminded me of living there, which reminded me of being there with my boyfriend, which reminded me of the fact that he had dumped me.'

I thought she was going to start crying, but she didn't. Instead she took her turn in what was quickly becoming a miniature self-help group for that small but vocal strata of society known as The Dumped. Her boyfriend – whom she refused to refer to as anything but 'my ex' or occasionally 'that heartless bastard' – had dumped her three weeks earlier, totally out of the blue. They'd been together for six perfect months.

'I lost the plot for a while,' said Kate, 'I really did. I used to lie in bed just staring at the ceiling. I even unplugged the phone just in case he ever tried to call me again. I didn't eat because I knew that I'd throw up. I didn't see anyone – not even friends – for nearly two weeks. I just stayed in watching telly and eating Hobnobs.' She laughed. 'Talking of which . . .' I listened to a packet rustle and the sound of an oat-based biscuit being delicately masticated. She made a satisfied kind of cat noise and continued: 'That's better. And then one day I just woke up. I said to myself, I can spend the rest of my life mourning his loss or I can get on with my life. Which is what I did.'

I marvelled at her confidence. She'd managed to do the one thing I could never do – she'd moved on. But the more I thought about it the less impressed I was. There was no way she could have loved her ex the way I loved Aggi, otherwise she'd be as crippled by misery as I was. The two cases weren't comparable.

Kate continued: 'I've never understood why people insist on saying things like, "There's plenty of other fish in the sea." My mum actually said that to me, you know, after I was dumped by the person formerly known as 'my boyfriend'. There's me crying my heart out and all she was offering me by way of consolation was a fish metaphor! She wouldn't have said that if that heartless bastard had died horribly in a car crash. She wouldn't have said, never mind Kate, there are plenty of other boyfriends out there who have the advantage over your ex of not being dead.'

She had a good point.

Just as I was wondering what to say next, out of the blue she said, 'Between grief and nothing, which would you choose?'

I recognised the quotation straight away. I knew it because me, Aggi, Simon and his then girlfriend, Gemma Walker (shelf-life three weeks, two days) had spent one Saturday afternoon, four years ago, watching *Breathless*, the Richard Gere version of Godard's *A Bout de Souffle* as research for an essay I was writing on Hollywood adaptations of non-English speaking films. I'd chosen the title because it meant I got to watch *The Magnificent Seven*, too, although the downside of that was having to endure *The Seven Samurai*, as well, which, to put not too fine a point on it, was about as meaningful as my moderately flabby arse. In one scene, Gere's girlfriend – played magnificently by Valerie Kaprisky – reads aloud a passage from a book and then drops it as she kisses him. Simon and I spent five minutes advancing that scene frame by frame to find out what the book was, because the passage made such a lasting impression on the both of us.

'That's from *The Wild Palms*,' I said excitedly, as if Kate was in a position to award ten house points *and* a gold star. 'William Faulkner.'

'Is it?' said Kate. 'I didn't know. That heartless bastard wrote it in a letter he sent after he finished with me.'

'Oh,' I said awkwardly.

'Well, what's your answer?' she asked.

I told her my answer would be nothing. She didn't believe me. But it was true. If I had to do it all again I wouldn't have gone out with Aggi. I would have walked straight out of Oxfam that day, albeit without my Elvis mirror, but thankful in the knowledge that at least my sanity and self-respect would be intact in years to come.

'But what about the good times?' probed Kate. 'You must've had some good times, surely?'

'Yeah, we had some good times,' I said, quickly flicking through some of them in my head. 'But at the end of the day what have I got? Nothing but memories. I'm twenty-six and I constantly live in the past. I've been without Aggi longer than I was with her and I still can't get over her. Ignorance, compared to this, would be bliss.'

Kate was beginning to tire of me. I could feel it. I wanted to tell her my whole life story. I wanted to tell her everything that was inside me. But I was convinced I was boring her.

'Am I boring you?' I asked, trying to make the question sound casual.

'No, why should I be bored?' Kate asked.

'No, well, maybe just a little bit,' I confessed. 'It's appalling that you have to listen to me droning on like this. Sometimes I'm so boring even I stop listening.'

She laughed. It still sounded like summertime.

'Kate, tell me about you,' I said, lighting up a cigarette. 'Tell me something I don't know about you.'

'Like what?'

'I don't know, anything you want.'

'I can't think what to tell you,' said Kate. She paused. I took a deep drag on my cigarette. 'Okay, I've got it. Ask me three questions that you want answers to and I'll ask you three.'

I agreed. My mind was racing, trying to think of questions that would be intriguing, sexy and yet devastatingly witty.

'Where do you live?'

'Good question,' said Kate. I tried to detect the irony in her voice. There was none. 'Let's sort the geography out.'

Kate lived in a flat in Brighton with her best friend Paula. Paula was out with her mates from work, which pleased me immensely because I liked the idea of the two of us being alone, talking conspiratorially late at night. Kate had stayed in because she had no money. She'd dropped out of her first year at the University of North London, where she'd been reading East European Studies ('We were known as the "Euro Studs"').

'So why did you leave?'

'Because I was going to get kicked out anyway,' said Kate, sighing. 'I hardly went to any lectures. I was in love. It seemed more important to be with my ex than learn about the history of the European trade agreements or have a social life. He was always having to go away and then I'd miss him so much that . . .' Her voice began to falter. She took a deep breath and the tone of her voice changed, as if she'd made a conscious decision to try and never think about him again. 'He's history.'

'Do you miss London?' I asked, adding: 'This is my second "official" question, by the way.'

She laughed and said: 'I don't miss London at all. It's too expensive, it's grimy, it's dirty and it's unfriendly. It reminds me of him. I like Brighton. My flat's only five minutes from the sea. And I love the sea.'

I thought long and hard about my third question. I thought of funny things to ask, I thought of poignant things too, but there was only one thing that I wanted, almost needed, to know. It was about her boyfriend. A subject that was now clearly off limits. As usual I succumbed to my compulsion.

'What was your ex like?'

'He was just a guy,' replied Kate without hesitation. 'Just a guy who thought he meant the world to me and was right. But between grief and nothing, I'd take grief.'

She refused to say anything more.

'I know you only said three,' I said, almost, but not quite, shyly, 'but I've got another question.'

'Ask away,' said Kate.

'Will you phone me again soon?'

'I don't know,' she replied. 'We'll have to see.'

11.45 P.M.

When she'd put the phone down I tried to dismiss her from my mind but I couldn't – she wouldn't go. Instead I went over the answers I'd given to her three questions.

Her: Who was the first girl you ever fancied?

Me: Vicki Hollingsworth. I was in my early teens. It didn't work out. Too many complications.

Her: What's your worst habit?

Me: Making pot noodle sandwiches. (Pause) Smoking. (Pause) Lying. (Pause) Thinking about my ex-girlfriend.

Her: Why do you want me to call again?

Me: Because.

Her: Because what?

Me: Because.

I considered returning to the entertainment of *The Barbara*

White Show, but the early morning rise to work – still some-thing of a shock to a body that preferred to run on dole time – was beginning to take its toll. It took roughly an hour, door-to-door, to get to school in the mornings. It wouldn't have been so bad if I could have strolled in at the same time as the kids, but it was frowned upon by Mr Tucker if members of staff weren't on site by 8.15. So unless I wanted his miserable, wart-ridden, beardy face chastising me on a daily basis, I had to leave the flat at 7.15 – requiring me to get up at 6.45! It was a killer. I tried a variety of methods to cut my getting-ready-to-go-to-work time down and thus lengthen the time spent in bed. I stopped brushing my teeth and instead squirted the toothpaste directly into my mouth; I showered in the evening instead of morning; and wore my trainers on the journey to work in case I had to sprint at any point. Somehow, no matter what I did, I always ended up leaving a half-eaten bowl of Honey Nut Loops in the kitchen sink and chewing a piece of toast while jogging up Holloway Road.

Off went my shirt and socks as I got back into bed. They landed in a crumpled pile next to my trousers. These clothes, my School Clothes, were completely alien to the real me. Until I started on my teacher training course, I'd managed to avoid going into branches of Burton's, Next or Top Man for over a decade. There was something about High Street men's shops that I despised more than fascism, landlords and neighbours who parked their cars outside my house. The combination of half-wit YTS trainees, terrible decor and the clientele – adolescent boys with clothing allowances, engineering students, and girlfriends with Zero Taste looking for a 'nice' jumper for their boyfriends – was all too much for me. All my clothes were second-hand, purchased from Imperial Cancer Research shops and the like. I had two wardrobes full of what Simon and I referred to as 'Dead Men's Clothes' – the sort of items only widows and bitter divorcees throw away. My whole wardrobe – consisting of literally dozens of items – had cost less than fifty quid in total, but it wasn't the money that mattered, what really counted was that it added to my sense of individuality. The look I was working towards was a cross between Clint Eastwood in *Magnum Force* and Richard Rowntree in *Shaft*. While I freely admit I wasn't exactly there, I was close enough to feel different from the rest of the crowd. Teaching, unfortunately, was about conformity, and even I could see that a complete fashion rethink was in order if I was ever going to get a job.

The trousers were from Burton's. They were black and had turn-ups. Looking down at them from the bed, I noticed that the seat was going shiny. The shirt was from Top Man (urrgh!) and was one of five purchased one size too small. As I handed over my money, the youth at the till had asked me if I was sure they were the right size. I said yes, because he was a seventeen-year-old with acne and I was a graduate in English Literature and Film Studies which, I considered, made me infinitely more qualified in the intricacies of shirt sizes than he was.

I got out of bed and turned off the light. Light from the street lamps in Friar Avenue, which ran along the end of the garden, made the curtains glow spookily, casting shadows around the room. As I put my head down I lifted it back up immediately and picked up the clothes off the floor to put underneath my head. One of the items I'd forgotten to pack was a pillow, and as I wasn't entirely sure which sort of shops sold pillows I'd managed without. I made a mental note to ask Kate about it if she ever phoned again.

Kate is definitely an interesting girl, I thought, hoping I might dream about her. *She sounds like she'd be fun to be with. She seems different from other girls. Not like . . .*

The phone rang.

'Hi, Will, it's me,' said a voice I knew only too well belonged to Martina. All things considered she sounded reasonably chirpy.

'I hope you don't mind me phoning so late,' she said meekly. 'It's just that . . . well . . . you haven't returned any of my calls this week. I thought perhaps it might be your phone playing up but I got the operator to check that the line was working properly.'

It was time for some quick thinking:

      a) Amnesia?
      b) Too busy?
      c) Answering machine not working?
      d) The truth?
      e) All of the above?

'I didn't know you'd phoned earlier,' I lied, trying with all my strength to sound surprised. 'I don't think the answering machine is working. I'm really sorry.'

'It's okay,' she said hushing my apologies, 'it's not your fault, I'm sure you'll have been too busy making new friends to call me back until the weekend. It must be so exciting, Will. More exciting than anything I could offer you.'

Martina had got into the habit of speaking to me like that – putting herself down in order, I think, to elevate me even higher in her esteem – from the moment I'd kissed her. It was a manipulative trick which pathetic people, myself included, used to make the object of their affections say something nice about them. Martina wasn't fishing for compliments – her earnestness was such that I just knew she was one of those people who meant every word they said and never said anything they didn't mean.

I ignored her bowing and scraping. 'So, how have you been doing?'

'Not too bad,' she sighed, making the 'oooo' in 'too' sound like an asthmatic owl. 'I still haven't found any work yet. I've signed on with some teaching agencies though – they think I might be able to get something quite soon. But as for a staff job, I don't think there'll be any of those going until after Christmas.'

I hated to admit it, but she did sound genuinely sad, lost and very lonely.

'How's it going at your parents' house?' I asked.

'I hate it, Will,' she said bitterly. 'I really hate it. I wish I was in London with you. Wouldn't that be brilliant? I could get a flat downstairs from you and I could make you dinner and we could watch that TV series you're always telling me about.'

'*Blackadder*,' I prompted.

'Yes, *Blackadder*,' she said wistfully. 'That would be my dream come true, Will. It really would.'

This wasn't some off-the-cuff remark, like 'Oh, wouldn't it be nice if . . .' She was serious. She'd probably transported herself to this scene in her head thousands of times as she sat in her bedroom filling out application forms. I knew this, of course, because I'd spent a lot of my own spare time imagining similar scenarios with Aggi.

'It won't be forever,' I reassured her. From my position on the bed, I craned my head trying to see the night sky through the bits of window that were visible because the curtains didn't meet in the middle. 'You'll get a job. You've got very good references. You'll . . .'

'I miss you, Will,' interrupted Martina.

There was no time for thought. The tone of her voice demanded an immediate reaction. Here was my chance. I could break her heart without saying a single word or I could make her day. I had this power – this all-consuming power – and I didn't want it. I didn't want it more than I'd ever not wanted anything because, metaphorically speaking, I was going to have to look down at this human manifestation of a seal pup, all big eyes and cuteness, and bludgeon its brains out.

'I miss you too, Martina,' I whispered quietly, hoping that neither her nor my conscience would hear me.

She sighed heavily with relief.

This couldn't carry on; I knew this of course. I'd made another huge mistake. She didn't want my pity – she wanted my affections. And I had none to give. I had to tell her the Truth.

'Martina?' This time the tone of *my* voice must have given the game away because she didn't reply. I could feel her tensing down the phone line, bracing herself for the blow, waiting for her world to end. I'd seen the family dog, Beveridge, do a similar thing when he thought I was going to tell him off. He refused to come when I called him, but waited, savouring the last few moments of Life as it Was before it turned into Life as it Is.

What was I going to say?

Martina, I'm sorry, but this just isn't working out.

Too harsh.

Martina, it's not you, it's me. It's all my fault.

Too soft. She'd just think I was having a bad day.

Martina, I don't know how to say this so I'll come straight out with it, this isn't working out.

Straight to the point. Firm but fair. Nice one.

'Martina,' I began, 'I don't know how to say this . . .'

'Don't say it, Will,' said Martina. 'I know exactly what you're going to say and I feel the same way too.'

'What?' I exclaimed.

'I feel the same way, Will,' she continued, spilling her confusion down the line. 'I know we've only been together since last weekend but what does time matter? Will, I love you too.'

I was well aware how large my active vocabulary was, and yet not a single word or phrase sprang to my lips in my own defence. I was speechless, although I'm sure she took the length of time I took to respond as a sign that I was inwardly returning the sentiment, too overcome with emotion to vocalise my affection. I just couldn't work out why she was telling me she loved me when all that we'd shared was the briefest of brief encounters over a week ago.

'Look, Martina . . .' I began, but stopped mid-sentence. Even fired by anger I couldn't allow myself to get straight to the point. 'Martina, it's late. I'm tired. It's been a really long week. I'd like to go to sleep now. I'll talk to you tomorrow, okay?'

'Dream of me,' she whispered sweetly.

'Yeah, all right. Whatever,' I said, shaking my head as I put the phone down.

Martina was bad news of the worst variety. She was a terrible idea that was even worse now it was running loose in reality. She was Satan in Gossard underwear. How had I ended up like this?

Nikki and Cathy, two girls from my teacher training course, were good friends with Martina. On a night out during the second week of our year-long course they'd told me about a number of complimentary comments Martina had made about me during lectures, which all added up to the fact that she fancied me rotten. At first I was flattered because Martina was far from ugly; she was tall, naturally blonde and had a manner about her so elegant that she almost seemed to float. That evening I'd tried talking to her a few times but it was obvious, even then, that though she was keen we had nothing in common.

I didn't say another word to her until the weekend before I came to London. I'd been discussing with Alice how soul-destroying it was looking for LOVE in the Nineties, when she suggested that the reason I hadn't found it had nothing to do with demographics, and everything to do with the fact that I was TOO UPTIGHT FOR MY OWN GOOD. I had to admit, she had a point. While, all around, my peers indulged in one-night stands, two-timing antics and three-in-a-bed-scandals, I was too busy to join in because I was searching for the Other One, to take the place of Aggi (the One). It was easy to see what Alice was getting at. I was practically walking around with a sign around my neck saying: 'Wife wanted.' I was looking for a replacement Aggi with a lifetime guarantee and nothing else would do.

So Martina was it. She was my experiment. The Franken-stein monster of my own creation. My one attempt at a casual relationship, and now I was paying for it dearly. One phone call was all it took. In the back of the taxi after an evening dining at Los Locos, she'd made it clear to me as I frantically stuffed my hand up her top and ran my fingertips along the edges of her bra, that *she* wanted a relationship. I'd mumbled something along the lines of, 'Yeah, me too,' before she swamped me in deep, passionate kisses. Now, because of that, my regret threatened to overwhelm me – which wasn't all that hard to do. On a good day, I felt guilty for things that most people didn't give a second thought – not giving to the homeless, not buying a Lifeboat sticker, killing moths trapped in net curtains: guilt had always been a key feature of my life. And now, thanks to Martina, I felt completely and utterly guilty for things I knew for a fact had nothing to do with me. Hiroshima. That was my fault. The sinking of the *Titanic*. That was me too. Han Solo getting stuck in carbonite in *The Empire Strikes Back*. Blame me for that one, Princess Leia.

Already my conscience was suggesting that I should go out with Martina as an act of penance. After all, Catholics had it sussed – erase all guilt by turning the pain of the guilt in on yourself, because at the end of the day, dealing with your own anguish is easy enough when compared to dealing with the pain you've caused. It was a nice theory, but it wasn't the answer. The situation would only get worse. This was my problem: I had to get rid of her, but I didn't have it in me to dump her. I'd never dumped a girl in my life. Yes, I'd behaved so badly that they'd had no option but to get rid of me, but I'd never done the deed myself. I just couldn't tell another human being that I didn't like them the way they liked me. Thanks to Aggi, sometimes I felt like I was the only person in the world who could say, 'This is going to hurt me more than it's going to hurt you,' and really mean it.

Martina, or more accurately, thoughts of Martina were denying me the right to sleep, as they raced around my head as if the inside of my skull were a miniature Silverstone. Inevitably, they slowed down, converging at one point – Aggi. How long had she wondered – just as I was doing with Martina – how to break it to *me* gently? She must have known that whatever she said, and however she said it, I'd be totally torn apart.

Weeks afterwards, when I could actually get my head around the concept of her not being there any more – about as easy as coming to terms with waking up a paraplegic – it occurred to me that she might have been trying to tell me how she felt for weeks, maybe even months, and I'd been too stupid to notice. It hurt to think that all that time I'd been under the illusion, thinking she felt the same about me as I did about her – and now I didn't know what to believe in. The questions I should have asked at the time never got asked, and by the time I'd got around to feeling I could ask them without falling to pieces, she'd cut off all contact.

Maybe she'd decided that very morning, or when I met her outside Shoe Express, or as the milk in our coffee began to separate in the café, or as she drove through the barriers of the car park, or as she pulled into Rilstone Road, or as she leaned over and kissed me to say . . .

71

That's enough. I closed my eyes tightly, hoping that sleep would come soon. *That's enough thinking for now.* I was never going to get to sleep at this rate. I looked through the gaps in the curtain, the night sky appeared to be fading into morning – I wondered if I'd fallen asleep without knowing it, and checked my watch. Night-time was still a very long way from being over. I lay back on the bed and stared at the Artexed ceiling, hoping to drop off out of boredom. I could barely see the ceiling without my glasses, the world was a blur and for this I would always be grateful.

I was twelve years old before I realised people were supposed to see the world clearly. My vision had been in a state of deterioration for at least two years. As a twelve-year-old that was a sixth of my life, or if I only counted the important bits when I could talk and at least do a portion of thinking for myself – at least a fifth. It wasn't like I was on the road to Damascus or anything, it just sort of sneaked up on me. I thought it was the way things were.

My first pair of glasses were a hideous affair that I bucked, railed and tantrumed against when informed of their impending entry into my life. I took one look in the mirror at the optician's and burst out crying. There were only two good role models for four-eyed youngsters back then: Brains from *Thunderbirds* or Joe 90, and even then, everyone assumed you were clever.

My peers, without any need for provocation, took it upon themselves to abuse both me and my spectacles at every opportunity. Even Sandra Law, who had a pink plastic pair, felt able to join in. I had to take the 'brassings', as we used to call it, for over a week until, thankfully, they found another child to torture. Craig Harrison's younger brother had shown his tackle to a group of girls in the gully that ran along the back of the school. Admittedly, they had goaded him into it, but that was no excuse. That boy had no shame.

During that dreadful week Simon had stood by me. This didn't exactly mean that he defended my honour – that would've only attracted abuse in his direction – but I always had someone to play with and knew that there was at least one person in the world who would never call me 'speccy-four-eyes'. It was during a lunch-time break, while playing Galactic Head with Simon, our personal vision of future space travel, that it dawned on me to incorporate my spectacles into the game.

I Sellotaped a Bic biro to the right arm of my specs and thus my glasses became an intergalactic communicator. It was an immediate success. I started off the biggest playground craze seen in years – bigger than the Slinky Spring, *Return of the Jedi* trading cards and fastening the top toggle of a duffel coat around your neck to make it look like Batman's cape. That afternoon my glasses were practically passed around the whole of the school. By the end of the following week people were bringing sunglasses into school for me to customise. The craze, and my popularity as a whole, took a nose-dive when Gareth 'Stiggy' Evans, brought in his dad's bifocals for me to transform. His dad later told the headmaster that Gareth had 20/20 vision, so it was 'no bloody wonder' he tripped over and smashed them while playing keep-it-ups with Arthur Tapp.

Four years after that my own glasses shared a similar fate during a Scout camping weekend in the Derbyshire hills. There were five of us to a tent and before we'd gone to sleep Craig Butler – who was sleeping in the middle – had convinced us that a man would try and sneak in during the night, and steal our body parts using a sharpened butter knife. By the time he'd finished winding us up only the unceasing clenching of buttock muscle kept the contents of my bowels from exploding. I was at the zip end of the tent, so there was no way I was going to take off my specs. When I woke up in the morning my glasses had disappeared but I didn't have to look far to find them. They were lying on the floor, crushed under the quivering buttocks of Fat Nigel.

The lead Scoutmaster, a man called Mr George, suggested Sellotaping the arm back on. Mr George had obviously never been a teenager because otherwise he would have realised how stupid his suggestion was. Sellotape may have been all right for Galactic Head, but I was only a kid back then. Now that I was thirteen, there was nothing on earth that could make Sellotaped spectacles cool. Thus, I decided, it would be far easier on my ego not to see anything at all, so I spent the rest of the weekend – that's all of Saturday *and* most of Sunday – being pointed in the right direction. When I got home, my mum made me go straight to the optician's to choose another pair of glasses. But how could I? It was like being asked to choose another nose. After three hours in the shop, trying on the whole range of children's spectacles, I settled on a black pair. I took them home and showed them to all my friends but I couldn't shake the feeling that they'd always be a second best to the pair I'd broken.

The thing about that weekend without glasses was that what I could see looked really nice. Nothing had any definition about it. Colours merged. It was like constantly being caught in the sort of cheesy soft-focus normally reserved for swooning heroines, all the rough edges smoothed away, all the blemishes blurred out of existence. Real Life seemed far away.

In my retrospective mood, lying in bed staring at the ceiling, I was reminded of the first time that Real Life and My Life collided in my head. I'd just completed a rather excellent picture of my mother. I'd painted her with a red smiling face and blue hair – most importantly of all I'd given her a neck. I'd noticed that those of my peers whose talents lay in the world of art rather than the sand pit, had drawn portraits of their mothers – specifically commissioned for Mother's Day – without necks. Some had big round heads, others even had hair, but not a single mother had a neck. I knew my mother had a neck, so I gave her a neck. It was a long slender green one. It made me very proud.

After painting time, we were forced into our afternoon nap. The beds were set out in rows across the far end of the classroom. I usually ran to the one by the door so I could feel the draught come in and pretend that I was on a boat at sea. This particular day, I ran to a bed that faced the large window which spanned the side of the room. It looked out onto the trees in the yard near the playground. I wasn't sleepy but I liked lying down. I could've run and jumped and played twenty-four hours a day, but I conceded this battle every time because the afternoon nap gave me a chance to think. Back then I rarely thought proper thoughts because I was too busy playing. Time was always NOW, in big, bold, upper-case letters. The future just wasn't my concern.

I closed my eyes tightly and waited until I saw the red and orange floaty things that always appeared before my eyes when I did this. They were beautiful, but I could never look at them directly otherwise they disappeared and would only reappear once I'd stopped looking for them. After five minutes or so, I began to think about my mum. She had dropped me off at the nursery, as she had done every day since September. I was completely happy with this arrangement. I had no problem with being left alone with strange adults and a bunch of children I didn't know. If my parents were trying to give me a head start on the advancement of my social skills then they should have asked me and I could have told them that I got along with everyone.

That morning I'd kissed mum good-bye but as I lay there that wintry afternoon, I began to think about where she was. I couldn't explain it, but I suddenly wondered if she was real. I'd sometimes dreamt things that felt so real that they couldn't possibly have been dreams. I once dreamt I could fly and, even now, can still remember what the city looked like from up in the sky and how the wind felt in my hair and against my skin. But when I woke up I couldn't fly.

Lying on the bed thinking these thoughts, I concluded that my mother was just a really nice dream. I could remember the softness of her cheek that I'd kissed that morning and how smooth the tissue that wiped away her lipstick felt. I could remember her smell, which was warm and summery in contrast to the bleak day it really was. I remembered it all, just like I remembered that I could fly. Right there and then, I convinced myself that my mum didn't exist, that both she and my dad, my bedroom and toys – all that I loved didn't exist. Nothing existed except me and what I could see.

I opened my eyes, looked out of the window, saw the branches of the trees blowing in the wind and started to cry. Not loudly for attention, but softly, very softly. My eyes filled up and warm tears ran across my cheek onto the hand resting beneath my head. Within minutes I was in full flow. I felt sad and empty. I was an orphan. The teacher, Mrs Greene, a lovely lady who smelt of Pears soap, gave me a hug and stroked my hair, but I was inconsolable. 'My mum's not there! My mum's not there!' I shouted through my tears, but it wasn't actually what I meant. What I wanted to say was, 'My mum's not real!' In the end I cried so much that she had to call my mum at work from the telephone in the school office. When she explained to my mum what the problem was, she passed the telephone down to my outstretched hands to let me speak to her. As soon as I heard her voice, the tears stopped. My mum was real. It wasn't a dream. Everything was all right.

1.05 A.M.

1.05 A.M.

I'm in my flat, only it's not my flat. It's a better one but not too flash – let's keep it within the realms of reality. And for argument's sake let's say that I'm still in London and I'm still teaching – although why I don't know. The flat's tidy and the cold water tap on the kitchen sink works. My records and CDs are in alphabetical order and I've got a state-of-the-art flat screen digital TV with cable.

Right. I'm busy in the kitchen. I'm chopping parsley and sprinkling it over a dish which I return to the oven for twenty minutes to crispen – well that's what it says in my Delia Smith cookbook, anyway. Playing in the background is Elvis – Live From Madison Square Garden – it just fits the mood I'm in tonight – triumphant, jubilant, ready to please the faithful. There's a knock at the door. I brush parsley from my hands and slip on my jacket which has been sitting on the back of a kitchen chair. As I enter the hallway I catch a glimpse of myself in the mirror. Looking good. I'm wearing a dark blue suit from Paul Smith. It looks expensive but not obscene, chic and 'with it'. No, scrub that. The suit's too formal – where am I going? A funeral? No. I'm in something casual that could only have been bought on a shopping trip to New York. Let's see. A checked Calvin Klein shirt and a pair of Chinos from

79

Bloomingdales. No, no, no, no, no. It's just not me – only models in GQ wear that sort of stuff. Okay, I've got it. I'm in a plain white T-shirt and a pair of old Levis and – here's the best bit – I'm not wearing any socks! Nice touch, she used to like my feet.

I open the door and there is Aggi.

For a millionth of a second neither of us moves, frozen in time and space, our eyes saying more than words can communicate. I'm overcome by a sick and dizzy sensation that doesn't last very long as it is soon overwhelmed by euphoria. I wrap her in my arms and squeeze. Her warm tears trickle down the back of my neck. I pull my head back, still pressing her close to me, and look deeply into those big, bad, beautiful, deep-green eyes I've missed so much.

'William . . . William!' she sobs. 'I'm sorry. I'm so sorry.'

Saying nothing, I increase the pressure of my grip so tightly that she almost feels faint, but she doesn't resist, in fact she wants me to hold her tighter, because my embrace is declaring aloud the one thing she most wants to hear – 'I forgive you.'

I relax my grip around her slender waist as she takes my hand and looks down, ever deeper, into my soul.

'I thought I could live my life without you,' she says, trying desperately to hold back her tears. 'I can't. I've tried and I can't do it, Will. I've been so unhappy for so long. I thought you'd never forgive me. These last three years without you have been awful. I've been to hell and back.'

No. Definitely too melodramatic. More Barbara Cartland than Brontë. Okay, take it from, 'these last three years without you have been awful . . .'

'As soon as I'd ended our relationship I knew that I'd made the biggest mistake of my life.' She stops, her eyes well up with tears and her bottom lip trembles. The pause is not for dramatic effect – it's for mercy. 'I wouldn't blame you if you hated me right now. Really, I have no right to be here. I gave up that right the moment I extinguished our love. But do you think that we could . . .? Do you think that we'll ever . . .?'

She notices how little I've said. The tears flow rapidly. 'Aren't you going to say anything?' she screams. 'You hate me, don't you? Don't you?'

I throw her a look I'd seen Nicolas Cage use on Laura Dern in Wild At Heart: intense, deep and unambiguous as if to say, 'Baby, you're mine – I'm yours – forever!'

She tells me she's grateful I've invited her around for dinner. She says that she didn't think I'd agree to see her. And I say something like, 'Why ever not?' And she looks down at her lap and then at her skirt, as if realising for the first time just how much she's let herself go. Though I hate to agree, she doesn't look like her old self. She knows it. I know it. And she knows I know it. It's almost as if she'd gone to her wardrobe and plucked out her best glad rags to realise that she was only half right. While reassuring her that she looks wonderful, I pull out a tissue from a box of Kleenex man-sized on the coffee table and gently dab the tears away. At one point, she smiles at me gently as my hand accidentally brushes against her cheek.

We move into the lounge. I offer her a seat on the sofa next to me. I get the feeling that she wants to move closer and very slowly she edges her body nearer to mine. Just at the moment she's close enough for me to feel the warmth of her breath against my skin, the radiation from her body and the smell of her perfume – Chanel No 5 – I evade her intimacy, announcing that I've got to look after the food.

Right, let's skip the boring bits and get to the point

where we're just about to eat. On the plates (from Habitat) are a wild mushroom and yellow pepper lasagne, and a selection of vegetables. Not your plain and simple peas and carrots affair, no, these are the kind of exotic veggies Sainsbury's have in little white containers covered with cling film. She tells me that I shouldn't have gone to all this effort because she's not a vegetarian any more, and I tell her that the effort was all for me, as I've not eaten meat in roughly three years.

I pour her a glass of red wine and tell her how this particular blend of grapes will complement the food wonderfully. I'm tempted to let her cup overflow symbolically but I don't. She says 'When' absent-mindedly, just as the wine reaches the edge of the glass. I pour myself one, our eyes meet, she raises her glass to her lips and is just about to sip when she says, 'What am I doing?' Her glass in the air, she says triumphantly: 'Here's to us! Here's to love conquering all!'

We clink glasses.

We're in the lounge again, back on the sofa. Two table lamps illuminate the room, creating a 'relaxed' atmosphere. There's no music in the background, although it does cross my mind to put on something laid-back like Tori Amos or Kate Bush. We sit down and I light a cigarette, not because I want one, but because I want her to know that I now smoke. Things have changed. Things have moved on. I'm the same man she fell in love with and yet different.

She tells me how dismal her life has been without me. How she gave up on her aspiration to be a social worker to work as an office junior in a firm of accountants. Recalling how her life lost direction after she dumped me, she sobs that she has felt adrift ever since. She even confides that despite her best efforts she has been unable to form a *relationship with anyone new – ANYONE AT ALL . . . okay, one bloke, but she didn't sleep with him . . . okay . . . there have been a few: Paul, Graham and Gordon but none of them understood her like I did, especially Gordon who had ginger hair and Paul who had taken her to see Chris Rea twice against her will. I hold back the information that I've been dallying with a few girls' hearts, but she can see – Aggi can see them dancing in my eyes. And what she can also see is that I was over her the minute she told me it was over. Maybe even earlier.*

The phone rings. I ignore it. Aggi moves to answer it and I hold my hand up, signalling that whoever is calling is nowhere near as important as she is. The answering machine clicks on and a refined voice – not altogether dissimilar to that of Audrey Hepburn – says, 'Hi, Will! It's Abi here. I just wanted to have one of our late-night chats but you're not in! What's a gal to do? Oh well. What are you doing next Thursday? I've got tickets for the theatre. It's Love's Labour's Lost. It'll be wonderful. Do say you'll come. We can have dinner at my place again afterwards. Ring me soon. Please! Bye!'

Aggi and I sit in silence. She takes my hand and places it between her two. They look small and artistic, just the right length for piano playing and stroking my hair. Thankfully she has stopped biting her nails. The wine flows freely and we chat and laugh and flirt with each other avidly until the Moment arrives. I know it's coming, I can see it a mile off. Once again, she slides herself closer to me, I feel the warmth of her chest pressing against mine, her eyes are closed, her faced turned towards me, her pale sensitive lips pursed to perfection and I prepare myself to relive all our kisses and . . . nothing. Nothing happens.

1.17 A.M.

The phone rang, denying me the opportunity to wallow in the depressing inadequacy of my imagination. I wondered who it could possibly be, but after a few seconds I made the decision to stop wondering, on the grounds that it was both pointless and stupid. I tried to argue back that neither of those reasons had ever stopped me before but I ignored myself and answered the phone.

'Hello?'

'It's only me.'

It was Martina.

I checked my watch, trying to gauge how outraged I should be. This late at night most normal people would either be a) not in b) fast asleep or c) having sex. As I wasn't normal I wasn't doing any of them – but I wasn't going to miss out on a sterling opportunity to lose my rag, dump Martina *and* fill the yawning chasm of boredom stretching out in front of me. This was obviously some sort of gift from above – maybe I'd done something right today.

'Martina,' I began. 'It's nearly three in the morning. Why are you telephoning me at three in the morning? Are you insane? I thought it was my mother ringing to say that my Gran was dead. How can you be so cruel?'

I don't know how I managed to say all that without laughing.

I especially liked the bit about it being 'three in the morning' – exaggeration always was my favoured weapon in wars of words.

Martina was so stunned that she literally didn't know what I was talking about.

'I . . . I . . .' was all she managed in her defence.

'You what, Martina?' I looked around for my conscience. It was nowhere to be seen. 'It's three a.m. Martina. You can't go phoning people at three a.m. Look, this has got to stop. Yes, I know we had a wonderful time last Saturday. And I'll always remember it.' I wondered where my conscience had got to and decided it must have had an accident and drowned in one of the many pools of self-pity dotted around my internal landscape. This was the kind of mean-spirited, hard-hearted, totally selfish, self-centred thing that Simon would do. Finally, after all this time I was totally and utterly devoid of guilt – I was Sean Connery as James Bond. I could love them and leave them and not care because, at last, I didn't give a toss about anyone but me. Shaken and not stirred! 'Martina,' I continued, limbering up for the kill, 'I've got to tell you something. Look it's not you it's . . .'

'I'm late,' said Martina abruptly.

'It's nearly four in the morning,' I replied, 'of course you're late. London's not in a different time zone, Martina, half four in the morning in Nottingham is half four in the morning here too. This isn't Australia, you know.'

She made small confused noises to herself. My efforts at biting sarcasm were obviously falling upon deaf ears.

Martina sighed heavily. 'I'm late, Will. As in, you know, *late.'*

I hadn't the faintest idea what she was on about. After some moments of confused silence I concluded she'd either finally parted company with the last of her depleted stock of marbles, or she'd been helping herself to her mum's Harvey's Bristol Cream.

'Martina,' I continued, 'I know you're late. I've got a watch. The big hand's on twelve and the small hand's pointing at the five. You don't need to tell me you're late.'

'Will, I'm . . .'

'If you tell me one more *bloody* time that you're . . .'

'Pregnant.'

I nearly coughed up my lungs in shock. This was quite literally the last thing I'd expected. The events of last weekend had been consigned to the annals of ancient history as soon as they'd occurred. And now I was being called back to take responsibility for something that, mentally speaking, happened decades ago. The entire point of one-night stands was supposed to be that they lasted *one* night. They were not allowed to come back seven days after the event and tell you they were . . .

'Pregnant?'

'Yes,' she whispered.

'But how?' I cried sulkily.

She started a sentence which I believe, had I let her finish, would've given me the text book explanation similar to the one I'd received thirteen years ago from Mr Marshall, my school biology teacher.

'Don't, Martina,' I said firmly. 'Just don't.' Huge droplets of sweat jettisoned from my every skin pore, so much so that my hands, wet with perspiration, lost all grip. The phone slipped from my grasp, smacking against the edge of the bed on its way to the floor. I sat and stared at it, carefully listening to the sound but not comprehending the meaning of the miniature Martina coming from the earpiece.

I picked the phone up. 'You're *late*?'

She didn't know what to say after the way we'd been

going round in circles. 'Er . . .' she began tentatively, 'yes, I'm late.'

'How late is late?' I barked. 'Later than I was to pick you up on Saturday? Later than the average British Rail train?' I started getting hysterical. 'I mean, should I start looking for a good secondary school for our child?'

'My period . . .' she began. I shuddered – an involuntary reaction cultivated in my youth intrinsically linked to the mere utterance of *that* word '. . . was due on Monday. I've never been more than a day late in my life.'

I crossed my fingers and hoped that this was the kind of biological freak of nature that would've gained her an entry in the *Guinness Book of Records* rather than the mundane result of a fertilised ovum.

'It's not fair. It's not fair. It's not fair. It's not fair. It's not fair. It's not fair. It's not fair. It's not fair. It's not fair . . .' I repeated, beginning what would've become a five minute mantra had Martina not intervened.

'Are you okay, Will?' she said kindly. 'Look, I don't want you to worry. Everything's going to be okay. I just don't want you to worry.'

I tried to think of something sensible to say, but, inside, my brain had turned to pure wibble. For all her faults Martina was being spectacularly calm, dignified, almost regal about the whole thing. I was entering my second childhood just as she was turning into the Queen Mother. She was unshakeable. This, I decided, was one of those moments that separated men from boys. And without a doubt I was standing on the prepubescent side.

'Don't worry,' she said again. 'Will, don't worry.'

I cast my mind back to The Event, but this time not through the eyes of the greatest fan of the most spectacular sexual athlete the world has ever seen. No, this time I went back as one of those disaster experts who sift through plane wreckage trying to piece together evidence of what went wrong.

While we had used a condom, I had to admit that I may have been just a teensy weensy bit careless. I kind of got carried away with the excitement of it all – after all, the one-night stand was uncharted territory for me. And for some reason the thought of doing it on her sofa while her parents slept in the room above us turned me on so much that I thought I'd pass out with the excitement. So, there *might* have been the slightest possibility that I *might* have torn the foil packet rather carelessly, but it had seemed okay to me when I'd wrapped it in its Kleenex coffin and flushed it away after The Event. I mean, I didn't put it through the sort of rigorous testing that had got it its kite-mark but it hadn't leaked. At least I hadn't thought so . . .

Part of me (that which would sooner hack off its own head than take responsibility for the fact that it may have screwed up) wondered if she was lying. After all Martina's favourite book was Hardy's *Jude The Obscure*. And while she probably fancied herself as the ethereal Sue Brideshead, she could well have been Arabella Donn trapping the unsuspecting hero with a false pregnancy. It was a nice theory but for the huge gaping holes in it. It just wasn't Martina's style to lie. She wasn't the kind to make waves even when trying to save herself from drowning. This was real. She was with child. I was the father. And it was highly likely that it was all my fault.

'Are you sure?' I said. 'I mean, do you know for sure?'

'No,' she whispered. 'I don't know for sure.'

'Then there's still hope.'

'Maybe.'

'So you haven't had a pregnancy test yet?'

'No.'

I couldn't believe what I was hearing. 'Why not? What's

wrong with you, Martina? Are you insane, woman? You are, aren't you?'

She fought back her tears but I could hear them in her voice. 'I . . . I don't know, Will. I'm scared. I'm scared what the test will say. I'll never get a job if I'm pregnant. I'll be stuck here with Mum and Dad, surrounded by nappies, watching gardening programmes for the rest of my life. I've been trying to phone you all week to tell you,' her voice faltered. 'I can't go through this on my own.'

I lay down on the bed, phone in hand, and stared at the ceiling. My earlier reincarnation as James Bond had all but disappeared by now. I'd had my licence to kill revoked. It felt good to be back in the familiar territory of the Realm of Regret, positioned on top of my favourite pile of ashes and sporting the latest designs in sackcloth. Martina had been worrying about this all week and I'd been too wrapped up in my own worries to notice. Lower than a snake's arse? Really, it just wasn't possible to feel more despicable.

I tried my best to comfort her, but at the back of my mind I knew something was up. I was carefully choosing every word I said, refusing to admit liability, in case one day soon it would be thrown back in my face. So I didn't say anything rash like 'I'll be there for you' or 'Let's see how our relationship goes' or 'I'll support you in whatever decision you make'. I made no mention of the future and instead opened my bumper book of meaningless platitudes and showered her with them from a great height. She seemed comforted. This, after all, was the nicest I'd been to her since promising to call as I'd warmly kissed her good-bye on her doorstep late on that fateful Saturday night.

We talked some more about things totally unrelated to the situation at hand: what was on telly right now; what she was doing in the morning; why teaching attracts such manic personalities; and then made ready to say our good-byes. She said that she was going to buy a test kit first thing in the morning and I told her to phone me as soon as she knew more. Before the call ended, reverting to her old self she said: 'Whatever happens, this doesn't change the way I feel about you.' And I said, 'Yeah, me too,' and put the phone down.

In a way I was both disappointed and elated at my sperm's performance. While in denial (which I surely was), it was quite possible to enjoy that exhilarating flush of pride in knowing that one of the little fellas had fulfilled its destiny. I'd kind of imagined them to be miniature versions of myself – slightly overweight, lazy, dysfunctional. It was hard not to laugh out loud at the mental picture I had: a group of them entering into a discussion halfway up Martina's cervix about whether it was time for a fag break. All, bar one diligent little fella, vote yes. 'I gave 'em up last week,' he says. 'No fags. No booze. I'm feeling so healthy that I think I'll carry on.'

It was funny. But not that funny. That one conscientious tadpole of love, so eager to live out its potential, was about to cause my downfall and there was nothing I could do about it. It was one of those classic moments when you wish that you really could turn back the clock. Even so, had I managed to go back in time, to that moment just as I was unzipping Martina's dress, not even the Ghosts of Christmas Past, Present and Future could've stopped me. Passion is depressing. A man in a French film once said, 'I resist my temptations in order to feel that I am free.' Though it was said by a character in a French film – which by definition means you can't take it entirely seriously – the truth of the words resonated clearly.

Sometimes the effort to resist can be as passionate as the compulsion to succumb.

The opening and closing of one of my close neighbour's front doors broke my concentration. I stood up and looked out of the window. Next door's dog – a black Labrador – barked at my window. Turning back into the room I scratched my stomach and tried to work out how I felt. I wasn't entirely sure. I looked at the alarm clock. It was late. Rather than being exhausted I had the munchies in a big way. Though not hungry enough to eat the proverbial horse, given two slices of bread, a bottle of ketchup and an hour or two longer without sustenance, even Champion The Wonder Horse would have looked snackworthy. My stomach specifically desired ice-cream. Then it occurred to me that perhaps I was having sympathetic cravings, just as some men have sympathetic pregnancy pains. Whatever the reason, I wanted ice-cream and I wanted it now.

This was one of the few instances I found living in the capital to have its advantages. Nottingham had nothing at all resembling the all night shop, which was a shame, because the 7-Eleven (so called because it's open 24-hours a day, seven days a week. Well done, Misnomer Man!) was a pretty good idea, probably in the top ten most brilliant ideas humanity has ever had – not as good as the Walkman or the answering machine, mind – but for that matter not that far behind either.

Fumbling through the clothes that constituted my pillow I located my trousers and proceeded to look for a jumper. The only one I found that would protect me from a bout of hypothermia was a cable-knit sweater Gran had made me a long time ago. It was during her frantic phase of making things out of wool: dolls for her next-door neighbour's kids, a bobble hat for my dad and a pair of trousers for Tom who, even at the age of ten, had the good sense to realise that woollen trousers were the kind of fashion mistake that followed you about for the rest of your life. Despite the cold I didn't bother with socks as I couldn't find any of the little sods. Instead, I pushed my bare feet into my laced-up burgundy brogues, ignored the sound of my mother tutting as she said, 'No wonder all your shoes fall apart if that's how you treat them,' and went out of the door.

The silence of early hours Archway was beguiling. Take away the sound of far-off traffic and the odd taxi or bus and this was the quietest North London ever got. The coldness of the night air heightened my sense of isolation – no one would be out in weather like this unless they were mad or in search of ice-cream. My ankles were so cold that they felt like they had ice cubes rubbing against them. Standing on the door-step, I watched the vapour from my first outside breath disappear heavenwards before launching myself into the night.

The streets were empty. Most of the revellers from the Irish club up the road would have been asleep for at least an hour or two. The chip shop on my side of Holloway Road was closed but the one farther down, past the dry cleaners, was still open, although technically speaking, it wasn't a chip shop – the name on the front of the shop being Mr Bill's Fast Food. The nearest they had to chips were French fries which, five minutes prior to ordering, lay in a bag with thousands of other grim-looking bits of frozen potato.

Walking briskly I reached the top of the road in a new personal best of eight minutes and thirteen seconds! A couple were huddled together in the doorway of the snooker hall near the intersection of Holloway Road and Junction Road. The man was in his mid-thirties, but it has to be said that I'm notorious for not being able to tell the age of most people over the age of eight. I once thought one of Simon's ex-girlfriends was fifteen, when she was actually twenty-five. I spent weeks congratulating myself on how liberal I was being, not asking her how she was getting on with her GCSEs or being less subtle and referring to her as jail-bait.

It began to rain as I walked along Junction Road and passed the Athena Kebab and chip shop opposite the tube station. There were no customers inside, but one of the men behind the counter stared at me menacingly as he diced cabbage. For some reason this scene seemed so ridiculous that I burst out laughing like some care-in-the-community patient.

Mr 7-Eleven didn't look up from his magazine as I entered, but I got the feeling that he saw me anyway. Simon once had a job working behind the till of an all-night garage off Jarvis Road. He insisted that while working night-shifts he discovered an uncanny ability to predict the make and colour of the next car to pull onto the petrol station forecourt. It was pure rubbish, of course – the sort of thing he'd write a song about one day – but, I supposed, it was possible to find out all manner of strange things about yourself if you spent all that time on your own while the rest of the world was sleeping.

Walking past the magazine rack and the early Saturday editions of the *Sun* and the *Mirror*, I made my way straight to the freezer chest, opened it up and sucked in the pseudo-Arctic air. The smells and tastes of all the produce that had ever been there lingered like spectres: I could taste the ghosts of frozen peas; I could smell the ectoplasm of spilt Alabama Fudge cake. It was spooky.

The choice was limited: Raspberry Ripple, Chocolate, Vanilla or Tutti Frutti. Tutti Frutti caught my eye but I suspected – correctly as it happened – that it contained melon. I felt the same way about melons as I did about girls who said they'd love me forever and then dumped me. A box of no-name choc ices in the corner of the freezer cried out for attention but try as I might, they failed to seduce me, forcing me to opt for a tub of Wall's Soft Scoop vanilla. You know where you are with vanilla. Its reputation, like that of Mother Teresa and Alan Titchmarsh, was spot free, which was highly useful, because at this particular moment, this close to the Edge, more than anything in the world, I couldn't afford to be disappointed.

The man in the kebab shop – keeping his steely glares to himself this time – had ceased cabbage shredding and was locked in conversation with his kebab-slicing comrade. The kissing couple had gone only to be replaced by an old man with matted – possibly brown – hair protruding from underneath a lime-green woollen hat. His overcoat pocket was ripped and, even in this light, I could see it was heavily stained. The closer I came to walking past him, the more I began to think I could smell him.

He's going to ask me for money.

At the height of my political awareness – five minutes into my first week at university – I'd made a pledge always to give to the homeless, even if it was only a penny. These days – since Aggi had left me, to be precise – in spite of my promise and acute sense of guilt, I no longer felt obliged to be nice to the needy. This wasn't so much a change in my personal politics as a sudden realisation that I didn't give a cack.

I set my eyes to a steely glare similar to that of the kebab chap, but the old man didn't say a word to me. I spent the rest of the journey wondering why he hadn't asked me for any money when he was so obviously in need of it. That thought carried me through the front door, into my flat and right into bed – leaving the object of my quest untouched and slowly melting on top of the TV.

SATURDAY

SATURDAY

I woke up with a start. I deliberately didn't move for what felt like a long time, trying to fake that just-woken-up feeling. I closed my eyes tightly, then relaxed them, repeating the action, squeezing out all traces of daylight from my irises, but there was no getting back to sleep. Instead, I pretended to be unable to move my limbs, and, after some moments of great concentration, even the slightest movement became an act of considerable determination.

Freshly squeezed thoughts dripped down from my brain, pleading for an audience. I put any questions re impending fatherhood to the very back of my mind. *Maybe I'll wrap them up*, I thought, while slowing down my breathing. *Wrap them up and put a note on them saying, do not open – ever. Some things are, after all, better left unthought.* None of the topics for debate that remained – familiar faces all – stood out from the crowd, which was pleasing because mornings, especially Saturday mornings, shouldn't be overwhelmed with stuff to think about.

Waking up the morning after the day Aggi dumped me – a Saturday morning no less – had been a terrible ordeal, not least due to the horrible taste in my mouth and the smell of sick on my pillow. I'd dreamt that Aggi and I had swum across a tropical ocean to lie on a Bounty chocolate bar type island.

I clearly remembered feeling the sun on my back and neck, the sand clinging to my feet and the cooling sensation of the wind against the droplets of water on my skin. It seemed so real. Then suddenly I was awake. The essence of the dream only lingered for the duration of the journey from deep sleep to total consciousness, but for that short time I experienced the sensation I imagined others felt when they said they were on top of the world. Then WHAM! The nail-bomb exploded. Aggi was gone. She didn't want me. It was finished. Over the following weeks, my first waking moments followed the same pattern – an overwhelming feeling of ecstasy followed closely by the distressing hollowness of reality. Gradually, the length of time it took for me to realise Aggi was gone grew shorter and shorter, until one day I woke up crying. By then, I think, the Message had finally made its way through to my heart.

I turned over, squashing my face into my makeshift pillow. It was too late. My brain was in gear. Saturday had begun.

> *I'll have to tidy the flat.*
> *I'll have to phone people.*
> *I'll have to mark 8B's books.*
> *I'll have to sort out my life.*

I rolled over onto my back. Staring out of my left eye I checked the time on the alarm clock. I'd set it for 1.00 p.m. hoping to sleep most of the weekend away. The digital display, however, confirmed with its authoritative blinking eye that I'd been way too optimistic.

A huge, unnatural, pulsating pain throbbed its way across the front of my skull as if the rear wheels of a Shogun were running backwards and forwards over it. The severity and suddenness of this migraine attack had me worried. As I rarely got so much as a headache, within half an hour I'd selected a brain tumour from a list of maladies that included: beriberi, encephalitis and Lhasa fever, as the chosen explanation for my throbbing temples. Death by brain tumour was, after all, an unfulfilling way to die. While the most popular characters in soap operas got to die in car crashes or at the hands of mad gunmen, those at the other end of the scale were always written out after coming down with a mystery illness that, surprise, surprise, turned out to be a brain tumour. One bald haircut and a chemotherapy storyline later, and they were gone forever. This was exactly why I was going to die this terrible death. I was being written out of existence by a medical condition that was the disease equivalent of a pair of flares.

Attempting to endure the pain by diverting my attention to the state of the room, the thought entered my head that, possibly, a little bit of suffering would make me a better person. This wouldn't have been particularly hard as, thanks to Martina, I was more overloaded with self-loathing than usual. Sometimes, I thought, *I'm born to suffer.* This, I noted, was the second time I'd contemplated Catholicism in the last twenty-four hours. I'd always thought I'd make a great Catholic. I quite liked Italy *and* found the smell of incense reasonably relaxing. If I had converted – from what I didn't know – I could've been up there with the greats: Joan of Arc, St Francis of Assisi, William of Archway – patron saint of crap housing.

Fortunately for me, my aching head and the Pope, my mother had packed a bottle of paracetamol in one of the boxes scattered around the room. Lacking the motivation to phone Nottingham to see if she could remember exactly where she'd put them, I found what I was looking for, but not before I'd emptied the contents of all four boxes on to the floor. My hand was forced. Now I really would have to tidy the flat.

I gazed longingly at the translucent brown bottle in my hand. The name on the front, Anthony H. Kelly, was my dad's. He'd had them prescribed for him when he'd had flu two years ago, which was precisely the last time he'd been ill and the first time in twenty-five years, so he told me, that he'd had a day off work through illness. The bottle was virtually full. That was typical of Dad, he loved to suffer more than I did.

I popped two paracetamols on my tongue and raced to the kitchen sink. The water which came out of it was brown and had been all week. I let it run – the two tablets now clung to my tongue like magnets – but there was no change. Cursing Mr F. Jamal for all I was worth, and myself for not reporting it to him the day I'd moved in, I managed to convince myself that brown water wasn't poisonous, but in the end I lacked the courage of my convictions. I was nearly sick as I struggled to swallow the tablets aided only by chalky saliva and a stomach of iron. I could taste their powdery slug-like trail along my oesophagus and into my stomach long after they'd gone to work alleviating my aching head.

Now that I was in the kitchen it seemed natural to start breakfast. Today, I decided, was not a Honey Nut Loop day. Instead, I opted to create a minor Sugar Puffs mountain in the only clean bowl left in the cupboard. Sat on the bed with my back propped against the back of the sofa, I pulled the duvet over my legs and turned my attention to breakfasting. I'd forgotten the milk *and* the spoon. Too hungry to wait any longer, I grabbed a handful of Sugar Puffs to satisfy my immediate craving and shoved them in my mouth; they too clung to my tongue like magnets, but *they* were sugary, satisfying and instantly cheering.

There were no clean spoons in the cutlery drawer, so the only option was to wash one using the brown tap water. Though, technically speaking, washing in the water was not the same as drinking it, my qualms about its safety remained, so I over-compensated in the cleaning process by using three extra squirts of Fairy Liquid as if it were some kind of germ napalm.

Opening the fridge door, I searched high and low for the milk. There wasn't any. It all came back to me. I'd thrown the last of it away yesterday, after pouring at least a quarter of its rancid contents over my Honey Nut Loops. There was no salvage operation. I had been so dispirited that I'd put the whole thing (bowl included) in the bin and had breakfast from the Italian newsagent's up the road – approximate waiting time for a Mars Bar and a packet of Skips: four minutes. Now I was going to be disappointed again.

Fully aware that this day was doing its very best to torture me with the constant dripping of small, but perfectly formed disasters, I placed two slices of frozen bread in the toaster. I hovered above the slot until the heating elements glowed orange, as this week's other little trick had been to pop in a couple of slices of frozen bread, go away for two minutes only to be greeted by – cue fanfare – frozen bread, because I'd forgotten to plug in the toaster.

Returning to the problem at hand, I tried to work out my next move. I couldn't possibly eat a whole bowl of cereal without milk – I just didn't have that kind of high-level saliva production in me. The other option was to dash to the shops to get some but, I suspected, if I was in possession of enough energy to 'dash' – which I strongly doubted – I'd probably have the wherewithal to have something more exotic than Sugar Puffs for breakfast. Out of the corner of my eye I spotted the answer to my problem. I opened the tub of ice-cream I'd been so desperate for the previous night – now a rich pale yellow froth – and poured the contents of my cereal bowl in.

Thoroughly pleased with my own ingenuity, I patted myself on the back and got stuck in.

Twenty minutes later, I finished about a third of my concoction and started to feel sick. As I lay back on my bed, letting the contents of my stomach settle, I listened to the postman struggling with the letter box downstairs. I got excited. As far as Birthday Cards that weren't going to be Late Birthday Cards were concerned, today was D-Day.

Reasoning that it was too early for the rest of the residents in the house to be up, I nipped out of the door and downstairs in a T-shirt and boxer shorts, only stopping to put my shoes on as I didn't like the look of the hallway carpet. There was a small hillock of letters on the Welcome doormat, most of which had been crushed mercilessly. There were yet more letters for Mr G. Peckham from the AA, a bundle of 50p off Pizzaman Pizza deliveries coupons, a postcard for the bloke in flat number four – Emma and Darren were having a wonderful time in Gambia – and a lot of other stuff I couldn't be bothered to look at properly. After flicking through the pile twice I found four envelopes addressed to me and one for Ms K. Freemans. Too lazy to put the discarded mail on top of the telephone where it normally congregated, I created a very poor artificial post hillock underneath the letter box, sat on the stairs and opened the cards:

Card 1
Description: Painting of a bunch of flowers.
Message: *'Have a wonderful day, son. All my love, Mum.'*

Card 2
Description: Gary Larson cartoon of cow leaning on a fence as car whizzes past.

Message: '*Have a wonderful day, Grandson, love, Gran.*'

Card 3
Description: Photo of Kevin Keegan circa 1977 with a full shaggy perm wearing a No 7 Liverpool shirt.
Message: '*Have a great birthday! Love and kisses, A.*'

Card 4
Description: Gustav Klimt's 'The Kiss'.
Message: '*Have a simply wonderful birthday. Thinking of you every second of every hour, ever yours, Martina.*'

I arranged the cards on the carpet in front of me, stood back and took stock of the situation.

Tomorrow I'll be twenty-six years old. For the first time in my life I'll be closer to thirty than twenty; I'll be officially in my late-twenties, and quite possibly a father to be. By no stretch of the imagination will I be young and if that's not enough this is what I'm reduced to: four cards. Two from relatives. One from a woman I'm trying to dump. And a crap 70s footballer from Alice!

I looked down at Alice's card again, an intense sense of disappointment slowly spreading throughout my entire body. This couldn't possibly have been what she meant by 'something special'. I could trust Alice. She'd never let me down. There had to be something wrong.

The postman.

I'd always had a deep mistrust of the British postal service ever since they'd returned a letter I'd written to Noel Edmonds when I was eight just because I hadn't put a stamp on it. Putting two and two together I decided that my postman had either lost, stolen or forgotten Alice's present. Whatever the reason, I was going to get it back.

A tall, wiry man in his mid-thirties was standing five doors away, shovelling mail through a letter box. The very sight of him sent me into a frenzy of anger, transporting me to a world where the only colour was red and there was no such thing as 'keeping things in proportion'. A yobbish 'Oi!' was all I needed to grab his attention as I ran towards him.

'Come on, where is it?' I asked, adopting the no-nonsense manner of the TV 'tec who uses unorthodox methods but always gets results.

The postman studied me nervously. 'Where's what?'

'My sodding present.'

I got the feeling that he wanted to run but terror rooted him to the spot. 'Your what?'

'It's my birthday tomorrow. Where's my present?'

He looked bewildered. A look of relief drifted across his face and his eyes darted about feverishly, presumably looking for the *Beadle's About* spy cameras. When he didn't find any his look of terror returned. 'Er . . . Happy birthday.'

'I don't want your congratulations. I want my birthday present.'

My eyes dropped down to his postbag. He followed my line of vision and draped his arm over it protectively.

'It's illegal, you know – tampering with the post. I'll call the police.'

'Not if I call them first.'

I was about to make a lunge for the bag when a red, white and blue Pizzaman Pizza moped pulled up next to us. Its engine purred with all the raw power of a Braun hairdryer.

'Nice day for it,' said the white jump-suited pizza delivery man, nodding in the direction of my boxer shorts.

I joined his gaze and then looked up at the postman sheepishly. As if awakening from a sleepwalk, the ridiculous nature of my temporary insanity became instantly apparent. 'Look, I'm sorry,' I said to the postman. 'It's just that a friend of mine was supposed to be sending something in the post. I jumped to the wrong conclusion when you didn't bring it. Sorry.'

The postman's whole body shook in a paroxysm of laughter. 'What do you look like!' he said, shaking his head. 'You need to work out, son. A couple of sessions down the gym will get rid of that.'

'Ah yes,' I said humouring him, 'very funny.'

He wiped a mirthful tear from the corner of his right eye. 'Tell us your name and I'll check my bag if you like.'

'William Kelly . . .'

'Flat 3, 64 Cumbria Avenue?' asked the pizza delivery man.

The postman and I both turned and looked at him.

He explained all: 'I only stopped to ask directions. House numbers around here are difficult to follow.' He got off his moped and handed me his clipboard. 'Just sign this for me, please.'

I signed.

He reached into the pizza carrier on the back of his moped and gave me a large cardboard pizza box.

'Cheers, mate,' he said mounting his moped, laughing. 'You've really made my day.'

The postman and I looked at each other in amazement.

'Go on then,' he said, pointing at the box.

I was about to open the pizza box when a Parcel Force van pulled up next to us.

'Everything all right, Tone?' asked the driver suspiciously.

'It's just that it's not every day I see you talking to a bloke in boxer shorts holding a pizza at . . .' he looked at his watch pointedly, '11.55 a.m.'

'Everything's fine,' said the postman. 'I'll tell you all about it when I get back to the depo. The lad's just having a bad day. We've all had those.'

Hoping to diffuse the situation I walked across to the van.

'Will Kelly,' I said offering my hand. 'Sorry about all this.'

'Will Kelly, Flat 3, 64 Cumbria Avenue?'

Despite the fact that this sort of occurrence was fast becoming commonplace the postman and I looked at each other in amazement for old times' sake.

'Parcel for you,' said the man in the van.

He handed me a small shoe box sealed with brown tape, waved to his colleague and drove off.

In the middle of our momentary not-quite-sure-what-to-do-next silence an Interflora van pulled up. The man in the van didn't bother getting out.

'Will Kelly, Flat 3, 64 Cumbria Avenue?'

'Yes,' I said warily.

'Thought so.' He handed me his clipboard to sign. 'I've got these for you.' I exchanged the clipboard for a large bouquet of lilies and he drove off.

'Looks like I can go now,' said the postman.

I offered him my hand. 'What can I say?'

'No problem,' he said, shaking my hand. 'This'll make a great story for the lads down the pub tonight.' He turned and began trudging back up the road. 'Many happy returns of the day!'

```
12.13 P.M.
```

Alice had excelled herself.

She'd completely transformed the formerly tedious birthday experience into a festival of happiness; a carnival of joy; a moment to remember for the rest of my life.

The Pizza

Extra cheese, pineapple, mushrooms, peppers, fish fingers and peas. The recipe of our Pizza – Pizza for the Dumped. Alice and I first created it when I visited her in Bristol a fortnight after Aggi and I had split up. I hadn't wanted to go, citing my newfound determination to grow a beard and forgo all human contact for the foreseeable future, as the reason. However, she had insisted to the point where she said that if I didn't arrive on her doorstep she'd drive up to Nottingham and take me back with her forcibly. (My hesitancy was odd, especially in the light of the fact that I ended up sleeping on her and Bruce's sitting room Futon for two whole weeks before reluctantly returning home.) On my first night at Alice's she'd asked me what I wanted to eat and I told her I didn't want to eat because I was too sad (Bruce, as luck would have it, had gone out so I could be as pathetic as I wanted). After much bullying on her part I relented and requested pizza. She flicked through *Yellow Pages* until she found a listing for a pizzeria that delivered. The entry read:

> **Luigi's – home of the pizza**. Luigi's Pizza
> Special: Two 7" pizzas and a selection of any
> six toppings, garlic bread and two soft drinks
> £7.99. Any delivery over thirty minutes late
> – FREE!

We called on Alice's speaker phone.

'A Luigi Pizza Special, please,' asked Alice.

'What toppings do you want?' enquired a distinctly un-Italian but disturbingly pubescent voice.

Alice turned to face me, her furrowed brow a visual question mark.

We took it in turns to make suggestions. As I was the guest I set the ball rolling.

'Extra cheese.'

'Pineapple.'

'Peppers. Only no green ones.'

'Mushrooms.'

'Fish fingers.'

'And peas,' said Alice with a flourish.

I laughed for the first time in what seemed like years (which was in fact only two weeks). For that brief moment Aggi didn't exist.

Baby Luigi tried to tell us that we could only order from selected toppings. Alice informed him that it didn't say that in their advert and if they refused to make our pizza she would be prepared to sue them for misrepresentation because not only was she a solicitor, she was also a solicitor who'd had a very bad day.

Forty-one minutes later (we'd set Alice's jogging stop watch the second we put down the phone) our free pizza arrived.

Reclining on the sofa, a slice and a Coke in our hands, we turned to face each other as though the situation required something momentous to be said.

Alice raised her Coke cup. 'May the mozzarella of our respective pizzas remain forever entwined.'

I took a sip from my cup before raising mine because I'd suddenly become incredibly thirsty. A mouthful of Coke and I was ready to speak.

'Ditto.'

When all that was left of my pizza were several crusts, fish finger crumbs and a number of peas that had managed to escape the glutinous grasp of the extra cheese I opened the shoe box.

The Shoe Box Parcel

Inside was a thick padded envelope and twenty packs of duty free Marlboro Lights. My entire stock of blood made a mad dash to my skull at the thought of being in such proximity to so many cigarettes. Alice was the world's healthiest person. She jogged, hadn't eaten meat since she was seventeen and even knew what her cholesterol count was. (It was low. Very low.) Not only did she not smoke, she was the most vehement anti-smoker I'd ever met, and yet her love for me was such that she was prepared to indulge me in my so-called filthy habit to the tune of 400 cigarettes! This act of charity propelled

Alice way beyond the parameter of best mate. She had excelled all definitions of cool. She was out there and unapproachable.

Propping my cigarettes on the window sill, so I could look and marvel at them wherever I was in the room, I tore open the padded envelope. By now Alice had whipped me up into such a flurry of excitement that I was half expecting to find it stuffed full of fivers with a note attached saying: 'Bruce and I had a collection for the poor. We don't know any poor, so we're giving it to you!' Sadly there were no bank notes only a colour photograph of a donkey, some stapled sheets of paper and a letter which read:

Dear William Kelly,

You are now the proud sponsor of Sandy the donkey.

Sandy, a twelve-year-old donkey, was discovered in a barn in South Wales by the RSPCA in July suffering from severe neglect, malnutrition and blindness in one eye. Following the rescue he was brought to The South Devon Donkey Sanctuary where he was looked after and nourished back to health.

Sandy is now a lot better and will be able to live out his days in the open fields of the Sanctuary grounds.

Thanks to your sponsorship we will be able to continue looking after the food and shelter needs of Sandy for a full 12 months.

Please find enclosed your sponsorship papers and special certificate. As a valued sponsor, your name will be placed on a plaque outside Sandy's stable for 12 months.

Thanks for your support,

Carol A. Flint
Director South Devon Donkey Sanctuary

I couldn't believe that somewhere in Devon there was a donkey with my name on it. I fixed Sandy's picture to the wardrobe door with Blu-tac and examined him in detail. Though donkeys are supposedly the most miserable of animals, Alice had somehow managed to find me a happy one. His good eye almost sparkled, although that might just have been the reflection of the camera flash going off, and his mouth was fixed in an expression much like a wry grin. His light brown coat looked healthy and sleek and from what I could see in the picture, he appeared to have more than enough field to roam around. Sandy was fantastic. He was better than fags. He might be a one-eyed donkey, but he was *my* one-eyed donkey and that was all that counted. I examined his papers and noticed that he was particularly fond of carrots. As I was now responsible for Sandy's welfare I decided that from now on his birthday would be the same day as my own. I made a mental note to send him a fiver's worth of carrots as a belated birthday present – a thought which resulted in the following miniature day dream:

I'm visiting Sandy for the first time. He's in a small paddock with some of his donkey friends. On seeing me he trots towards the fence. I reach down to get his birthday carrots out of a carrier bag and realise that there's a small child standing next to me. I offer her a carrot, pick her up and let her feed Sandy. I look down at her smiling face and she says, 'Thanks, Daddy.'

I shook my head violently hoping that the image would somehow fall out of my ear and disappear into the farthest, darkest reaches of the underneath of the sofa-bed. Once the coast was clear I took a deep breath and examined the flowers.

Ten White Lilies

The lilies were perfect. But not as perfect as the message written on the card which had accompanied them:

> *Dear Will,*
>
> *Ten years of whingeing, sarcasm, toilet humour, cynicism and misanthropy. Here's to ten more!*
>
> *All My Love*
>
> *Alice*

Simon had been in my life longer than any of my friends and yet he still wasn't even sure when my birthday was. Only Alice would have done something like this; the flowers, donkey, fags and pizza – things she knew would please me immensely – delivered to my door within minutes of each other. I wondered what I'd done to deserve her and after a number of minutes concluded that I'd done nothing whatsoever. She was in my life without reason. She was there in spite of myself. Good things could happen to not so bad people.

I put the flowers in the only receptacle in the flat that looked anything remotely like a vase – the electric kettle – and climbed into bed with the telephone so that I'd be comfortable while I thanked Alice for her presents. I dialled her number but her answering machine was on, so I left her a message telling her to ring me asap because she was wonderful.

I looked around the room again at the fags, flowers and donkey and tried to imagine my life without Alice. Without her I'd be a rambling bearded tramp yelling expletives at young women and children while trying to beg enough money for my next can of Special Brew. The fact that she was always there to listen to me made a real difference to my life, especially at times of crisis – when Aggi dumped me my self-confidence completely imploded. It was Alice who had rebuilt it brick by brick, until I was back to my miserable and bitterly sarcastic old self. Of all the damage repair work she had undertaken on my bruised, battered and bloodied psyche one thing in particular had helped me more than anyone or anything to realise there was life after Aggi.

She had sent me a letter.

It arrived the day after I told her that Aggi had dumped me. It came in a sky blue envelope which my dad had put on the bottom of my bed as I lay there, pretending to be asleep so that he wouldn't ask how I was, because I didn't want him to see his twenty-three-year-old son crying like a baby and telling him that he felt like dying.

I took the letter out of a folder in my suitcase. It was one of my most prized possessions. I read it whenever I woke up feeling crap and wondered what the point was.

The paper was wearing thin along the edges where it had been folded. I flattened it out carefully and re-read it even though I was as familiar with every word as I was with Alice herself. The letter captured perfectly the rhythm and pattern of her speech. It was almost like having her here with me.

Will,

There's a part in Frank Capra's It's a Wonderful Life®, *right at the end when all of the families are bringing in money to save the Bailey Building and Loan company which gets me every time I watch it. I think it's his brother that says it: 'Here's to George Bailey – the richest man in town.' I hear that one line and I'm in tears. I tell you this because I suppose in a way that's how I feel about you. I think you're the richest man in town. There's a lot more I could say but I won't because I don't want your head to swell.*

Alice

PS
I've always thought that Aggi was a silly bitch with an over-inflated sense of importance who didn't appreciate how lucky she was and now she's proved it!

That last bit in Alice's letter always amused me. Up until then Alice had put on such a convincing show of civility in Aggi's presence I'd been convinced they were on the verge of becoming best friends. Strangely I'd never really got to find out what Aggi truly thought of Alice, as she'd always changed the topic of conversation whenever her name came up. I'd pretended to get the message and left her to it, reasoning it was some sort of 'women's thing'.

My thoughts were full of Alice, Alice and more Alice when it suddenly dawned upon me that I was probably experiencing one of the best birthdays witnessed since records began.

And then the phone rang.

1.33 P.M.

Simon and I were mates from way, way back, even further than primary school. On our first day at nursery school he had tried to steal a packet of tomato-flavoured Snaps from my lunch-box while I was completely engrossed in a game of *Stingray* in the water bowl with Stephen Fowler. Something, possibly a sixth sense, made me look over at my satchel at the very moment Simon's thieving digits were delving into it. With the spirit of Troy Tempest within me, I ran across the room, snatched back my snack and punched him in the mouth. Mrs Greene didn't take kindly to me taking the law into my own hands but there was no further trouble. Because from that day forward Simon and I were best mates.

Twenty-odd years later, Simon was more interested in singing and playing guitar in his band, Left Bank, than women, life or tomato-flavoured potato snacks. Music was his life. He once told me that if forced to choose between music or women he'd sooner Bobbitt himself with a Bic disposable than give up his guitar. According to him it was only a matter of time before they, as he said in his own words, 'made it big'. I was both amazed and ashamed on his behalf when he'd said this, because not only was he deadly serious, he'd also managed to say 'make it big' without even the faintest nod in irony's direction.

While I spent my youth watching TV, reading books and going to the cinema, Simon had spent his – at least from the day he saw Duran Duran on *Top Of The Pops* sporting more make-up than Max Factor – studying and emulating the eccentric and obsessive personalities of rock 'n' roll folklore. In his final year at Beechwood Boys' Comprehensive, he took to wearing an earphone – not even attached to the pocket transistor radio it had come with – because it was the nearest thing he could find to the hearing aid his beloved Morrissey was sporting at the time. In the sixth form he discovered reggae and literally overnight every sentence he spoke started with the words 'I and I'. Within a week he was referring to anyone in authority – the head of sixth form especially – as 'Babylon'. He knew people thought he was weird, but he was also well aware that these same people, especially girls, thought he was cool in a sort of 'out there in deepest space' kind of way. It was all part of his master plan. One day a music magazine would ask him about his school days, and he'd pause, take a deep drag on his Silk Cut and say, 'I always felt like an outsider.'

He knew everything there was to know about music, and yet, it was this fact that was his band's downfall. Left Bank were dull, plodding and overly worthy because Simon was so steeped in rock 'n' roll history that he found it impossible to distance himself from it. It wasn't enough for him to write a good song, he wanted, in fact he needed, to write a 'classic' to impress all the musical heroes that lived in his head; lyrics that would make a pre-electric Dylan raise an eyebrow, tunes that would make John Lennon tap his toes seven-feet under, and a stage presence that would blow away Hendrix at his playing-guitar-with-his-teeth best. Nothing short of Beatlemania would do. I was firmly of the opinion that Left Bank mania would never become a word the music purchasing general public, let alone the *Oxford English Dictionary*, would ever become aware of. It was an awful name, conjuring up images of berets, fifties jazz, filterless cigarettes, beatnik poetry and tosspots who discuss Sartre without having read him (which Simon hadn't but I had – and was none the wiser for having done so). They were lumbered with this ludicrous moniker by Tammy, Simon's girlfriend and Yoko Ono in-waiting. She was three years younger than him and not his usual type at all. He always claimed to be 'a bit of an arse man' but she was a beanpole, with about as much arse as a stick insect.

Mine and Tammy's hatred of each other was pretty much instantaneous, but we were civil to each other because we had Simon in common. While he and I were pretty open with both our conversation and criticisms of each other, there was an unwritten rule never to make comments about each other's girlfriends. Even after I'd split up with Aggi he understood that only I could slag her off; if he'd joined in I would have felt obliged to beat him to a pulp or die trying.

When Simon called around to my house the day after Aggi had finished with me, he was completely unaware of all that had occurred. There wasn't a lot he could've done if he'd known anyway, apart from giving me 'space' and lending me his favourite Leonard Cohen album. To console, he needed to be a good listener and Simon didn't like to listen as much as he liked to talk; the ability to cook wouldn't have gone amiss either, although the key feature he lacked was a pair of attention-diverting breasts – to rest on, hug against and admire from a distance. I wanted Alice but she was in Bristol. When Simon asked where Aggi was I lied and said that she'd gone to see her cousin in Wolverhampton. The truth would come out sooner or later. It had to. I just didn't want to be there when it happened.

On his way out, having borrowed my brand new CD (*Elvis*

– *That's The Way It Is*) which I'd purchased with the sole
aim of cheering myself up, he'd asked me what Aggi had
got me for my birthday. It was then I remembered what
had unsettled me so much when I'd met her outside Shoe
Express – she hadn't brought a birthday present with her.
Like the Dutch boy with his finger in the dam I tried my
hardest to keep my tears at bay but the pressure behind my
eyes rose steadily. Finally, when I could take no more, the
most painful, animalistic, high-pitched squeals and groans
released themselves, and before I had time to even think
about being self-conscious I was crying like a baby. Snot
gurgled loudly at the back of my nose as I opened and
closed my mouth, attempting to form a sentence: '*Snort-
gurgle-snort*-she's-*snort-snort-gurgle-gurgle*-duuuuuu-
mmmped-*gurgle-gurgle*-meeeee!*' Simon had looked around
the room for something, anything, that might help me get
through this anguish. Drawing a blank, he'd taken a deep
breath, put his hand firmly on my shoulder and said: 'It'll
be all right, mate.' With snot running down my chin and
bent double in convulsion, I'd nodded in agreement, and
told him I'd be all right and that we ought to go for a drink
at the weekend. It never happened, a band practice came up
at short notice. When I finally saw him weeks later, part of me
wanted to thank him for being there, but the majority of me
wanted just to forget it.

'You definitely missed a blinder,' Simon boomed down the
phone, referring to the previous night's gig. 'Things are looking up for us.'

And they were too. Earlier in the week, Left Bank had
received an excellent review of their last London gig in *Melody
Maker*. Simon had blown it up on his dad's photocopier on to
an A3 sized sheet of paper and sent me a copy, underlining

in blue felt-tip pen phrases like; 'Kerosene fuelled attitude', 'the perfect antidote to the post-modern condition', and, my favourite, a sentence describing Left Bank's songs as, 'ergonomically crafted for those who like their music to fit the late twentieth century snugly'. Worse still, was the fact that Left Bank actually had a record deal. Last year they'd signed to Ikon, an off-shoot of EMI. Their first advance brought in enough money for Simon to buy a new guitar and sign off. The dole office almost threw a party when he told them the good news.

'That can't be your earth shattering news, surely?' I said incredulously. 'Come on, what's so important?'

Simon coughed shiftily. 'Listen, forget it. Temporary madness – that's all. It's no biggy. Forget it.'

And so I did because that was exactly what Simon didn't want me to do. If he felt the need to play games, the least I could do was annoy him with fake apathy.

'So how's it going?' I asked, not really wanting to hear the answer. I wasn't in the right frame of mind for Simon, or to be more accurate, I wasn't in the right frame of mind to hear he'd had an excellent week.

'Great. Really cool,' enthused Simon. 'You know we'd been demoing new material in London for the last couple of months? Well, it's all finished. A little bit of polish and our first single will be ready to be unleashed. I was talking to our press officer last week and she reckons we're creating a real buzz in the industry. Some woman at the *Guardian* might even do a feature on us. Wicked.'

'Yeah,' I said, trying to imitate sincerity but falling far short of the mark. Until the record deal, Simon's life had been my sole source of comfort when feeling guilty about Not Getting A Life. While languishing on the dole in Manchester I was constantly cheered by the thought that though I wasn't doing anything constructive, at least I wasn't him, at least I wasn't killing myself, putting all this energy into something so hopelessly futile as a band. *We hate it when our friends become successful.* Indeed. It was frustrating. I had more talent than Simon could ever dream of. I just didn't know where my genius lay, and in my latest incarnation as a secondary school English teacher it wasn't likely I'd find out either.

'How are things between you and Tammy?' I asked.

'Couldn't be better, my son.'

He was lying. Tony, Left Bank's drummer and West Bridgford's most notorious alcoholic, had told me over a double whisky chaser in the Royal Oak, that Tammy and Simon had been fighting with alarming regularity for the last couple of weeks.

'Oh,' I said casually, but not all that casually.

'Oh what?' said Simon coolly – his interest piqued.

'Fifteenth letter of the alphabet. At least I think so.'

I didn't need to say any more. My job was done. Happier, now that he wasn't quite so smug any more, I allowed him to change the topic of conversation.

'How's school?' Simon enquired. 'It sounds weird saying it like that. Like you're back at Beechwood Comp.'

'Fine,' I lied. I wanted to give him a run for his money in the fantastic-week-stakes. 'School's good. The kids think I'm cool because I've got a pair of Nike trainers. London's not as bad as everyone makes out y'know, there's a lot going on. I've been so busy I haven't been in a single night all week.'

'Sounds good,' said Simon. 'If things work out then the band might move down your way soon. I've been down there so long in the last six months, what with gigs and recordings, that it almost seems like home.' He hesitated as if weighing up something in his mind. 'How's the flat?'

'All right,' I said, wondering where his question was leading.

He was strangely silent. I wondered if he wanted me to thank him again for helping me get a roof over my head.

'Oh, don't forget to thank Tammy for finding the flat for me,' I said. 'It was uncommonly kind of her.'

'Yeah it was,' replied Simon absent-mindedly. He paused. 'George Michael signed his first record contract with Innervision at a café on Holloway Road just down the road from you. I always fancied going down there to see if there are any early eighties Wham vibes floating about, but I never got round to it.' He paused again, more than a little embarrassed, and fired off a diversionary question intended to win back the point lost by my earlier volley. 'So, anyone new in your life?'

Whether I'd had someone new in my life or not, I would've conjured up the perfect woman instantly, just to deny him his moment of self-satisfaction. However, as fate would have it, there was no need to break the truth when bending was all that was required. 'I've been seeing a girl called Martina. Stunning. An absolute babe. We met in Bar Rumba, in the West End. She's one of the reasons I'm so knackered. I've seen her every night this week, in fact she'll be coming round here soon.'

The only reason I even knew there was a club called Bar Rumba was because Aggi had once talked about driving to London just to go there and I'd said that I didn't fancy it, and she said she was going to go on her own, and I said fine, and she said fine, but she ended up not going anyway.

'That's good news,' said Simon. 'It's good to see you happy again.'

'Why?'

'Well, because it is.'

He meant Aggi.

'Oh, you mean Aggi?' I said.

'Yeah, well I didn't want to mention her,' he said, fumbling

127

over his words. 'I know how sensitive you still are about her.'

'I'm not sensitive,' I said. 'Aggi? Lucky escape, if you ask me.'

'Come on, Will,' sighed Simon impatiently, 'you can't mean that?'

'Oh, yes I do,' I replied. 'She was a total control freak. No, this was definitely a lucky escape, mate. Martina's definitely the girl for me. Nice, down to earth and very beautiful.'

I carried on like this, rubbishing Aggi and extolling the virtues of Martina, so that soon it began to sound like a truth, if not quite up to the same standards as the Truth. It had been *three years* since Aggi and I had been together – a lifetime ago to any normal twenty-six-year-old. She was nothing but memories to me, and for what it was worth *she* might as well have been a figment of my imagination. Martina, on the other hand, was real. She was real, quite stunning and most of all I didn't have to do anything to please her because she liked me the way I was.

The more I spoke, the more I realised that if I could get Simon – who had heard me moan about missing Aggi all this time – to believe I had never loved her, then maybe I could pull the wool over my own eyes too. And then I'd finally defeat Aggi and drive her from my head and my heart for good.

'I never loved Aggi.'

The words cut dead the thread of our conversation. It sounded so unreal that I said them again.

'I never loved Aggi. I just thought that I did. I think that at the end of the day I'd just grown used to her. It was nice having her around, and yeah, losing her and leaving university did kind of turn my world upside down for a while, but I'm over it. Those three years we had together meant nothing to me. Nothing at all.'

'Nothing?' asked Simon. The tone of his voice indicated that he didn't believe me for a second.

'Not a thing, mate.'

It felt good to lie.

Simon put on his agony uncle head and I wondered whether he'd been listening to *The Barbara White Show* too. 'Are you sure that you're not just saying that because you think that you've finally got to get over her?'

I hated the way he thought he could suss out a situation in seconds. He was the only person in the world allowed to be unfathomable. The thing was, everything he'd learnt about life had been culled from music. That was his biggest failing. He hadn't realised that life couldn't always be reduced to a three and a half minute pop song.

'No,' I lied again. 'Not at all. Look, she was all right, I'll give you that, and we did have some fun times.' I looked at her photograph on the wall and considered tearing it up as a show of strength. 'And, yes, I was distraught when we split up, but you've got to remember that I'm the man who went into mourning when I heard there wasn't going to be another series of *Blackadder*.' I chickened out of tearing up the photo and instead grabbed a marker pen, blacked out a tooth and drew a beard, a pair of glasses and bushy eyebrows on her face. 'Me and Aggi, well, we had different agendas right from the start. She wanted to be ethereal and I wanted to be down to earth. She wanted to go out and experience life and I wanted to stay in and watch it happen on TV. We were doomed from the start. We had nothing in common.'

I gave myself a standing ovation.

Simon's only response was, 'Well I'm glad you're over her.'

'Over who?' I joked.

We both laughed but Simon's sounded forced, as if trying to bolster my spirits.

'Listen,' he said. 'I'm glad you've told me all this.'

'Yeah,' I said, mellowing not only to Simon, but to the thought of being without Aggi. 'It's been good to get all this off my chest. You know how it is when you keep things bottled inside. It's not good for you.'

'No, you're right, it isn't,' he admitted.

Simon paused theatrically. More theatrically in fact than the entire cast of a Harold Pinter play. His sense of drama was another extension of his rock 'n' roll persona. Life to him was something that happened so that he'd have something to write songs about. He was always in search of an Experience he could dilute into a verse-chorus-verse structure. I was sure that was why he'd had so many different girlfriends and behaved like a git to all of them. There wasn't a lot of song mileage to be had from successful relationships and a nice personality.

'I've got to tell you something,' he said. 'It's the reason I called last night.'

I wondered whether he was cheating on Tammy again; it wouldn't have surprised me as he'd done it before. As far as I knew, he hadn't been seeing anyone on the side, he'd been too busy working on his masterpiece in London to bother with women.

'I'm sorry, mate,' he continued, playing the scene for all he was worth. 'I don't know how to say this, so I'll just come out with it. I had a bit of a "thing" with Aggi.'

'You did what?'

I'd heard exactly what he'd said and understood it all too clearly, but I needed to hear it again if only to torture myself more than was strictly necessary.

'I had a bit of a "*thing*" with Aggi.'

His voice was throaty, like he needed a glass of water and a good cough to clear his air-passages.

I asked him, 'What kind of a *"thing"* did you have with Aggi?' My voice was emotionless, at least, that's the way I remember it.

'The kind of *"thing"* that you wouldn't have been very happy about at one time,' he replied.

Strangely, my emotions appeared to have gone AWOL. My brain was getting ready for a bit of a scene but there was nothing happening on an adrenal level. Maybe I'd got my wish. Maybe I *was* finally over her. I stared across at her graffitied photo and smiled weakly.

'It's no skin off my nose,' I said. 'What Aggi does with whomever is her business. I just thought . . .' This time it was my turn for a dramatic pause, because I hadn't got a clue what I thought. 'I just thought that perhaps you could've been a bit more sensitive about it. I know it's been three years since she and I split up but even so, it's a bit much. You're meant to be my mate. What are you going to do next? Jump in my grave before I get there? And what will you say, "Oh, sorry, Will, didn't know you were going to use it"?'

'It's been and gone,' he said, refusing to react to my sarcasm. 'It's all over. It happened a long time ago. I just wanted to tell you because it's been weighing on my mind recently. I only wanted to be fair. We've been mates for too long to let a girl come between us.'

'You should've thought about that before you started . . .' I couldn't bring myself to say it. Giving it a name would only have made it more real than I could handle.

'I'm sorry,' said Simon quietly. 'Will, I really am sorry.'

'Forget the apologies,' I said, ejecting one of Left Bank's early demos from my cassette deck and throwing it to the floor. 'I told you, I'm over her. All I want to know is exactly how long ago was it?'

'A while ago,' he said, barely audibly.

My brain was in overdrive but my emotions were still nowhere to be seen.

'Exactly how long ago is "a while ago"?' I asked.

'It was . . .' He was loving every second of this. 'It was while you were still going out with her.'

Suddenly, my emotions returned home from their package holiday. The pain was physical and emotional all at once, as if a huge invisible fist had sent me across the room like in the 1982 Spielberg-produced horror film, *Poltergeist*. I felt sick, I felt faint, my knees went weak. I couldn't understand why he was telling me now after all this time. Ignorance wasn't just bliss, it was the pillars that kept the roof of my sanity from crashing down.

Simon, meanwhile, was waiting for a response. I didn't know what to say. He was right, a response *was* called for, something brutal that would cut him down to size, something that would make him feel as low as I felt, a guilt trip so far off the map he'd never find his way back. I drew a deep breath and put the phone down.

2.38 P.M.

When Simon had given me the copy of Left Bank's demo tape which I now held in my hands, he'd described it as 'a piece of rock 'n' roll history' that would one day be priceless. Clearing a space amongst the clothes, dirty crockery and exercise books, I placed the tape on the floor and looked feverishly around the flat for an instrument to aid me in my actions. In the kitchen I discovered a bread knife and a saucepan which had the remains of Thursday's spaghetti hoop dinner encrusted to its non-stick surface. I smiled at them both maniacally like Jack Nicholson in full 'Here's Johnny' mode.

Standing with Simon's 'priceless' work of art positioned at the foot of the bed, I raised the saucepan over my head and brought it crashing down against the tape, repeating the blows until it shattered into a million pieces. On roughly the twentieth blow the saucepan and its handle parted company, at which point I fell to my knees panting heavily. Someone, presumably the bloke from downstairs, whose roof was my floor, knocked on my door loudly. Ignoring him I began bundling together what was left of the magnetic tape before attacking it with the bread knife – shredding it into three weddings-worth of confetti. This complicated procedure took ten minutes to complete because halfway through, my temporary dementia still raging, I had decided that no piece of magnetic tape should be longer than half an inch and forced myself to begin again. Once I'd finished, I gathered the bits into a pile and scooped them into an envelope – the one I'd stolen from the school stationery cupboard specifically to send to the bank with my begging letter – and, using the same marker pen I'd used to graffiti Aggi, I scrawled Simon's address on it, sealed it with Sellotape, and added a first class stamp.

I got dressed and pulled on my heavy grey cashmere over-coat (bought from a jumble sale at Beeston Methodist church hall for £2.20, knocked down from £5.00) though I hadn't a clue what the weather was like. In my head it was the harshest Siberian winter on record, and in my heart it was a rainy night in Georgia – it had to be heavy grey overcoat weather. I picked up the envelope from the floor, slipped my *A–Z of London* into my coat pocket and walked out of the flat.

I needed to walk. I had too much anger in me to sit and watch TV, which was the only other thing I could think of doing bar getting the train to Nottingham, borrowing my dad's car and leaving tyre marks across Simon's chest. As a rule I wasn't a violent person, but I amazed even myself by the murderous thoughts rocketing around my head. Smashing the tape had helped to a degree, but I wanted something more, something that would bruise, bleed and make him beg for mercy. Simon was considerably bigger than me, but I felt invincible, like I was in full Jackie Chan *Drunken Master II* kick ass mode. I would've smashed his face in.

> I wanted to know when it had happened.
> I wanted to know how it had happened.
> I wanted to know why it had happened.
> I wanted to know everything.
> But most of all I wanted Aggi back.

Simon's news at least had an upside: I now knew how point-less it was trying to pretend that I didn't still feel something for her. It didn't make sense to love her. I'd weighed up the pros and cons a million times, and the results were always the same: I needed her. She was no good for me, she didn't want me to be part of her life, but there was nothing I could do about how I felt. I loved her. I couldn't lie to myself, though it was the one thing I wished I had the strength to do. I couldn't forget about her. The passage of time had, if anything, made her more important to me now than ever. I couldn't replace her with another girl without constantly comparing them to her and finding them lacking. I couldn't move forward and I couldn't reclaim the past. I was stuck in an ex-lover's limbo with nothing but happy memories to keep me company.

Looking around me for the first time I realised my feet had taken me to the Italian newsagent's near the top of Holloway Road. I put the envelope in the post box outside, decided against going into the shop to buy chocolate and continued up the road. My mission, petty as it was, had been accomplished, but I didn't want to go home. That was why I'd brought the *A–Z* with me.

Simon thinks that all Archway's got to offer is some café where George-bloody-Michael signed a record contract, I'd thought, while getting my coat on, ready to leave the flat. *Well, Marx's grave is near here somewhere. Now's as good a time as any to find it.*

With my *A–Z* open and my finger on Archway Road, I crossed the traffic lights at the tube station and navigated my way to Highgate Road. As I came to Whittington Hospital, an ambulance pulled out in front of me which led me into a long and protracted daydream:

Simon has contracted a rare blood disease. I'm the only

*person on earth that has the right blood type to save him.
'Will, you're the only one who can save me,' he whispers
weakly, clutching at my hand.*

*'Should have thought of that before you started poking
my girlfriend,' I reply.*

Five minutes and a fag-break later, I checked the *A–Z* again.
It didn't look too far now. Across the road I could see an
old church marked on the map which had been converted
into a set of yuppie apartments and a bit farther up was
the entrance to Highgate Park. The park was empty apart
from a middle-aged woman in green Wellingtons walking a
Yorkshire Terrier. As I passed the pond in the middle of the
rolling landscape, I walked into a swarm of midges, inhaling
quite a few of their number. Normally this would've set me
off on a tirade of abuse against the animal kingdom but even
this didn't phase me. I was a man with a mission and Marx's
grave was my holy grail. There everything would become
crystal clear.

I came to the gates on the far side of the park and turned
left. There it was – Highgate Cemetery. There was a small white
hut positioned two yards past the gates, on which was pinned
a small hand-written sign revealing that tickets were 50p per
person.

*What has the world come to when you can't even visit
deceased left-wing thinkers without having to pay for the
privilege?*

Disgruntled, I paid the far too chirpy elderly woman residing
within her blood money. She asked me if I needed directions,
I said no, in case she wanted to try and sell me a map.

The cemetery was peaceful and almost as silent as Archway
had been the previous night except, if I strained really hard, I
could hear the occasional lorry, so it kind of made sense to

stop straining. Ridiculous as this might seem, it occurred to me that this was definitely a cemetery. All around me were graves. Marx was in the company of a lot of people whose deaths spanned over two hundred years. Time had caused the older gravestones to blend in with nature; ivy and erosion now made them seem at home. The newer headstones, though, looked depressingly incongruous, like shiny marble bookmarks stuck into the ground. I made a mental note to remind my mother that I wanted to be cremated. If I left my funeral arrangements up to her she'd get me the shiniest marble headstone money could buy, with the specific intention of embarrassing me for eternity.

Wandering aimlessly around the cemetery, occasionally stopping to read the odd inscription, I stumbled across the grave, or rather tomb, I was looking for. There was no mistaking it, a huge metal cast of a balding, bearded man's head rested on top of the pale stone tomb. Even if I'd never seen a picture of Marx I would have known who it was; he looked exactly how I expected the father of modern Socialism to look: a little sad, a little world weary; sort of a cross between Father Christmas and Charlton Heston, but with a twinkle in his eye, as if he was constantly on the verge of working out the meaning of life. The inscription on the tomb in gold lettering read:

'The philosophers have merely interpreted the world. The point is to change it.'

As expected, his tomb had become a Mecca for Marxists worldwide, just as Jim Morrison's grave in Paris had become a home from home for half-arsed Euro-poets. Scattered around the edge of the marble base were a number of artificial roses and scraps of paper containing messages. I stood over one and read it:

> *'Thank you, from those of us still fighting for freedom all around the world.'*

It wasn't signed.

I studied the inscription on the tomb again and felt ashamed. Marx had tried to change the world and make it a better place. He wanted workers to be able to study philosophy in the morning and go fishing in the afternoon. He wanted an end to tyranny, based on the belief that all men were equal. All I wanted was to get my ex-girlfriend back. It was a selfish pursuit benefiting no one but myself. Even as these self-chastising thoughts entered my head, I felt my shoulders automatically hunching up into a 'so what' shrug. I wondered if every man was like me. Give a man a noble cause and he would fight to the death for what he believed in, but get the woman he loves to leave him and his once honourable principles would cease to be quite so important.

I was standing so quietly, wrapped up tightly in my thoughts, that a robin flew down from the branches of the oak above Karl's head and landed on the ground right beside my feet. Straight away it began tugging at a twig over twice its own body length. For over five minutes it struggled, lines of determination etched onto its beaky little face, before it gave up and flew off to a silver birch branch four trees to the left to recuperate. That robin was me. I was that robin. And Aggi was that twig. Those five minutes the robin had spent tugging at that twig, well, those were the three years I'd spent trying to get her back. Like God and McDonalds, Aggi was everywhere.

```
3.00 P.M.
```

I decided it was time to go when huge raindrops fell from the sky in their thousands, drenching me in seconds. My hair was soaked through and small rivulets of water ran down the back of my head, along my neck and into my shirt. I turned the collar on my overcoat up and pulled my head into its protection as far as I could, which didn't really help because now I couldn't see anything as my glasses had completely steamed up. To make matters worse, for the last few minutes I'd been monitoring a distinct rise in the smell of old men coming from my coat. Too cheap to bother getting it dry-cleaned when I'd bought it, I was now paying for the tightness of my wallet as the essence of the coat's previous owner came back to haunt me; it was sweet and musty, like stale urine mixed with the contents of a cat's litter tray.

I was wet, cold and smelling like the tramp from my late-night 7-Eleven trip. It was the rain that depressed me most of all. A walk in the rain might possibly have been fun if I'd had somebody to get wet with. I could've splashed gaily in puddles, swung on lamp-posts and sung a song or two, but I was alone. Drowning in torrential downpours on my own had no romance about it whatsoever. Gene Kelly wouldn't have been quite so annoyingly smug if he'd just found out his best mate had been sleeping with *his* girlfriend.

By the time I reached the house I felt lower than I'd done all week. Oblivious to the elements, I waited shivering by the garden gate, unsure about what to do next. It was still only Saturday afternoon, roughly speaking there were another thirty-six hours to fill until Monday. Even if I slept for as much of it as possible, there was still too much time, time I would spend imagining Aggi and Simon together: having sex; exchanging secret glances; laughing conspiratorially. Once I opened the front door the outside world would be locked out, leaving just me and my thoughts.

The hallway was depressingly dusty. Mr F. Jamal had promised me all communal spaces would be cleaned every Friday. I eyed a scrap of silver paper from a pack of Polos that had fallen out of my pocket onto the carpet yesterday morning, and shook my head sadly. Walking up the stairs I strained my ears, listening out for evidence of life in the other flats – people alone like me – people who might like to talk. The house was silent. Dead. When eventually I reached my door I fished around in my soggy overcoat pockets for my keys and also discovered the following:

> Three squashed Rolos (still in wrapper).
> Two bus tickets.
> Bakewell tart crumbs.

I scattered the crumbs on the threadbare carpet outside my door. A year ago I'd carried a solitary Bakewell tart in my coat pocket for less than a minute and since then I'd been removing crumbs by the thousand like modern day loaves and fishes.

I looked around the flat. Nothing had changed. N-O-T-H-I-N-G. I wasn't sure what I had expected to happen (someone to have fixed the kitchen tap? A miracle? A message from

Aggi?) but I'd desperately wanted something, anything to have changed. Instead, time had stood still and waited for my return.

To keep my brain ticking over I tried to work out who the last human being I'd spoken to in person was. There was one proviso, I could only count people whom I'd choose to go for a drink with. I'd left Nottingham the previous Sunday from my mum's house. Technically speaking, my mum and my brother had been the last human beings I'd spoken to. But while I liked them both, I didn't know whether I'd go as far as to say that I'd go for a drink with either of them. Next in line was Martina on Saturday night, but as I was trying to erase that encounter from my memory, she didn't meet the requirements. Casting my mind back further I recalled that on Friday I'd gone for a quick one in the Royal Oak with Simon, but as he officially no longer existed as far as I was concerned he didn't count either.

I pulled the emergency cord on this particular depressing train of thought and turned my attention to the phone. There were no messages on the answering machine. It wasn't even on, I'd forgotten to set it. After dialling 1471 – the number that tells you the last person that called – I wished I hadn't. At 2.42 p.m. precisely, Martina had phoned. She had to be pregnant. I called her parents' house but she wasn't in. They asked me if I wanted to leave a message and I said no. Shifting a pile of clothes and books aside, I made myself comfortable on the carpet, lying stomach downwards, and concentrated on the phone, willing it to ring.

For a while Aggi and I had lived under the delusion that we were psychic, after one occasion when we tried to phone each other at exactly the same time. The thought of our separate electrical impulses simultaneously hurtling down a fibre optic cable towards each other had meant so much that we spent a whole afternoon trying, quite seriously, to project images into each other's minds. It never worked.

I emptied the pockets of my jeans onto the floor because my keys were jabbing into my groin. After two minutes of intense concentration the phone still hadn't rung. I thought perhaps it was because I was being too general, trying to get anyone (bar Simon) to call.

Minutes passed and nothing really happened. Next door's dog, for some unknown reason, began howling like a wolf, but with the exception of that minor interruption life continued to pass me by. More minutes passed uneventfully. I considered calling Martina again and maybe leaving a message like 'Tell her everything's going to be okay' – something that would bolster her spirits if she was feeling scared or lonely, something that would imply that I cared without going overboard. It was wrong of course. I couldn't give her hope where there was none. If she thought she'd found true love after a drunken sexual encounter seven days ago, her warped mind would turn a message of solidarity into a proposal of marriage.

The telephone that I had in my hand was one I'd bought in Argos during my final year at university. It had come in three colours: grey, cream and white and I'd chosen grey because I thought it wouldn't show up the dirt as much as the others (although the grubby mouthpiece caked in minuscule deposits of dried saliva was testament to the fact that most things show up dirt if you don't clean them). Everyone in the house I shared had chipped in to buy it, but I'd got to take it home when we graduated because I won it in the house lottery. Tony (whom I hadn't seen or heard from since we all moved out) won the toaster, Sharon (whom I hadn't seen or heard from since graduation) won the plug-in TV aerial, and Harpreet (whom I hadn't seen or heard from since I left Manchester) won the electric kettle. I was really chuffed to win that phone; the hours I'd clocked up on it talking to Aggi probably ran into months. Some of our best conversations had been on that phone, like the one when she'd told me I was the kind of man that she wanted to marry one day. That phone had made me very happy.

It rang.

'Hello?'

'Hello.'

It was Kate.

'Hi, Kate. How are you?'

'I'm fine. I hope you don't mind me calling.'

'No, not at all,' I replied, happy that it was Kate and not Simon seeking forgiveness.

'Are you sure I'm not disturbing you?' she asked. 'You answered the phone very quickly. You must've been sitting on it. Were you expecting a call from someone else?'

'No, I was just passing,' I lied. 'I've only just got in. I went to Highgate Cemetery with some friends to see Marx's grave. Very cool. Definitely worth seeing.'

I wished I hadn't described Marx's grave as 'cool'. I was sounding too nerd-like for words.

'Do you know I lived in that flat for over a year and never got around to going there? It's a shame, I'll probably never get to see it now.'

'Maybe I'll let you visit me some day,' I replied, only half joking.

She laughed.

I laughed too, but only because I was wondering whether I was stretching the point to describe her laugh as 'flirtatious'.

'You'd better be careful what you say,' she said wistfully. 'I might take you up on that.'

Simultaneously I ran out of saliva and witty come-backs. I changed the subject. 'So, what've you been up to today?'

'Nothing much,' she said. 'I watched kids' TV this morning and then went into town. I managed to get an extension on my overdraft, so I spent most of it on a pair of trainers and a skirt. I shouldn't be spending money like I do but it cheered me up.'

'I think your cheque came today,' I told her, spying her letter on top of the TV. 'Well, there's a letter for you anyway.'

'Brilliant. That's fantastic news. Oh, what time is it? Quarter past three? I've missed last post then. Oh well, at least it'll get here on Tuesday. Better than it not coming at all, I suppose.'

She sounded happy.

'So would you like to talk some more?' she asked.

'Of course,' I said. 'How many times did I beg you to call back yesterday?'

'What do you want to talk about?'

'Anything,' I said happily. 'Anything at all.'

I actually had a topic that I wanted to discuss if she couldn't come up with one. It was a question I'd been mulling over on the journey from the cemetery. I wanted to know whether she thought the most beautiful people in the world (Cindy Crawford, Mel Gibson *et al*) ever got dumped. And if so, did this mean that no one, no matter who they were, was safe from getting dumped? I was thankful when she said she'd got a question, because I was sure mine would've eventually ended up about Aggi.

'This is kind of related to what you did this afternoon,' said Kate, revealing her question. 'Where do you stand on death?'

'I'm against it,' I joked.

We both laughed.

'You know what I mean,' she said. 'What do you think about death?'

'I think that when you're dead you're dead,' I said matter-of-factly. 'This is it as far as life goes, so we'd better make the most of it while we've got it. Although having said that, I think I'd be kind of disappointed if what I've spent the last twenty-six years experiencing was really all there was to life.'

'Okay, well my question for you is this: how would you like to die?' said Kate, as if she was a waitress asking a diner how they liked their eggs done.

'This is all getting a bit strange, isn't it?' I said.

'Strange? You should hear the things that me and Paula talk about at five in the morning after our eighth triple vodka! Question is, are you man enough?'

'I'm more of a man than you,' I protested mockingly.

'I should hope so!' said Kate.

'You'll never find out,' I retorted, wondering if this banter we were engaging in constituted flirting or simply joking around.

'Seriously, how would you like to pop off?' she asked.

'I don't know,' I said, gratefully returning to the subject of death. 'I'll need some time to think about this one. In the meantime, what about you? How would you like to die?'

'I thought you'd never ask!' she said laughing. 'Me and Paula have discussed this many times during our late night chats. My answer is all ready. Are you?'

'As I'll ever be.'

3.20 P.M.

PART ONE OF A TWO PART CONVERSATION ON DEATH: HER WAY OF THINKING

Now this is going to sound morbid, in fact it's going to sound very morbid. I suppose it is morbid, really. What must you think of me? You don't know me that well, so I suppose you're probably not thinking all that much. Well, here goes. Every now and again I like to think about my own funeral. I know it sounds weird but it's true. People don't think about death very much these days, do they? They seem to spend their whole lives avoiding it. Pensioners on the other hand think about it constantly. They've definitely got the right idea. I suppose it's because they're so much nearer to the End than the rest of us. They keep a little bit of money in a post-office account to make sure there's enough cash around to pay for a decent funeral, coffin and finger-food for afterwards. That's how it should be. Then of course you've got the ancient Egyptians. They spent their entire lives thinking about death and when they went it was like the biggest party ever: good clothes, possessions and even slaves buried in the roomiest coffins in the world. Egyptians, old people and me – we've all got our priorities right.

The first thing to work out is exactly how I'm going to die.

147

Sometimes it's drowning, other times it's an aeroplane crash, but at the moment it's dying in any manner at all as long as it's for someone I love.

Okay, so you want me to explain? It's really simple. I'm desperate to die for someone I love. That's all there is to it. I don't know what the situation is. The important thing is that when I die the person I save lives on because of me. That's all that matters. I know it won't surprise you to know that I've already constructed a purpose-built scenario for this!

I'm nearly twenty. I've not done an awful lot with my life so far. I've been to school, gained a couple of A levels, gone to university and dropped out, and, um, that's about it. Pretty self-centred, wouldn't you say?

I got the idea from a black and white film I saw one Saturday afternoon the week before I moved out of the flat.

Here's the sitch: there's a cad, a French aristocrat, and a beautiful girl who's madly in love with the aristo. Anyway, the Cad falls in love with Beautiful Girl. On a trip to France the Aristocrat gets caught by the children of the revolution, who put him in the Bastille. The Cad goes to France and visits the Aristocrat in the Bastille. Now here's the good bit: the Cad knocks out Aristocrat, swaps places with him and goes to the guillotine in his place! D'you see? Cad loves Beautiful Girl so much that he's prepared to sacrifice his own life so that she can be happy with Another!

That film left me in shock. I've only seen it once. I don't even know what it's called – I mean . . . well . . . I did know, but now I don't. Being dumped does that to your long-term memory, doesn't it? Oh, it doesn't matter what it was called, it moved me. It really moved me. I mean, what does it mean? Is that love or is it obsession? Will any man want to do that for me? I'm asking a lot of questions. I apologise. I think Dirk Bogarde was in it.

Where did we begin all this? Oh yeah! My funeral.

It's been a great worry of mine that all of the people that I want to invite to my funeral won't be invited due to my own lack of foresight. There's no one person amongst my friends that knows all of my other friends. My friend Lizzie knows most of the people who went to our school who were friends with me, but she wouldn't know people like Pete or Jimmy or Karen or any of the small number of friends I made at university, and she wouldn't know any of the people from when I lived in Cardiff last summer like Mrs Grosset, or the lads who used to come into the Lion on a Tuesday night. A couple of times I've made a definitive list and posted it to Lizzie with strict instructions for it to remain sealed until my death. Lizzie is a mate, but I just know that she's opened it. Well, you would, wouldn't you? But it doesn't matter because I revise the list every now and again when certain people get too much for me. I'll add you to it if you want me to.

I suppose with all this talk about funerals you'll think I'm being really vain but it's something we're all guilty of. I just want to know that my passing will be mourned big time. I don't want people to be philosophical about my death. I want them to grieve for a decent period. It's good for the soul, you know?

3.42 P.M.

PART TWO OF A TWO PART CONVERSATION ON DEATH: MY WAY OF THINKING

It'll be of little comfort to you but you're no weirder than me. I know what you mean when you say you want to die for someone else. When you look back at your life you want to have meant something. I've got a friend, or rather had a friend, and it's just possible that through some quirk of fate he might become famous. And I bet he thinks that if he gets this goal, i.e. fame and fortune, his life will have meaning. But it won't. The only way life can really mean something is if you give it away. It's a shame though because if you do give it away, you don't get the chance to fully appreciate the splendour of it. That's the main flaw of the ultimate selfless act – you never get the chance to be around to take your bow.

I had my first encounter with death at the age of five. I'd been given a junior gardening kit by my parents which consisted of a small shovel, rake and watering can. My mum had bought me some red Wellington boots to go with it and my dad had let me choose a packet of carrot seeds from a huge row of seed packets at the local gardening centre. At the time I had a big thing about carrots. I thought that if I grew some they'd lure Bugs Bunny to my garden. I lived in

151

hope that one day I'd see my carrots disappearing under the ground and then I'd know that Bugs was real. Then I'd peer down the hole where my carrots had been and he'd look up at me, twitch his whiskers and say, 'What's up, Doc?'

It was an incredibly hot summer's day when I decided to do my planting – my dad completely ignored the advice on the packet, which said to sow from March to late May – just to make me happy. Within half an hour of starting work I'd dug the soil, planted my seeds and watered them. My job was done, but I carried on digging for the sake of it in a patch of ground away from the carrots. Once in a while I'd find a worm. The first one startled me a little – I think it was because they didn't have eyes – but after that, every time I came across one, I picked it up on the edge of my spade and popped it in my little yellow bucket. I decided to have a competition to see how many worms I could collect in an afternoon. I promised myself that if I'd collected enough by the end of the day I'd try and make my own wormery like the one I'd seen in the solitary copy of *The Encyclopaedia Britannica* (Washington – Yam) we'd received free for joining a book club.

At about one o'clock my mum called me in for lunch. I was quite relieved to finally take a rest because I was beginning to feel a bit dizzy from the heat. Inside, the house was cool. On the table was a ham, lettuce and tomato sandwich and a glass of Ribena. I drank and ate and felt content. In fact I felt so content that I fell asleep on the living room sofa. Two hours later I woke up. By now it was time for the kids' programmes on telly. I watched my favourite cartoons until my mum ordered me to sort out the mess in the garden. It was then that I remembered the worms. I examined the bucket expecting to see a writhing mass of slimy worms bent on revenge. Instead all I saw were very grey, very stiff, very dry, dead worms. Why weren't they moving? I wondered. Why had they stopped being worms? Eventually I worked out that their few hours in the sun might not have been particularly beneficial to their welfare, so I rushed to the kitchen and filled a Tupperware beaker with water from the hot tap, poured it into the bucket and waited. I expected the worms to be instantly re-animated, but they weren't. Instead they floated on the surface of the water, rocking gently to and fro as steam rose up against my face.

I asked my mum why the worms had died and she gave me the technical answer about them losing moisture and dehydrating. But that didn't really answer my question. Why were they dead? The real answer, and the answer that I kind of worked out there and then, was this: the worms died because everything dies eventually. That's what life is all about.

The only attractive prospect about dying is that if I do it soon enough there's the possibility that Aggi might finally see that she and I were meant for each other. Of course, her realising this once I've popped my clogs makes the whole thing kind of pointless, but at least this great wrong would at last have been righted.

And now to funerals: I've done more than plan the guest list. First off there'll be twenty-two wailing women, dressed in black, standing at my graveside; girls whom I've fancied at various points in my sad life but who had ignored my advances, only to realise, now that I was dead, that I had been their perfect man all along.

My mum would be weeping like mad; I can't imagine that she'd be in any state other than suicidal. I think she's desperate to die before either my brother Tom or me, and I'm inclined to agree that it might be for the best. My mother takes great comfort in the status quo, as does my dad; they like things to be just the way they found them, though that didn't stop them getting divorced last year.

I find it hard enough to deal with twenty-six years of life, so the thought of dealing with an eternity of death fills me with dread. I can barely motivate myself to get out of bed these days. I wasn't always like this. I wasn't like this at all.

Look, I'm feeling a bit tired now. Thanks for calling. You're certainly an interesting person to talk to, but right now I've got to go. And no, it's not because I want to be a moody boy loner, although any mystique, even hackneyed moody boy loner mystique, would be useful. It's just that I'm talking all manner of weirdness to you straight off the cuff. I need to sit down and work everything out a bit. I found out today that the only girl I had ever loved cheated on me with my best friend and it kind of shook me up. Look, I promise I'll phone you back soon.

4.41 P.M.

My neck was killing me.

During the course of the conversation I'd changed position several times and, by the time I'd put the phone down, I was lying half on the bed and half on the floor with my neck supporting more weight than it was designed to. It was a little unsettling to be suddenly thrust back into The Real World. A gust of wind sent a sheet of rain crashing against my window, as if I needed reminding that I wasn't meant to be happy. I picked up the phone again to see if Kate was still there. Sometimes, if the other person hasn't put their phone down, they can still be connected. When I discovered this, I used to do it to Aggi all the time. She'd always be the first to put the phone down and then she'd pick it up seconds later to call someone else and I'd still be there. When she cottoned on to what I was doing, she made me put the phone down first whenever we spoke. With hindsight, of course, she probably did it so she could phone Simon.

I reflected on the conversation I'd had with Kate. I hadn't told her the whole truth – I hadn't told her about my fantasies about Aggi's untimely passing. For ages the only way I could cope with Aggi's absence from my life was by pretending she was dead. I scattered her ashes by our oak tree in Crestfield Park, and when I occasionally visited her, I'd lay a few daisies at the base of the tree and tell her how life was. It was great when she was dead because at last I was free from worry. I always knew where she was and what she was doing; she always listened attentively and never argued.

Her funeral was wonderful. Lying in the coffin at the crematorium, her face was pale and fragile, her body stiff and wax-like – the complete opposite to how she'd been alive. Many of her previous boyfriends were present at the service but while they were all grim-faced and stiff-upper-lipped, I was the only one who openly shed tears because she would've liked that. Like Kate said, the last thing you want at your own funeral is people being reserved – the more wailing and gnashing of teeth the better.

Mrs Peters had cried too. She was one of the few people who could understand the pain I was going through. Although we hadn't spoken at the crematorium, when she'd bumped into me in town weeks later, she revealed how she'd always had a soft spot for me and said things like Aggi must've taken leave of her senses to dump me. She promised to put in a good word for me with Aggi when she got back home, unable to grasp the concept that her only daughter was dead.

Aggi had died from natural causes. I admit I'd considered murder, but it wasn't very me, although for a while it was. 'If I can't have you then nobody else can either!' It would've been amusing to have seen the look of horror on her face as I uttered those terrible words while haphazardly shoving cartridges into a shotgun. I'd have seen the terror in her beautiful green eyes as she realised that finally, after all these years, I did have a backbone and, unfortunately for her, my new Arnold Schwarzenegger-like persona would be the last thing she'd ever see. I couldn't shoot her though – too messy – and I couldn't stab her – which is what a crime of passion really called for, because that was messy too, and if I'd used a blunt instrument, I would've ruined that face that I loved so much. No, Aggi had died naturally from something the doctors didn't have a name for. Of course there was no antidote or cure but I didn't let her suffer. I offered her the choice of any of my organs if they could help matters, but alas they couldn't. After a week of suffering I kissed her good-bye and she fell into a coma. A month later Mrs Peters and I turned off her life-support machine to give another human being the chance of life.

I was devastated – the love of my life, felled in her prime by a mysterious disease! I spent morning, noon and night crying and shaking uncontrollably. My dad had said things like, 'It'll be all right in the end, son,' and told me to keep my strength up. Tom hadn't known what to say, but had given me a small smile of solidarity whenever our eyes met. Mum was the best of the bunch. She'd been very understanding, saying that whenever I was ready to talk, she'd be there to listen. Alice had phoned and told me that although she hadn't liked Aggi she was sad she was dead, and I had said it was okay and that it was good just to hear her voice. I'd telephoned the dole office and told them I wouldn't be in to sign on for the next couple of weeks, and even they, Nazis that they are, were extraordinarily nice, saying it was okay, rather than asking me to bring her body in as evidence, as I thought they might.

I rubbed my neck. It still felt sore. As I raised my arms to rub further I caught a whiff of my armpits that made my nasal hairs recoil. School sweat smells like nothing else on earth, the nearest thing I can compare it to is the smell of rancid milk and grass cuttings. I hadn't showered since Thursday evening – I had over thirty hours' worth of school sweat plus three hours' worth of its fouler smelling cousin, gym sweat, clinging to my skin. Fortunately, the shower was the one thing in the flat that had been modified since 1970. The water blasted out of the nozzle of my Gainsborough 1500 series like a mini police water cannon. I stayed there, enclosed by the shiny plastic shower curtain, for half an hour, lost in a world of steamy waterfalls, cleanliness and soap with labels that remained stuck on until the very end.

Standing on the cold lino post-shower, I rubbed myself down with a green hand towel – the only towel in the flat, because I'd forgotten to pack any others. Every time I showered I'd leave it hanging on the wardrobe door, praying that it would dry in time for use next day. By Wednesday morning it couldn't have been any wetter if it had been in the shower with me.

Dressing leisurely, I pulled my jeans back on and slipped on a clean, dark blue shirt. As I did the top buttons up, my hand brushed against what felt like the beginnings of a spot on my chin. I wanted to give up. I was undecided as to which was the more depressing thought: the fact that at twenty-six I still got spots, or that I was wishing I was at home so I could borrow my mum's foundation to cover it. It was impossible to tell exactly what stage it was at – minor blemish/hurts like buggery/custard pustular/bleeding scab – because I'd broken my Elvis mirror on Monday, the only mirror in the flat, having trodden on it as it lay hidden underneath a pile of clothes. *Seven years' bad luck*, I'd thought to myself. I added them to my last three years of misery, to make a nice round number.

The phone rang.

I gazed at it emptily, still wrapped up in thoughts about spots and my Elvis mirror, as if unsure where the sound was coming from. Once my brain got into gear, I whispered a silent prayer. I don't know why I hoped it was Kate. After all I had been the one who'd finished our last conversation prematurely and, as well as that, she'd given me her number so I could call her any time. No matter, I still hoped it might be Kate.

'Hi, Will, it's me.'

Like a spoilt child in need of – as my dad would put it – 'a good slapping', I was unreasonably annoyed that Martina had been out when I'd called. So out of sheer spite I pretended not to be sure who it was.

'Who?'

'Will, don't you recognise me? It's me, Martina.'

'Oh, sorry. I didn't recognise you for a second. You sound different on the phone.'

'Oh, do I?' she said, genuinely surprised. 'I just wanted to find out if you received my card.'

I tried to work out whether she sounded pregnant or not. There were no signs of stress in her voice but neither were there signs of relief. What's more she was asking me pointless questions about birthday cards when she knew full well that I was waiting to find out whether I'd fertilised one of her eggs and was going to spend the next thirty years in mourning. There was no way, of course, that I was intending to ask her. That was out of the question. She was playing games but I didn't care. If she'd ever seen the ruthless way I played Monopoly she'd know it wasn't worth her trying.

I cast my mind back to the birthday card and briefly con-templated denying its existence, because what Martina was really asking me was had I read and fully comprehended the ramifications of the message she'd written in it? She was making sure that the escape route marked 'Ambiguity' was blocked off for good.

'Yes, I got it,' I said.

'I've always wanted to send that Klimt card to a special person,' she said. I pictured her in my head, long blonde hair falling over her face. I'd watched her in lectures almost hiding behind that hair, as if it made her invisible. It was one of the few endearing things I'd noticed about her. 'Someone like you, Will. I think it's a really beautiful picture, don't you? It's got so much passion in it. I've got a poster of it in a clip frame. I spend hours looking at it.'

As she continued to sing the praises of Klimt and several other classical painters, I wondered whether I'd been too harsh with her. After all, she was kind and meant well. It wasn't her fault alone that she might be pregnant. She was certainly attractive and most of all she thought incredibly highly of me, in spite of everything I'd done to persuade her otherwise.

'Martina . . .'

I'd never used her name like that, not with any sort of softness or tenderness behind it that wasn't driven by lust. To her, my saying her name like that was a prelude to heaven. Wielding this sort of power was unsettling – I felt like a god, albeit a minor deity – all I had to do was utter a few small words and I could make Martina's wildest dreams come true.

'Martina, how would you like to die?' I asked, eventually.

'What do you mean?' she said, obviously confused. This wasn't what she had been expecting at all.

'I mean exactly what I said,' I replied gently. 'Taking aboard the fact that one day we're all going to die, when the big event comes – how would you like it to arrive?'

'I don't know the answer to that sort of question,' she said uncomfortably. 'I don't like thinking about, you know . . . passing away.'

'Yeah, well think about it now,' I said. My gentleness and sympathy evaporated. I was annoyed but only momentarily, because a second later I was overcome with guilt.

'I'm sorry,' I apologised. 'I didn't mean it.'

'No, *I'm* sorry,' she said bitterly. 'I'm obviously annoying you. I'll have a think right now. Let's see . . .' She paused, and made audible thinking noises. 'I'd like to go in my sleep,' she said, once she'd regained her composure. 'I don't want to know about it when it happens. I had a great aunt who died in her sleep and she looked very peaceful, like she was enjoying a good nap.'

I didn't know what to say next. I'm sorry to say that I didn't care about her answer. Martina wasn't Kate and she wasn't Aggi. We were never going to work out. It just wasn't meant to be.

'The test,' I said firmly.

'Negative,' she whispered. 'I'm not pregnant. I wanted to tell you. I just didn't know how. I'm sorry I dragged it out. I know you're angry. Please don't hate me, Will. I wasn't trying to upset you. I just didn't know . . .' She started to cry. 'Will, I was so scared. I really was. I was terrified. I wish you were here.'

I stood up and looked out of the window. It was raining. Next door's dog was sheltering underneath the silver birch at the bottom of the garden.

I was disappointed. Yes, I was disappointed. I wasn't going to be a father. I wasn't going to have to think up exotic middle class names for our child. There'd be no trips to Mothercare. My parents wouldn't be Gran and Granddad, nor for that matter would Gran gain her stately 'Great' prefix; Alice wouldn't become a godmother. After all that mental speculation everything would remain the same. I thought I'd have had a little girl. If Martina had voiced no objections we would've called her Lucy. When she'd reached five she would've gone to my junior school – hopefully Mrs Greene or someone equally nice would have been her teacher.

This is so hopeless.

'Will, I've got something to ask you,' whispered Martina,

ignoring my silence. 'I know you've probably been really busy this week, going out with your new London friends and all that, but I wonder . . .' Her voice grew quiet. An endearing blend of shyness and humility. 'I wonder if I could come and see you next weekend? I really miss you. I haven't been out all week because I've had no one to go out with. Nearly all of the friends that I managed to keep in contact with have moved away, and I swear if I have to spend another Friday night watching gardening programmes with my parents I'll go mad. I won't come if you don't want me to. I know that it's quite early on in our relationship and, well, with this scare things haven't been easy but . . .'

That 'but' hovered in the air for an unreasonably long time. I couldn't work out if she'd actually intended to finish her sentence or whether she'd left her 'but' lingering with intent. I decided she wasn't cynical enough to be that manipulative. I was genuinely moved. This girl was displaying a distressing lack of self-respect that only a master of these kind of indulgences such as I could truly appreciate.

I told her that I didn't really know what I was doing next weekend and that I had a lot of school work on. It was only after I'd said this that it occurred to me I might sound a little insensitive, what with her being an unemployed newly-qualified teacher. I told her that the best thing would be for me to ring her during the week and see how things were looking then.

She seemed to believe me and didn't say anything more about it. Before I said I had to go I promised her again that I'd call during the week. She sighed quietly, more to herself than anything, but clearly enough to let me know that she was disappointed I hadn't just said yes. Seizing the opportunity to start an argument in which I could end it all, I asked her if there was anything wrong. She hesitated before carefully answering 'No' in the chirpiest voice she could muster – which was in fact exceptionally chirpy. I said good-bye and put the phone down.

4.57 P.M.

Martina had depressed me.

I really did want to make her happy. I did. But if her happiness involved my being with her until death did us part, there was nothing I could do for her. Pointless as it was, I bitterly wished I hadn't got off with her. I wished it hadn't happened at all. At least then, maybe I could have been her friend and helped her out; spoken to her on the phone for hours at a time; said yes immediately to her coming to stay; drunk too many bottles of wine and showed her my very poor impression of Sean Connery. But now none of this could ever happen. She'd never be satisfied with a demotion to being 'just good friends'.

Hunger drove me to the kitchen in search of sustenance. The best I could muster from a frantic search through the cupboards was an unopened bag of Tilda brown rice. In the end I opted for a cigarette and two slices of bread which I slipped into the toaster while I went to the toilet.

With my trousers around my ankles and the initial push of the first defecation of the day almost upon me, Martina's tearful face flashed inside my head with the persistency of a Belisha beacon. *That's how she'll look when I give her the push. Tearful. Like I've killed her Mum's Yorkshire Terrier with my bare hands and she's next on the list. Why can't she just get the message? Why is she making me do this? Why hasn't she got any self-respect?*

Get some, Martina. Get some self-respect before you end up like me.

Two days after Aggi had kicked me out of her life I was still very much in denial. The afternoon of the day in question, I found myself wandering along the booze aisle in Safeway, working out the most economical way to numb the pain with over a week left until my next Giro. Traditionally speaking, the situation – spurned lover seeking brief alcoholiday – cried out for vodka or whisky, but getting intentionally drunk on spirits, early in the morning, lacked the romance of, say, cheap wine, as it smacked too much of the real desperation of tramps and alcoholic wife-beaters. Plonk could always be explained away to my conscience as nothing more sinister than over-indulgence and so wine it was, two bottles of Safeway's own brand of Lambrusco. I barely got through the automatic doors at the exit before I'd unscrewed the cap off the first bottle and taken a deep swig. By the time I'd reached home on the bus over half the bottle had disappeared.

Wobbling up to my bedroom, I had dumped Aggi's letters out of the Nike trainer box where they lived and spread them over the floor. In between sips, I pored over each one, ninety-seven in total. This was the first time I'd ever read them collectively. Beginning with her first (twelve pages of feint-lined hole-punched A4) and ending with the last (a single sheet of green writing paper sent to me three weeks earlier), I built up a picture of our relationship different to the one in my head. The letters reminded me of how our relationship had really been, untainted by the events of the past few days. While the themes varied, after a year, they were pretty much all about the same thing: how much she loved me. I remember thinking to myself that the girl in these letters adored me and it was that girl, and not the girl who had dumped me, whom I loved so deeply. The other girl was just an impostor.

Hours went by as I filed them all in chronological order, even though some of them weren't dated. I amazed myself by working out when she'd written them by the kinds of things they mentioned. For example two letters were signed, 'Love, Mary Jane'. At the time that she'd sent them to me (March, roughly two-and-a-half years ago) I'd had a real thing for *Spiderman* comics and Mary Jane was the web-slinger's girlfriend. This and thousands of other tiny details sparked off so many wide-screen Technicolor memories that I felt like they'd only been written yesterday. By the time I'd re-read them all, I'd finished both bottles of wine and floods of tears were silently streaming down my face. I went for a walk to get some fresh air and ended up on Aggi's front door-step.

Mrs Peters opened the door, ushered me into the front room she kept for best and offered me a cup of tea. She told me that Aggi wasn't in but that she'd be back in half an hour as she'd only nipped out to the library down the road. She chatted at me (rather than to me) for every minute of that excruciatingly long half-hour, while I barely spoke a word in return, the Lambrusco having wreaked havoc with my ability to form simple sentences. She asked if Aggi had invited me over for Christmas dinner, which told me at least that Aggi had been too scared to tell her mum she'd dumped me. Her mum thought the world of me, and I of her. It took all the strength I had to stop myself accepting the invitation on the spot.

The scratch of key finding keyhole signalled Aggi's return, and in what felt like an instant we were standing in front of each other. She looked as beautiful as ever. She was wearing jeans, a checked shirt and a wine-coloured corduroy jacket that used to be mine. She was so shocked when she saw me that she almost dropped the books she was carrying. Mrs Peters slipped out of the room, sensing that we'd had some sort of tiff and were in the process of making up. Before leaving the room she said, 'Do you want another cup of tea, love?' I told her I didn't.

'You're drunk,' said Aggi aggressively. 'I can smell it all over you. How dare you come to my house in this state.'

I motioned drunkenly to her to sit down, which only served to infuriate her even more. I didn't say anything for a few seconds. The floor was spinning so wildly that I was desperately searching with my eyes for something solid to hang on to.

'You're beautiful,' I slurred eventually, gripping onto the arm of the sofa, 'but at least I'll be sober in the morning.' I thought I was so funny that the resultant fit of hysterics caused me to fall back into the sofa.

She moved towards the sofa until she was standing over me. I looked down into my lap to avoid her gaze, ashamed that we'd come to this. She told me I'd got to go and tried to pull me up by my arm. The sulky five-year-old that dwells within every melancholy drunkard freaked out and told her that she wasn't allowed to touch me any more. I think that scared her, she sat down in the armchair opposite me and did her best to hold back her tears.

'What do you want from me, Will?' she asked, taking her turn to avoid making eye contact. I searched her face for signs that she recognised me – the man she used to love – and found none. 'What can you possibly want to say to me? It's over and there's nothing that you can say to change my mind.'

'Nothing at all?' I asked, still trying to catch her gaze.

I told her that I wanted answers, I needed to know what I'd done to make her stop loving me.

These were her exact words:

'It's not you, it's me. I've changed. I thought I could be the person that you wanted me to be. For a while it was what I wanted too. I wanted to feel love like it is in the movies and you gave that to me and for that I'll be grateful forever.'

It didn't make sense. She was saying all these wonderful things about me but the message she was sending added up to little more than, 'Cheers, I had a really nice time.'

'But what did I do wrong?'

'You didn't let me grow, Will. I've been going out with you since I was nineteen. I'm not the same girl! You've stayed the same though, you haven't changed at all – you didn't grow with me – that's why we're different people. And now I can't breathe. I feel stifled. I feel like you're trying to trap me.'

I tried to explain to her that I wasn't trying to trap her. I told her that whatever freedom she wanted she could have. But she told me it was too late. She wanted a new beginning.

One thing she said really cracked me up though. 'It's like that song,' she said, completely straight-faced, '"If You Love Someone, Set Them Free."' I couldn't believe it. It wasn't enough that she was wrecking my whole life. She was quoting Sting to me too.

To be crueller than was strictly necessary I began singing in what I thought was a close approximation to the former Police star's vocal style. She wasn't amused. I knew our conversation would draw to a permanent close unless I could do something, anything, to make her see what a huge mistake she was making. As hard as I tried, I couldn't think of anything. Worst of all, I was beginning to sober up when all I wanted was to be drunk again, if only to give me an excuse for crying in her sitting room.

She stood up as if to say that she'd had enough. I stood up too and walked to the front door and opened it. She followed me into the hallway. Standing outside on the door-step, with eyes full of tears I said to her, 'Aggi, what do you want? And why aren't I it?'

She looked at me blankly and closed the door.

I flushed the toilet and pulled my trousers back up. Back in the kitchen, the toast had long since popped up and gone cold.

I hate cold toast.

5.47 P.M.

In my reckoning if Aggi and I hadn't split up when we did, we probably would've remained together. At least I hoped so. With the combined income from two professional jobs maybe we'd even have had the London equivalent of Alice and Bruce's place, a smart flat in nearby Highgate, instead of a poorly decorated shoe box in Archway. Of course, I didn't know this for a fact, but I often liked to imagine that somewhere out there existed a parallel universe where things had turned out okay.

I'd always longed to take my turn at playing house. At the age of thirteen (although, looking back, I could well have been fourteen) I was deeply besotted by Vicki Hollingsworth, to such an extent that I felt ready to make a huge commitment to her and I told her as much. It was a Tuesday dinner-time, I was in the canteen watching, mesmerised, as one by one, she consumed the jam sandwiches that constituted her lunch. A smear of strawberry preserve adorned her top lip and I remember feeling an overwhelming urge to lick it off. Instead, keeping my adolescent awakening in check, I got up from my table and strode across the room until I was standing in front of her. Emma Golden, Vicki's best friend, had just got up to scrape the remains of her dinner into the huge bin by the main door, leaving the two of us alone. With my eyes to the ground, I spoke to her. 'Vicki,' said the teenage me, 'I don't know if you realise this but we were made for each other.'

I'd heard those very words spoken, less than twenty-four hours earlier, on the Monday evening episode of *Crossroads*. The second they'd come out of our Pye television set and into my world, they seemed to me the most magical, beautiful words ever spoken. Momentarily looking up from my shoes, I studied her face as she mulled over my proposition. I could almost see my words tumbling from one ear, past the back of her hazel eyes, to the other ear and back again, as she vacantly tipped her head from side to side. After a minute of this she met my gaze briefly, before running off in the direction of the main exit. My eyes remained fixed on the chair where the buttocks of this vision of loveliness had once been. I sat down in Emma Golden's chair and surreptitiously placed my hand on the seat Vicki had vacated. It was still warm.

In any one of the thousand times I'd played this scene over in my head, Vicki had been so overcome with emotion at my line that she'd clutched me to that region of her chest that would one day become her bosom and whispered, 'I love you.' I'd imagined happy teenage years, safe and secure in the knowledge that I had someone to love who loved me in return.

When, minutes later, I saw Vicki walking back across the canteen I snatched my hand away from her seat guiltily and stood up. Gary Thompson, a confirmed head-case from the year above, and unfortunately the nearest thing Vicki had to a boyfriend, was by her side. He was a whole twelve inches taller than me, never smiled and had small marks on the back of his hands where, rumour had it, he'd stabbed himself with an HB pencil trying to give himself lead poisoning. As Gary took a step towards me, I shuffled backwards to accommodate him.

'I'll count to ten,' said Thompson menacingly.

'Okay,' said the teenage me, resisting the urge to tell him it was lucky he wasn't wearing mittens.

'And if you're still here, you're a dead man.'

I didn't need to be told twice.

I didn't say another word to Vicki for the rest of my school career. When I saw her in the Royal Oak, two years ago, I still half expected Gary Thompson to pop up from nowhere and give me a Chinese burn for being in the same pub as she was. After a protracted period of exchanged glances she came over and spoke to me. She asked me what I was doing with my life. At the time I was very much on the dole, so I told her that I was a surgeon at a teaching hospital in Edinburgh. She was impressed. When I asked her how she was doing, she told me she was married to a forty-six-year-old lorry driver called Clive and had three kids, one of whom wasn't Clive's but he didn't know that. I asked her if she'd got what she wanted from life. She looked at the gin and tonic in her hand, raised her glass and said, 'Yes.'

Gary Thompson, I thank you.

The thing is, I never learned my lesson. Even after Vicki, all I ever wanted from a girl was stability. My sole aim in life was to find a girlfriend who would make me feel so secure that I'd never have to worry about relationships again. But it was always my fault that it never worked out with the girls I dated. I always underestimated the depths of my insecurity. It had nothing to do with poor self-image – I actually considered myself quite a catch – the problem was, I never trusted the women I was involved with to tell the Truth, because the Truth never changes, but as I knew so well, people did. I knew it wasn't everyone, some women did have Staying Power, but it was impossible to tell which ones they were.

Women should come labelled – it would make life so much simpler.

If Aggi and I had still been together, I would've asked her to marry me. She would've turned me down, of course, because in our final year together she'd told me that she didn't believe in marriage any more. I was informed of her decision while sitting in the middle row of screen two at the Cornerhouse cinema, right in the middle of a screening of a new print of *The Seven Year Itch*.

'Will,' she whispered into my ear, 'marriage is a stupid idea. It'll never catch on.'

'It already has,' I told her.

'Not with me, it hasn't.'

And that was that. I like to think she said it to stop us from drifting into matrimony by accident, as so many couples do after university, but it was probably more of a built-in escape clause, a bar-code on our relationship which, while giving me the impression that our love was open-ended to eternity, was in fact doing the opposite, stamping a coded sell-by date on our love that only she could read.

After I graduated, I actually did ask her to marry me anyway. The conversation went a little like this:

Me: Aggi, let's get married. I mean, will you marry me?

Aggi: (Firmly) No.

Me: Why not?

Aggi: I wouldn't like it. It'd be too constraining.

Me: How do you know? You've never been married.

Aggi: No, but I did live with a lover for a while.

Me: You did what? You had a . . . you lived with a . . .

Aggi: I shouldn't have told you. I knew you'd be uptight about this.

Me: (Angrily) Uptight? Uptight? I think I've every right
to be 'uptight' since discovering that my girlfriend
has in fact been 'shacked up' with some bloke.
Who was it? Have I met him?

Aggi: No . . . well, yes.

Me: Who? Come on. Which one of them was it?

Aggi: Martin.

Me: (Ranting) Martin? Martin! But his eyes are too
close together. You can't have lived with a man
whose eyes are too close together! You've
obviously made some mistake.

Aggi: Will, you're being hysterical.

Me: I'm not being hysterical. I'm being me. You ought
to try it some time.

I knew about all her ex-boyfriends because I'd made her tell
me about them after our fourth date. Out of all seven of them,
Martin was the one I liked least. Aggi was only seventeen when
she met him at a night-club in Nottingham. Three weeks later
she moved into a room in his student house, and eventually
into his bedroom. He was twenty and was studying Politics at
the poly. He was a walking tragedy, the best reason to Eat
The Rich I'd ever seen. He'd spent the ages between zero
and eighteen at boarding school where he collected stamps,
rowed and played Dungeons and Dragons. Rejected by Oxford
after dismal A-level results, he ended up at what was then the
Polytechnic. Realising that he was liable to be beaten to death
by the mob of Socialist Workers who stood guard outside
the student union selling *Militant* every day, Martin – posh,
useless, waste of space Martin – decided to reinvent himself
as the Ultimate Smiths Fan. Out went his chinos, V-necked
jumpers, button-down shirts and nondescript haircut, and in
came all things Mozzer-like. He had the stupid Morrissey quiff,

the stupid Morrissey overcoat, the stupid Morrissey shoes but how he ever found a pair of stupid Morrissey glasses to fit his beady, too-close-together eyes I'll never know.

The reason I knew so much about Martin was that on my third coach trip to London in search of accommodation, the gods of misfortune allocated me a seat next to the git. We'd met once before, about four years earlier in the Royal Oak, when Aggi had been forced to introduce us because, unbeknown to Aggi and me, his Smiths' tribute band, The Charming Men, were playing a gig there. For the entire journey to London (five sodding hours!), all he talked about was Aggi and how much she'd changed his life.

What really offended me about Aggi's 'shacking up' experience was the fact that she didn't think it was a big deal. She'd lived with him for three months before she dumped him for another student, at a different night-club, and moved back to her mum's. I saw the whole episode as a threat to everything we had. When all you have is 'you', to give 'you', seven days a week, twenty-four hours a day, so casually, *is* a big deal. She'd been prepared to do that for three months with beady Martin, so why wasn't she prepared to have a go at spending the rest of her life with me?

If I had known that one day I'd be in a flat with Aggi for the rest of my life I could have relaxed – I'd have been happy. I'd have taken up a hobby. Maybe even tried and liked football. I'd have been NORMAL. But Aggi wasn't here and chances were she never would be. She was the one I wanted. The only one. She was made for me. I was made for her. She was my Legendary Girlfriend and I'd miss her for as long as I lived.

I got up from the bed, opened the window and sat on the ledge with my legs hanging outside. Lighting a cigarette I gently let out a silent fart. Chuckling heartily I sucked in some of the cold, damp air with my nicotine, causing me to cough and gurgle phlegm. It felt good to open up the window. I hadn't realised it, but the air in the flat had grown so stale I could almost see it trying to escape. The glowing end of my ciggy looked warm and inviting. A long column of ash fell onto my jeans. I brushed it away and after a while I thought about food again. Stubbing out my cigarette, I left my perch and went into the kitchen. Opening a can of spaghetti hoops and dropping them into a pan I turned the heat on the cooker up to maximum. I was just about to light another fag when the phone rang.

'Are you all right, dear?' said Gran.

'Not too bad,' I replied. 'Can't complain. Are you all right, Gran?'

'Yes, thank you, dear. And you?'

'Not too bad. And you?'

'Fine. And you?'

'Dandy. And you?'

'Lovely!'

My Gran wasn't senile, and neither was I. This was just our little joke, although I wasn't all that sure whether Gran was quite up on the concept of irony. As far as I was concerned, this was our way of defusing tension caused by the fact that we had nothing in common, other than Francesca Kelly (my mother). We could talk to each other perfectly well face-to-face for hours on end, but on the phone, the importance of words always got blown out of proportion. I like to believe we spoke in clichés because it was much safer that way, but if my Gran wasn't entirely in on the joke, all it probably meant was that I was an evil grandson with a crap sense of humour.

'Your mother's not in,' said Gran.

'Isn't she?'

'So where is she then?'

'I don't know, Gran. She's probably out or something.'

'Oh.'

'Oh.'

'Oh.'

I introduced a new topic. 'Nice weather we're having, aren't we?'

'Not particularly,' said Gran. 'It's raining cats and dogs here. Mrs Staff across the road says it's the coldest September on record.'

'Is it really?'

'Coldest on record.'

'Well I never.'

'Happy Birthday for tomorrow,' said Gran. 'I would've phoned you tomorrow dear, but Mrs Baxter has managed to persuade her husband to take a couple of us up to the Lake District. I hope you're not offended, my love.'

'Of course not, Gran, don't you worry. Have a great time. Bring me back some Kendal Mint Cake, eh?'

Gran got excited. 'Oooh, you like Kendal Mint Cake? I shall have to get you a job lot!'

'Yeah. That'd be nice.'

'Well, I'd better be going, son. Take care and have a lovely birthday.'

'Yes, Gran, I will.'

'Oooh, before I forget I must tell you that your card will be late. I was trying to phone your mother all day yesterday to get your address. I've missed last post now anyway. It'll get there by Tuesday. Never mind, eh? Better late than never.'

'Yes, Gran. Better late than never.' I glanced across the room at the card she had sent which was perched on top of my hi-fi. Perhaps she was going senile after all.

As I put the phone down wondering what exactly to do with the lifetime's supply of Kendal Mint Cake she was sure to purchase, I realised that my spaghetti hoops were burning. The reason why

I'd suddenly recalled my dinner was that the smoke currently working its way under the kitchen door had already reached the smoke alarm, which was now belting out the mother of all high-pitched screams. I'd been in the flat five days and already heard it six times. It was far too sensitive; let toast crispen a little too much and on came the siren. Once this happened, the whole household played the I'd-rather-burn-to-death-than-leave-my-poxy-studio-flat-and-turn-off-the-alarm game of endurance. The rules were simple, if a little cavalier: see how long you can stand the alarm before you're compelled to get out of bed and turn it off at the control box on the ground floor. There were six residents in the house – I'd done it once, the residents of the two ground floor flats had done it twice each and the old man on the top floor had done it once. The man at number four on my landing, and the woman at number six on the top floor, hadn't done it at all, which to my mind either meant that they were deaf or took the playing of bloody-minded Russian Roulette-style games very seriously.

In spite of the noise, the problem at hand still had to be dealt with – the burning spaghetti hoops. Opening the door to the kitchen fully, I half expected to be faced by a scene from *The Towering Inferno* and was pleasantly surprised merely to choke violently on thick black smoke. My eyes began to water almost immediately; I shut them tightly, reached out to the cooker controls and turned off the ring. Using a souvenir Bournemouth tea towel of my mother's, I carefully manoeuvred the saucepan out of the kitchen, opened the window in the main room and laid it to rest on the sill outside, closing the window behind it. There was nowhere for the smoke to escape to now, it lingered in the flat like one of those ridiculously foggy evenings in the Basil Rathbone Sherlock Holmes films. It was time for another walk.

As I reached the front door, the woman from downstairs

came out of her flat, dressed in a white towelling dressing gown and huge Garfield slippers, a black cloud of pure annoyance hanging over her head like a garland of hateful intent. Standing on the tips of her toes – poor Garfield's head squished unhappily against the grime-laden carpet – she attempted to press the reset button on the control box. I smiled at her in a neighbourly fashion. She scowled back. Within seconds of reaching the garden gate, the alarm stopped.

It was raining again. Archway looked more miserable than usual, all its colour had drained away, leaving only shades of grey and dog poo brown. I pulled my neck as far as I could into the collar of my coat (which still smelt) and headed in the direction of the newsagent's up the road.

The newsagent's on Holloway Road was owned by an old Italian woman with white hair and skin like a barbecued chicken. According to the sign on the door her sons were also involved in the operation, but as I'd never seen them, I couldn't exactly confirm this. My problem with her, and the reason she was on my mental hit-list (sandwiched in the lower ranks between my bank manager and Foster menswear) was that she had the kind of attitude problem Mussolini would've been proud of. Every morning that I'd gone into her shop she'd been umbilically attached to a pay-phone on the counter, wilfully ignoring customers until an appropriate pause in her conversation, which as I'd found on Tuesday could be anything up to six minutes. I hated that woman, and still fuelled with Simon-inspired bitterness, reasoned that now was a particularly good time to exact revenge.

As usual, she was behind the counter, and as usual she was talking very loudly into the pay-phone, every now and again repeating the same word in Italian, while shaking her head emphatically. No one else was in the shop. It was just the two of us. *Italian Granny Vs William The English Teacher. Ding! Ding! Round one.* I don't know what came over me but I secreted two Yorkie bars, a pack of Rolos and a copy of *Cosmopolitan* into my overcoat pocket and walked out without paying, not even bothering to pretend that I couldn't see the item I'd wanted to purchase. Though she didn't look up from her perch as I made my way to the door, this didn't stop me, once outside, from running like the proverbial clappers all the way to the flat, imagining that she'd suddenly realised my crime and stopped her conversation mid-sentence, in order to summon her sons to stab me to death because the honour of their family name was at stake.

I hadn't shop-lifted sweets in over sixteen years. Not since Simon and I had grabbed a handful of fizz bombs each from the newsagent's around the corner from our junior school, and stuffed them down the front of our trousers, reasoning that should we ever get caught, the police would never think of looking there. It felt good to have a bit of raw excitement in my life again, a bit of cut and thrust, a bit of living life by the seat of my pants. Stealing a pack of Rolos wasn't quite Raffles' standard, but I was happy nonetheless. The important thing was that I'd got one up on Crusty Old Italian Woman. 1–0 to me.

Back at the flat most of the smoke had managed to escape to the place where smoke goes to die. I checked the answering machine (no messages), and took a look at the spaghetti hoops on the window ledge. The saucepan had stopped smoking now. Not all the spaghetti hoops had died in the fire, there were a number of survivors floating on a sea of ruby sludge. I dipped my fingers in to taste a mouthful. They were cold and wet with rain rather than tomato sauce, but as long as the carbonised seam of hoops underneath remained undisturbed, they didn't taste too horrific. The saucepan on the other hand was knackered, which was unfortunate, as I'd 'borrowed' it from a set of three, against my mother's express wishes. I ate the Rolos and Yorkie too and then felt sick and sorry for myself.

I searched for the phone, called Alice's number again and left another message telling her to call me as soon as she got back in even if it was 3.00 a.m. because it was an emergency.

I turned on the TV, an action which I'd been trying my very best to avoid all week. As much as I loved to watch TV, the very thought of wasting hours doing it made me feel sadder and even more desperate, as if I were giving in to becoming a total loser without a fight. My mum had bought the portable TV for me as an early birthday present before I went to university. She'd said, and I quote: 'It'll be like a friend. Something on in the background in case things seem a bit empty.' It was a nice thing for her to say but ever since I'd been terrified that, if I wasn't careful, the day would come when I really would consider the TV to be my friend.

There was nothing on anyway. I flicked across the channels waiting for something good to happen. Sport, something about art history, news, horse racing and a nappy ad. Desperate, I decided to look for amusement elsewhere, but left it on in the background while I composed another letter to the bank:

Dear Sir,

I am writing to you to explain my current financial position. I have just started a job teaching in London. Due to the expense of moving to the capital and the fact that I will not be paid until the end of September, I would be very grateful if you would further extend my overdraft by £500 until the end of November.

Sincerely

William Kelly.

As I put the full stop after the 'y' in Kelly, and wondered if it actually warranted a full stop, I glanced up at the TV and then scanned the room searching for confirmation of what I was feeling. I returned my eyes to the page, having found my answer. I was bored. When I was small and I used to tell my dad I was bored, he'd tell me that one day I'd find out what boredom was really about and then I'd be sorry. At that moment, sitting there in the flat, with the will to do anything at all almost crushed out of my body, I realised that I'd finally found out what it was like to be bored and I *was* really sorry. When I was bored as a kid, I had a whole lifetime ahead of me. I could easily afford to spend a few years here or there doing Nothing. But now, with a twenty-sixth birthday looming in the background, I no longer had time to waste that wouldn't come back to haunt me, as those two years on the dole did every time I heard about someone from my degree course getting a job writing on *Empire*, earning over £30,000 pa, or simply getting a life.

I changed channels. The walls of the flat were far more interesting than what was happening on screen, so it was there my eyes lingered, soaking up the years of desperation caked on to the wallpaper, before finally coming to rest on Aggi's defaced photograph. Crawling underneath the duvet, shedding trousers and socks on my journey to the pillow, I settled in bed. And there I lay, not thinking about anything at all, for quite a long time.

6.34 P.M.

In the right-hand corner of the room, just above the curtains, a cobweb caught my attention as a steady draught whistling its way through the poorly-constructed window frame tried its best to dislodge it from the wall. It looked a bit flimsy, as though it existed for decorative rather than practical purposes. Whichever spider had created this silken trap I decided was going to go hungry because no self-respecting house fly was going to be caught in a web as crap as this one. Even Mother Nature it seemed was capable of creating creatures as lazy, apathetic and half-hearted as me.

The telephone rang, preventing me from taking thoughts of spiders, flies and cobwebs any further. It rang three or four times before I climbed out of bed to answer it, as I was busy working out the odds of who it might be:

> Aggi (1000–1)
> Alice (5–1)
> Kate (3–1)
> Martina (2–1, odds on favourite)

'Hi, it's me.'

'Hi,' I replied, ashamed that in spite of myself I'd still backed the rank outsider. 'What've you been up to?'

'Nothing,' replied Kate. 'How about you?'

I recalled my promise to phone her back and considered feeling guilty, but then it occurred to me that she had phoned me in spite of my non-action. Kate actually *wanted* to talk to me. I instantly felt more relaxed. In the distance I could hear the siren of a police car.

'I'm sorry I didn't call back when I said I would. I fell asleep.'

'I love sleeping,' said Kate. 'It's kind of a hobby of mine.'

She gave a little laugh and I joined her, but whereas hers was joyous and summery, mine was nervous and shifty because I'd been busy wondering whether she slept naked or not.

'What are you doing tonight?'

'Nothing,' replied Kate. 'I've got no money. Anyway I don't fancy going out. I thought I might stay in and watch TV.'

'Good idea,' I said, nodding needlessly.

'What's on?'

I located the remote control hiding under a pair of grey M&S pants. The red light on the front of the TV flickered momentarily, and there before me was an episode of *Dad's Army*. I relayed this information to Kate and together we watched in silence; she in Brighton, I in London, unified by the wonder of television. Private Pike was on top of a huge pile of furniture on the back of a lorry next to a telegraph pole. As far as I could work out there was a bomb lodged up there and it was his job to get it down.

'I love *Dad's Army*,' I said quietly, half hoping that she wouldn't hear me.

'Yeah,' said Kate. 'It really makes me laugh.'

We sat in silence (apart from occasional laughter) watching Private Pike get stuck up the telegraph pole, and Captain Mainwaring's attempts to extricate him from this situation. It wasn't an uncomfortable silence at all. I felt as close to her as if she had been sitting on the bed next to me, absent-mindedly offering me crisps from a packet of cheese and onion, with her head resting on my shoulder, happy to be doing something as mundane as watching TV.

'What else is on?' asked Kate after a while.

Switching channels, I discovered a documentary on BBC2, about hi-tec thieves stealing computer chips from companies in Silicone Valley and was instantly drawn in. Excitedly I told Kate to turn over and join me and in the following quarter of an hour we learned about the Mafia's involvement in the multi-billion dollar black market in stolen chips. Kate wasn't half as interested in the programme as I was, and despite wanting to return to *Dad's Army* almost immediately, she continued watching BBC2 for my sake. I was touched. Eventually (once the micro-chip programme had finished), we switched over to Channel Four because the news was on ITV and neither of us considered news entertainment, which was all we were looking for. While a car advert played, Kate and I tried to think of as many ridiculous names for cars as we could in a minute. Our top three were:

1. The Nissan Nipple.
2. The Vauxhall Prostate.
3. The Ford Oooh!.

The ad break finished and the voice-over woman said something like, 'And now for something completely different,' in a soft Southern Counties accent she probably considered amusing. The credits for a TV show I'd never seen before came on. It was obviously some kind of fashion/music/style/youth-oriented programme because brightly coloured graphics were flashing up on the screen, battering my irises into submission in time to the thumping bass line of the theme tune. What it was called I never found out, because just as I was about to switch over to *Noel's House Party*, I caught a glimpse of something on the screen that instantly crash-landed all feelings of contentment.

'Dave Bloomfield!' I screamed at the TV.

'Who?' said Kate.

'The biggest tosser in the universe.'

Dave Bloomfield, aka 'the biggest tosser in the universe', I explained, was on my course at university. He was tall, half Spanish and a quarter Iroquois (so rumour had it), with hazel eyes and floppy, jet-black hair that made him look like some kind of Edwardian fop. He used to sit in the canteen on the top floor in the English Department reading the *Guardian* from cover to cover – always a sign of a tosser in the making – sipping black coffee and smoking filterless Camels. The female population of the department (lecturers included) doted on his every word, so much so that he even pulled *and* dumped Annette Francis, the most gorgeous creature on our course, a woman so aloof that the one occasion I plucked up the courage to talk to her by asking her the time, she point blank refused to tell me. Oh, and to make matters worse he got a first. Kate couldn't quite understand why seeing an over-achieving former university colleague presenting his own TV show was winding me up so much and so I tried to explain.

'Some things just come too easily for some people,' I raged. 'While the rest of us mere mortals have to make do, *they* get it all on a plate.'

I was surprised at my bitterness, particularly as I'd never harboured any urges to be a TV presenter. My problem with Dave Bloomfield was that he represented everything I hated about the successful: he was good-looking, clever, witty and, worst of all, motivated. Dave Bloomfield was everything I wasn't. Dave Bloomfield was the anti-me.

I explained this to Kate. 'It's just like anti-matter and matter, if Dave and I ever meet again we'll explode, killing thousands.'

Kate laughed. 'You put yourself down too much. You know you can do whatever you want if you put your mind to it.' She paused, as if thinking. 'What do you want, Will? What do you really want to do with your life?'

I lay down on the bed and pulled the duvet over my legs. I hadn't thought about what I wanted to do, in any serious manner, for such a long time that the answer didn't come quite as speedily as I felt it should have.

'I'd like to make films,' I said with a lack of conviction. I was ashamed that I'd done so little to push myself in that direction. I once filled out, but never posted, an application to Sheffield University for an MA in Film Production. It was still in the drawer of my desk at home.

'Really?' said Kate. 'That's brilliant. Why don't you do it?'

'Well, it's not that easy, you see,' I began. 'You need money and you need to be in with the right people. It's full of nepotism, the film business, and with my mum working at the retirement lodge and my dad doing whatever it is he does all day for the council, I can't imagine that either of them can open the doors of Paramount for me.'

'What about writing scripts?' offered Kate. 'Those don't cost a thing and you could do them in your spare time. A mate of mine's brother works on *Coronation Street* and his dad runs a chippy.'

I wasn't encouraged. 'I've enough problems teaching without trying to do anything in my spare time other than complain,' I said, getting out of bed and finding a comfortable space to lie on the carpet. 'Have you ever tried marking thirty poems on snowflakes? Believe me, if you had you'd be praying, just like I am, that global warming's going to get a lot worse.'

I wondered whether my excuse sounded like an excuse.

'That sounds like an excuse to me.'

I ignored her comment. 'So what about you? What do you want to do?'

Taking a deep breath she told me how she had always wanted to be a nurse. That was one of the reasons (apart from her ex) she'd dropped out of university. She'd realised that her course was pointless and wanted to do something that would help people. In five months she'd be starting nursing college at a hospital in Brighton which was why she was currently languishing on Boots' perfume counter. The more she spoke, the more I found myself admiring her spirited determination to lead a fruitful life and I even told her so. I think she might have blushed but I couldn't be sure over the phone.

'Do you mind if I ask you a question?' said Kate eventually.

'No. Not at all.'

'Are you sure you won't be offended?'

I wondered if it was going to be an embarrassing question along the lines of 'When was the last time you saw a man naked?'

'Look,' I said, 'at the rate of excitement I've been indulging in this weekend, being offended would be positively welcome.'

'What are you scared of?'

I paused, relieved that I no longer had to tell her about the occasion when I'd disturbed Simon and Tammy on their kitchen table, naked but for the melting contents of a tub of Cookie Dough Dynamo Häagen-Dazs.

'You think I'm scared of life, don't you? Well, I'm not. I'm not scared of failure either. After all I'm a failed teacher and I haven't killed myself yet. What I'm scared of is this: that at twenty-six, I'm too old to make my dreams come true. It's so hard not to feel envious of you. I know I'm going to sound like an OAP, but at least you've got the potential to do what you want to do.'

'Whereas you . . .'

'Whereas I haven't. My course is set. Unless something drastic happens this is it for the rest of my life.'

'What about becoming the next Scorcese?'

She wasn't getting the message. 'Orson Welles had written, produced and directed *Citizen Kane*, one of the world's greatest films, by the time he was twenty-six.'

'Forget Orson Welles,' exclaimed Kate. 'The TV genius that is Tony Warren was only twenty-three when he came up with the idea for *Coronation Street!*' Kate stopped herself, immediately realising she wasn't helping matters. 'I'm sorry. I'm not being very helpful, am I? My mate's brother who works on *Coronation Street*, he told me that amazing fact. It's been waiting there for the chance to escape ever since.'

'I'm not getting into a debate about whether *Coronation Street* is better than *Citizen Kane!* That's not the point. The point is, I'm twenty-six! All I've done is smoke cigarettes, watch TV and moan about my ex-girlfriend. Even if I started now, I'd be lucky to direct a school production of *Joseph and his Technicolor Dream Coat* before I'm thirty. Sometimes you've got to face facts.'

Kate wasn't convinced. 'You can do anything you want. If you've got talent it'll shine through in the end. You've got to believe in yourself.'

Her positivity was depressing. The similarity of her words to those I might have uttered at her age was surprisingly accurate. Little did she know that I was she, six years down the line.

'Look, Kate,' I said in my best let-me-give-you-a-few-words-of-advice voice. 'It's taken me this long to just get here. How long is it going to take to get anywhere else? Three years ago, maybe I had a chance. Maybe I could've done all the things I wanted.' My voice became higher, louder, more aggressive. 'It's too late. Sometimes you've got to know when enough is enough!' Out of frustration I kicked the ice-cream tub containing my Sugar Puffs breakfast and immediately regretted it. Creamy yellow froth and puffed wheat seeped onto my overcoat, which had been lying on the floor next to it. Now I really would have to get it dry-cleaned.

'It's never too late,' said Kate quietly. 'Not while you still believe.'

I was moved by the kindness of her words and for a few ecstatic seconds, deep in my heart I was convinced she was right. Then my brain kicked in. She was wrong. In spite of everything I'd done to prevent it, my course *was* set and there was nothing I could do about it. I'd spent the whole of my life wondering what I was going to 'be': at the age of five I'd wanted to be a lorry driver; at eight I'd desperately wanted to be Noel Edmonds; in my teens I'd flirted with every profession from a psychic to a chef, before deciding in my twenties that I sort of, possibly, wouldn't mind making films. So what had I done to set myself on the right path? I'd sat on the dole and then done a teacher training course. And because of that one mistake I was going to 'be' a teacher even if it killed me.

'Thanks, it was nice of you to say that,' I said kindly. I wanted to apologise for getting so wound up but I couldn't find a way to say it comfortably, so I changed the subject. 'What's your favourite film?'

This was a naff question, only surpassed in naffness by, 'So, what music are you into?' but I was desperate to know. Kate and I were sharing so many things that I felt were binding us together. It was hard to believe that as someone who adored films I hadn't asked her already.

'It's *Gregory's Girl*,' she said despondently. 'I know it's not as cool as some of the films that are bound to be your favourites. It's not *Taxi Driver*, *Reservoir Dogs* or *Apocalypse Now*, but I like it all the same. It's sweet, it's . . .'

I tried to contain my excitement. 'You're wrong, Kate. So wrong. *Gregory's Girl* is my favourite film. It's fantastic. Better than *Taxi Driver*, *Apocalypse Now* or even sodding *Citizen Kane*!'

Time ceased to have any meaning as we tried to recall the best bits of a film full of best bits. Her favourite parts were when Dorothy, the object of Gregory's desire, was being interviewed for the school paper in the dressing rooms, followed by the bit where the lost penguins keep getting redirected around the school.

'Let's dance,' I said.

She knew what I meant immediately.

Lying on my back, elbows resting on the carpet and wrists in the air, I began to move as if dancing as Gregory and Susan had done in the park scene near the end of the film. My ear kept moving away from the phone, but there was no mistaking the fact that Kate was participating because she was laughing so loudly that I could still hear her.

'What if Paula comes back? She'll think I've completely lost it!'

'Don't worry!' I yelled at the receiver, still dancing and feeling the happiest I had in a long time. 'Just go with the flow.'

7.39 P.M.

I was on a roll. My words couldn't trip out fast enough. Kate made me feel like jabbering away until Monday morning. What was most impressive was the fact that she wasn't bored, sitting there in her Brighton flat, listening to a complete stranger talk about his life. I wanted to confess everything: how I couldn't swim but could bend my thumb back until it touched my wrist; and how, until my first day at Wood Green Comprehensive, I'd never bought a pre-packaged sandwich (I don't know why, I just hadn't). I wanted her to know everything.

'Tell me some more,' said Kate.

'What?'

'Tell me more about you.'

'Er, well. No,' I said uneasily. It was hard saying no to a girl who made me want to say yes to anything she suggested, but one of the cover lines on my 'donated' copy of *Cosmopolitan* kept flashing up in my head: 'Why men love talking about themselves.' Now, I decided, was my turn to listen.

'Tell me about *you*,' I said, smiling needlessly. 'You've heard enough of me surely? Anyway, my mother always told me never to talk to strangers and until I know more about you, a stranger you will remain.'

'It's quite nice being a stranger,' said Kate. 'I could be

197

anyone I want to be. Unfortunately I'm me. I work at Boots. I have to get there at 8.00 a.m. and I leave at 6.00 p.m. I work every other Saturday and get one day off during the week if I've worked a Saturday. That's it really.'

'I worked in a pub for a couple of months shifting crates of beer from the cellar. I hated every second of it. If it's anything like that, I bet it's soul-destroying.'

'Not really,' she said chirpily. 'A mate of mine, Daniel, he works for a firm of accountants in Oxford, and his job is what I'd call soul-destroying. He's constantly under pressure to produce results. Last week his doctor told him he's got a stress-related ulcer. He's only twenty-four. He earns quite a bit, mind. But no amount of money is worth all the rubbish he has to put up with. I'd never want a job like that. Boots wouldn't be so bad if I didn't have to get up so early. Anyway, I told Daniel this and I'll say it to you. There's no point in getting stressed about work. If a job gets on your nerves then leave it. No one's got a gun to your head.' There was a knocking noise down the phone line followed by a loud click. Kate's voice disappeared. I panicked. I thought she'd gone forever. 'Sorry about that, Paula's just come in. She took me by surprise. I dropped the phone! Where was I? Ah, yes. I used to want to have a high-powered job. I can't remember what kind exactly; I mean, I had phases where I've wanted to be everything from a news reader to a Crown Court judge, but I came to the conclusion that I couldn't really see the point. Do you know that I once got it into my head that I wanted to be a professional tennis player?'

'Were you really good at tennis?'

'No, I hated it,' said Kate dolefully. 'I just liked the skirts.'

We both laughed. I wondered what she looked like in a tennis skirt.

Kate continued. 'My driving ambition now is to fall in love, be a nurse, and have babies. That's all I want my life to be about now. Once I've got those three things in that order I'll have everything I want. It's true.'

I wasn't convinced. 'How are love and babies going to make everything all right? Aren't you forgetting some key points here, like babies costing money, love being hard to find, people falling out of love as easily as they fall in?'

'I know all these things,' she said, testily. 'But that's my ambition. I didn't say it was practical or even possible. We've all got our dreams.'

'Yeah, you're right,' I said, by way of apology.

'Do you think I'll get what I want?' asked Kate.

I couldn't help looking at the photograph of Aggi's bearded, bespectacled, scarred, toothless face on the wall. Even a defaced Aggi was better than no Aggi at all.

'Yeah,' I said. 'The babies part is easy enough. The world's crawling with sperm donors, as long as you're not too choosy. And the job seems to be sorted. It's the love part that I think might be problematic. In my opinion, you can only say that love truly is love once you're both dead, because it's only then, once you've managed to go your entire lives with each other and there's nowhere for you to go off to or anyone to go off with, that it finally becomes real. Anything else is more or less just infatuation. I'm serious.' The door to one of the neighbouring flats slammed shut, shaking my windows. I crawled into bed. 'Everybody loves a lover but too many people lack Staying Power. Love should be fatal. You should never recover from it. If you can, then it wasn't love.'

'Really?' said Kate, as though she had another question lined up. 'So what about you and Aggi? Was what you had love?'

'It was love. I loved her and I continue to love her, despite everything I do to make myself stop.'

'*You* might love *her*, but what about the fact that *she* doesn't love *you*? Is love really love if only one person stays true to the cause? That sounds more like infatuation to me. No offence intended.'

Kate was showing a side of her that I hadn't noticed before. She was capable of seeing straight through my sweeping statements and had by now probably realised that my authoritative manner was as fake as everything else about me.

'I don't know,' I said, lost for words. 'I think you've actually made quite a good point there. This must mean that I'm as sad as every other loser out there.'

'You made up the rules,' she joked.

'Yeah, I did.' I was getting tired of this now. 'He who lives by the sword dies by the sword. What goes around comes around. I've made my bed so I'd better lie in.'

'It?' prompted Kate.

'No, just in.'

We both laughed.

'I tell you what though,' I said. 'Aggi did love me.'

'How do you know? Did she tell you?'

'Yeah, she told me a million times but . . .'

I was going to tell Kate about something Aggi had done which proved beyond any reasonable doubt how much she felt about me, but I couldn't get the words out. This was a private memory and neither time nor space had made it mean any less to me. What Aggi and I had done was ridiculous in a silly sort of way, but I had forgiven myself long ago on the grounds that we're all allowed to be 'silly' once in a while, especially when in love. And I suppose it's true that even the most ridiculous things can carry more poignancy than all of Shakespeare's sonnets rolled together.

At the time of the event I was thinking of, I was twenty-one and Aggi was twenty, ideal ages to be hopelessly romantic. It was a Tuesday afternoon during the summer holidays, a year after we'd first met. Aggi had called around at my house. I was still in bed even though it was two in the afternoon. The sun was shining brightly through the chocolate fabric of my bedroom curtains, turning everything inside golden brown and warming up the air until it felt like a greenhouse. All the sounds coming in through my open bedroom window – birds chirping, next door neighbour's kids playing Swingball; the far-off jingle of an ice-cream van – were surprisingly life-affirming. And yet, there I lay, sweating under the duvet flicking through a number of books looking for ideas for my dissertation.

Tom must have let Aggi in because I only realised she was there when she knocked on my door from inside the room. She must have been standing there for ages because she didn't say anything for a minute or two and seemed a little embarrassed when I looked up from my book, completely avoiding all eye contact. She'd said, 'Let's go to the park.' And after I'd put on some clothes and had a brief wash, that's exactly what we did. On the way there she didn't say much, as if going over something in her mind that she was trying not to forget. When we got to Crestfield Park by the large oak tree – the very same oak tree where I'd later scatter her imaginary ashes – she sat down on the freshly mown grass and tugged at my sleeve, signalling me to take a seat. And this is what she said:

'I woke up this morning and knew that I loved you more than ever. Sometimes I get scared that this feeling will slip away into something less than the wonderfulness it is now. So I've got a plan. Let's capture how we feel right now and keep it forever. I've got some scissors in my bag and I'm going to cut off a lock of my hair and then you'll cut off a lock of your hair and we'll twist them together. Then on a scrap of paper I'll write down everything I feel about you and then you'll do the same. Then we'll put the lot in one of those plastic containers you put film in and we'll bury it right here. What do you say?'

What could I say? It didn't seem a 'silly' thing to do at all. It seemed like the only thing that made sense. It's easy to feel that everyday love isn't like love in the movies because successions of mind-numbingly dismal, modern romantic comedies – stand up *French Kiss*, *Sleepless in Seattle* and *While You Were Sleeping* – have succeeded in turning everything that's wonderful about love into cheese. People are too literal about love now and it's all because, thanks to these films, there's little space left for symbolism in real life. What Aggi and I did was slightly strange and the kind of thing that only lead characters in a Shakespearean tragedy could pull off convincingly, but I loved every second of it.

Aggi took her mum's orange-handled scissors from her bag and chopped off a lock of hair, scribbled on a piece of paper and put it in the container. I cut off some of my hair from the back, wrote on my piece of paper and then twisted our hair together and dug into the dirt with my hands. The hole, as deep as my hand, was more than big enough for the container. Together we packed the leftover soil on top of it, then stood up and stared at the mound, not speaking. We kissed right there and then went back to Aggi's.

I didn't know what Aggi had written and she didn't know what I had written, and that was what made the whole thing so mystical. Looking back, sometimes I like to joke with myself that the whole thing was some kind of voodoo trick, and that our messages and twisted hair were what was keeping me bound to Aggi all this time, but even I couldn't take it that seriously.

Over the next few days I couldn't get what we'd done off my mind. I had to know what Aggi had written about me. Nearly a week after we'd gone to the park, I returned, determined to dig up the container. I felt awful. I was betraying her trust. But I needed to do it. Because I needed to know.

When I reached the spot I immediately knew something was wrong because the mound had been disturbed. I clawed at the soil, but the container wasn't there. Had Aggi dug it up because she'd changed her mind? Had she been afraid that I might do what she'd actually done herself? Had someone else dug it up? I didn't know and I never found out. It was another of those questions that I never got to ask Aggi. Something inside me makes me think that she had second thoughts and just didn't like the idea of our declaration being out there – because then I would've had evidence that I was as important to her as she was to me.

We'd been talking for a long time. My lips were as close to the phone as humanly possible. A small but not insignificant pool of moisture had formed in the mouthpiece. I swear if I could've slipped into that pool and slid down the telephone line right into Kate's flat I would've done. Gladly. To be with her, to be touched by her presence would've made my day. It would've made my decade. A huge wave of loneliness sprang up from nowhere, threatening to overwhelm me. *I think it's time to go.*

'I think it's time to go,' I said.

Kate was hurt. 'Oh, I'm sorry.'

'No, it's not you,' I said, desperately wanting her to believe me. 'It's not you at all. It's me. I've enjoyed every second talking to you. You're really . . .' I couldn't finish the sentence without saying something totally clichéd. 'You're really . . .'

'I'm really . . .'

'You're really . . .' I flicked through my lexicon of top quality compliments. Thanks to a world brimming over with cheesy films, cheesy books, cheesy music and cheesy TV – reducing the greatest human emotion to the lowest common denominator – they all sounded too jaded, too un-Kate, too, well, cheesy.

'You're special,' I told her. 'I think you're special.'

She laughed.

'And you're wonderful. I think you're wonderful, Will.'

'Goodnight.'

'Sleep tight.'

Back to reality.

The phone had never looked as lonely as it did when I ended that call. Lying there stiffly in its cradle, after it had had so much life flowing through it, it looked like it was dead rather than dormant. I picked it up and dialled Kate's number to make sure it was still working but put it down before it had a chance to ring. I felt bleak and empty, as if it wasn't quite worth the effort to take another breath. In these kinds of situations, I'm embarrassed to say, I often indulged myself in a little fantasy, believing myself to be a tortured poet rather than just a sad git with too much time on his hands. I once wrote fourteen volumes (i.e. fourteen W H Smith exercise books) of oh so very terrible poetry, entitled *To Aggi with Love*. I put them out for the bin men the week before I came to London as part of the first stage of my New Start policy, which I later abandoned when I realised it meant getting rid of my photo of Aggi too. Fortunately, the urge to conjure up a bit of blank verse for Vol. 15, was beaten to the finish line by the impulse to take a slash.

Before the house was turned into flats, my room had obviously been a large bedroom, part of which Mr Jamal had sectioned off to construct a plasterboard prison otherwise known as my bathroom, which was the reason it didn't have any windows. So, in order to see what I was doing in the bathroom, I had to switch on a light, which automatically started an extractor fan. I wasn't dead keen on stinky smells as such, but the extractor fan was the main cause of my flat-inspired frustration; it drove me up the wall. Every time it came on my heart sank. Something inside it was broken, so instead of a gentle hum like a far-off mosquito, I had to endure a sound similar to a tabby in a Moulinex liquidiser, and worse still, the fan continued to extract air – and my patience for that matter – for the next twenty minutes, even after I'd switched the light off. By Wednesday, I was so obsessed with never hearing it again that I attempted crapping in the dark. While it was nice to enjoy the silence, there was something disconcerting about sitting on the toilet, trousers and boxer shorts around ankles, in a darkened room. I once read a newspaper article that said the average rat was quite capable of swimming up a toilet U-bend from the sewer. The thought of coming cheek to cheek with a rodent depressed me so much that, in the end, I saved all bowel movements for the privacy and comfort of the school staff toilets which, I hasten to add, were virtually the same standard as the kids', but with marginally better quality toilet paper.

While washing my hands in the kitchen sink using a bar of soap I'd found under it, I was suddenly struck by the significance of my actions. The bar of Imperial Leather that I was fondling, caressing and generally playing about with had probably been left here by Kate. Looking at that gorgeous rectangle of glycerine resting in the palm of my hand, I smiled warmly and consciously indulged myself in thoughts of Kate. Five minutes I took over washing my hands – five of the best minutes I'd had all day. When I finally came to my senses (the warm brown water in the tap having reached coffee-making temperature), I began to feel claustrophobic. The walls of the flat weren't exactly closing in on me, but I did feel incredibly constrained by them. I was in a prison where I had the key, but no reason to use my freedom. *I need to go out*, I thought. *I need to go out to the pub where I can mix with real people instead of the ex-girlfriends who haunt me and strange women at the end of the telephone*. Before I could change my mind I was out of the front door.

The public house I had in mind was only ten minutes away from the flat but far enough from Holloway Road not to attract tramps, drunks, nutters or any permutation of all three, which that dreadful stretch of road regurgitated late at night. I'd discovered it earlier on in the week while trying to find out how many off-licences in the area sold Marlboro Lights (answer: none).

It was so cold outside that I was able to watch my breath rise gently in the dark blue sky, so I whiled away the majority of the short journey attempting to defy the laws of nature by blowing smoke rings without smoke. When I reached my destination, the Angel, I stood outside and peered into the huge windows that spanned the side of the building. From what I could see it looked reasonably friendly, by which I mean it wasn't so empty that I'd feel any more conspicuous than I was already feeling, but not so full that I'd feel like a loser even before I walked in the door.

I'd never felt the need to go to a pub on my own before. There had always been someone to go for a drink with, even if it was only Simon or friends from my teaching course. My experience of what I was about to do was strictly second-hand, and yet I felt quite confident, having watched one too many American movies where sad (in both senses of the word) men in trilbys drown their private sorrows in public bars, talk drunkenly to bar-tenders, and offer to buy wanton women (they were always wanton) drinks because it's their birthday even though it isn't. Well it was as good as my birthday, and as I pushed my way through the swing doors into the lounge area, I hoped the next hour would offer me an interesting chat with a barmaid or two, a couple of pints to take the Edge off life and, of course, my allotted quota of wanton women.

I tried not to meet anyone's eyes as I made my way to the bar, but I couldn't help looking at a couple of denim-clad Heavy Metal-type blokes playing pool noisily in the corner of the room. Their significant others were sitting at a table behind them, casting the odd glance at the table but essentially more interested in their nails than in who was winning. I felt sorry for these women, not because they'd made such poor choices in their love-life, but because they were both probably really happy. Vicki Hollingsworth Syndrome was everywhere. Sometimes I got the feeling I was the only person in the world wondering if there was a meaning to life, and people like these girls were undermining my faith that it was a question worth finding an answer to. *Maybe I should ask them if they're happy*, I thought.

Or maybe I should just shut my mouth and get a drink.

Two men were being served at the bar as I got there. Bald Bloke on my left was being served by Weasel Man (features too small, beard too thick) while Bomber Jacket Boy on my right was being served by a woman whom I was instantly attracted to. She wasn't my usual type – by this I suppose I mean that she didn't look like Aggi – she was some considerable years my senior and far more womanly than any female I had ever known. She looked a lot like Kim Wilde in her *Kids in America* phase – all blonde highlights and heavy make-up, yet strangely lithe and earnest but, of course, a lot older. *I want to be served by her*, I decided. *I need to be served by her.*

Weasel Man was pulling two pints of bitter while Archway Kim Wilde was serving two pints of lager. They were both neck and neck, which depressed me greatly; if Bald Bloke got his pints first, I decided, I was definitely going to be upset.

Plan A

1. *Weasel Man finishes first.*
2. *Pretend to tie shoelaces until he finds something else to occupy himself with.*
3. *Failing that, head for the Gents' and try again later.*

Plan B

1. *Archway Kim Wilde finishes first.*
2. *Ask what bitter she recommends and then order a pint of it.*
3. *Engage her in conversation at every opportunity but play it cool.*

Archway Kim Wilde finished her pints first. I nearly let out a whoop of joy, which would've been premature because Bomber Jacket Boy, obviously a student, was holding her back from the finish line by fishing about in his pocket for change. Bald Bloke had handed Weasel Man a crisp tenner and received his change before Bomber Jacket Boy had even finished counting out his coppers. I'd turned towards the toilets, already attempting to convince my bladder that it needed to go, when Bald Bloke turned back to the bar and said to Weasel Man, 'Oh, and a pack of ready salted crisps, please.'

I glanced hopefully at Archway Kim Wilde as Bomber Jacket Boy walked away from the bar with his two pints.

Hurrah!

Her: What can I get you?
Me: A pint of bitter, please.
Her: Which would you like?
Me: Which would you recommend?

Her: I don't know, I don't drink bitter. Most people like
the Griddlingtones though.

Me: A pint of that then.

Her? Nothing. Not another word. Not even when I gave her
the money. What a miserable cow. I wondered whether a
tip would change her mind but as I'd only given her two
pound coins I strongly doubted whether she would've been
all that impressed. She didn't even look at me when she
gave me my change because she was too busy smiling at
a new bald bloke now standing at the bar smoking a thin
cigar. Out of the corner of my eye I angrily looked him up
and down. He was wearing a grey leather blouson jacket, the
type which you only ever see in clothes catalogues, and a pair
of grey trousers which were the epitome of the word 'slacks'.
I wondered, if it came to violence, whether I stood a chance.
As he moved his hand to his mouth to take a deep drag on
his cigar, the tattoo across his knuckles which read 'ACAB',
drained me of my entire stock of bravado. She chatted to him
about football: goading him playfully about West Bromwich
Albion's recent performance while he in turn cast aspersions
on Spurs. I listened to him crack an abysmal 'joke' about a
rabbit going into a bar, which had Archway Kim Wilde on
the verge of wetting her knickers, before I decided to leave
them to it.

I looked for a seat well away from the bar because I was
scared I might 'say' something in a casual glance, offensive
enough to get my head kicked in. I ended up sitting next to
the fruit machine and the door to the Ladies'. I settled myself
down and searched for my fags and then sighed as I realised
I'd forgotten them. I stared at my solitary pint, the head of
which was already beginning to go flat. For the first time in
over a year I felt like crying. Not big, manly tears like the

soldiers who had faced death, pain and man's inhumanity to man in Oliver Stone's *Platoon*, but small childish tears that didn't make sense and didn't need a reason; the kind mums have an incredible knack of wiping away so well that it almost seems like they never existed.

The table in front of me was bare. No cigarette butts, empty glasses or crisp packets. It would be obvious to everyone in the pub that I was here Alone. I didn't even have the energy to go into the pretence of being early for a date. It was written all over my face anyway: 'It's my birthday tomorrow. I have no friends. I hate my job. I can't get over my ex-girlfriend. Shun me. For I am a latter-day leper.'

This, I thought to myself, *I can safely say is the lowest point in my life.* As if to prove this proposition I began to search through my mental catalogue of disasters.

- Losing my Action Man at the age of six.
- Accidentally leaving my Maths homework at home when I was thirteen.
- Failing my O-level French at sixteen.
- Being dumped by Aggi at the age of twenty-three.

In five minutes that was all I could come up with. I felt something was wrong, they were all a bit obvious, really. None of them seemed depressing enough, even though I'd been devastated by them all at the time. I'd made myself immune to them by thinking about them so much that they had ceased to have any effect on me. There were other thoughts, however, thoughts floating around my head, locked away in boxes marked 'Do Not Open. Ever' and abandoned on the less-travelled byways of my mind. Things which I hadn't forgotten but had instead simply learned to ignore. I couldn't do it with large-scale events like Aggi's dumping me – only small things that were easily hidden. These tiny thoughts were like stagnant pools that would only smell if the horrors putrefying in their deeper waters were disturbed.

I took a sip of flat bitter and dived in.

Stagnant Pool No. 1 (Eau de Abandonment)

Dad left us when I was about nine. (About the same time that Action Man went MIA. Although I don't think the two events were connected.) And if I'm being honest he didn't just leave us, he 'went to live with another lady', which was how I put it to Simon the following Monday on my way to school. My parents had thought they'd protected me from potential psychological damage caused in the build-up to this event by cloaking their bitterest arguments in geniality, as if I was too stupid to work out what was going on. Then one Saturday morning Mum took me and Tom to Crestfield Park. On the way she bought me a brand new plastic football that had all the signatures of the England football team printed on it – I knew they hadn't really signed it but I was impressed nonetheless. Tom didn't get anything because at fourteen months old he wasn't capable of making her feel guilty.

When we got home all of Dad's things were gone. I asked Mum where Dad was and she said he'd gone to live with another lady and then began crying. As young as I was, I could see that she hadn't dealt with the situation very well at all. For the next three months I saw my dad every other weekend, when we'd go to the park or eat chips in a café in town, and then one day I arrived home to discover he'd moved all his stuff back in and everything returned to normal.

Then last year my mum announced that she wanted a divorce. She said she'd got tired of being somebody's wife and wanted to be herself. Dad said it was all for the best, then three days later moved out. They were really laid-back about it, as if it was something Tom and I should've been happy about.

Stagnant Pool No. 2 (Eau de Paternity)
A new entry.

This morning I was nearly a father. This evening I'm still just a loser.

I couldn't help but feel that I'd lost out on something. It was like I'd caught a glimpse of another place – a place that didn't look as depressing as the one I was in – a place that looked like heaven.

Stagnant Pool No. 3 (Eau de Fidelity)
Aggi's infidelity had completely thrown me. I didn't know what was real and what wasn't. Talking to Kate had taken my mind off it for a while but now this thought was back and refusing to be ignored, boxed away or submerged: *I had the best time of my life with her. Does her cheating on me mean I have to throw it all away? Kate's right. Is love really love if only one of you believes in it?*

I didn't much feel like finishing my pint now. I couldn't quite see the point. I was perilously close to crying in a public space. If I'd been a woman I would've had the right, culturally speaking, to nip into the Ladies', find a comfortable stall, pull off a few sheets of loo roll and have a good bawl. The best on offer in the masculine world was the smell of carbolic and stale urine as found in the Gents' – not really my idea of a comforting environment. I went in there anyway, just to get away from humanity for a while. To pass the time and give myself an excuse for being there, I took a leak, concentrating the contents of my bladder on a crushed fag packet in a valiant effort to make it move.

I returned to my table to see a young, trendy-looking couple hovering by it predatorially, their faces wildly exaggerating the effort it took to hold a pint glass and stand up at the same time. Ignoring them, I sat down and finished my pint. I considered lingering just to annoy them, but I still felt like crying, so instead I made ready to leave, casting a last glance in Archway Kim Wilde's direction that said: 'This is your last chance, babe. I'm walking out that door now and I ain't ever coming back.' My visual reprimand went unheeded – the delights of serving watery beer to the dead-beat regulars of the Angel were obviously more alluring. The trendy couple virtually threw themselves in my seat.

Walking back home through the debris of Henmarsh council estate, I kept my eyes glued to the pavement, scanning for dog crap. I didn't know anything about this estate, but the graffiti, up-turned dustbins, discarded armchairs and occasional syringes provided sufficient evidence that this one was as dangerous as any I had come across in Nottingham or Manchester. I was, of course, classic mugging material: four-eyed, weak-willed and middle-class with a cash-card. It was a wonder there weren't queues of long-limbed teenage miscreants waiting to take a swing at me. Although I was feeling apathetic towards most aspects of my life at this moment (including personal safety), getting beaten-up, I reasoned, wouldn't exactly improve my frame of mind and so I speeded up my pace.

Just before I reached my road I spotted the pale light of an off-licence, tucked behind a row of shops that I had somehow managed to miss on my Get To Know Your Locale tour of Archway. On a whim I entered and purchased the following:

> 2 packets of salt and vinegar Hula Hoops.
> 1 packet of barbecue beef Hula Hoops.
> 1 box of Swan Vestas.
> 1 bottle of tequila.
> 1 small bottle of lemonade Panda Pop.
> 1 bottle Perrier (sparkling).

I paid for the booty on my credit card, because the man at the till didn't have one of those swipe machine things, so I figured that he wouldn't be able to tell that I'd reached my card limit. Anyway, save for the thirty-seven pence change

I'd received from Archway Kim Wilde, I didn't have any real cash on me.

Plastic bags in hand, I made my way to 64 Cumbria Avenue, where I was welcomed by the cheery glow of a naked electric bulb emanating through the net curtains of the front ground floor flat. Peering through the window as I walked along the front path, all I could distinguish were the vague outlines of a man and woman sitting at a table, possibly eating.

Inside my flat nothing had changed. The answering machine had no answers on it and the flat, with my clothing strewn everywhere, looked like the community centre jumble sale from hell. I turned off the lights and fell onto the bed, hoping beyond hope that the day had been sufficiently exhausting for me to fall asleep before my brain could kick into gear again. Meanwhile, some twelve feet underneath me, the man in the flat below whom I'd seen dining turned his quiet meal for two into a very loud meal for two. I listened as a record needle was dragged across side one of Led Zeppelin's *Houses of The Holy*. (I recognised it immediately. Once when Simon's parents kicked him out briefly after they'd caught him smoking dope in his bedroom, he'd slept on my bedroom floor for a month until they took him back. *Houses of The Holy* was the only record he listened to.) When the 'DJ' finally left the needle to rest, Jimmy Page's amazing guitar-smithery was immediately interrupted by a slow, steady knocking – the unmistakable sound of headboard against wall. With nowhere to run or hide, I resigned myself to depression once more. I felt around on the floor in the dark until I found a mug that at some point during the week had contained Vimto, and after locating my tequila poured some of it in. I took a sip, switched on the radio and turned up *The Barbara White Show* until it was loud enough to reduce Mr Doing-it Downstairs' sexual workout to no more than a gentle thud.

Barbara was as amusing as ever. Thanks to her, within five minutes of listening I felt considerably better. There were a lot of people out there (and I do mean 'out there') who were in a far worse state than I'd ever be. Her first caller, Mary, was undergoing a course of chemotherapy for breast cancer while coping with the recent loss of a husband from cancer of the throat. On top of that she was worried about her teenage daughter who she feared was agoraphobic. I had to give Barbara her dues, even the hardiest of agony aunts would've been fazed by a caller so obviously without hope, but not she. Without pausing for breath she set her empathy zap gun to ooze-factor ten and swamped Mary in a sea of sympathy. But that wasn't her job done, by any means. In a world where there are so few certainties, Barbara, unlike politicians, wasn't afraid to put her neck on the line and say she had the answer. She was definitely growing on me. She advised Mary not to feel guilty for worrying about her own problems and gave her the phone number of a bereavement counselling group. As for the depression, she advised her to see a doctor, extolled the virtues of Prozac, herbal tea and soap operas and finished off by telling her to give her daughter a jolly good talking to. I was impressed.

I switched off the radio.

Silence.

I switched it back on and listened to an advert about a new Eddie Murphy film.

I switched it back off.

Silence again.

The man downstairs must've finished.

I poured myself another tequila, turned on the light and reached for my phone book, scanning through the lists of numbers as if they were meals on the menu of a Chinese takeaway. I found the number I was looking for and dialled.

An answering machine clicked on, there was a crackle and high pitched squeal before a section of film dialogue played: 'Life moves fast. If you don't stop and look around once in a while you might miss it.' It was Matthew Broderick in *Ferris Bueller's Day Off*. Simon was so predictable. 'Hi, you're through to Simon and Tammy,' continued the tape. 'Leave a message after the beep!'

A deep breath and a swig of tequila and I was ready.

'Simon, you're not in right now but I'd like to leave a message,' I gurgled quite magnificently. 'I hope you're horribly maimed in a terrible car accident. What's more, I hope you catch a gruesome tropical disease that causes your genitals to dry up like the seaweed in a Chinese restaurant, and that what you're left with crumbles and blows away in the wind. I wish every kind of nastiness I can think of and while I'm at it give me back that twenty quid you borrowed from me last May.' Tears worked their way into my voice. 'Give me back that twenty quid you sodding sod and everything else I ever lent you. Give me back that twenty quid. Give it me back now!'

It wasn't until I'd finished my rant and wiped the tears from my eyes that I realised I'd been cut off. Most answering machines stop recording after thirty seconds. I knew this, because I once drunkenly tried to leave the lyrics to The Velvet Underground's 'She's My Best Friend' on Aggi's mum's answering machine. I hadn't even managed to finish the first verse.

I called back and finished the message.

'This is me again. What was I saying? Yes, that's it. Give me back my twenty quid you git. You've had my girlfriend and now you want my money? Give me back my twenty quid or I'll phone the police. I'm not joking, you know. Poking my girlfriend might not be illegal but theft is!'

I slammed the phone down and laughed. I'd stopped crying now and felt a little bit better.

The journey to the kitchen from the bed – once only a few jaunty steps away – had now become a long and dangerous expedition, requiring me to stumble drunkenly into the few pieces of furniture I had, banging my shins hard enough to make the left one bleed onto my jeans. Ignoring the pain I searched through all the cupboards until I found what I was looking for: the equipment I needed to make the mother of all tequila slammers – a Tupperware beaker and a salt cellar. Racing back to my bed I poured a quarter of my tequila into the beaker, added a generous dash of lemonade and shook the salt cellar near the rim. Drawing a deep breath I covered the beaker with my left hand, raised it to shoulder height and then, leaning over the edge of the bed, slammed it down onto the carpet. Tequila spilled all over my jeans. I laughed maniacally and took a huge gulp from what was left.

It was not long before I was well and truly on my way to not knowing what planet I was on. My next mission, I decided, was to open two of the packets of Hula Hoops and endeavour to throw their contents, hoop by hoop, directly into my mouth. I scored four direct hits and crushed the rest under my feet, forming a huge powdery desert of reconstituted potato. Still hungry, I opened the third pack, barbecued beef flavour, and consumed them in the conventional manner – but only after I'd worn every single one of them on my fingers, waving them in the air. This was good. I felt happy. I was Forgetting. Only one thing could make me happier. I turned on the TV and put *Star Wars* in the video. When Simon and I had first seen the film at the age of six we thought it was real. We used to talk about Darth Vader and Luke Skywalker as if they lived at the end of our road rather than in a galaxy, far,

far away. This strong belief in the film had lingered with me throughout my life, to the extent that I even involved it in my final year dissertation: *Star Wars – Better than Shakespeare?* Eight months' research, 15,000 words written in the six days prior to the deadline with only twenty-three hours' sleep, and all Joanne Hall, Head of the Film Studies faculty, gave me was a 2:2!

Fast-forwarding to the scene where the Imperial Guard are attempting to board Princess Leia's ship, I pressed pause just as she was about to put her hologram message for Obi-Wan Kenobi inside R2D2. Carrie Fisher looked gorgeous – she was vulnerable, trusting, desperate, lonely. All the things Aggi never was. *Princess Leia needs a hero but Aggi doesn't need me.*

The phone rang.

I ignored it, I was having a Princess Leia Moment. The picture was perfect – The Viceroy and First Chairman of Alderaan frozen in time and space. *Princess Leia*, I thought, *I love you.*

The phone continued to ring.

Grudgingly, I answered it.

'Hey, Will, it's me.'

I pressed play on the remote control without saying a word. My Princess Leia Moment was gone. Soon storm troopers would arrive and spoil everything.

'Will, I know you're there,' said Simon, 'I'm really sorry, man. It was a really stupid thing to do. It was really stupid. If I could have my time again I swear I wouldn't do it. I wouldn't go anywhere near her.'

I didn't know what to say.

'Will, come on, talk to me.'

'What do you want, Simon?' I yelled hysterically. He must've thought I was well and truly off my rocker. I calmed down.

'What could you possibly want from me now? You've had it all, haven't you? You've had my girlfriend, what else do you want?'

'Look, it wasn't like that,' he said, trying to be earnest.

'It wasn't like what?'

'It just happened,' he said, clearly uncomfortable that I wasn't making it easy for him. 'It only happened the once. And neither of us wanted it to happen again.'

At the back of my mind a question was lurking. Every second it loomed larger on the horizon, but I knew I had to resist it, because I didn't think I had the guts to gamble everything I believed in just so I could hear something as nebulous as The Truth.

'When did it happen?' I asked. My hands were shaking. I didn't want to hear his answer.

'When I came to stay with you at university.'

He was being vague on purpose. 'You came to stay a lot of times. Which time?'

'At the start of the second year when I came up to see U2.'

I should've listened to my instincts. My brain immediately flashed to that fantastic scene in *A Few Good Men* where Tom Cruise demands to hear The Truth from Jack Nicholson. Nicholson in full menacing mode looks Cruise straight in the eye and tells him he can't handle the truth. I was in the same boat as Mr Cruise. Aggi had got off with my best mate five months into our relationship. It hurt.

'How did it happen?' I asked, more to myself than to Simon, as I knew he'd never go into the details.

Surprisingly, he answered my question.

'Do you remember that night?'

I had to say that I did, but not all that much of it. I'd been drinking all night with my mate Succbinder (whom I haven't seen or heard from since I graduated) because we didn't really like the band, but we thought it might be a laugh anyway. Aggi and Simon were really into the music so they went off to the front of the stage while Succbinder and I propped up the bar at the back, sipping expensive watered down lager from plastic cups.

According to Simon's version of events they'd tried to find me and Suc at the end of the gig but we hadn't been where we'd arranged to meet, which was in front of the merchandise stall at the back of the hall. Bored of waiting, Aggi and Simon had decided to go to 42nd Street, a club in town, and it was there that they first kissed.

They'd got a taxi back to mine and Simon admitted that he'd tried to persuade Aggi to sleep with him but she'd said no. And then they started kissing so passionately that 'No' turned into 'Will used the last one yesterday' and when a team of wild horses couldn't have kept them apart, Simon had sprinted to the all-night garage up the road in three minutes, shaving a good thirty-two seconds off my own record for that desperate dash. They did it on the sofa downstairs. Twice. Afterwards, Aggi had crept upstairs and slept on the floor in my room, because I'd been sick on the bed and was lying across it fully clothed.

In the morning I woke up in my underwear and remembered the horrific journey home and the ten pound cleaning levy the taxi driver had charged before he threw me out. I looked around, the bed had clean sheets on it and Aggi had even tidied up my room. I felt so guilty for getting drunk and not meeting her after the gig that I tried to be especially nice to her all day. I bought her chocolates, took her to see *Metropolitan* at the Cornerhouse and cooked her dinner in the evening. She in turn didn't complain that there was sick in her make-up bag and bought lunch for the two of us. We must have been driving each other insane with guilt.

Simon finished unburdening himself by telling me that Aggi had told him the day after, that if he ever breathed a word of what had happened to anyone she would kill him. Not because she was scared I might be angry, but because she knew it would break my heart.

I could tell by the tone of Simon's voice, as though he were confessing his sins to a Catholic priest, that he thought I'd forgive him there and then, as if the pain of being so frank about his treachery was penance enough. He probably was genuinely sorry, but I couldn't help thinking that some part of him was enjoying this scene. Here he was getting to play the sterling role of the blackguard with a heart. I told him to write a song about it and slammed down the phone.

After five minutes swearing at the phone I ran out of expletives and tequila. I tried to call Alice again because now, more so than ever, I needed her. Her answering machine was still on. I left a completely incomprehensible message and searched for a diversion. An English exercise book belonging to Susie McDonnell which had fallen out of my school bag caught my attention. I picked it up off the floor and considered marking the whole of my year-eight's class work. Although I probably would've got through them a lot quicker than usual I knew I'd only have to do them again in the sober light of day. Flicking absent-mindedly through the back of Susie's book I noticed a couple of badly spelt messages to her friend Zelah Wilson, who sat next to her in class, and quite a good sketch of Terry Lane, the year-eight Lothario, underneath which were the words: 'Terry Lane! Give me one, please!' I laughed and turned over the page, and there written in green Biro in Susie McDonnell's unmistakable handwriting were the words, 'Mr Kelly is a twat.'

I marked Susie's essay and gave her three out of twenty and wrote 'See me' in very large letters.

Turning to the back of Susie's exercise book again, I found two blank pages and across the top of them in large sprawling capital letters I wrote the words, **'I WANT . . .'**

I WANT . . .

1) I want to get over Aggi.

2) I want to move to a better flat.

3) I want to leave teaching.

4) I want adventure.

5) I want to be stronger (physically).

6) I want to like people more.

7) I want to talk to John Hughes over lunch.

8) I want more Hula Hoops.

9) I want to make a film better than *Good-fellas*.

10) I want to grow old gracefully.

11) I want to dump Martina without breaking her heart.

12) I want to live in Brazil at some point in my life.

13) I want world peace (please).

14) I want to know what was so wrong with me that Aggi could even consider getting-off with Simon.

15) I want to know why the sky really is blue.

16) I want my parents to get back together.

17) I want to stop smoking.

18) I want to get married.

19) I want Alice to be here.

20) I want a cat.

21) I want a film to be made about my life.

22) I want a clean towel.

23) I still want Simon to die a horrible death.

24) I want to never run out of fags.

25) I want to be somebody's dad (one day).

26) I want to believe in something that can't be explained.

27) I want Princess Leia.

28) I want to be able to play guitar better than Simon.

29) I want to be a hero.

30) I want to sleep.

SUNDAY

My eyes cracked open and my head shuddered violently as the telephone yanked me into consciousness. Though still disorientated by sleep, I managed to reach down to the floor, locate the source of the noise by touch alone *and* flatulate silently, all before picking up the phone in the middle of its second ring. All the same, it took at least a minute or two of grunting and stretching before my brain, still some two laps behind my body, was able to catch up. Someone was talking to me, using words that I recognised to be English; now all I had to do was arrange them in some sort of order and I'd be able to have something roughly approximating a conversation.

'Sorry I didn't return your calls, Will. It's just that . . .'

I didn't recognise the voice.

'Don't be sorry,' I said weakly, scratching my groin. 'Just tell me who you are.'

'It's me, Alice.'

'Oh yeah. Nice one,' I said, confirming her statement. 'What time is it?'

'Ten past eight. Sunday morning.'

'I'd heard the rumours, but I didn't know such a time really existed, you know. Ten past eight: Sunday morning. Well I never.'

I finished my bout of primary school sarcasm and was about to go off on a surreal tangent about the various theories I'd been contemplating in recent weeks about time travel and the nature of reality, when Alice started to cry.

'Oh, Alice, I'm sorry,' I apologised. 'I'm a git. Just ignore me.'

'It's not you,' she said.

Holding the phone close to my ear, I slipped out of bed, opened the curtains and looked outside. It was raining. Next door's dog had just finished his morning dump and was haphazardly flicking soil over the steaming deposit with its hind legs.

'It's Bruce,' she said, between sobs. 'He's left me.'

I listened carefully as she explained what had happened. Bruce had arrived back at the flat on Saturday afternoon after supposedly being 'at work' and, cool as you like, announced that he was leaving Alice for another woman. After a lot of shouting and crying on Alice's part, he was decent enough to admit that the other woman was, in fact, Angela, his project supervisor. When she'd asked how long it had been going on, he'd refused to say anything more than that he was moving out immediately and would be back to get the rest of his things. And that, as they say, was that. Five years of relationship demolished in under half an hour.

Armed with all the information, there should've been nothing stopping me from taking up the role of best friend and stalwart, as Alice had when Aggi had dumped me. The job of making her feel better was entirely my responsibility, but much to my shame I didn't feel up to the task. Every sentence that came to my lips sounded either too stupid or insensitive – the sort of thing that would've worked wonders for someone like Martina but would be an insult to Alice. She deserved better than meaningless platitudes, but that was all

I had in stock. She was my best friend and she was hurting and there wasn't a word in the English language that could make it stop.

Still, clichés are clichés for a reason. They exist to fill in conversational gaps, to make the person who says them feel marginally less impotent than they are and most importantly of all, to cause as little further upset as possible. To this end I imagined what Barbara White would do in my situation. First off, I had to ask a great number of questions, no matter how obvious, to show that I cared.

'Are you okay?'

'No, I'm not okay, Will. I feel crushed. Completely crushed. I never thought this would happen to me. He said he loved me. He said he wanted to marry me. He said that he'd always love me. He lied. He lied.' She began to cry again.

My mind remained blank. The spirit of Barbara White took control once more. 'You must be pretty cut-up about it.'

'I can't believe he's gone,' said Alice oblivious to my inanity. 'He's gone. What am I going to do now? I haven't done a thing since he left but cry. The cat's crapped over the bathroom floor, I'm supposed to be preparing for a meeting with my senior manager tomorrow and I was going to paint the kitchen this afternoon too.' She laughed sardonically. 'I hate that sodding cat anyway. She always liked Bruce more than me.'

'Perhaps she'll like you more now he's gone,' I said sagely.

Alice began to cry again.

I abandoned Barbara White mode, as it wasn't doing me or Alice any good. Instead I did what I should have done from the start: relied on my natural ability to tell It the way It is. 'Y'see, Alice,' I said crawling back into bed, 'it's like this: life is a load of old arse. Always has been and always will be.' I felt cold. I pulled the duvet up to my neck. 'I know how you feel. I do, I really do. There you are living life safe in the knowledge that the only thing that keeps you sane, the only thing that makes it all worthwhile is the person you love and then *vroooooooom!*, he clears off faster than the Tasmanian Devil with a rocket up his bum. And all that's left to remind you he was ever part of your life is a pile of photos, a few letters and too many memories.'

Alice didn't say anything. I didn't know whose benefit my little speech was for, so I changed the subject.

'Did you manage to sleep at all last night?'

'No. I lay awake all night thinking and crying. I would've phoned you earlier but it was really late when I felt able to call.'

'Look,' I said gently, 'you can phone me whenever you like. Morning, noon or night. It's like Diana Ross once said, "Ain't No Mountain High Enough".' I cleared my throat and presented her with my best impression of that former Supreme's soul stirring hit.

'Cheers,' said Alice laughing. 'You're a mate.' She paused as if catching her breath and then started crying again. 'Why has he done this, Will? I met her, you know. We all went out for dinner when she gave him the promotion to her department. She was exceptionally nice to me too. All night she kept saying that we must go out together some time. She must be about forty-two but she's really beautiful. She's got her own personal trainer. I don't know . . . what's wrong with me? Why doesn't Bruce love me any more? He must really worship her to do this to me after all the time we've been together. This kind of thing doesn't happen overnight. How long has he felt things were wrong and not told me? How long has he been sleeping with her and then coming home to sleep with me?' She broke down, violently sobbing into the phone. This was my closest friend, the only person in the world I could actually rely on, and there was nothing I could do or say to heal the pain. So we sat not speaking, wrapped in our own thoughts for close to an hour. Our connection via the telephone representing the closest two people can be when separated by 120 miles' worth of fibre optic cable.

Next door's dog began barking violently, waking me up from my trance-like state. I shook my head, trying to remember what I'd been thinking about in the time that had elapsed. I couldn't remember. I thought perhaps I'd fallen asleep.

'Hello?' I called down the phone line. 'Hello? Alice?'

'Oh, Will!' said Alice sleepily. 'I just dreamt that Bruce was here with me. We were lying in bed, his arms wrapped tightly around my waist, and he kept kissing me gently on my neck and telling me that he loved me.' She began crying again.

'What time is he coming back?' I asked, once her tears had subsided to a gentle whimper.

'Some time this evening,' she said. 'He's at her house now . . . wherever that is.' I could tell it took all her strength to hold back another flood of tears, but she did it. 'What can I do? I can't take this any more. He's just walking all over me and I feel like I can't do anything to stop him. I feel so helpless.'

'What do you want to do?' I asked. 'Do you want me to beat him up?'

'Yes,' she said bitterly.

'Oh,' I said, swallowing hard as I pictured all six foot, four inches of Bruce. 'While it would give me the greatest pleasure to kick all kinds of crap out of Bruce on your behalf, I think you ought to take on board the fact that given my weak stature the letting of blood would be all mine.' Alice laughed. 'You're my best friend though, so I'm quite prepared to bleed over his Armani suit for you. Anything to make you feel better.'

Alice became serious again. 'I want him to hurt, Will. I want him to hurt as much as I do. He wouldn't care if I started seeing someone else. It'd probably make things easier for him. I just want him to hurt like I hurt. I want him to feel my pain.'

It was up to me to make things all right. I felt like Hannibal from *The A-Team*. 'So hit him where it hurts.'

'I'd never get near enough to get a kick in,' said Alice, only half joking.

Taking out my imaginary cigar, I shook my head and wondered if George Peppard had ever tried it on with Audrey Hepburn.

'No, I don't mean that,' I said. 'I mean destroy all that he holds dear. Exactly what time is he coming back?'

'I don't know. Around five maybe. I said I wouldn't be in and I won't. He'll probably have that bitch waiting for him outside.'

'Right,' I said. I searched around on the floor for a pair of socks for my cold feet. 'There you go, you've got plenty of time to have the locks changed and make him regret ever wanting to see his boss naked.' The duvet slid off the bed as I made myself comfortable. The flat was freezing. The plug-in electric radiator by the front door was at least three feet too far away for me to consider it worth the effort of getting out of bed. I pulled the duvet back onto the bed, covering myself right up to my neck, relaxed and checked the details of my plan. 'You've got a cordless phone, haven't you?'

'It's what I'm talking to you on.'

'Excellent,' I said – which would've been sufficient in itself – but I couldn't resist adding, 'Let's party.' I smiled involuntarily, my body's way of telling me that on my internal scale of attitude, I was much closer to corny than ironic. 'Which room are you in right now?'

'I'm in the sitting room.'

'What can you see?'

'The sitting room.'

'No, I mean what can you *really* see?'

I listened to the rustle of Alice's hair brushing against the receiver as she looked around the room. 'A sofa, a TV, a pack of B&H, a coffee table, some magazines: *GQ, Marie Claire, The Economist*, a fish tank, a hi-fi . . .'

'Stop right there,' I interrupted. 'Is it Bruce's hi-fi?'

'His pride and joy. One of those high tech jobs. Ludicrously expensive.' She sounded distant. 'It's Bruce's pride and joy.' More tears were right around the corner.

'Right. Pick it up!' I shouted, hoping I could generate enough mystery to stop her thinking about Bruce.

'Why?'

'Just pick it up!' I yelled. 'Have you got it?'

'Yes.'

'Take it to the bathroom.'

Alice made her journey to the bathroom in silence. All I could hear was a very faint buzz of static from the phone line.

'Don't walk!' I commanded. 'Run!'

'I'm in the bathroom,' said Alice breathlessly, after some moments. 'This thing's a bit bloody heavy. What shall I do now?'

Another involuntary smile spread across my face. 'Put the hi-fi in the bath, put the plug in and turn on the tap.'

Alice laughed nervously.

'You *are* joking?'

Yet another involuntary smile emerged because I desperately wanted to say, 'No, I'm deadly serious.'

Fits of shrieking and laughter filled my ear drums.

'Excellent,' said Alice giggling. 'Shall I add some Radox?'

The sound of running water and laughter seemed to be everywhere. As we waited for the bath to fill up, Alice reminded me that I'd promised to visit her this month. I said I'd love to but couldn't afford it. She offered to pay for my train ticket. I was genuinely moved.

'It's full,' shouted Alice excitedly.

'Right,' I said. 'Let's take a look at his clothes, shall we?'

'I'm heading into the bedroom now!' screamed Alice in full *Challenge Anneka* mode. 'I'm opening his wardrobe. I can see his favourite jumper that he bought from Duffer of St George, a couple of hand-painted silk ties, two Agnes B shirts and three Armani suits.'

'Anything else take your fancy?'

'Oh, there's a pair of black Katherine Hamnet trousers that he used to jokingly call his "pulling strides" and a limited edition Tommy Hilfiger T-shirt he adores that he got on a work trip to the States. Come to think of it, Angela was on that trip too. Bitch. What are we going to do to them?'

'Head for the kitchen.'

'I'm running through the hallway,' said Alice, unaware that this was the longest she'd gone without crying since our call began. 'Hang on, I've dropped the T-shirt. I'm going through the living room. I've just spotted his vinyl copy of the *Enter The Dragon* soundtrack. It cost him a fortune.'

'Good, bring that along too.' *Enter The Dragon* was Lalo Schifrin at his very best. A loser like Bruce didn't deserve it. 'Right, are you in the kitchen yet?'

'Yes.'

'Find the biggest pots and pans you can. Throw in some water and bring Bruce's stuff to the boil. Anything left over, toss it in the washing machine with some bleach.'

'Wonderful,' said Alice, genuinely elated.

'Feel any better?'

'I feel ecstatic!'

Next door's dog began barking again. A man's voice shouted, 'Will you be quiet, Sultan?' I laughed, because for a few seconds I thought he'd said Satan.

'What are you laughing at?' asked Alice.

It wasn't worth explaining, so I didn't. 'Take the rest of his belongings and chuck them in a black bin bag and leave them by the front door.'

'Front door? What about the rubbish chute?'

'Nice one. Oh, and if you've got any paint throw that in too.' Over the next hour we painted Bruce's black Patrick Cox shoes in the white emulsion meant for the kitchen walls (Alice's idea); cut the toes out of all his socks (Alice's idea again); cut his face out of every photo in the flat and burnt them while I played the soundtrack to *South Pacific* down the phone (my idea); rubbed his toothbrush in the cat crap in the kitchen (my idea, obviously); and threw his leather briefcase, including all of the work-related documents within, off the bedroom balcony (a joint effort).

Alice let out an exultant yell once she had frisbeed Bruce's briefcase out of the window. I listened to her fall to the floor and let out a heavy sigh of exhaustion and though I'd barely exerted myself I distinctly felt in need of rest and recuperation too.

'Do you ever wish you'd done this to Aggi?' said Alice, her voice muffled, as if she were lying face down on a sofa.

'No.' I immediately paused and reconsidered the question. 'Well, yes. I suppose sometimes I do but then I still kind of hope that one day we'll get back together. Thing is, Aggi always took her clothes very seriously. If I'd ever messed with them I guarantee she would've had a lobotomy rather than take me back.'

'Do you really think you'll still get back together?'

'I dunno,' I lied.

'That's it for me and Bruce. I never want to see him again.'

'Do you mean that?' I glanced over at Aggi's photo on the wall next to me, resisting the temptation to see if the marker pen would wipe off. 'Do you *really* mean that?'

'Yeah, I do.'

'Well, you're a braver man than me.'

There was an awkward silence in which neither of us knew what to say next. It was Alice who spoke first.

'Work. I'm fed up of it. I've been working so hard for so long and it's not worth it. I've made a decision. I'm booking a flight – one of those three month round the world things – as soon as possible. Bruce and I used to talk about it all the time . . .'

She started to cry again.

I imagined not being able to talk to her for a quarter of a year. I imagined trying to cope with life without her. I imagined telling my television how much I hated my job. It was really too depressing for words. I stopped imagining.

'You can't go,' I said only half joking. 'It's my birthday.'

'Oh yeah,' said Alice perking up. 'Happy birthday!'

I thanked her for the card and the presents and told her about the episode with the postman. She laughed and said that she didn't trust the Royal Mail either.

'I'm glad you liked the presents,' she said warmly. 'My favourite thing was the donkey. It reminds me of you.'

I laughed. 'Cheers.'

'I think it's important that you've got this donkey,' said

Alice thoughtfully. 'You've got a lot of love inside you, Will, and it's got nowhere to go. Maybe you can love and care for this donkey. You've both been neglected.'

I eyed Sandy's picture suspiciously. I was fond of my mange-ridden donkey but I wasn't about to fall in love with it, at least not quite yet, though I appreciated the thought. I told Alice that she'd given me the best birthday I'd had in a long time and that without her I would be lost. She accepted my thanks silently and then said: 'What are you going to do today? Anything special?'

'Well,' I said, wondering whether to tell the truth, construct a plausible lie or make a joke out of it. 'I thought I'd throw myself a surprise party, the surprise being the fact that I won't bother going.' Alice laughed. 'No, I think I'll just be staying at home enjoying the day with my favourite people: Mel and Choly. Ho ho.'

'Will, let me come to London,' said Alice seriously. 'Please. I can get the next train. We could go and celebrate your birthday in style, have a laugh and forget what a "load of old arse" life is.'

Of course I wanted to say yes, but we both knew it was a recipe for disaster: take two consenting adults, add a dash of vulnerability, a bottle of wine or two and a few 'just hold me's' and before we knew it Plato would take the night off and leave us to deal with the disastrous consequences of two friends settling for second best.

'Thanks for the offer but I'd rather not today,' I said, strongly believing that I'd probably live to regret this decision. 'Next weekend maybe, at least then we'd have more time together. If you came now and went Monday morning I'd be more depressed than if you hadn't shown up at all.'

'Okay,' she said, obviously disappointed, but probably nowhere near as disappointed as I was. 'Have a great day, won't you, Will?' Almost under her breath she added, 'I love you.'

'I love you, too,' I replied.

There was a world of difference between Alice's 'I love you' and Martina's. Alice had only wanted to say 'I love you' because when you had someone to say 'I love you' to, you miss saying it when they're gone. I knew that and Alice knew it too. It didn't mean that anything special was going on here. It was just the sound of two desperate people being desperate.

Alice made ready to say good-bye. 'Look, thanks for . . .'

'Yeah,' I said. 'No problem. What else are friends for?'

11.57 A.M.

As I sat flicking backwards and forwards between a gardening programme, a repeat of *Grange Hill* and *The Waltons*, a speckled grey and white pigeon momentarily sat on my window sill, spread its wings and cooed before disappearing into the late morning sky. It had stopped raining, and the sun was shining brightly off the hundreds of raindrops on the window pane, making them sparkle like stars. I opened the window and got back into bed.

This was quite possibly the worst and best birthday I'd ever had. On the one hand, if I actually cared about birthdays this could have been the depressing episode which broke this particular dromedary's back. After all, I was now twenty-six, still recovering from the fallout of a pregnancy scare, the focus of a mad woman's unrequited love, in an awful excuse for a flat, in a less than salubrious area of London and all alone on the anniversary of the date I was born and the day I was dumped. But it was this fact – the fact that I was on my own – which I considered the silver lining in my otherwise dismal dark cloud. I'd spent my twenty-fifth birthday with Simon and Tammy in the Royal Oak. It had been awful. There I was immersed in my own private tragedy, deeply lamenting the passing of youth and my failure in life, while my companions' sole topic of conversation was how Ray and

Sophie, the couple they shared a house with, hadn't bought a communal toilet roll for over a fortnight.

The phone rang.

My brain was alert to the call a split second after it had rung, but my body wasn't interested in speedy responses. The distance between myself and the phone, which had been abandoned under a pile of clothes near the wardrobe, seemed so utterly overwhelming that I never thought I'd make it. In fact, my movement was so sloth-like that the answering machine had turned on before I even got there.

'Hi, you're through to me,' said my machine, in its flat East Midlands accent. 'Leave whatever you want after the beep.'

It beeped accordingly.

'Hi, Will,' said Kate's voice. 'I was just phoning for a chat really. I'll probably try you later.'

I ceased all effort to get to the phone, and lay on my stomach on the carpet, my legs resting uncomfortably against the side of the bed. *Should I pick up the phone?* I wondered. *If I answer I'll have to talk to her and as much as I like her, I'm not sure I want to communicate with the world today. Today – my birthday. Today – the third anniversary of my being dumped. Today – today. I still like Kate, I just need a breather. I can always phone her later. Yeah, that's what I'll do, I'll call later.*

I picked up the phone and apologised. 'Sorry about that.'

'I thought you weren't in for a minute,' said Kate. 'That would have really spoilt my Sunday.'

'Well, we can't have your Sunday spoilt, can we?' I said, wondering if I'd ever learn to control my guilt. 'How are you?'

'I'm okay, I suppose,' she sighed. 'After I got off the phone with you last night I did my washing down at the launderette. I was going to stay in like I told you, but then Paula and a bunch of her mates persuaded me into town for a drink. I ended up going to a club and then we finished up the night back here with four bottles of Martini, watching the end of *An Officer and a Gentleman*. Richard Gere can whisk me away on his motorcycle any time he wants.'

I attempted to laugh, but it came out halfway between a snort of derision and a clearing of the throat – I was already regretting picking up the phone. Kate wasn't cheering me up, she was depressing me beyond belief. I should have listened to my instincts. I wasn't feeling very talkative, and recognising this mood from previous encounters, I soon realised that unless this conversation was brought to an end quickly, I'd become more obnoxious than usual, which could only lead to trouble.

'What did you do last night?' asked Kate.

'Oh nothing much.' I licked my lips and scratched my head. 'A couple of mates came over and we went for a drink in the West End. Bar Rumba. Do you know it?' She said she did. 'It was good. I ended up with some girl called Annabel.'

'I take it she's not with you now,' said Kate. 'What was she like?'

I tried to detect any trace of emotion – there wasn't even the palest shade of jealousy.

'How do you know she's not still here?' I asked.

'The flat's not really big enough for you to refer to a woman you've just slept with as "some girl called Annabel" is it?' said Kate. 'I used to live there, remember?'

I laughed. 'No, she went early this morning.'

I expected Kate to put the phone down.

'I said, what was she like?' repeated Kate not quite aggressively, but not all that far off either.

I answered her question. 'Not really my type. She was a

247

bit stupid. I asked her who was her favourite out of *Starsky and Hutch* and she said, Hutch, when everybody knows that Starsky was far cooler because he had a better car, better jumpers and, anyway, Hutch was a tosser.'

'I think you're the one being a tosser here, Will.'

'Possibly.'

'Unequivocally.'

'Maybe.'

'Incontrovertibly.'

'So what do we do now?' I asked.

'I put down the phone,' she replied resolutely. 'And we never speak again.'

'Good-bye then.'

'Have a nice life.'

She slammed the phone down.

I got out of bed and closed the window. The sun had stopped shining, and next door's dog was going berserk at a squirrel in a tree. I thought about getting dressed or eating breakfast, anything apart from the subject of Kate and what an idiot I'd been. I got back into bed and pulled the duvet over my head.

On the surface, the ambiguity of our peculiar relationship might have allowed my conscience to remain untroubled, but that wasn't to be. Just because what was happening between us didn't have a name it didn't mean that it could be ignored. My lies were bound to have hurt Kate, because I knew that had they been said to me I would have been devastated. So instead of nurturing our blossoming relationship, I'd simply rounded up all the worst clichés of my sex and thrown them in her face. I wanted Kate's forgiveness, but more than that, I wanted her back as a friend. I had her phone number. I'd scribbled it on the back cover of one of my students' exercise book, Liam Fennel's, to be exact, during our mammoth conversation on death. I remember feeling at the time that her offering it to me represented a turning point: she was letting me in, making me part of her life; showing she trusted me in the only way she could. It was an action as intimate as any kiss.

'Hello?'

'Hi, Kate, it's me,' I said quietly. 'I'm sorry. Look, I'm really sorry. Please don't put down the phone.'

'Why not?' said Kate angrily. 'You don't want to talk to me, do you? What do you want?'

'I want things to be like they were,' I said. 'Can we do that?'

'No.'

'Why?'

'Because.'

I understood her 'because' and she knew that I knew I understood it too. 'I know. I'm sorry. I lied. I lied about going to the West End last night. I lied about having friends to go to the West End with last night. And I lied about meeting a girl last night. I went to a local pub on my own. I got depressed and drunk (in that order), came home, made an abusive call to my former best mate and fell asleep.' I paused. 'I just wanted you to know.'

'And now I know,' said Kate as if she didn't care.

'I know it's no excuse . . .'

'Too right.'

'I give new depth and meaning to the word "arsehole".'

'And the phrase "self-deprecation",' added Kate.

The ice between us slowly melted and things eventually got back to their usual rhythm and energy. I told her about the previous evening in great detail – although skipping over any mention of Archway Kim Wilde – and she was highly entertained but, I think, more than a little disturbed.

'Will,' said Kate cautiously.

'Yes?' I responded.

'You do know your behaviour's pretty strange, don't you?'

'What do you mean?' I asked. 'I'm not *that* weird, am I?'

'Well . . .' she began.

'Well . . .?' I said expectantly.

'I don't mean to be insensitive, but somehow, I think that if I stopped one hundred members of the general public and told them that yesterday you smashed your best friend's demo tape and mailed it back to him, called him up and left abusive messages on his answering machine, sat depressed in pubs on your own . . .'

'Don't forget being obsessed with my ex-girlfriend three years after she's dumped me,' I interjected.

'Yes, that too. Added to the fact that you talk to strangers on the phone and give them fictional accounts of your evening's activities – you lied about going to Marx's grave with friends too. You went alone, didn't you?'

I said yes and added helpfully: 'Don't forget scribbling moustaches and thick eyebrows on a photograph of my ex-girlfriend and helping a friend destroy her cheating boy-friend's possessions this morning.'

'You helped a friend destroy her boyfriend's possessions?' asked Kate in genuine wonderment.

I told her everything that had happened, missing out the part about the frisson of sexual tension in the air between Alice and me. She was especially shocked by the episode with the toothbrush and the cat crap.

'You're mad!' exclaimed Kate. 'You really are mad!'

'Steady on,' I joked. 'I wouldn't go that far.'

'Will,' said Kate. 'Can't you see this isn't normal behaviour?

All one hundred members of my general public survey would've had you in a straitjacket quicker than you can say Mental Health Act.'

I scratched my head and decided it was time to get out of bed. *Kate*, I thought to myself, as I pulled on my jeans, *may have a point*.

'You know the Edge,' I explained to her.

'The what?'

'The *Edge*,' I repeated. 'As in "close to the . . .".'

'Yes.'

'Well, I think I'm about as close to it as it's possible to get without going over. You don't have to tell me about my behaviour, plenty of others have mentioned it, but none of them have told me a single thing I don't already know.' I stopped for a second, pulling a T-shirt on over my head. 'I know I must seem weird to you, but believe me, it all makes sense from where I'm standing. It all stems from Aggi. It really does. She told me that she'd love me forever. I took her at her word. And now she doesn't want to know.' I picked out a shirt from the wardrobe and started putting it on. 'Take Alice, for example. If she started bombarding Bruce and his new girlfriend with threatening phone calls he'd be able to get a court order to stop her. But where is her recourse? Society – I do hate that word – hasn't provided any form of protection for her. His behaviour is deemed okay by their standards but her behaviour will just get labelled obsessive. But isn't love obsessive? Isn't that what it's all about? It eats you up, controls your mind, takes you over and everybody says, "Oh, that's so beautiful, they're in love." But when it's over, and you start sending your ex-lover letters written in chicken blood, you're suddenly labelled "insane" because you're willing to do anything – absolutely anything you think will bring them back to you. Now tell me, is that fair?'

There was a long pause. Kate coughed nervously. 'You didn't really send Aggi letters written in chicken blood, did you?'

'What do you think I am?' I joked. 'A voodoo priest?'

'Good,' said Kate with a sigh of relief, '*that* would just be too weird.'

I was about to confess to Kate how, at my most 'insane', I'd briefly entertained the thought of murdering Aggi, when the phone made a double beep, which broke my train of thought. I ignored it but it did it again seconds later. For a minute, my heart sank because I thought I'd broken the phone, until Kate pointed out that a double beep meant I had a call waiting. When I'd phoned BT to take over the line, the operator had asked me if I wanted the Call Waiting service. It was probably a bit decadent of me but as it cost nothing and was at a point in my life where I actually thought I might have more than one call at a time, I'd said yes. Following Kate's instructions, I pressed the star button.

'Hello? Is Will there?'

It was my brother.

'It's me here, Tom,' I replied, wondering what he wanted. 'Who were you expecting?'

'I don't know,' said Tom in his monotone voice, which hadn't just broken at fourteen, it had completely collapsed, losing all sense of expression along the way. 'I thought you were sharing with someone.'

I cast my mind back to the twenty-minute conversation I'd had with my brother where I'd told him I was getting a place on my own and he'd said, 'Nice one, I'm gonna get me a bachelor pad some day,' and I'd said the day he'd get a bachelor pad would be the day Mum and Dad died, and he'd moaned at me for making jokes about our parents' mortality and I'd told him that there was no point in sticking his head in the ground because it was the same end waiting for us all, and he'd raced upstairs to his bedroom and played his Bob Dylan albums loud enough to disturb the neighbours.

'I did tell you,' I said. I remembered Kate. 'Listen, I'm on another call at the moment. I'll phone you back.' I went to press the star button but changed my mind. I'd talked to Kate for a long time, and now I thought – especially after my earlier performance – was my chance to quit while ahead. 'Hang on a second,' I said to Tom. 'I'll be right with you.' I pressed the star button and got Kate back on the line. 'Hello, Kate? Sorry about that, it's my kid brother. Can I phone you back later?'

'No problemo, Mr Spaceman,' said Kate. It was the second time she'd called me this. I was about to ask her what she meant by it when it clicked, it was an obscure reference to *Gregory's Girl*. I felt like I'd just discovered the meaning of life.

'No problemo, Mrs Spacewoman,' I replied happily.

'I'll speak to you later.' She giggled and added: 'Oh, and Happy Birthday!'

Tom and I weren't exactly close. It was only in this last couple of years that I'd even considered him part of the human race. There were eight years separating us; what my parents had been thinking I don't know. Maybe he was a mistake. Even so, recently he'd turned into a reasonably personable mistake. Yes, he was nosy, lazy and prone to borrowing things without asking, but there was something about him that was incredibly likeable. We rarely fought because he was just too laid-back to get uptight about anything. When he was born, I was determined to let him know who was boss and spent the next few years trying to discover more and more ingenious ways to make him cry, like stealing his dummy, pulling faces at his cot, telling him he had an allergy to ice-cream which would make him choke to death, but everything I did simply washed over him. My theory was that he'd received from my parents a double helping – that's to say my helping – of the genes that control the ability to give a toss, which, I reasoned, explained without any loose ends, my complete inability to be carefree.

'So, what can I do for you?' I asked Tom.

'Just wishing you a happy birthday and all that,' he replied. 'What've you been up to?'

'Nothing much,' I said casually. 'I went out with a couple of people that I know down here. Nothing special. We just went up the pub, had a couple of pints, went back to a mate's house and watched some Hong Kong action flicks: *Drunken Master II*, *A Better Tomorrow II* and *Fist of Legend*.'

It wasn't that I hadn't learned the lesson that lying was neither big nor clever, I had. Very much so. But as Tom's big brother, and quite possibly the only stabilising influence in a family that was falling apart around his ears, I felt a responsibility to be someone he could look up to; possibly even aspire to be, just as Simon's older brother Trevor had been when Simon and I were growing up. For many years, even after Trevor had died in a car crash at the age of twenty-one, mine and Simon's only ambition was to grow a moustache, drive a decrepit Mini Cooper and 'score' with 'chicks' in tan tights. I remember Simon once captured the essence of our admiration succinctly, when years later he described his brother to Tammy as: 'Like the Fonz, only you could touch him.' Trevor was cool. He made the world sound easy.

'Where's my card?' I asked Tom.

'The same place as my seventeenth birthday card,' he retorted.

I ignored him and set about finding a topic of conversation that he wouldn't be quite so cheery about. 'How are your A levels?'

Tom tutted loudly. 'Oh them,' he said absent-mindedly. 'They're all right, I suppose.'

He'd had his heart set on going to Oxford, I think, because Amanda, his hippy chick best friend/potential love interest, had applied there. My mother had called me up at the start of the week and told me the results of his mocks, which to put it kindly, weren't exactly the kind of grades that got you into premier league educational establishments. I kind of felt sorry for him, and Mum said she thought he'd be really lost without Amanda.

'Have you decided about which universities you're applying to?' I asked, in full big brother mode.

'So Mum's told you then?' said Tom.

'What is it I'm supposed to know?'

'It doesn't look like I'm going to Oxford,' he said, not even revealing the slightest hint of emotion in his mono-tone voice.

'Not if you carry on getting grades like that,' I said. 'What did your teachers predict?'

'Three A's.'

'What did you get?'

'A B and two U's.'

On his behalf I tried to look on the bright side and told him the myth about Nottingham having the highest ratio of women to men in the country. He wasn't impressed. Instead he began to list the pros and cons of his five places of study. It was tedious to listen to, truly painful. I diverted his attention. 'Where's Mum?'

'She said that she'd call you this afternoon,' said Tom, now mumbling.

'Are you eating?'

'Yeah, Sunday dinner,' he explained, munching on another bite. Clearly I was boring him as much as he was boring me. 'Roast chicken and fried egg sandwich,' he added. Though I felt like throttling him for his lack of manners, I couldn't help but find him amusing. 'Mum's gone to Aunt Susan's,' Tom continued, 'and then she's picking up Gran from her day out.' I nodded pointlessly as I remembered the Kendal Mint Cake episode. 'She won't be back till about four or five.'

'Anything else to tell?' I was going to ask him how Dad was, but I didn't bother. Dad had apparently gone up the wall over Tom's exam results. It wasn't worth stirring.

'I saw that girl you used to go out with a while ago,' said Tom clearly. Either he'd put his sandwich down out of politeness – which wasn't likely – or he'd finished it. 'What was her name again . . .?'

'Aggi,' I said, feigning a lack of interest. 'She was called Aggi. She's probably still called Aggi.'

'Yeah, I saw her last Saturday in Broadmarsh Shopping Centre coming out of the Index catalogue shop.'

'Did she say anything about me?'

'No. She asked me how I was and what I was up to and then went off.'

'She didn't say anything else?'

'No.'

'Was she on her own?'

'Yeah. She's quite good looking, you know,' said Tom, as if he'd arrived at this fact using the latest scientific calibration techniques.

'Yeah, I know,' I said impatiently, thinking to myself that if he was mentally undressing my ex-girlfriend I'd give him the punching of a lifetime when I came home for Christmas.

I tried to resist the temptation, but I couldn't keep my

tongue still any longer. 'So, you're sure she didn't ask about me?'

'Yes, I'm sure,' he sighed theatrically. 'No messages, no secret handshakes and no mention of you.' I sighed in return, although not loud enough for Tom to hear.

'Well, that's all my news,' said Tom. 'Happy birthday. I'll see you next time you're home maybe.'

'Yeah,' I said. 'See you later.'

I thought about Aggi and birthdays. As an exercise in self-flagellation, I made a list of all the things she'd given me as presents in the past:

20th Birthday

Bottle of Polo after-shave.
Rebecca, Daphne du Maurier.
Monty Python and The Holy Grail.

21st Birthday

Best of Morecambe and Wise Vols. 1 and 2.
The Edible Woman, Margaret Attwood.
An Action Man.
An anthology of poetry by e. e. cummings.

22nd Birthday

Let It Bleed, The Rolling Stones.
The Greatest Hits of Burt Bacharach.
A packet of Liquorice Allsorts.
A pair of boxer shorts from M&S.

23rd Birthday

She dumped me.

I made another list of all of the things I'd bought her on her birthdays:

19th Birthday

Fame annual (1982).
England's Dreaming, Jon Savage.
It's a Wonderful Life.

20th Birthday

Star Wars.
A dress she wanted from a second-hand stall in Afflecks Palace in Manchester.
The Greatest Hits of The Smiths Vol. 2.

21st Birthday

A bottle of Bailey's Irish Cream.
The Empire Strikes Back.
Oliver Stone's *The Doors*.
A plain silver ring from Argos.

22nd Birthday

The Best of Scott Walker and The Walker Brothers.
Betty Blue.
The Best of Hancock Galton and Simpson.

I never gave her the twenty-second birthday presents. By then she'd already dumped me and wasn't returning my calls. I still had them at the bottom of my wardrobe under a pile of clothes that I didn't wear any more. They were still wrapped up in the gift paper designed by a female artist Aggi liked. Once, in a maniacally depressed mood, I considered ceremonially burning all the presents Aggi had given me, but I really would've been cutting off my nose to spite my face. The only thing I couldn't look at were the books, as she used to write messages in them; things about the book or how much she loved me. When it all ended I took them off my bookshelf and gave them to the Oxfam shop in West Bridgford.

Bizarrely, Aggi and I had never got around to doing The Exchange of the Carrier Bags – that curious post-splitting-up ceremony, where former lovers attempt to behave like mature adults as they return each other's belongings; records, hair brushes, books, etc., in a plastic carrier bag – it's always a plastic carrier bag – without falling apart. One of the parties, of course, always fouls up the genteel nature of proceedings by being totally devastated that the relationship is over. Aggi knew I would be that party. I tried to force her hand and arrange it through her mum, saying that I'd left some important stuff relating to a job I was after in her daughter's room, but after The Calling Round The House Drunk Episode her mum said she'd have to check with Aggi first and she, of course, said no. And so, in our great love war, these were the items belonging to me that went Missing In Action:

- A compilation tape of sixties music Simon had made for me.
- The spare key for the lock on my mountain bike.
- *Nevermind*, Nirvana.
- 1 black T-shirt.
- *The Beauty Myth*, Naomi Wolf.
- A pair of red baseball boots.
- An Action Man.
- A first-year essay from History module one, entitled: *Discuss the Origins of the Second World War* (52%. Well structured but would

have benefited from more original research.).
- Dad's watch.
- A videotape with four episodes of the third series of *Blackadder* and an episode of *The A Team* recorded on it.
- My copy of *Catcher in the Rye*.
- *Unreliable Memoirs*, Clive James.
- *The Unbearable Lightness of Being*, Milan Kundera.

On the other side of the coin, the following were my prisoners of war:

- *Star Wars*.
- *The Empire Strikes Back*.
- Three pairs of earrings.
- *Fame* annual (1982).
- *The Complete Works of Shakespeare*.
- *The Murder of Roger Ackroyd*, Agatha Christie.
- *Fear and Loathing in Las Vegas*, Hunter S. Thompson.
- *Riders*, Jilly Cooper.
- Her copy of *Catcher in the Rye*.
- *The Greatest Hits of The Pretenders*.
- New Order, *Technique*.
- Four editions of *Marie Claire*.
- A calculator.
- 25 A4 envelopes.
- A pair of Marks and Spencer 60 denier black tights (unworn).

2.42 P.M.

I wanted to call Kate back straight away. I missed her more than I'd missed anyone since Aggi. The more I thought about her the more relaxed I felt. If I concentrated, I could recreate the comforting nuances of her voice in my head as she talked to me about life, films, funerals, careers and love – it was almost too wonderful for words, which led me to think that perhaps the outer reaches of my brain were beginning to obsess. I had to stop my head from taking over my life and learn to take things one day at a time. As an exercise in willpower and something of a diversionary tactic, I promised myself that before calling Kate, I would sort out the mess in the flat once and for all. It was disheartening not being able to locate anything I needed. I had all but run out of clean crockery and the smell of festering food – melted ice-cream on the carpet, half eaten sandwiches curling before my eyes, spaghetti-hoop-encrusted plates simply crying out to be put out of their misery – was as low as I could go. I cleared the dirty crockery into the kitchen and got down on my hands and knees and tried to scrub the ice-cream out of the carpet – it wouldn't budge, it had bonded to the fibres. Moving on, I put all of the kids' exercise books in neat piles against the wall, and emptied the contents of my suitcase into the wardrobe, which required me to push the doors shut with both hands and lock them, as if the clothes inside were lunatic hordes trying to escape their asylum. The room was now beginning to resemble the flat that I had signed a six-month lease for only a fortnight ago. I filled the empty plastic Asda carrier bag that doubled as my bin with all manner of detritus: a half eaten Mars bar, crushed Hula Hoops, invitations from Barclays to receive a credit card and much more. I was about to add a letter from the TV licence people that had arrived on Wednesday when I thought the better of it. It was addressed to The Occupier. Instinctively I reached for my marker pen and wrote 'Not Known Here' and crammed it in my overcoat pocket ready to be posted back to them – the name in my passport did not say The Occupier, and I wasn't about to start responding to it now just to satisfy lazy TV Licensing Authority bureaucrats. It was a stroppy, mean-spirited and more than a little pathetic thing to do, but I must say, I really did enjoy it.

All week I had been freezing in bed because Mr F. Jamal had made the mistake of positioning the sofa-bed underneath the windows, which wasn't a good idea, particularly as the windows were in such a state of disrepair that the draughts coming through them could have filled the sails of a small yacht. To rectify this situation, I dragged the sofa-bed across the room and positioned it against the opposite wall, stopping every now and again whenever the carpet snagged itself under the bed's wheels. Although its new location meant that I couldn't open the bathroom door to its full extent – the only other alternative meant blocking the sole exit out of this tiny hell hole – I decided to leave it in its new home. Sweating profusely after this brief exertion, I considered it time for a fag break, but my conscience would have none of it. Instead, I continued my rearranging frenzy while my momentum was up. The room's two wardrobes, I decided, would look far more pleasing to the eye, on the wall opposite the kitchen door, as where they currently stood made them look too imposing. After a short debate as to whether it was worth emptying their contents first (it wasn't), I began struggling with the smaller of the two wardrobes.

At first I rocked it from side to side, but disturbing creaking noises emanating from the joints indicated that this wasn't the way forward. Instead, lowering my shoulder against one side, I pushed hard, as if in a rugby scrum. It took a great deal of exertion before it moved, but as it finally did so something fell, scraping against the wallpaper. Leaving the wardrobe where it was, my fertile imagination took hold, suggesting that it might be a rotting hand, which would of course have accounted in some part for the smell of my room. Although only half joking, at the back of my mind it had occurred to me that it would be typical of the kind of misfortune which had dogged me this last twenty-six years, that Kate, the Kate whom I was obsessed about to the point of possibly falling in love, would turn out to be a serial killer. I was relieved and yet a little disappointed to discover not one, but two objects, neither of which was a severed limb. Lying at the base of the wardrobe were an envelope of pictures from SupaSnaps and a hairbrush.

The object in my hand (the photos, not the hairbrush) took my breath away. I felt dizzy and nauseous and so sat down clutching them to my chest. I could feel the adrenaline caused by my excitement whizzing its way around my body. Somehow I knew that these photographs would contain pictures of Kate, my Kate, the Kate of my dreams – the Kate I'd never seen. A hand-delivered argument from my conscience lodged itself in my head.

'Looking through someone else's photographs,' it said, 'without their consent constitutes an infringement of a person's moral rights and is tantamount to the deplorable act of reading a diary, or private letters. I strongly recommend that you leave these photos well alone – especially as I know you're hoping she might be naked in some of them.'

'What a load of old arse,' said my brain, in an alarming show of bravado. 'We want to look. And we want to look now!'

I had neither the will nor the inclination to leave the photos unseen. These weren't just photos – they were photos of the person in the world I most wanted to see.

This must be what it's like when blind people have operations to give them sight, I thought . . . *For the first time in their lives, they can just see and believe.*

The photos were holiday snaps which, as far as I could tell, had been taken one summer in Paris. The majority of them featured either one of two girls in their late teens or early twenties, although there were a few bottom halves of the Eiffel Tower and shots of the Arc de Triomphe and the Louvre thrown in too. There were two good head shots of the girls, which I separated from the pile to study closer. One girl had long dark brown ringleted hair which, though tied back away from her face, still appeared unruly and untamed. She wore no make-up though her skin was quite pale. Her lips, however, were a healthy pinkish colour and she had small silver studs in her ears. In some of the other photos she was wearing a plain white T-shirt and jeans and it was clear that she was taller than the other girl. The only other detail I noted was that she had a nice smile.

The other girl, as far as I could tell, had naturally blonde hair (or a very good hairdresser) which was cut into a sharp bob. Despite the fact she was pushing out her tongue, which screwed up her face, it was obvious she was very attractive – more attractive, in fact, than her brown-haired companion. Her skin was tanned and her eyes were the bluey-green of tropical oceans. A white chiffon scarf adorned her neck and she too had small silver studs in her ears. She was wearing a yellow halter-neck top with a short royal blue checked skirt. The only other detail I noted was that she had legs to die for.

If I had to choose one of them just on looks, I said to myself, *then I'd like Kate to be the blonde.*

I phoned Kate.

'Hi, Kate? It's me, Will.'

'Hello,' said Kate cheerily. 'How was your brother?'

'Okay,' I replied, fingering the corner of the blonde girl's photograph. 'He's trying to work out which university to go to.'

I was impatient to find out which of the girls she was, but I didn't want to bring the subject up out of the blue. I don't know why. I suspect my conscience had a great deal to do with my unease.

'Tell him not to bother,' said Kate. 'Look at me.'

I did. Well, at least I looked at the photos of the two girls in my hands. Kate began talking about how a lot could be learned about life from just living but I tuned out, concentrating on the photos instead. I moved off the bed, over to the wall where Aggi's photo was. I positioned the two possible Kates on either side of Aggi and wondered if, one day, I'd be compelled to deface one of these photos too.

I couldn't wait any longer.

'What colour's your hair?'

'My hair?' said Kate quizzically. 'I don't get you. What's that got to do with Keynesian economics?'

'Nothing at all,' I replied sheepishly. 'But please, tell me what colour your hair is.'

'My hair?'

'Yes, your hair.'

'It's a reddish colour,' said Kate. 'Why do you ask?'

'It's not brown?'

'No.'

'And it's not blonde?'

'No.'

'It's not brown or blonde?'

'No.'

'Oh.'

Neither of the girls in the photo was Kate. As always I had let myself run headlong into disappointment. I tossed the photos into my carrier bag bin and made ready to cut this conversation short as I felt the black clouds of my sullen nature descending.

'It's not naturally red, of course,' announced Kate after some time. 'It's a dour brownish colour by nature. I inherited it from my dad.'

'I thought you said it wasn't brown,' I snapped.

'It's not brown,' said Kate, her voice revealing a distinct edge of worry that I should consider her hair colour to be so important. 'It was brown. But now it's red. It's quite simple, you know.'

Reaching into the carrier bag I plucked both photos from the rubbish and examined them closely. Instantly the scales fell from my eyes. The brown-haired girl was, to me, the most gorgeous creature that had ever existed. I returned the blonde girl to the bin and lay back on the bed, holding the real Kate's photo above my head, staring in wonderment.

'I have a confession to make.'

'Sounds juicy,' said Kate. 'Let's hear it.'

'I think I found some of your holiday snaps,' I announced, still gushing.

'The ones where I'm in Paris?'

'Yeah, I think so.'

'I wondered what happened to those,' said Kate ponderingly. 'Were they behind the wardrobe?'

'Wow.' For a nano-second I imagined hidden cameras. 'How did you guess?'

'It's not that big a flat,' replied Kate. 'I checked everywhere except there. I couldn't be bothered to move the wardrobes. You'll probably find my favourite hairbrush there too. Weird things backs of wardrobes, things always drop behind them.' She paused. 'So what do you think? Are you disappointed?'

'No. Not at all. Who's the blonde girl?' I asked, immediately regretting having opened my mouth.

'That's my flat mate, Paula. It's okay, most lads fancy her. She's very pretty.'

'She's all right, I suppose,' I said casually. 'Not really my type. To make things even, do you want to know what I look like?'

'No, thanks,' said Kate. 'I think you're nice whatever you look like. I'm trying to imagine that you look totally hideous. That way I can only be impressed.'

'I'll send the photos back to you, shall I?' I said, even though I was desperate to keep them.

'Nah. You keep them,' said Kate. 'It was a terrible holiday anyway. We spent two weeks getting chatted up by loads of really slimy blokes. One guy even told me that I looked like his mother. Now is that pervy or what?'

We spoke for at least an hour, in which time she told me all about the holiday to Paris which she'd actually taken this summer. In return I told her about the holiday to Tenerife I'd taken back in July with Simon and Tammy. We'd rented a one bedroom apartment on the agreement that the living room would be *my* bedroom. Instead, I ended up sharing it with Simon three nights in a row after Tammy had thrown him out simply for being a git. And when they weren't arguing, the living room, with its paper thin walls, wasn't nearly far enough away for me to be saved from hearing them thrashing about in the throes of passion. It was a very depressing holiday.

I was beginning to get hungry as I drew my holiday narrative to a close and on top of that a niggling worry about the cost of all these phone calls had wormed its way into my head. I'd been on the phone for hours. As it was, I already owed the bank millions, my dad £300 which I'd borrowed for the holiday and Tom £30, and he hadn't even got a job. I rounded things up and said good-bye, telling Kate that I'd give her a ring at the end of the day to tell her how the rest of my birthday had gone.

I plucked my beautiful lilies from the kettle and placed them on the bed as I was in need of hot water to make a Spicy Tomato Pot Noodle (discovered hidden behind the Honey Nut Loops). Brown water was still on the menu so I used my initiative and filled the kettle with the sparkling mineral water I'd purchased the previous night. While waiting for the water to boil, I flicked through the photos in the main room again, separating them into two piles: 'Kate' and 'Not Kate'. I took the pile of 'Kates' with me into the kitchen, which was now full of steam, and poured the hot water up to the marked level on the Pot Noodle and then added a touch more for good luck. Usually I hated the three minutes it took for the noodles to soften, but time flew, engrossed as I was in flicking through my 'Kate' pile again and again, studying each one for clues about her personality.

With half the Pot Noodle I made a sandwich, adding some of the soy sauce from the sachet and then wiping the Pot Noodle dust from my hands onto the seat of my jeans, I made my way to the bed but not before returning my flowers to their 'vase'. Between mouthfuls, it slowly occurred to me that there was a high probability that in spite of myself, I might actually be happy. In the last hour or so I hadn't thought a single negative thought. *Maybe this is what happiness is*, I wondered. Part of me reasoned that I should sit back and relax and enjoy this sensation, fleeting as it was bound to be. The rest of me – that part of me that tried to touch the grille on the front of the gas fire when I was three, despite the fact that I'd been burnt by it before – wanted to investigate this feeling. Would it, could it, stand the test?

I thought about school and Alec Healey in year-eleven, the most evil child I had come across so far.

I was still happy.

I thought about the worksheets that I had to do by third period on Monday morning.

And I was still happy.

I thought about Archway and all the dog crap therein.

And I was still happy.

I thought about my twenty-sixth birthday and how as of today I was officially nearer to thirty than twenty.

And I was still happy.

I thought about all the money I owed the bank and even added two years' worth of student loans plus an extra year for my teacher training.

And I was still happy.

Then I thought about Aggi.

Here's the scene: *I'm sitting on the sofa bed with the phone in my hand pointed at my temple as if it's a loaded weapon I'm about to use to blow my brains out.*

Before reaching this stage, I had spent a considerable amount of time – in between peaks and troughs of maudlin inactivity – agonising over what I was about to do. In the end, like most major decisions in my life, I made a list, hoping logic would throw up a reason to hold back.

Three reasons why I should phone Aggi

1. I think I'm feeling something for Kate. Something that's got an air of permanence about it. If I get involved with her now it's going in one direction. Forever. Kate could be everything I've ever wanted. I don't want to lose her now. I owe it to myself to put a full stop at the end of this thing between me and Aggi. No other kind of punctuation will do.

2. Deep down I'm not even 100 per cent sure I still love Aggi. This thing between Simon and her has only high-lighted what I would've known if I'd been paying attention – that maybe I don't actually love her any more. Maybe

273

I am over her. Maybe I've blown her importance out of proportion. In my head she's become this huge thing – My Legendary Girlfriend. If I don't find out what she really means to me, how am I ever going to be sure I'm over her?

3. I can't think of another reason. I don't think any more reasons exist.

Three reasons why I shouldn't phone Aggi

1. I may discover that the reality lives up to the legend and then I'll want her back more than ever but she still won't want me.

2. If I make a decision based on how she reacts to me, doesn't that mean that she wins again? I don't want to turn Kate into a runner-up prize. She deserves better than that.

3. It's just a bad idea. And if there's one thing that I've learned it's that bad ideas should just stay bad ideas.

The last in-depth news I'd heard about Aggi's whereabouts was from her oldest school friend, Sally. When Aggi and I had split up Sally, overcome with compassion, had informed me that even though I was no longer with Aggi, she really did want to remain friends. Seizing the opportunity to have a mole within Aggi's ranks, I took up the offer and went for a drink with her despite the fact that she was exceptionally dull. She worked as a computer systems analyst, but never spoke about computers, as her real passion was fell walking, a subject which she could, and indeed did, talk about for hours on end. In between discussions endured on the merits of various youth hostels in the Lake District, I would pump her mercilessly for information on Aggi, which was forthcoming, up to a point – she never spoke about Aggi's personal life. According to the last Sally update, given some time after Easter, Aggi had moved to London after securing a job as a junior press officer for Amnesty International and was living 'somewhere in Barnes' (Sally would be no more specific than that). There was no point in asking Sally for Aggi's number, although I'd endured more hiking talk than I'm sure my ex-girlfriend ever had, for Sally's loyalties lay with Aggi. Instead, I called Aggi's mum and asked her for the number. I could hear the worry in her voice when she heard my request. 'The Calling Round The House Drunk Episode' was probably still as fresh in her mind as ever. Whatever her misgivings, she gave me the number, although it saddened me greatly to hear the doubt in her voice. Before ending the call, she asked me what I was up to. The fact that I was a teacher not only impressed her but seemed to make her more relaxed. The last thing she said to me was, 'You will take care, won't you, dear?' She meant it too.

I am not feeling confident about this at all.

I dialled. The phone rang five or six times.

'Hello?'

It was a male voice that had all the authority of someone who earned three times as much as I do. I also noted traces of solicitor who spends his weekends playing rugby.

'Hello,' I said in a thinly disguised, well-spoken voice. 'I'd like to speak to Aggi if I may.'

'She's in the kitchen,' he gruffed. 'Who shall I say is calling?'

'Tell her it's Simon,' I said, reasoning that it would be

Mike Gayle

sheer folly to say, 'Tell her it's Will, her ex-boyfriend. She's probably told you about me. No, I'm not the one with the stupid Morrissey glasses. I'm the one who is completely off his rocker.'

'Hi, Simon,' said Aggi warmly. 'What a surprise!'

'Look, Aggi, it's not Simon, it's me,' I confessed.

She paused, briefly stunned, but bounced straight back totally unfazed. She was good at this.

'Hello, Will,' she said calmly. 'How are you? And why are you pretending to be Simon?'

'I'm fine.' I nervously twiddled the phone cord around my wrist. 'How are you? You all right?'

'Oh, not too bad,' she sighed. 'Work's really busy but that's the way I like it. What are you doing with yourself these days?'

'I've moved to London,' I said coldly. I didn't want her to think this was leading up to some sort of 'Why don't we meet up for a drink' type of proposal. This was strictly business.

'Oh really, where abouts?' she asked.

I was about to drive my mental removal van to somewhere more upmarket when I told the truth. 'I've got a place in Archway. It's only temporary. Flat 3, 64 Cumbria Avenue.' Saying it aloud made it sound less of a hovel than it was. If it hadn't been in Archway, the toilet of the universe, she might have been impressed.

'I know it,' said Aggi. 'A friend of mine used to live in Leyland Avenue, which runs parallel to your road. She was broken into thirteen times in four years.'

Defeated, I changed subjects. 'I teach English at a comprehensive over in Wood Green.' I lit up a cigarette. 'I doubt if you'd know it. It's pretty small. Five hundred kids tops.' I inhaled and coughed violently as if I'd never had one before. 'Sorry about that. I'm just recovering from the flu.' I coughed

276

again, this time a little less abrasively. 'Where were we? Yeah. English teacher. That's me.'

'That's great.'

'Why?' I asked abruptly.

'Because you must be good at it. I always said you'd make a great teacher.'

I grew impatient. We were pretending to be old friends who spoke regularly on the phone. It was disturbing me greatly, because if there was one thing I was certain of, it was that I wasn't her sodding friend.

She was prepared to let the conversation drift along until I got to the point. I took control. 'I can't do this right now. Was that your boyfriend?'

'Yes.'

'Are you in love?'

She finally lost her cool. 'What's it to you, Will? Three years and you still know how to drive me up the wall. What do you want? You don't really honestly want to know, do you?'

'No,' I replied calmly, hoping that the serenity of my denial was needling her. 'I don't, but you want to tell me, don't you?'

She didn't say anything.

'Look,' I said, 'just tell me, okay?'

Playing me at my own game, she calmed down.

'Yeah, I suppose I do,' she said. 'We get on well. We have a lot in common . . .'

I interrupted. 'Like?'

'You want a list?' She was angry now. 'Well, we both like being part of the human race. We both like taking things as they come. Neither of us are obsessives. We both real-ise there's more to life than what's on TV. We both like to have a laugh. We both know where we're going. We're prepared to give each other space. We both want to do what we can to fight injustice. Do you want me to carry on?'

The only thing I could think of to say was: 'A match made in heaven.' It was an empty, facile statement. It didn't make me feel better.

Aggi's tone changed. No longer fired by anger – instead it was powered by sympathy. Not sympathy for me, but for the man she had been in love with all that time ago. 'Will, are you drunk? I know it's your birthday. Why are you ringing me today of all days?'

'Because.'

'Because?'

'Yeah, because.'

Her patience finally ran out. 'I'm going to put the phone down. I'd really like it if you didn't phone me again.'

'No,' I said sulkily. I flicked a long stem of ash from my cigarette onto the carpet. '*I'm* going to put the phone down.'

'You're being childish.'

'I'll take that as a compliment coming from you.' I stubbed the cigarette out against the side of the bed. 'Don't worry, I won't phone you again. I've got what I wanted.'

'And what was that?'

'To topple you off that pedestal I put you on,' I said confidently, 'and baby you're gonna come crashing down!'

She put the phone down.

Looking back at the conversation I like to think that I won – use of the word 'baby' without the faintest degree of irony notwithstanding– I mean, I got quite a few blows in, I thought. But deep down, as always, it was Aggi who had won. She hadn't given me a second thought in the last three years. I didn't mean anything to her at all. And this was the first time I had really understood this. I'd spent nearly three years of my life with her and she'd binned them without a second thought. *I bet she can't even remember getting off with Simon*, I thought to myself. *Why hadn't I asked her about Simon? That would've scored me some points.*

I felt relieved. In a way I couldn't believe I'd carried a torch for her this far – I should have used it to set fire to her years ago. For three years it had been my constant hope that one day she would come back to me. I had even purposely chosen relationships that I knew would have a limited shelf-life because I wanted to be able to dump them at the drop of a hat – at the first sign from Aggi. I never wanted any of them. I just didn't want to be alone. I was a user. At school being called a 'user' was the third worst insult, only surpassed in grievousness by '. . . and your mum' and 'No mates'. It meant you didn't like people for who they were but what you could get from them. In a way I suppose I'd used Aggi. I got someone to listen to me moan about life, watch episodes of *Blackadder* with, someone to kiss when I needed warmth, someone to understand me and someone to make it All Right when everything was All Wrong. She got nothing. She was my Legendary Girlfriend but I wasn't her Legendary Boyfriend. And it was only now that it was too late that I realised this.

I called her back. Her boyfriend answered.

'Is Aggi there?' I asked, completely unsure of what it was I was going to say to her.

'She's in the bathroom. Look, who is this? Is this Will?'

There was little point in lying. 'Yes.'

'You've really upset her, you offensive piece of crap. I've a good mind to come round to your place and beat some politeness into you.'

I lost the plot. 'You don't know what an evil bitch she is. You don't know. But you will. You'll find out when she sleeps with your rugby playing mates. She's probably already started on the scrum half. Then it'll be the tight head prop, then the loose head, then the hooker, then the wingers, then the full back . . . what am I talking about? She's probably had 'em all by now, one after the other. Yeah, she'll be starting on the opposing team next . . .'

I didn't hear what he had to say in reply. I slammed down the phone. It was an evil, spiteful thing to do but I didn't care – just like she didn't care about me. My eyes locked on the scrap of paper where I'd written Aggi's number. I picked it up and moved to the kitchen, pulling her photo down off the wall as I passed. Turning on a cooker ring I simultaneously set fire to the photo and her phone number. As the flames licked their way up to my fingers I let the ash fall in the sink, watching the fragment embers until they burned out. I half expected the fire alarm to come on but it didn't. I turned on the tap. Soggy jet black ash blocked up the plughole.

To celebrate my freedom, I lit another Marlboro Light, opened the window and sat on the ledge even though it was drizzling outside. I wanted to feel like a huge weight had been lifted off my shoulders but I felt exactly the opposite. I'd always secretly credited myself with a little bit of intelligence. I thought I was smarter than the average bear. So it came as a bit of a shock to discover that I was as much of a mug as anyone else.

Ash fell onto my leg. I made a move to flick it off but didn't bother because it didn't hurt.

After a while it got too cold on the ledge, my jeans were soaked through to my underwear and I could barely see out of my glasses. Back inside and lying in bed under the duvet, I wondered what Aggi was thinking about this very second. She must have thought I was mad calling her out of the blue after three years. She was half right, I suppose, I did call because of my birthday. Maybe it was the symmetry of it all. A reunion three years after she dumped me would've fitted in well with my romantic view of her. What a gal, eh? Comes back to me on the anniversary that she chucked me away – now that's what I call stylish. I wanted to blame someone but the only person here was me. I sat down and did some calculations. Three years I'd spent wishing she'd come back to me – roughly 11.5 per cent of my life. I searched the room for a suitable metaphor and spied a half drunk can of Coke. It took a while but I calculated that 11.5 per cent of a 330ml can of Coke was – roughly speaking – three mouthfuls! *Sodding sod! I've wasted three mouthfuls of the only can of Coke I'm ever going to get!*

In the bathroom, the light on and the extractor fan in full swing, I gave myself a pep talk. Half talking to my Audrey Hepburn poster and half talking to the mirror above the toilet, I told myself that this was it. I wasn't going to take life lying down any more. Nothing was going to stop me from doing all the things I talked about doing but always found an excuse for never bringing to fruition. For the last three years I'd been living in a state of limbo. I'd been going to the same places, hanging out with the same people, listening to the same music – doing the same everything as a living monument to Aggi. I'd become chief curator in the National Museum of Ex-Girlfriends. I was stuck in the past unable to get on with the future because everything I ever wanted *was* in the past. No. Enough is definitely a-sodding-nough.

Back in the main room, I lit another cigarette, and stood on the bed to get as close as I could to the smoke alarm. Taking a deep drag, I blew right into the sensor and under the cover of the siren I yelled: 'Things are going to change!'

My hands trembled as I picked up the phone. I didn't know why, really – there was nothing to be nervous about at all. I'd already envisioned what would happen: I'd say hello, she'd say hello, we'd talk about life, the universe and everything; I'd make some facetious comment that would make her laugh; we'd have a good time; I'd forget all about Aggi. I'd feel human again.

'Hello?'

'Er, hello, is that Kate?' I asked an unfamiliar voice.

'No, it's her flatmate. Who's this?'

'Oh, it's Will,' I said, taken aback. It hadn't occurred to me that Kate's flatmate ever answered the phone. 'Is she there?'

'Oh, you're the guy she's been talking to all weekend,' said Paula, lacing her voice with mock surprise. 'She's off her tree, is that one. She's been talking about you non-stop. I'm surprised she didn't pick up the phone herself, she's been hovering by it all afternoon. You said you'd phone her back straight away, you lying sod. Tell me, why *are* men so crap?'

If Kate's flatmate was trying to embarrass me she was doing a particularly good job of it. The thought of someone this shallow being conversant with the intimacies of mine and Kate's relationship annoyed me greatly; she was sullying the beautiful thing we'd created. I grew impatient. 'I don't know why men are so crap. I only know why I'm crap. Could you put her on, please?'

'You're keen,' said Paula, clearly pleased to discover she was capable of winding me up. 'That's a good quality in a man. Have you got any friends?' Not a single decent witty comeback or insult came to my lips, my wittiest barbed comment: 'Oh, just sod off, will you?' seemed rusty and dull in comparison.

'Paula!' yelled Kate. 'Get off the extension, will you?' Paula giggled maniacally. 'Stop teasing him.'

I let out a sigh of relief. 'Hi, Kate?'

'Yeah, it's me,' she replied. 'Sorry to have put you through all of that. Paula's in a bit of a mad mood today. Must be something to do with the moon.'

Kate's voice sounded magical, as if it had the power to do whatever she commanded, and right at this moment she had told it to provide me with comfort. I felt like I'd been rescued from the clutches of an evil dragon by a knightess in shining armour. If it had been possible for her to have lifted me up in her arms and carried me to safety, I honestly believe I couldn't have thought of anything I wanted more at this very moment. I took a deep breath.

'Kate, will you marry me?'

'You what?'

I cleared my throat needlessly, hoping that a simple cough would somehow steel my reserve.

'I said, will you marry me? I've been doing a lot of thinking and I've worked out two things: one is that I love you and the other is that I have to act on this new feeling as soon as possible.'

She laughed nervously. 'Are you joking? Because if you are, Will, it's not funny.'

'I am not joking.' My heart smiled as I paused. 'I've never

been more serious in my life. I decided this afternoon that I love you, it's as simple as that. You've changed my life, Kate, you've changed my life more than anyone I've ever met. I need you. I know it sounds melodramatic but it's true.' I bit my lip. I had a lot more to say but I was scared of overwhelming her like I'd done thirteen years ago with Vicki Hollingsworth. 'Look, you don't have to answer me right now if you don't want to . . .'

'How long have I got to think about it?' interrupted Kate, her voice barely audible.

'Three minutes.'

We both laughed.

'Okay,' said Kate still giggling. 'Synchronise watches . . . now!'

For the duration of the three minutes we were silent, lost in a world where only we existed. I listened intently each and every time she inhaled or exhaled. At one point I nearly broke out in laughter, when, for the second time this weekend, I thought about a Sting song, 'Every Breath You Take.' For once, a crucial moment in my life wasn't overwhelmed by thoughts of what might be or might not be. Nothing came in or out from the moment she'd said, 'Okay'. I was so without grounding, floating out of my body, out of this world's experience, that it wasn't until I was well into the second minute that I noticed I hadn't been breathing – listening to her respire seemed sufficient in itself – and it made me happy.

I looked at my watch. The three minutes were up.

'Okay,' said Kate

'Okay, what?' I asked hesitantly.

'Okay, I will marry you.'

'Are you joking?'

'No, I'm more serious than *you'll* ever know,' laughed Kate. 'You're the most important person in the world to me. I love you. Do you know how I want to die? I want to die saving your life.'

I was speechless.

'Don't worry, I was only joking,' she reassured. 'I do love you though. I spent the afternoon making you a birthday card. Can I read it to you? It's got a picture of Jimi Hendrix on the front that I cut out of *Q* magazine. I've put a speech bubble in his mouth that says, "I say a little prayer for you". Inside, it says "Dear Will, Happy Birthday. My prayer for you is that I hope you never have to spend another birthday without me. Ever yours, K."'

I was touched, the thought of her cutting things out and gluing them down solely for my benefit brought tears to my eyes.

'Thanks. It's a really nice thought.' I looked around my room despairingly. 'I'm just sorry I haven't got anything to give you.'

'I've got you,' said Kate. 'What else does a girl need?' She paused as if she'd run out of words. 'So what do we do now?'

'I don't know, I hadn't planned this far ahead.' I stood up and paced around the edge of the room as far as the telephone cord would allow. 'I suppose we should tell our parents.'

'My mum will be overjoyed,' said Kate. 'I spent the whole of my teens telling her I'd never get married and look what you've made me do. My dad will be impressed too. He's never liked any of my old boyfriends but I know he'll like you. I just know he will.'

I gazed out of the window. A thin covering of grey dirt coated the pane. The garden was overrun with tall yellow flowered weeds and stinging nettles. Next door's dog was nowhere to be seen. I could hear kids playing football but couldn't see where they were. 'Both my folks will be pretty stunned,' I said quietly. 'My mum will think that . . . well . . . you know . . .' I paused, embarrassed at the thought of being accused of getting someone pregnant for the second time this weekend. 'How's that for irony? I've got you in the club and we've never even shaken hands.'

'What do you think all this business on the phone has been about?' said Kate earnestly. 'I know more about you, and feel closer and more intimate with you, than any boyfriend I've ever had, even my ex. I've seen the real you, Will. You didn't bother putting on an act because you thought you'd never meet me! What kind of bloke on the pull starts off by talking about his ex-girlfriend?'

'I suppose you're right,' I said, wishing she hadn't mentioned Aggi. Just thinking about her made me feel sick. I changed the subject. 'We've still got to come up with a plan. Where are we going to live and all that?'

'It doesn't matter. I'll come to London . . .'

I stopped her there. I didn't fancy staying here at all.

Samuel Johnson said: 'When a man is tired of London he is tired of life . . .', I thought to myself. He was only half right. I was tired of This Life, and with Kate I'd have the chance of resurrection and redemption.

'No, I'll come to Brighton first thing in the morning,' I said. 'I've always fancied living by the sea. I'll hand in my notice. I'll say I've had a bit of a mental breakdown or something. It won't be too hard to convince them.'

'Okay, whatever makes you happy. Paula's going off on a course in Cheltenham for the week so we'll have the flat to ourselves. What do you like to eat?'

Her question took me by surprise. I was about to say anything with pasta in it but I held back because I didn't know if she liked Italian food. But deep down this was bigger than pasta dishes, this was about fate. I knew that if I said pasta and she didn't like it I'd interpret it as some sort of sign from above that we were completely and utterly incompatible.

'Anything,' I lied. 'I'm not fussed really.'

She paused, audibly mulling it over. 'Okay, I think I'll make you tagliatelli in a spicy tomato sauce. I love it.'

Before I had a chance to register my delight a flood of thoughts erupted from the ground, smashing through the mental dam I had erected. I needed to know she was as serious as I was. 'Look, are you sure you want to do this?'

'Of course I'm sure,' said Kate, so surely, so steadfastly, so assuredly, that I felt the kind of admiration for her normally reserved for pensioners reminiscing over Winston Churchill's 'Fight them on the beaches' speech. 'I'm even surer than you are,' she continued. 'Just because you've been with someone, say, ten years, doesn't mean that your marriage is any more likely to succeed than if you met and married someone ten minutes ago. There's no way that you can accurately predict the future, so why bother trying?'

'But you can reduce the odds of everything going a bit pear-shaped, can't you?' I said, nervously. Next door's dog barked wildly. The palms of my hands began to sweat at an alarming rate. I wiped them on my jeans but within seconds they were literally dripping with perspiration again.

'Everything about love is random,' said Kate calmly. 'So why try and bring order to it? It's not worth worrying about. I know we could just move in together and that would make everything much easier, but it works both ways. It's easier to walk out, it's easier to be unfaithful, it's easier for everything to just disappear. If I'm going to invest my emotions in another human being again then I'm going to make sure if it doesn't work out it'll be the messiest, most savage divorce ever.'

'Like *The War of the Roses*,' I joked. 'Kathleen Turner's finest performance.'

She ignored my aside. 'Splitting up shouldn't be amicable. Not if what you had was love. It's not the way love works; well, at least the kind of love I'm talking about.'

Kate really was Winston Churchill and I was the British Nation. I would fight the enemies of our love on beaches, street corners or supermarket car parks. In short, I was roused.

'I love you,' I said.

'I love you, too,' replied Kate. 'I can't bear to be away from you. I miss you. This is going to sound weird but even though we've only known each other a weekend, I feel like we've created a million memories together. I've gone over everything you've ever said to me again and again in my head. I love your voice. It makes me feel safe.'

'When did you realise?' I asked.

'That I loved you? When you told me the story about the worms dying and how you tried to save them. I thought to myself – that's the man for me!'

I could hardly believe what I was hearing. 'Really?'

'Yeah, really. I like the way you talk about your childhood. You seem incredibly fond of it. I like that. I can tell that you're special. You notice things differently to other people. You torture yourself for not being this go-getter kind of person, but you are what you are, so why change? Even though you don't think so, you *are* important and you *have* made a change. Look what you've done to my life in three days. Before I spoke to you the biggest thing on my horizon was trying to work out how I was going to afford to pay back my grant cheque. Now all I've got to worry about is you.'

Kate asked me when I'd realised that I was in love with her. I rolled the question around in my head, momentarily sitting down on the bed to aid my thinking processes. 'I didn't decide,' I said shakily. 'It just happened. When I picked up the phone I realised that out of the billions of people on the planet, you were the one I wanted to speak to the most. It was like the deepest part of me took control and said what it felt, unafraid of embarrassment or rejection or any of that other stuff that normally leaves me paralysed with fear. I didn't think. I just was. Normally I find it necessary to have a three hour debate with myself just to decide what flavour crisps to buy, and here I am making the decision of my life purely on instinct. I kind of feel like Stone Age Man. Quick, I feel the need to hunt and gather.'

Kate laughed. 'I know exactly what you mean. Y'know, I didn't need three minutes to think about my answer. The minute you asked me I knew the answer was yes. A mate of mine, Becky, does psychology at Cardiff and she told me this fact: apparently when you're asked a question, whether you want to or not most people answer straight away in their heads and then spend the time available to them trying to make sure they're right. The instant you asked me I knew the answer was yes.'

'So what do we do now?' I asked.

'You ask me properly,' replied Kate.

'What do you mean? Get down on my knees?'

'Yes. And be quick about it.'

'Okay. Kate . . .'

'Are you down on your knees?' enquired Kate doubtfully.

I was astonished at the depth of her insight into my personality. 'How did you know I wasn't down on my knees?'

'Well, were you?' countered Kate.

'No, but that's beside the point,' I laughed. 'You ought to trust me, you know. I'm your husband to be.'

'And I'm your wife to be so you'd better watch out. Hurry up.'

I got down on one knee.

'Look up as if you were gazing straight up at me,' said Kate.

'Okay, I'm looking up as if I was gazing up at you,' I said. My knee began to wobble. I focused my attention on the right-hand corner of the curtains. 'I've even got my hand outstretched as if I were holding your hand. "Would you do me the honour of becoming my wife?"'

'Yes,' said Kate matter-of-factly. 'Now it's my turn. I'm down on my knees and I'm holding out my hand as if I'm holding yours and gazing up at your beautiful face. I love you, Will. Will you marry me?'

'I, Will, will.'

We both laughed.

There was a long moment of silence when I felt neither of us really knew what to say or do next. Kate wasn't playing around, this was for real, which made me feel excited and exhilarated. I had so much adrenaline shooting through my veins that it wouldn't have been enough to simply pace around the flat trying to expend it, I wanted to run, to Brighton preferably. Over the moon? I was high jumping the Milky Way and sprinkling star dust in my hair!

'We've got a lot of things to sort out,' I said, drawing a deep breath in an attempt to steady my breathing. 'I've got to tell my parents about this and sort out how I'm going to tell the school that I'm leaving. I know this is going to be hard but I think we ought not to phone each other again today. Let's just wait until I come over to Brighton tomorrow morning. Then we can talk until we're blue in the face. I think we both need some time to get our heads around this; plus, I'm afraid the phone bill is going to end up so large we'll have to take our honeymoon in Skegness.'

'I like the sound of a week in Skegness with you,' said Kate joyfully. I closed my eyes and tried to encrypt that enchanting sound in my head. 'But I suppose you're right, we do need to calm down a bit. Okay, let's make a pact we won't call or speak to each other until you come to Brighton . . . unless there's an emergency.'

'What sort of emergency?' I asked.

'You know, deaths, births, fires, pestilence, irate parents.' There was a brief pause. 'I love you,' said Kate as a good-bye.

'I love you, too.'

6.34 P.M.

I was so filled with *joie de vivre* that I wanted to tell the world that I – yes, me, William Kelly, cynic *par excellence* – had found love. In the end, however, I decided against informing the inhabitants of Archway of my newfound love. Instead, for some considerable period of time I lay very still on the bed, listening to the sound of my heart beating until hunger drove me into the kitchen. My evening meal consisted of two slices of dry toast as I didn't have the energy or inclination to 'cook' and I'd used the last of the Flora in the construction of my Pot Noodle sandwich.

The piles of exercise books propped against the wall which all required marking pricked my conscience, compelling me to propose the suggestion that even if I wasn't going to school tomorrow, I should at least fulfil this small requirement of my job description. I didn't mark them, of course, as in truth my motivation had less to do with professional pride or guilt than it had to do with avoiding calling my parents, my mother in particular. My newfound positive attitude to life, however, wouldn't let me kid myself – not any more. I was determined not to worry. I could tell my parents, my brother, my Gran, my friends – without fear of what they might say – because finally, I had something I could believe in.

My mother

'Mum, listen,' I said, employing the same tone of voice I'd used four years ago to tell her that Tom had broken his leg playing football.

'What is it?' she gasped, immediately recognising the gravity of the situation.

I cleared my throat to postpone the inevitable temporarily. 'I'm getting married.'

My mother was silent. She wanted desperately to believe I was joking. 'What for? Who to? Do I know her?'

Questions. Questions. Questions. This reaction was typical of my mother. When faced with a problem her natural instinct was to interrogate her subject until she was better informed than even they were. It was like *Mastermind* only in reverse: her chosen speciality was my love life, but it was she who got to ask the questions and I who had to answer them. This was very weird.

I told her the story from beginning to end. She listened attentively, but it was clear that the story made little sense to her. In her world, things like this just didn't happen.

My mother's first words were: 'Oh, Will, what is it? You haven't got her . . .' I knew she wouldn't finish the sentence. I contemplated finishing her sentence for her just for a laugh, but I feared the missing word's shock factor had the potential to put her heart in arrest, if not kill her on the spot.

I comforted her. 'No, you're not going to be a gran. You're going to be a mother-in-law.' She let out a sigh of relief. 'It's nothing like that. It's love. I love her more than I've ever loved anyone.'

'But what about your job?' she questioned. 'You've only just got going. Won't they have something to say about running off to Brighton?' Again, this was classic 'my mother'. Practical considerations were always top of her list; while all things spiritual were right at the bottom, just below embroidered toilet roll covers.

I explained to her what I was going to do about my job and even as I spoke it was plain to me how flimsy and ill conceived my 'plans' were, but it did nothing to shorten my stride towards making them happen. I told her more details about Kate: how her laugh sounded like summer; her breath like the breeze on a beautiful day; and most importantly of all, how I truly believed she thought the world of me. My mother remained unmoved.

'Don't go throwing your life away, Will,' she said losing control of her voice. She was close to the Edge. I decided to be more careful with my words. She had never thought it necessary to need much of an excuse to cry, and with a situation tailor-made for the shedding of tears on her door-step, unless I could convince her what I was doing was the right thing, she would break down. I'd never made my mother cry before. And I didn't want to start now.

'I'm not throwing my life away, Mum,' I said warmly. I looked around my sad, messy little flat. This was my life. This was what I was giving up. Nothing. I became angry that she couldn't see for herself how unhappy I was here. 'I'm not throwing my life away,' I said acerbically, 'I'm getting married. There's a difference, you know.' Before I'd even come to the end of the sentence I regretted it. At first Mum didn't say anything in reply; I thought I'd managed to escape retribution, but then she started to cry.

I felt awful. 'I'm sorry.'

'It's a big step, you know,' she said sobbing. 'You shouldn't do things like this lightly. Look at what happened to me and your father.' I wanted to say I'd rather not look at them because it would've been a clever thing to say, but I didn't because I'd already hurt her more than I thought I could endure. Instead I kept quiet, dwelling upon my parents' marriage. As much as I loved them both, they weren't particularly good advertisements for holy matrimony, but neither were they particularly good advertisements for joining the human race. In the end, I decided, it made no odds.

'Yeah, I know it is,' I said. 'And I'm not doing it lightly, Mum. I won't be any more sure in ten years than I am right now, because I am 100 per cent sure.'

'What's her name?' she asked.

'Her name's Kate.' The words came out so quietly that I wasn't sure she'd heard them.

'Kate what?'

My mother wanted more details, they were the only things that made sense to her. Facts, figures, information – The Tangible.

'Er, I don't know,' I said faltering. I tried desperately to remember. 'It's Freemans. Like in the catalogue. Kate Freemans.'

My mother couldn't believe this. 'You're getting married to someone and you're not even sure about their surname?'

I looked at my watch. The second hand *was* moving, the watch's mechanism *was* ticking but time felt like it had stopped.

'Listen, Mum,' I said, deciding I'd had quite enough. 'I've told you now. You're obviously upset. We're not getting married right this second so there's plenty of time to get used to the idea.'

She didn't say anything.

'Look, Mum,' I added, 'before I go I've got something else

to confess. I think I've knackered that saucepan you told me not to take.'

She put down the phone.

My father

'I'm getting married.'

My dad remained silent. Unfazed, I continued talking, though it was like communicating with a brick wall. 'Look, Dad, there's nothing to worry about, okay? I'm twenty-six years old. When you were twenty-six you'd already been married two years and you had me to look after. I know you think I'm being rash but I'm not. Do I sound like I don't know what I'm doing?'

He remained silent. And from past experience I knew why. My dad never liked being put on the spot. He liked to consider things in his own time before passing judgement on them. Not that his considered reaction would have been any more promising than his unconsidered, but at least given his own time he would have known exactly what he wanted to say.

'Marriage?' he said, unsure of his words. 'Why? Why this way? Is it because of the divorce? The divorce had nothing to do with you. I thought you were okay about it.' It wasn't like my father to use pop psychology to come up with a causal link between the divorce and my getting married. He didn't believe in conditioning or the influence of environment. He once told me that everyone should be responsible for their own actions and not getting enough love or attention was no excuse for being a thug. 'You can't excuse Hitler everything he did just because his mother made him wear short trousers,' he announced one day, more to the television programme which had provoked this reaction than to us, his family.

'I don't know, it just is,' I said, focusing on why marriage was the answer to all my problems. 'I'm fed up with all the what-ifs life throws up, Dad. I'm fed up of them all. I'm fed up with waiting for life to happen before I can have a life. If I don't do this one thing the way I want to do it then I really will be a failure. She's everything I've ever wanted. I can't let go.'

'Can't it wait a while?' he said, bitterly. He was angry now and so was I, but not about what he was saying. I was angry because it had taken me so long to work out where I'd been going wrong all along. *All this wasted time that I'll never get back again.*

'Wait for what, Dad?' I retorted angrily. 'Wait for you to talk me out of it? Wait for me to talk me out of it? Haven't you ever felt the need to trust your own judgement? Just this once I need to listen to what *I'm* saying. It's like there's a voice inside me that I've always shouted down or ignored, but for once I'm going to listen to it. I have to listen to it because I think it's making sense.'

I laughed inwardly. This was *Pretty In Pink*, *East of Eden*, *St Elmo's Fire* and *The Breakfast Club* rolled into one. Be that as it may, I couldn't hold in what I had to say just because I was treading on the same hallowed ground as James Dean, Molly Ringwald, Emilio Estevez, Judd Nelson or thousands of other celluloid coming-of-agers trying to navigate their way through to adulthood. My life would resemble a teen movie until the day I died – I guarantee I'll be the only eighty-year-old man in the world suffering from teen angst.

After my speech, my dad refused to say anything for a while. I told him about all of the beautiful things I saw in Kate and how she made me feel, but I was fighting a battle that had been lost before the first bullet was even fired. His silence did nothing to hide his feelings, he was angry and disappointed (in that order). Still, I felt pleased that I'd had the guts to tell him – the old me would never had done that.

'It's a real shock,' said Dad, finally breaking his silence. 'But if you really do love this girl then what can I do? I just worry. That was the job I was given when you arrived twenty-six years ago. I suppose you're not the only one with an inner voice, son, I've got one too. And it's telling me I've raised a fine son. Happy birthday.'

My brother

'I'm getting married.'

'I know. Mum and Dad both went ballistic,' said Tom excitedly as if my life was a *Sun* exclusive. 'Mum started crying and Dad came around and said he thinks you're mad. Mum was straight on the phone to Aunt Susan to see if she could try and persuade you out of it.'

'Why hasn't she phoned then?' I enquired suspiciously.

'She told her that she wouldn't do it,' he said. 'Mum didn't say why, but I think Aunt Susan thinks Mum should mind her own business.'

It was good to know that someone was on my side. Aunt Susan was right, it wasn't anyone's business but my own. *I'm twenty-six*, I thought to myself, *I don't need anyone's approval*.

I asked Tom what he thought.

'I think it's a bit weird but it's cool,' he said absent-mindedly. 'To tell you the truth I never thought you'd ever get over that Aggi bird.'

'Are you playing that sodding computer game?' I asked threateningly.

I heard him put it down on the table next to the phone.

'No,' he said defensively. 'Well, what about Aggi?'

'It's over.'

'This girl, Kate, did you really meet her this weekend or are you just winding them up?' he asked. I retold the story adding a few details that I hadn't thought my parents would have been interested in. Tom was completely unmoved by it all but listened intently. When I finished all he said was: 'I don't get you.' He wasn't being thick on purpose, he'd inherited my mother's literal mentality. The concept of higher love eluded him too.

'I've only ever talked to her on the phone,' I told him.

He laughed, still unsure whether to believe me.

'It must've been an excellent conversation,' said Tom.

'It was,' I replied.

My Gran

'I'm getting married.'

'I know, dear,' said Gran. 'Your mother told me not ten minutes ago.' She sounded sad. I hated disappointing her.

'I'm sorry, Gran,' I said.

'What for, dear?'

'For doing this all wrong. Mum and Dad are furious . . .'

'Never mind them,' she interrupted. 'The important question is are *you* happy?'

Whereas my mother asked every question but the important ones, Gran asked the important questions and worried about the details later. Apart from her narcotics fixation, my Gran was all right.

'I am, Gran,' I said happily. 'Yes, I am.'

'Then that's all that matters. Your parents have got every-thing all muddled up. They don't know what's really impor-tant in life. At least it looks like you've got your priorities right, Will.'

'Kate's lovely, Gran,' I said. 'You'd really like her.'

'I like her already,' she said.

Those four words cheered me up immensely.

'Do you know what?' continued Gran. 'They've forgotten what it's like to be in love, your parents. No disrespect to them, I suppose it's their way. During the war with so many young men going off to fight, never sure if they'd ever come back, people got married as soon as they knew it was love. Straight to the church and no messing. When you don't know how long your next minute's going to be you soon learn to take time seriously.'

Alice

Before I had a chance to tell Alice about Kate and me, she told me she had some news of her own: she'd not only managed to book her three-month world trip, she'd booked on a flight to New York leaving on Monday afternoon at 4.00 p.m. too. I was shocked at the speed of her actions. I hadn't had the opportunity to give her leaving much thought, but in the split second available to me I gave it my fullest attention. It was a bad idea. The worst she'd ever had. Right up there with going platinum blonde (for three weeks when she was nineteen – I'd called her Andy Warhol for weeks afterwards) and going out with Simon. She thought she needed space but I knew she needed friends – me especially. That was my considered reaction. I took another split second to reconsider it. I was being selfish. It wasn't about her happiness, it was about

301

mine. I didn't want her to go because I didn't want to miss her. I wanted her to be here for me. All I could think to myself was that I'd already lost one friend this weekend. I couldn't afford to lose another. My conscience was well aware of the fact that I wasn't considering for a second that she might need something different. She'd decided to deal with Bruce's leaving in a more constructive way than spending the next three years moping, moaning and miserable. I felt ashamed of myself and told her in an overwhelmingly enthusiastic manner just how happy I was for her. She gave a short, sharp but unsteady laugh and joked about sending me a postcard. I told her not to send it to London. She asked me why not and I told her the reason.

'I'm getting married.'

She didn't say anything.

'Alice, I'm getting married. It's true.'

She remained silent. Rather optimistically I hoped that she was simply lost for words so I began the story which by now had formed itself into a ten-minute after-dinner speech – all that was missing were the cigars and the ten-year-old brandy – but before I could tell her I was going to Brighton, however, she started to cry. I wondered whether I was being insensitive, what with Bruce leaving her earlier this morning.

'I'm sorry,' I began.

'What for?' said Alice.

'I don't know. Being happy. You've had a terrible day and the last thing you need is me being so bloody cheerful. It's enough to make anyone sick.'

'It's got nothing to do with you, okay? The whole world doesn't revolve around you, even though you might think it does. You're so self-centred sometimes . . .'

'I thought that's what you liked about me.'

'Yes, go on. Make a joke about it, why don't you?' Alice

was really angry now. 'You're such a bastard, Will, you really are.'

She started crying again. I was at a loss what to do next. This wasn't what I'd expected. I thought she'd be pleased. Three years I'd been moaning to her about Aggi, and now that I was happy Alice thought I was public enemy number one. I thought she'd be happy for me. After all, I was happy for her. We were both finally sorting out our lives and moving on – she had her trip of a lifetime while I had wedded bliss. It was like she'd thrown all the rules of logic out of the window and was making up new ones as she went along. This was very un-Alice. This was uncharted territory.

She stopped sobbing. 'You can't marry her. You just can't.'
She started sobbing again.
She stopped sobbing. 'Why can't you see how wrong this is?'
She started sobbing again.
She stopped sobbing. 'Please don't do this.'
She started sobbing again. This time her tears were even more heartfelt than they'd been this morning.

I patiently waited out her tears as if they were a passing storm and eventually she 'explained' all. She said that she didn't want to see me unhappy and that if I married this girl then I would be unhappy because I was doing it on the rebound. I said three years is a long time to be on the rebound and I was bound to bump into someone sooner or later, but she didn't laugh – she just cried even harder. When those tears passed she told me that Kate was probably after my money, which brought a moment of levity that we both enjoyed. I told her that Kate was as wonderful as a person could be, and that if she could only meet her she'd be bound to like her. Alice disagreed and said that I was just like every other man and that I only thought with the contents of my boxer shorts. I asked her why, when she'd been in support of so many of my ridiculous plans, was she so opposed to this one and she said because this one was the stupidest I'd ever had. I asked her why she was being so weird and she said she didn't know. And I asked her if it was Bruce and she said no. I asked her if she was having her period. Her reply was both physically impossible and potentially unrewarding.

'Listen,' I said, hoping what I was about to say would miraculously change her view of the situation, 'you will come to the wedding, won't you, because . . .'

'Over your dead body!' she hissed.

'That's a no then?'

She started to cry again.

'It's just that with me not talking to Simon and not being on particularly good terms with the rest of the human race, I was kind of hoping you'd be my best man. Your speech would be much funnier than his would anyway.'

'Cheers,' said Alice through her tears, 'but I won't be coming. Everything's going to change, Will! Everything's going to change!'

'Nothing's going to change,' I reassured, even though I wasn't entirely convinced I was telling her the truth. In a way she was right, we'd reached junctures in our lives that would take us in different directions. I couldn't quite see why my marriage should make such a difference to our relationship, when she'd been living with Bruce for five years, but for some reason I knew that it would. One day soon the circumstances that we now found ourselves in would take their toll. It was just a matter of time.

After a moment's silence she sighed wearily and said, 'You've got to do what you've got to do.'

I tried to think of something comforting to say but the only thing I could think of to say was: 'Ditto.'

Martina

'I'm getting married.'

Martina didn't say a word. I wondered whether she'd misheard me. 'Martina, I'm really sorry but I'm getting married.'

It was entirely in my imagination but I was certain I heard her heart break.

'Martina, I'm sorry,' I said. And I truly meant it. 'I'm really sorry. Are you all right?'

She put the phone down.

Simon

As Simon's phone rang for what seemed like years I thought deeply about how much I hated him. Granted, for best mates we had never been particularly close, but we were all each other had and he hadn't seen that. And that's what hurt. And so now I wanted him to die. I really did. But before his death I wanted him to know that I'd finally found happiness. Because now, more than ever, I could see that Simon – irrespective of whether success or failure lurked around the corner – would one day wake up to discover that he was Fat Elvis, bloated by excess, talent slashed up the wall, wearing totally ridiculous clothes and lonely as hell.

His answering machine clicked on. I didn't want to leave a message – I wanted him to hear it from me. Just as I was about to put the phone down he picked up.

'Will . . .' He started crying.

I didn't say anything. I was getting tired of people crying on me. I decided he was either having some sort of premeditated crisis to get back in my good books or was exploring new emotional avenues to inspire material for the album.

'Will, me and Tammy have split up.'

This was no big surprise and certainly nothing for Simon to get all weepy about. He didn't care about anyone but himself – these tears weren't for Tammy.

He stopped crying and told me what had happened. Simon had come home to find Tammy crying (yes, she was at it too) on the sofa. In her hand was a packet of three condoms which she'd found in the case of his acoustic guitar – there was only one condom in it. Tammy had been on the pill since she'd met Simon so she concluded that two missing condoms added to one boyfriend whose eye for the ladies was well documented, equalled infidelity. Despite Simon's uncanny ability to tell the most outrageous skin-saving lies convincingly, just like his previous confession to me, he'd felt compelled to tell Tammy the truth. Yes, he had cheated on her; yes, he had been sleeping with someone else and no he didn't love her any more. She'd packed her bags and left without saying another word.

'Why did you do it?' I asked.

'What, go off with someone else?'

'No. Why did you tell her the truth? What's the thing you've got with the truth? Why did you tell me about you and Aggi?'

Simon paused, but it wasn't theatrical. He seemed genuinely lost for words. 'I don't know.' His voice sounded croaky. He coughed. 'Hang on a sec. I need a fag.' He coughed again. 'The reason I told you and Tammy the truth is that I fell in love. It sounds stupid and I know you think I'm talking out of my arse but it's true. The band were playing at a university gig down in London. I met a girl there. At first it was just a bit of a laugh, just like it always is, but then suddenly it wasn't. I used to tell her the band were touring a lot so she never hassled me about being away so much. I saw her for about six months. And then one day I was flicking through "S" in the rock and pop section in HMV when I thought about this girl and I couldn't get her out of my head. That's when I knew I had to do it. I called her up and dumped her. And then I wrote her a letter in case she didn't get the message.'

In spite of my hatred I was hooked. The thought of Simon being in love was just too much to contemplate. I lit a cigarette and told him to continue.

'I realised I was falling in love and I didn't like it. I've only got to look at you to see what love can do. It's such a crap, pointless emotion. All that intensity, all that demanding, no one could voluntarily want to be in that sort of condition.'

I laughed. Simon had a heart? This was too weird. It was a given. One of those irrefutable laws of the universe. Energy cannot be created or destroyed. All barbers are mad men. Simon doesn't give a toss about anyone but himself.

I still didn't understand. 'But why did you tell me and Tammy the truth?'

'I told Tammy the truth because I'd never loved her. I'd never even told her I liked her. So the least I could do was tell her the truth. And I told you because this weekend I realised I'd made a huge mistake. The biggest mistake of my life. I'm still in love with the girl that I dumped and I don't know where she is or how to contact her. I've never felt like this before. I can't sleep. I can't eat. I can't listen to music. I even split up the band today. The record contract, the album, everything I've spent my life working towards is history. On Friday I realised that if I'm like this after three weeks without her then what you've been going through this last three years must have been torture – and so I owed you the truth. I'm sorry, I really am. Will, I love this girl so much I don't know what to do.'

Simon was being real. He meant every word. It was hard not to feel sympathy for him but I managed it. I was glad he was hurting. I was glad that he knew what it was like to be in pain. I silently whispered a prayer of thanks to the gods of malice who had obviously heard my pleas and come up trumps. I had to rub it in. I didn't even need to tell him about my forthcoming nuptials, Simon's life was falling apart, and that was all that mattered.

'What's her name,' I asked, wondering what kind of girl could bring the mighty, magnificent Simon to his knees.

He took a long drag on his cigarette. 'Kate,' he said. 'Her name's Kate.'

```
10.04 P.M.
```

The world's not that small. Of course it was her. I checked all the details. Where did she go to university? The University of North London. What was her surname? Freemans – like in the catalogue. What colour was her hair? Reddy brown. What was her favourite film? *Gregory's Girl*. Where did she live? If I had any hope at all that our Kate Freemans were similar but separate Kate Freemans, cast into the public arena by the gods of fate just to pull my plonker more than was necessary or indeed, healthy, Simon's answers crushed it instantly. Kate had lived in my flat. When Simon had dumped her she'd told him that she was going to leave London. As I was in need of a flat Simon, callous bastard that he was, had passed this information on to me but lied about his source. He asked me why I was asking all these questions so I lied, and said it was because I thought it was really funny. I put the phone down and fell into a deep shock.

> *Kate and Simon.*
> *Kate and Simon.*
> *Kate and Simon.*
> *Kate and sodding Simon.*

The whole concept was too much to bear. It was impossible

even to begin to comprehend the sheer scale of devastation Simon's revelation was wreaking inside me. I just couldn't face it. So I didn't. I locked 'Kate and sodding Simon' in a box marked 'Just don't – all right?' and tossed it into the darkest corner of my mind, promising myself on pain of death that I would never go there. Some might call it denial but the only word I had for it was survival.

I needed a diversion and I needed one quick. I turned on the radio. *The Barbara White Show* had just started. She was telling the listeners (aka 'you gorgeous people') they were the most important part of the show: 'You can have the best experts in the world,' she said drooling over each word, 'the best Agony Aunt money can buy, but without you and your problems, it doesn't mean a thing.'

'. . . and thank you, Patricia. I hope everything works out okay for you and the children. Okay, next on the line is Will, from Archway, North London. Hi, Will, or is it William? You're through to *The Barbara White Show*. What can I do to help you?'

'Hi,' I said nervously. I looked around the room for something to drink. There was a tiny splash of yesterday's tequila in a Tupperware cup that hadn't been cleared away. I took a swig. 'You can call me Will, Barbara.'

'I know you feel nervous,' gushed Barbara. 'I am too. Just tell your story in your own time.'

It was an utterly inane thought, but it suddenly occurred to me that she really did sound like she did on the radio. I took another sip of tequila, coughed and wondered what the thousands of listeners 'out there' thought I sounded like. When I was a kid I used to cup hands behind my ears and try and imagine what I sounded like to other people. It never worked, not unless of course I actually did sound hollow and echoey.

Barbara mechanically peppered my narrative with reassuring 'uh-huhs' and the odd 'hmmm yes' – the same as she did with every caller – but as soon as I said the word 'marriage' she abandoned auto-Barbara.

'Will, let me stop you there!' exclaimed Barbara. 'I need a recap!' She let out a sigh of mock exasperation. 'So let me get this straight! You got a call from the girl who used to live in your flat and after a couple of hours of conversation you've decided to get married?'

'That's right,' I said, pleased at having got her attention.

'Will, let me tell you, this is a wonderful story!' She clapped her hands and let out a little whoop of joy, the kind only Americans could get away with. 'So let me guess, you're worried that you might not be doing the right thing, huh?'

'Yeah, that's right,' I said, considerably less smugly than before, because I was now feeling more than a little bit stupid and exposed.

'Can I ask you when you first realised that you liked this girl?' asked Barbara.

I considered her question. It was hard to believe it was only a few hours ago. *This morning I was me and now I'm someone else*, I thought to myself. *Or is it this morning I was someone else and now I'm me?*

'Some time this afternoon,' I said staring around the room until I located what I was looking for. 'It wasn't anything in particular that she said.' I put Kate's photo up on the wall next to my bed with Blu-tac. 'Something clicked in my head and I knew she was the one.' The Kate in my photo smiled down at me radiantly.

'Can I ask you how old you are?' enquired Barbara.

Barbara, I felt, was suddenly beginning to get on my nerves. Her fake politeness, accent and probing, grated against me immensely. 'Yeah,' I said, almost spitting. 'I'm twenty-six. Today's my birthday.'

'Many happy returns for the day,' said Barbara paying no heed at all to my annoyance. 'Have you ever been in a long-term relationship before?'

My anger subsided. 'I went out with a girl for three years from roughly when I was twenty to when I was twenty-three,' I said, hoping she wouldn't ask for Aggi's name.

'Was it a mutual break-up?'

I wanted to lie. I needed to lie.

'No,' I said remorsefully. 'She wanted out of the relationship. I think she wanted more freedom. Maybe I was boring her, I don't know. I loved her a lot. I thought she was the one, but I could never get her to think long-term. She got over me straight away, which really hurt. She got on with her life as if I was a minor interruption.'

I'm pleased I've told the truth, I thought. *It's another sign that I have changed. The old me is dead. Long live the new me!*

'Is there anything else I should know?' asked Barbara.

I paused before answering and wondered what kind of details she required. Simon and Kate's box rattled in its secret hideaway. I ignored it.

'She also got off with my best mate while she was going out with me,' I confessed, picturing Aggi and Simon in an embrace. I wondered, too, if I ought to have explained the phrase 'get off' but decided against it. 'I only found this out yesterday.' I paused again. 'Oh, and she also dumped me three years ago today.'

'She dumped you on your birthday? That must've been terrible,' sympathised Barbara.

'It was,' I replied.

'Have you dated other people since?'

'I didn't for the first year,' I confessed. 'I couldn't face even thinking about other girls. In the last two years I've been out with a few, some of them I quite liked too.'

'Can I ask you what went wrong with these relationships?'

'I don't know.' A montage of ex-girlfriends' faces swirled inside my mind. What a question! It would have been easier to tell Barbara the meaning of life than to work out what had gone wrong with them all. I knew the problem was always me, but what it was *about* me I didn't know. 'They fizzled out, or they had to move away,' I told Barbara while still trying to figure it out. 'I thought I was cursed for a while.' I conjured up a reason. 'I think it all went wrong because at the back of my mind I always thought to myself, what would I do if the girl I loved came back and I was going out with someone else? I suppose that's why they all failed.'

'Will, can I stop you there? We're just due for a commercial break. You hang on the line and we'll talk to you just after this . . .'

I was forced to listen to four adverts: Double glazing, a specialist bed company, an athlete's foot cream and an agency that you pay to pay your bills for you. This was hell. I was in hell. I had sunk this low. I wanted to put the phone down but couldn't. This was the first time I'd told anyone the full story. The director's cut of My Life with all the scenes my parents didn't want to know about, and the scenes my friends wouldn't have understood.

'Before the break,' announced Barbara, 'we were talking to Will, from North London, who has asked a girl he's never met to marry him after speaking to her on the phone on Friday. Will, can you continue your story?'

'What else do you want to know?' I asked.

'Why do you think that this relationship will work when all the others failed because of how you felt about your ex?'

'I wasn't sure about that either,' I admitted. 'Which is why I phoned her up this afternoon.'

Barbara could barely contain her excitement. 'What did you say to her? Did you tell her that you were getting married?'

'No. I called her . . .' I paused, searching for the right way to say it. 'I called her to give her one last chance. I didn't tell her that, but that's what the call was about.'

'How did she respond?'

'Well, I hadn't spoken to her for three years. She's living in London with her boyfriend.' I added absent-mindedly: 'She was surprised to hear from me.'

'But how did she respond?' repeated Barbara eagerly.

I stared vacantly into the bottom of the empty Tupperware beaker in my hand. 'I don't know. I think I managed to get her back up. I was fed up that the fact that I'd been a major part of her life for three years didn't mean a thing. I ended up being a bit sarcastic, I suppose.'

'And she didn't stand for it? How did you feel after the call?'

'Devastated. All this time I'd been thinking that there might be a chance that we would get back together . . .'

Barbara interrupted. She couldn't wait to get stuck into that one. 'What made you think that? Did she tell you that?'

'Well . . . no, not really,' I replied. 'She'd told me it was over and that there was no chance that we'd ever get back together,' I said blankly, realising how stupid it all sounded.

'So why did you think that you'd get back together?'

Barbara, in her own 'subtle' way was trying to imply that I was stupid for living a lie, and she was right. I helped her out.

'I don't know,' I said. 'I'm stupid. Perhaps I'm an optimist. I don't know. It's three years today that we split up. I suppose she was on my mind.'

My Legendary Girlfriend

'So, Will, this girl you're going to marry, does she know about all this?'

'She knows about my ex,' I said. 'But she doesn't know that I called her today.'

'Why didn't you tell her?' asked Barbara.

'Because . . . because . . . because,' I paused and examined the empty Tupperware beaker again. 'I . . . er . . . don't know . . . okay . . . er . . . I do know.' I gave up. 'I didn't tell her because then she'd think that I only asked her to marry me because my ex didn't want me back.'

'But isn't that the case?' asked Barbara accusingly, sounding for all the world like a hot-shot lawyer in a court room drama.

'No,' I stumbled. 'Well, yes. But it isn't as simple as that. I had to know one way or the other about my ex in order to get on with my life. I must have had the idea of marrying my new girl in my head all the time. I knew that it wouldn't work if there was a chance I could get back with my ex. I needed to know that my ex didn't want me so I could get on with my life, otherwise I'd just keep thinking about her.'

'Round and round,' said Barbara wearily. 'Just like a roundabout in a children's playground. So what would've happened if your ex had said that she'd take you back?'

'I probably would've gone back to her,' I confessed dejectedly.

'And what about this girl that you were going to marry forever and ever, forsaking all others 'til death do you part?'

'I suppose I wouldn't have married her.'

'How can you consider marriage to someone if there's another partner who looms so large in your past, Will?' asked Barbara.

She had hit the nail on the head. I got out of bed to take a look out of the window because my room felt like it was

315

shrinking. My knees started to buckle before I could reach my destination and so, instead of continuing my journey, I opted to sit on the floor under my own steam before gravity came into force.

'After all that time I'd invested worshipping that woman,' I told Barbara, 'don't you think I owed it to myself to try and get her back? I'm glad she doesn't want me. I want to move on. And now I can.'

'Will, do you want to know what I think?' offered Barbara. 'I think that your ex has confused you so much you don't know whether you're coming or going. Sometimes when you're the partner that has been left, you find it hard to get on with life. You ask yourself the question "Why aren't they hurting as much as I am?" It's not unusual for people in this situation to see hope in the relationship when there is none. I did it myself with my ex-husband. After we divorced I felt that if I was there for him one day he'd realise that he needed me like I needed him. Do you know what happened? He married a girl half my age and invited me to the wedding because he thought I was over him! Can you believe the nerve of that guy? I understand how you're feeling, Will, more than you know. But you've got to ask yourself, why do you want to marry this girl?'

I surveyed my tiny room. I had my answer. 'Because she's made me realise that I can move on. I can finally live my life and think about the future.'

'Marriage is a big step,' said Barbara. 'I know that this girl sounds like the answer to your problems, and she may well be. But I think you've got to ask yourself why this girl you've never seen is so important to you. This kind of thing happens all the time, Will. I had a caller last week who thought she'd fallen in love with the man she ordered office stationery from. When you're on the phone you can be someone different. You can flirt and have fun, secure in the knowledge that you don't have to meet this person face to face.'

'It's not like that,' I protested.

'I'm not saying it is, Will. But what I am saying is that you have to check that it's not. Can I give you some advice? Try and work out whether you've really been *you* on the phone or whether you've been the *you* you wish you were. The girl at the end of the phone is in love with the person she spoke to. But will she be in love with you?'

A gust of wind blew a heavy sheet of rain against the window. Kate and Simon were making another attempt to escape from their box. I shivered. I placed the receiver on the floor and cradled my head in my hands. In less than half an hour Barbara had managed to crumble my rock solid faith into dust.

'Right, that's all we've got time for, Will,' said a tinny sounding Barbara from the floor. 'Thanks for calling. Please, please, call me, Barbara White on *The Barbara White Show*, in the next couple of weeks and tell me and the listeners at home what happened. We found your story riveting.'

1.13 A.M.

The doorbell awoke me from a nightmare in which I was a US Marine being held prisoner in a bamboo hut by a combination of the Vietcong and Aggi. At least I thought it was the doorbell. As no one had rung it during my week's residency it was hard to know exactly what the noise could be. I attempted to ignore it, assuming it was just some dipsomaniac Archway dropout playing funny buggers, and hoped that they'd get bored before I'd be forced to go downstairs and throw water over them. It continued, long, shrill, angry bursts of doorbell for minutes at a time. I stared at the television and wondered if the TV licence people had the technology to monitor TV sets even when they were off. What can I say? It was 1.15 a.m. and I wasn't really thinking straight. I turned over and pulled the duvet over my head. The TV licence people could just sod off too.

Consciousness was once again slipping from me, taking with it the worries of the day, when there was a knock at the door. I checked my watch again. It was now 1.23 a.m. Someone had either let the dipsomaniac dropout in or I was about to get fined £600 for having a TV in my room that was switched off. I pulled the duvet up a bit higher, determined to ditch reality as soon as possible before it all got too much. This time, the rain of blows that smashed against the door nearly took it off its hinges. I crawled out of bed, not even bothering to put on any sort of proper clothing, pulled the door slightly ajar and peered through the gap. The woman from downstairs (she of the Garfield slippers) peered back at me angrily. She wasn't wearing her usual towelling dressing gown. Instead she had on these fluffy sky blue pyjamas with elasticated ankles that made her look like she was wearing a romper suit. Her face was all red and blotchy and her hair was flying off in all directions. Honestly, it would have been impossible for anyone, even the angriest man in Angryland, to have looked more thoroughly enraged.

Peppering the rather short question, 'Do you know what time it is?', with an unfeasibly large number of expletives, Garfield woman began tearing strips off me. Bewildered as I was at being woken up in the middle of the night, I couldn't resist the opportunity to indulge in a spot of neighbour baiting. 'You're banging on my door because you haven't got a watch, you mad cow? Away with you before I call the police!'

She didn't laugh. In fact I was sure that if the door had been open any wider, I would've received a swift Garfield in the crotch.

'It's not enough that you never take your turn with the fire alarm, now you want me to be your personal man-servant! Next time, pal, answer the bloody doorbell when it's for you!'

I attempted to look suitably chastised but in reality I think I probably just looked puzzled. 'I take my turn with the fire alarm! If it's fire alarms you're moaning about, ask the bloke over there,' I pointed across the landing, 'that bugger's never done it.' The expression on her face was one of purest anger. I attempted to calm her down. 'Look, I don't know what you're on about, okay? There was some mad person ringing my bell too, but as I don't know any mad people I reasoned that it couldn't have been for me.'

'I think I can explain,' said a voice just to the side of Garfield woman. 'I thought I'd got the wrong number. I rang this woman's doorbell by accident after you didn't answer yours.'

I opened the door a little wider to take a look at the mystery woman. It was Aggi.

I looked her up and down, not believing my eyes. She was wearing black leggings and a purple kind of smock thing. Her hair was messy. While she wore an expression as uncompromising as Garfield woman's she was still as beautiful as ever.

'I think you'd better come in,' I said warily. I threw a stern look in Garfield woman's direction in case she thought the invitation included her.

Aggi came in, closing the door behind her, but remained standing. I sat down on the bed and felt ludicrously self-conscious. Not only was I wearing nothing but boxer shorts and odd socks, but they happened to be a green pair with Subutteo sized golfers all over them, a farewell gift from my mother. What's more, there was nowhere for the flab around my midriff to hide, so instead it just hung there dejectedly, waiting for me to get The Message. This was the way that the love of my life saw me for the first time in three years – looking like a bucket of lard in novelty underwear. While I pulled on a T-shirt, Aggi averted her eyes, content to gaze despondently around the room, admiring the decor and saying nothing.

I finished dressing, looked up and smiled. 'Hello.'

Aggi's face suddenly contorted with anger as if she'd just turned on a switch marked 'Screaming Mad Banshee

Woman from Hell'. I was scared. The kind of woman that could get angry at a slightly overweight but cuddly bloke in silly boxer shorts, was the kind of woman that would get a six month discharge after pleading temporary insanity.

'I am sooooo angry,' she screamed.

I winced, assuming that she was still smarting from the comments made in regard to her popularity with sportsmen. I considered reminding her that I was wearing glasses but thought better of it.

'Toby wanted to kill you, you know. He wants to smash your face in, and he would, you know. He knows how weird you are. He's waiting in the car outside so don't get any ideas into that warped head of yours.'

'Is he a solicitor?' I asked timidly.

'Yes,' she spat.

'Does he play rugby?'

'Every weekend.'

'Oh,' I said.

I felt about this small, which is to say just a bit smaller than a gnat's knackers. It was like being scolded by my mum, only worse because I didn't have any trousers on and well, my mum would never threaten to get her boyfriend to beat me up, even if she had one. The only good thing was that as far as I could gather, Aggi's boyfriend hadn't told her exactly what I'd said, although I was sure she'd heard enough to get the general impression. It was totally embarrassing. Aggi was unrelenting in her attack – she paced the room saying all kind of nasty and venomous things about me all of which, unfortunately, were true. Every sentence she said began with 'How dare you . . .' I didn't have a leg to stand on. I'd phoned her out of the blue three years after I had any right to and assassinated her character in front of her boyfriend, who could clearly beat me to a pulp with both arms tied behind his back. It was ridiculous. I sat there, head bowed, and took it, if not like a man, then the nearest approximation I could conjure up – a creature half adolescent and half sheep.

When I thought she'd finished I looked up. But I was disappointed to discover that she was far from finished. 'If you ever try and contact me by phone, letter or even try and send me bad vibes, I will go to the police, you bastard. Don't think I won't!'

She turned and opened the door without even looking at me. *This is it, this is her hello and good-bye. Surely I deserve more than this*? It was better to have her shouting at me in my flat than living in the knowledge that the second she walked out all memory of me would be wiped clean – she'd ditch the lot. The good and the bad. It was too terrible to contemplate because if I didn't exist in her head then I didn't exist at all.

'What about you and Simon?' I said, in a manner ranking lower than mumbling.

She turned around, her hand still on the door handle, the expression on her face puzzled. 'What?'

I coughed and studied the soles of my feet. I had a verruca the size of a five pence piece on my heel that I'd never seen before. Without looking up I repeated the question. 'I said, what about you and Simon?'

Slowly she came back in and closed the door carefully with both hands, crossed the room and sat down next to me on the bed.

'He told you, then?'

I nodded.

'When did he tell you?'

'Yesterday.'

'Why did he tell you?'

'Because he's in love.'

Aggi's eyes filled slowly with reluctant tears. I watched them roll down her perfect nose, along the edge of her perfect upper lip and onto her perfect chin. I didn't want her to cry. Everyone was crying this weekend.

'I never meant to hurt you, Will.'

'But you did.'

'It just happened. I was angry that you weren't there.'

I swallowed hard. 'So you got off with my best mate.'

'It was just sex. I didn't love him. It didn't happen again.'

'Does that make a difference?'

She was staring into her lap now, but she met my eyes briefly and said: 'No. I suppose not. At least not to you.'

I edged away from her and began to shake, as if just being in her proximity would cause irrevocable damage. Here she was sitting in my room reminding me of a betrayal that, though it had happened years ago, was as fresh in my mind as if it had happened yesterday – which in a way it had. 'I worshipped you from the moment we met. I adored you. You were all that I wanted. What did I do wrong?'

She started crying. I put my arms around her shoulders. Holding her felt exactly the same. Nothing had changed. It was like travelling to the past in the present – none of it seemed real. I tried to brush away her tears but she just cried even more into my neck, making the collar of my T-shirt damp. She lifted up her head and stared right into my eyes.

'I'm sorry, Will. I'm so sorry.'

I didn't say anything. I wasn't trying to be the martyr, I just didn't have anything to say. She looked so pitiful, her eyes were red and puffy. All I wanted to do was make everything all right.

'You know me. I've never regretted anything,' she said, 'and don't think for a minute that I regret ending our relationship. I don't. We were dead. Going nowhere. But if I could have my time again I would never have done that to you. You don't need to tell me that you loved me. I always knew it. You were my best friend for those three years, Will. I can never repay you for all the wonderful things you did for me. I don't know . . .'

Her words trailed off as she buried her face into my shoulder. I looked down at the top of her head, studying her crown sadly. In a perverse sort of way it was almost worth letting Simon sleep with her just to know that after all this time she really did care – albeit in an abstract fashion. She hadn't forgotten – there was some small part of her that cared enough about me to believe in the concept of regret. I was locked in her head – the one thing she could never get over. This was beautiful. This was more than I could ever have hoped for.

Aggi gradually lifted her head up until her eyes were directly in line with mine, her lips parted, her nose barely an inch away from mine and her head tilted in that magical manner that only ever means one thing. I cast a glance at the door, I couldn't help myself, my thoughts had already raced downstairs in fear that fifteen stone of rugby playing brute was about to burst in and beat me to a pulp. Aggi, seeing my distress, pressed her index finger up to my lips. 'I lied,' she said. 'I just didn't want you to get the wrong idea.'

And then she kissed me.

All at once the universe seemed to make sense. The weight of the world was no longer on my shoulders. This was the feeling that I'd been pining for all this time, and yes it was worth the wait. I couldn't kiss her fast enough. I kissed her face, her hands, her neck – everywhere that was available – but within seconds I was overwhelmed by feelings twice as powerful, twice as destructive and twice as painful as those I'd just experienced.

I pulled away from her in shock. 'I can't do this.'

'I told you Toby isn't here.'

I shook my head. 'It's got nothing to do with him. It's to do with me. *I* can't do this. *I* can't cheat on Kate.'

Aggi's face changed immediately. All the sadness seeped away leaving an expression of quiet defiance. 'Is Kate your girlfriend?' she asked with a touch of sarcasm clearly evident in her voice.

'No,' I replied. 'She's my fiancée.'

I explained the whole story to her even though it hardly made sense to me any more. She nodded at the appropriate moments and laughed at a few inappropriate ones. When I finished I could see that she still didn't believe me. *Seven days ago I wouldn't have either.* I weighed up the situation:

Aggi	Kate
Aggi was here in my room.	Kate was in Brighton.
I'd known Aggi six years.	I'd known Kate two days.
I knew every detail of Aggi's body.	
	I knew every detail of Kate's photo.
I loved Aggi.	But I loved Kate even more.

There was no explanation or rationalisation except to say

that it wasn't guilt talking, it was me. It wasn't that I was over Aggi – three years of intense high-level obsession does not disappear overnight – but it was like this: I'd thought Aggi was the ceiling of my love but Kate had shown me there was something even higher. Overwrought? Yes. Melodramatic? Possibly. The brain-addled words of a troubled soul in love with love itself? No.

'So that's the way it is,' I said after some moments of very uncomfortable silence.

Aggi laughed. 'I can't believe you're doing this, Will. I really can't. But don't insult my intelligence with your pathetic stories. I knew you were bitter but I didn't know it ran this deep.' She stood up, straightening her top and wiping the stray mascara from her cheeks. 'I suppose it's what I deserve. Well, the score's even now. I'll never have to feel guilty about sleeping with Simon again and you get your imaginary girlfriend.'

I looked up at her dejectedly from the bed. 'Yeah, whatever.'

MONDAY

MONDAY

5.45 A.M.

For a few seconds the end of the world was no longer nigh – it had arrived. I, as fully expected, had gone to hell and besides not being quite as warm as I expected, the most notable thing about Hades was that it was very noisy and looked like my flat. I glanced at my watch, it was 5.45. Monday morning. Thanks to Mr F. Jamal's dodgy smoke alarm, The Rest of My Life had begun an hour earlier than anticipated. In less than five hours I'd be in Brighton with Kate, and the smoke alarm, flat, Archway, Wood Green Comprehensive, Italian newsagent's, Simon, Aggi and everything else that sought to rain on my parade would be nothing more than a bad dream.

The fire alarm stopped ringing.

The front door belonging to one of my downstairs neighbours slammed loudly, the vibrations causing my windows to rattle. Peace was restored. I bathed in the silence.

Today is going to be the adventure of my life.

This was the kind of thrill I'd been looking for all my life, a book with an ending you couldn't guess – a Rolf Harris sketch that you couldn't work out until he'd scribbled in the last details with his squeaky marker pen.

Last week I could have predicted my every movement down to the very last detail weeks in advance. 10.00 a.m. Tuesday – English with my year eights. 8.15 a.m.

Wednesday – running up to the school gates attempting to finish early morning cigarette. 11.00 p.m. Friday – in bed asleep dreaming about ex-girlfriend. Now thanks to Kate I don't have a clue what's about to happen to me, but at least I know who it will happen with. Security and adventure – the best of both worlds.

The duvet, which had slipped off the bed during the night, was lying perilously close to the ice-cream stain in the carpet that had refused to die. I pulled it back on the bed, tucking the edges underneath my bum to form a misshapen cocoon, with my head poking out from the top. The draught coming through the windows, seemingly unhindered by the curtains, indicated that the day of my emancipation was a cold one. Straining intensely, I listened out for any other meteorological news. There was no mistaking the gentle yet unrelenting tapping of drizzle against window pane.

My thoughts automatically turned to breakfast but excitement caused by the day's forthcoming events constricted my stomach to a tight ball of muscle – no Sugar Puffs or Honey Nut Flakes, frozen bread or toast without margarine would make it in there today.

In the bathroom, Audrey Hepburn, hand aloft, cigarette-holder drooping daintily from her fingers, greeted me with her usual wistful smile. As I closed the door behind me I turned on the light, positively encouraging the extractor fan to lurch back into life. While in the shower I occupied my mind trying to imagine the Kate in the photo on my wall in three dimensions. Post-shower, I dried myself off using the Towel, wandered into the kitchen and dropped it into the bin. For some, redemption was out of the question.

Cold and naked I stood on the bed to prevent dust, dirt and carpet fibres clinging to my damp feet and meditated on what to wear. First impressions, I reasoned, counted for an awful lot, in spite of what Kate had said. I wanted her to be attracted to me the moment she saw me so that there could be no doubt in her mind that she had made the right decision. Following several changes of clothes I went with a pair of navy blue trousers that I'd bought from Jigsaw's summer sale – a minor blip in my strictly second-hand policy – and an ancient chalk blue Marks and Spencer shirt with huge collars purchased from Aggi's Oxfam. I examined my ensemble in the largest shard of broken Elvis mirror I could find: I looked good enough to eat.

Checking my watch, I began hurriedly packing my ruck-sack, throwing in the remainder of clean underwear – roughly three pairs of pants. I say roughly, because I had included a black pair that my mum had purchased when I was younger than some of the kids I teach now. It had been my intention to go to the launderette over the weekend – it had been one of the things To Do – which, sadly, I never even got around to thinking about let alone doing. I threw in an assortment of T-shirts and jumpers, and cursed my lack of clean socks, throwing in a couple of dirty ones instead, swiftly followed by my duty free cigarettes and picture of Sandy the donkey. My eyes scanned the room in search of things I might have forgotten, while in my head I ticked off a mental list of things I usually forgot: toothbrushes, soap, shampoo – stuff that Kate would be bound to have in her flat. Thinking about Kate reminded me of her cheque. I slipped it into the side pocket of the rucksack.

Sitting on the edge of the bed, staring at the ceiling, I attempted to prepare myself mentally for the day ahead. A radio alarm clock in the next door flat went off and Thin Lizzy's 'Waiting For An Alibi' broke my concentration. A random thought entered my head: I wondered whether I ought to take a present for Kate. Within five minutes this thought had taken precedence over all others and turned itself into a national emergency. I scrambled around the flat searching for something that might constitute a present. My eyes fell on my *Star Wars* video. If she liked *Gregory's Girl*, I said to myself – my reasoning faculties had all but disappeared by now – then she'd probably like *Star Wars*. Genuinely at a loss for a better present, I dropped it into the rucksack and made a mental note to look out for a florist's at Victoria Station.

Ready to brave the elements and with my essentials on my shoulders I took a final look at what I was leaving behind. This flat which had been my worst enemy for over a week now felt like a close friend. We'd shared good times, bad times and mad times. But somehow I was grateful to it.

I was halfway down the stairs before I got the feeling I'd forgotten something important. I tried to fight it – after all, Lot's wife had been turned into a pillar of salt – but the feeling would not subside. I returned to the flat. I checked that the lights were off. They were. I checked the cooker was off. It was. I checked the toaster was unplugged. It wasn't. As I unplugged it I laughed to myself. I had finally become my mother. Every family holiday as far back as I could remember always commenced with the ritual of my mum running around the house maniacally unplugging household electrical items. 'If the house gets struck by lightning,' she used to say, 'anything plugged in will go up in flames and burn the house down.'

Before closing the door I glanced down at the phone. The answering machine wasn't switched on. After rectifying the situation I closed the door, walked out of the flat and stepped into a brand new day.

'Right,' I said, addressing my year eights as they shuffled into the classroom, knocking over chairs, tables and anything else that stood in their paths, 'get out your copies of *Wuthering Heights*, please, and turn to where we left off on Friday.' This simple request resulted in a flurry of fruitless activity: Kitty Wyatt, a tiny mousy-haired girl whose diminutive stature and continually flushed cheeks gave her a remarkable similarity to a garden gnome, ran out of the room crying, swiftly followed by her friend Roxanne Bright-Thomas, who informed me that Kitty was having 'women's problems'. Colin Christie, a thug whose reputation preceded him all the way to the staff room, and the child most likely to have spat on my back, hadn't got his book and was locked in a struggle with Liam Fennel who, quite rightly, wasn't pleased that his own copy was being forcefully commandeered. I ignored them all.

'Lawrence,' I said, pointing to an overweight boy sitting next to the radiator by the window, 'I do believe it's your turn to read today.'

'But, sir,' he complained, 'I read last week!'

'And you did such a good job of it that I'm going to get you to do it again this week,' I replied tersely.

He was right, of course, he had read last week but given the mood I was in since returning from Victoria Station, I

335

didn't really care about being fair, nor was I ever likely
to.

As Lawrence commenced reading and the class settled
down into some semblance of peace, I sat down at my desk
and took the opportunity to gaze out of the window and study
the afternoon sky. In spite of earlier meteorological activities,
the day had in fact turned out very pleasantly indeed: the sun
shone brightly through the oaks, ashes and silver birches
lining the playing fields, cottonwool clouds were dotted about
the heavens, even the oases of grass amongst the sea of mud
that constituted the football pitch appeared to have an added
lustre to them. I opened the window to let a little air in. *Today*,
I thought, as the dark clouds of depression slowly lifted from
me, *is a day possibly worth living.*

I'd actually been sitting on my freedom train. Not at the
ticket office or even the platform – on the sodding train –
rucksack in the rack above my head; in my right hand, the
latest issue of the *New Statesman* (working that 'I give a toss
about politics' look to the max), a Marlboro Light in the other
and both feet resting on the seat opposite. I was literally five
minutes from leaving Victoria Station and fifty-five minutes
from becoming the happiest man alive. But it had felt all
wrong. Not right. Just All Wrong.

I tried not to think about it. I looked out of the window,
speed-read an article on European federalism, counted the
change in my pocket but nothing could shake this feeling.
Within minutes I was back on the platform watching the
last carriage of the 8.55 to Brighton disappear into the hazy
distance.

I called Kate. Dialling her number felt as natural and as
necessary as breathing. I almost forgot why I was calling her
– I just wanted to hear her voice. It was some time before she

answered. She was just on her way to meet me – too excited to wait any longer – and she'd heard the phone ring just as she closed the door. She'd rushed back thinking the worst – that I'd had an accident and was calling her from hospital, or even worse, that the police had found her number on the body of an unidentified corpse in the Thames. I was sorry to disappoint her.

Straight to the point was what the situation called for, any side-stepping of issues was only going to cause more pain in the long run. I took a long, slow breath and patted all over my body trying to locate my cigarettes. 'Kate . . . Listen, Kate. You know that I love you, don't you? I love you more than anything, but I've got to ask you something. I need to know this: if your ex-boyfriend wanted you back would you want to be with him and not me?'

She was honest enough to mull over the question, which many, myself included, would never have dared. It was strange, she had become so used to the more bizarre aspects of my personality that the question and its abruptness didn't faze her for a second. I was odd but she loved me. I was bordering on being unhinged and she didn't care.

She took her time, which was nice of her. She really was weighing up her answer, in spite of the fact that I was so obviously the low fat option. She'd loved Simon so fervently that it would be impossible for her to lie without my knowing. Her love for him hadn't fermented into bitterness. Neither had she stopped loving him. She'd simply filed her love away in a box similar to the one I'd put her and Simon in, and now it was open there could be no stopping it.

'Will, I don't know why you're putting yourself through this. I love you. Nothing's changed since yesterday. My ex isn't going to come back to me. I haven't got a clue where he is. He could be anywhere. And he certainly hasn't got any way of contacting me. There's no point in discussing it, Will. Don't you see? We've been let down by other people but finally we've got someone that we trust. We've got each other.'

I was silent. I was right. I lit a cigarette and slipped another fifty pence piece into the pay-phone. Over the station Tannoy a nasally voiced BR employee announced: 'This is a reminder: Victoria Station is a no-smoking zone.' I returned my mind to the call. I could think of nothing more to say.

'Will, don't go all moody on me now,' said Kate anxiously. 'We're nearly there. You'll be getting on the train. I'll meet you and everything will be all right.'

I wanted to believe her. 'All right?'

She sighed lightly. 'All right.'

I checked my timetable for the next departure. There was another train at 9.35. I slipped the timetable back into my pocket, then took it out, screwed it up and tossed it on the floor. I wouldn't be on the 9.35 or any other train.

'No, it won't,' I said in response to her efforts to comfort me. 'Everything will not be all right. It's not happening, Kate. It's over.'

'Will, don't do this,' she said, trying to stop herself from crying. 'Don't do this. It's not fair. It's not fair. If Aggi told you she wanted you back you'd be there in a shot, wouldn't you? You can't deny it!'

'No. I can't,' I lied. 'And neither can you. But at least you've got hope.'

Kate didn't understand. 'Will, what's this all about?'

Leaning against the back of the telephone booth I slipped gradually to the floor as the will to remain upright left me. The person in the booth next to me, a middle-aged balding man with a sad, pathetic boyishness about his face looked at me with a puzzled expression. I met his eyes – not defiantly, not even passively – I just met them. He removed his gaze straight away and turned his back on me. I returned my attention to the phone.

'Your ex-boyfriend,' I began lifelessly. 'His name's Simon Ashmore. He's in a band – Left Bank. He used to be my best friend. He's not now. He wants you back. He says he's sorry. He says he loves you.'

Kate began to cry. I stood up. I wanted to run after the train just so I could be there to make everything okay.

'But he said he hated me. He said he never wanted to see me again. Why's he come back into my life?'

'Because he loves you.'

'But I love you,' she said.

'And I love you and will always love you. But this isn't meant to be. It's not just about love. You said that love's a random act. It's true, it can happen anywhere at any time with anyone. But this, this is about being in love with the right person – the right person doesn't come along twice in a lifetime. You've found yours, and it's Simon, and that makes me happy.'

She cried her heart out. I told her his number but she wasn't in a state to listen. When she finally regained her composure I had to wait listening to the sound of telephone static in one ear and London commuters in the other while she searched for a pencil. I gave it to her again. She cried some more. I was determined not to make a scene – I didn't want there to be any guilt, but neither did I want to belittle the selflessness of this act – so I held back my tears as best I could, which was right up to the moment when she said: 'I'll miss you forever.'

And then I broke down.

The balding man was so intrigued by my sobbing that he chanced another glance in my direction. Our eyes met but

I saw through him, through the telephone booth, through Victoria Station and through London – out into the world at large and the everyday activities that make up people's lives. This was the end. Through my tears and sobs I heard the pips. I searched maniacally for coins but found none and so resigned myself to saying good-bye in the seven seconds that remained.

> 'Sir, I've finished the chapter. Shall I start the next one?'

> *Six.*
> *Five.*

> 'Er, Mr Kelly?'

> *Four.*

> 'Sir! Mr Kelly!'

> *Three.*
> *Two.*
> *One.*

> 'Mr Kelly! I've finished!'

> *End of call.*

> 'Sir! Sir! Mr Kelly!'

Lawrence had stopped reading and was now trying to get my attention by waving his arms.

'What do you want?' I barked, annoyed that he'd disturbed my train of thought.

'I've finished the chapter, sir,' he said hesitantly. 'Shall I carry on?'

I stood up and approached the blackboard at the front of the classroom. A brief gust of wind caught the letter of resignation I'd been working on and sent it spiralling to the floor. I hastily put it back on the desk and commanded my pupils' attention.

'You've just heard Lawrence read one of the most famous passages in English Literature on the subject of love,' I said, carefully examining their expressions to see whether Ms Brontë had managed to penetrate their stony hearts. 'Catherine Earnshaw has just explained to her servant, Nelly, the difference between her love for Linton and her love for Heathcliff. What, if anything, has this made any of you feel?'

A wall of thirty-two pairs of eyes returned my gaze blankly. I was alone on this one.

'Okay, so that probably *is* asking a little too much of you,' I said, surprised that my sense of humour was still functioning. 'Cathy's talking about two types of love here: the first is her love for Linton which she says is "like the foliage in the woods. Time will change it. I'm well aware. As winter changes the trees."' I paused, studying the activities of my students: Kevin Rossiter was scraping the inside of his ear with a plastic pen lid, Sonya Pritchard and Emma Anderson (now quite ordinary girls in their school clothing) were passing notes to each other and Colin Christie was attempting to suck back a carefully manufactured thread of spittle all the way from his chin to his mouth. 'But,' I continued wearily, 'her love for Heathcliff was like "the eternal rocks beneath. A source of little delight but essential." Now here's the good bit; she says, "Nelly, I am Heathcliff!" My question to you, 8B, is this: which kind of love would you prefer?'

Although I hadn't intended it as a rhetorical question I hadn't expected anyone to answer either. In fact I was halfway to writing some suggestions on the board when a solitary arm waved diffidently in the air – it belonged to Julie Whitcomb, the girl who'd been so cruelly spurned by Clive O'Rourke on Friday. Her fellow students shuffled their chairs in order to stare at her in amazement. I smiled at her, giving her the nod to answer.

'I'd like the kind of love that lasts, sir,' she said, avoiding all eye contact. 'I'd like the kind of love that lasts forever. It doesn't matter if it's plain, it doesn't matter if it's ugly. It just has to be there.' She stopped and fixed her eyes on the novel in her hands, her face glowing redder than Kitty Wyatt's on a cold day. 'I'd have Heathcliff's love over Linton's any day, sir.'

I thanked Julie for her contribution. 'That was an excellent observation. But I have another question, 8B: what about Heathcliff in all this? I don't want to spoil the book's ending for you – but let me tell you, if you're a tall, brooding, gypsy boy made good, it isn't a happy one. The thing I'd like to ask you – a question I'll admit I don't know the answer to – is this: was he right to love her so much when he knew she'd never love him the way she loved Linton?'

'What do you mean, sir?' asked Julie.

'I mean it's all very well Cathy loving Heathcliff "like the eternal rocks beneath", but isn't he being just the teensy weensiest bit naive to think that the "higher" nature of the love they shared was in any way a substitute for having her there in his arms? Heathcliff let her marry the man who brutalised him!'

Julie Whitcomb put her hand up again, shouting, 'Sir! Sir! Sir!'

I looked around the room, there were no other signs of life.

'The thing is, sir,' began Julie, quite obviously speaking from the top of her head, 'I think that love's more complicated than we think it is. Sometimes you fall in love with someone that's just no good for you. It's not your fault and in a way it's not their fault either – it just is. And I think that's what happened here. Heathcliff fell in love with the wrong person. I . . .' She looked down at her desk sheepishly. 'Sorry, sir, I finished the whole book over the weekend, sir. It's just that once I started I couldn't stop.' I smiled at her reassuringly. 'Anyway, I like to think that Heathcliff would've found the right person if he'd only looked. I think the right person's out there for everyone, but you can only see them if you want to see them. The thing is, Heathcliff couldn't see anybody but Cathy.'

She buried her head in her book, overcome by self-consciousness. Most of the class were dumbfounded by the depth of her perception, although out of the corner of my eye I observed Kevin Rossiter sucking on the very pen lid he'd been using to clean his ears, Colin Christie eating a packet of crisps and Susie McDonnell and Zelah Wilson leaning back on their chairs whispering to each other – probably remarking how much of a twat I was.

I looked at Julie Whitcomb, so small, so helpless and yet so wise beyond her years and was moved. Here was someone who wanted to learn, someone who was reading a text and responding to it. This was why I'd become a teacher. I felt a flush of pride and wondered if I was responsible for inspiring her or whether she was merely a freak of nature.

I agreed with everything she said. It wasn't just about being in love, it was about being in love with . . .

'The right person!' I yelled aloud, thinking back to my conversation with Kate. 'You're right, Julie. It's not just about being in love. It's about being in love with the right person! The right person was there all the time! She was there all the time!'

The entire class thought I'd taken leave of my senses but as it meant that they didn't have to listen to me witter on about a book bearing as much relevance to their lives as a Latvian bus timetable, they didn't care. Smiling enthusiastically at Julie Whitcomb as I approached the classroom door I shouted, 'Carry on reading by yourselves,' and ran into the corridor in search of the nearest phone.

'I need the phone,' I said. 'It's an emergency.'

Margaret the ancient school secretary examined me with an air of studied uninterest. When I was introduced to her at the start of term the first thing she'd said to me, after looking me up and down disapprovingly, was, 'Don't think you can use the photocopier willy-nilly, young man.' Later in the week she'd point blank refused to give access to the stationery cupboard without her being there, and on Thursday she'd told me off for slouching in the corridor. She was pure evil in a tweed two-piece. There was no way she'd let me use the telephone to make a private call, even one that might change the entire course of my life.

'Is it concerning school business?' she bellowed. 'The headmaster doesn't allow private calls, you know.'

'It's a matter of life and death,' I said patiently.

'Whose life?' she replied tersely.

I studied her face: her thick grey hair in a tight bun; her mean, snaky eyes; her sallow cheeks, thin, tight lips and saggy liver spotted neck. She would've looked more compassionate if she'd been carved out of stone. Lacking the energy to even make an attempt to change her mind I ran out of the door and across the playground to the school gates. It took five minutes racing around Wood Green High Street before I finally found a telephone box that hadn't been violated by Wood Green Comprehensive kids.

I checked my watch. It was 2.24 p.m. I dialled the number and waited. It rang three times before the answering machine picked up:

Hello, you're through to Bruce and Alice . . .

I checked my watch again. Her flight wasn't until 4.00 p.m. I still had a chance. I fumbled through my phone book and found her mobile number. It rang six times before directing me to her voice mail.

I was too late.

I had no more tears left to cry. I'd finally become immune to life and was comforted by the lack of emotion. It wasn't that I didn't care – I did – I just ceased to see hope where there was none. It was a lesson I was learning three years too late, but it was necessary all the same. As I walked back into school, up the stairs and towards my classroom, I promised myself that I'd never let this happen again. Never.

As I approached the classroom door, my hand about to press down on the door handle, I noted that the rabble inside were strangely quiet. 8B were never this quiet voluntarily. I decided they were either dead or being babysat by the headmaster. For my own sake I hoped they were dead, because the only other option was that the school secretary had told the Head I'd gone mad and abandoned the class. This, I decided, was the end of the line for me and teaching.

I was going to get sacked for sure, which scared me even though I'd made up my mind to resign. I was half tempted to carry on walking down the corridor and go home, but cowardice, I reasoned, was just another form of denial and I'd had about as much as I could take of not facing the facts.

I opened the door and there in front of the class was Alice.

She was wearing black jeans and a dark blue fleece-lined jacket, the kind that people who participate in outdoor pursuits wear. Her hair was out of place, as if she'd been running, and her cheeks managed to look flushed in spite of her perpetual tan. She had a rucksack on her left shoulder which she was keeping in place with her right hand. She released her grip, allowing the bag to slide off her shoulder and hit the floor. She didn't look down, she just stared at me.

As I took my first step towards her my breathing started to deepen. I looked down at my hands, they were shaking. She took a step towards me, her lips tightly pursed. She put her hand to her mouth and took another step. Every second it took until we were face to face, close enough to touch, seemed too long. It was a magical moment, but for once not one that was a product of my imagination.

She wrapped her arms around me. And slowly, very slowly all the pain and worry locked within my frame flowed away. My senses were filled by her perfume, her body. We fitted together perfectly. Her face was buried into my shirt, next to my lunchtime tomato ketchup stain, the existence of which she was thankfully oblivious to. I took her hands and squeezed them gently. My hands still wouldn't stop shaking. I was terrified. Absolutely bloody terrified. And she seemed terrified too. We stood there motionless, staring at each other, hoping beyond hope that what was happening was as real as what we were feeling.

'What are you doing here?' I asked stupidly.

'I've come to save you,' she replied.

'Save me from what? Kate?'

'Lung cancer, eating biscuits in bed, growing fat and old and lonely without me.'

We both laughed.

'It's a long story but Kate is history,' I explained guiltily. 'She's history but happy.'

'And Aggi?' asked Alice, her smiling face converting to a stony seriousness.

'Aggi?' I repeated, as if I wasn't entirely sure who she was talking about.

'Yes, Aggi.'

I smiled. 'She's ancient history.'

Alice didn't laugh or for that matter return my smile.

'How can you be so sure? I've heard you say a thousand times that she was your perfect woman. You've always had such high standards when it comes to love. You were telling me only a few weeks ago that your perfect woman had to be this, had to be that – it was just short-hand for she had to be Aggi.'

'Sometimes, you're as divorced from sanity as I am,' I began, mock chastising her. 'You've got it all wrong. You are the standard. Before Aggi there was you. She had to fit *your* standard. I know I thought Aggi was The One but I was wrong. You were The Original One. She was The Wrong One. And now you're here.'

'And now I'm here,' she smiled, relaxing.

'But you know it'll never work,' I said softly.

'It's doomed from the start,' she laughed, tears gently rolling down her cheeks.

'We might as well give up now,' I said, shrugging my shoulders.

'We'd be fools not to,' she nodded.

I wiped away a tear and kissed her eyebrow. 'Friends should never be lovers.'

Standing on tiptoes she reached up and lightly pressed her lips against my ear. 'Or lovers friends.'

Colin Christie made puking noises. Sonya Pritchard and Emma Anderson shouted, 'Give her one, sir.' Kevin Rossiter flicked the pen lid he'd been cleaning his ears with at my head and Julie Whitcomb, star that she was, stood up and gave us a round of applause.

EPILOGUE

In a world where the accumulated wisdom of thousand of centuries still exists – everyone from Socrates to Sair Paul through to Freud and Stephen Hawking – it migh seem crass to quote Oprah Winfrey in order to explai where I'd been going wrong in life all this time, but that the thing about common sense, it appears in the oddes places.

I came across the nugget of wisdom in question on afternoon a couple of years ago, while I was on the dol and living at my mum's. Having just watched *Escape Fron The Planet of The Apes* on video for the third time that week I happened across an episode of *Oprah*. Too lazy to chang channels and, dare I say it, intrigued by the show's title: '*Mei who love too much; Women who love too little*', I openee a packet of milk chocolate Hobnobs to share with my faithfu hound, and settled down to enjoy the programme. As I bit into my biscuit Oprah said something so profound that I inhalee a large fragment of Hobnob, resulting in such a violent fit o coughing that I was nearly sick over poor Beveridge. This i what she said:

'Love ain't supposed to feel bad.'

Of course, like most profound statements (including the biblical 'Love your neighbour', Marshall McLuhan's 'The medium is the message' and Morecambe and Wise's 'More tea, Ern?', it made an impact on my life for approximately three seconds before it was consigned to the dustbin of history. Until now.

You see, sometimes I'll catch Alice looking at me while I'm watching TV and she'll have a huge inane grin on her face that really doesn't become her. I'll ask her what she's doing and she'll take her time before answering my question with silence. Then she'll ask me if I love her. I'll pretend to take *my* time thinking over the question and then she'll throw a cushion at me. This is my cue to tell her that I love her with all my heart (which I do), then she'll tell me that she loves me more than anything (which she does). Then it will be my turn to joke that because we're 'friends' and 'more than friends' it kind of makes her my best girlfriend. And then she'll laugh, look me in the eye in a manner which still makes me go weak at the knees and say, 'No, I'm your Legendary Girlfriend.' Whenever she makes this statement I always nod and smile in agreement – but the truth is I'm not so sure one way or the other. The one thing I am sure of is this: our love doesn't feel bad.

And that is all that matters.

Don't miss Mike Gayle's new novel, MR COMMITMENT, available in Flame from August 1999.

Duffy is engaged. He accepted Lara's proposal. But the trips to Ikea, dinner parties for couples and talk of babies are giving him itchy feet and now he's not sure if he can say goodbye to his extended adolescence and face up to that final walk down the aisle. How does he know if she's The One? Can he cope with responsibility? Does he have what it takes to become Mr Commitment? Because if he doesn't, he may just find that he's lost Lara – forever . . .